LONG BEACH

A NOVEL OF INTRIGUE AND SUSPENSE

NORM OLSON

outskirts press

Long Beach
A Novel of intrigue and suspense

v3.0

This is a work of fiction. The events and characters described herein are imaginary and are not intended to refer to specific places or living persons. The opinions expressed in this manuscript are solely the opinions of the author and do not represent the opinions or thoughts of the publisher. The author has represented and warranted full ownership and/or legal right to publish all the materials in this book.

Outskirts Press, Inc.
http://www.outskirtspress.com

ISBN: 978-1-4787-9347-2

PRINTED IN THE UNITED STATES OF AMERICA

PROLOGUE

It's 1947. I'm about to become claustrophobic and here's the reason. The Minnesota winter was back in high gear, snow coming down hard and blowing sideways. Snowflakes feeling like razor blades were cutting across my face. The banks of the coulee were covered with scrub brush, three to four feet high in the summer. In the winter after a heavy snow, they were covered with snow and created a hollow world beneath as a hard crust would form after the storm.

Recess at the Riverside one-room school was hide-and-seek time. As I ran over the mounds of hard-pack snow, suddenly the crust broke and I plunged head first into the hollow, snow-covered brush, trapped, upside down, struggling to get out, and only inching deeper as I struggled.

Snow packs in my eyes, mouth, and nose. I'm unable to move and trying to scream for help. I'm buried alive. I feel someone grab both my ankles and start pulling me up. I was never so happy to see the school bully Donny Hoff in my whole life. "Should have left ya there," he grins.

It's now 1982, and I am dreaming of that moment. When I awake it feels like every bone in my body is broken. My face is still buried in the snow. But, it's not snow, its dirt.

My hands are tied behind my back and I can't move. I'm buried alive. I try to scream, but I only choke on the dirt. I feel someone grab both my ankles and start pulling me up. I feel my hands being cut free and someone wiping the dirt from my face. I open my eyes and see a smiling face. Thank God it's not Donny.

She asks me, *"Como Esta Senor? Como se llama? "* My head is spinning and throbbing with pain, I have no idea what she just said, and then that one year of Spanish I took in college kicks in.

So I respond *"Si, Si! Comprende Espanol, uh poquito. Mi llamo es Marc. Marc Ryder."* I know I just murdered that phrase trying to tell her I understood a little Spanish and that my name is Marc. Marc Ryder.

She responds in English, "Your name is Marc Ryder?"

"You speak English, thank God! Yes, yes, my name is Marc Ryder. Where am I?"

"You are in the jungle near Tequila, Mexico. We saw some men carry you from a van and into the jungle. So, we waited until they were gone and came to find you and found you buried."

"I am so grateful. I was in Puerto Vallarta, and I was kidnapped. How far are we from Puerto Vallarta?"

"About four hours by car," says the man with a knife who cut off my bindings.

"Four hours? Can you take me to a telephone?"

She says, "We will tell you where you can find a phone, but we cannot go with you. It will be too dangerous for us."

Dangerous! What the hell have I got myself into now? And I thought Donny was bad news.

Part One

1

JUANITA

JUNE 1970

Afternoon in the jungle is filled with sounds of birds and monkeys, and who knows what other creatures called it their home. The canopy covers everything, and the air is heavy with the smells of jungle plants. The walk through the jungle from Tequila is pleasant and relaxing.

Juanita has worked at one of the distilleries in Tequila since she was 14. She works long hours but is happy to have a job where she can help her mother take care of her five brothers and sisters. Her father had gone to America, and she had no idea where exactly he was, but he sent periodic money orders to help support the family. The money orders never seemed to come from the same place. Today, she looked forward to getting home early. Her brothers and sisters were still at school, and her mother would not be off work for another four hours. It was precious time to herself.

As she walked the path from Tequila through the jungle and past the small airport carved out of the jungle, her thoughts were of Benny and their plans to get married. She had just turned 16 and was ready to start her own life.

Just as she walked into the clearing where the family home stood, she was roughly grabbed from behind and thrown on the ground. Her face was shoved into the dirt, and she could not move. The man forcing her down was too heavy. He gruffly growled, "Do not attempt to fight me, or I will kill you." One hand kept her head shoved down, while the other ripped off her skirt and underwear. He forced himself into her, groaning as he did. He finished, and keeping his hand on her head, he leaned in close to her face, "Tell anyone of this and I will come back for you another day. Or maybe your mother or sister." He then got up and disappeared into the jungle.

Juanita got up trembling with fear. Her clothes were ripped and dirty. She sobbed uncontrollably as she ran for the house. She could not fix her skirt, so she changed and tried to figure out what to do with the soiled one. She went to the sink to wash the dirt off her face. In the mirror, she saw a bruise on her cheek. She worried, how am I going to explain that? Anger began to well up inside her, and she thought, I will find this pig and kill him, but I cannot let anyone know what happened, anyone.

Meanwhile, the man followed the path back into the jungle and then followed another path to the main road. He brushed off his uniform, got in his police cruiser and drove towards Tequila. He pulled up in front of the police station and parked in a spot with a sign. The sign said Chief Humberto Gonzalez. He got out of his car and walked into the Tequila police station and was greeted by the desk officer, "*Hola,* Humberto. Chief, did you fall? You have a small tear in the knee of your slacks."

2

LONG BEACH HARBOR

AUGUST 1978

Tequila, Mexico, is a long way from California. California, that's where this story really begins. I got out of the Army in the early '70s and immediately got offered a job with the Department of Defense, Defense Foreign Liaison Office. Most people have never heard of this outfit, nor had I, but they offered me a job as a Special Agent and *mucho* opportunities for advancement and travel. Plus, my office would be in Long Beach, California. I'll have to admit I really didn't know where Long Beach, California was, but it was a place I had dreamed about since I was a kid growing up on a farm in northern Minnesota. I mean beautiful white sand beaches and nothing but clear blue skies; a year round climate to die for—but not in Tequila, Mexico.

As I said, I got out of the army in the early '70's. I trained at the Infantry School, Fort Benning Georgia and became an Infantry officer, Ranger and Airborne qualified. A trained killer. Just what my mom had planned for me.

When I left the Army and signed on with DFL, no that

does mean Dead Fucking Last, I was sent to train with FBI recruits at Quantico, Virginia. I advanced to the next level of being a trained killer. I also became an expert marksman with my new best friend, my Smith and Wesson revolver. Although I was authorized to carry a weapon, I rarely did due to nature of my work.

Now a trained killer I was sent to Monterrey Language school to be trained in Russian. My ability to speak Norwegian and just enough Spanish to get me in trouble, somehow made me an ideal candidate.

I finished language school and reported in to DFL Regional HQ in Long Beach, California. My office consisted of four special agents and a secretary. We were each "Specialists" in a certain area and mine happened to be Russian Counter-Intelligence. I know what you're thinking, not a lot of Russians in Southern California. It's true there were not but there were over four hundred defense contractors in Southern California. That aught to get your attention. It sure got the attention of some of the United States Cold war contestants. After four years I got bumped up to the next level, and became the Deputy Assistant Director, DFL. Most people who ask what I do for Uncle Sam change the subject when I begin to describe the Defense Foreign Liaison office.

Now Long Beach has an interesting history, and I won't bore you with a long history lesson, but its climb into prominence began back in the 1920s. The 1932 Olympics bolstered that prominence, helped by the arrival of the United States Navy. Long Beach was designated the "Navy Capitol of the United States" with the establishment of the Long Beach Naval base and shipyard.

The Navy brought almost twenty nine thousand officers and men to Long Beach and it became the fastest growing city in the US. This is probably why I heard about it up in Minnesota, dreaming of living in a place like Long Beach. So, what we got here is a Navy town and not a place where we want ships bearing the flag of the Soviet Union. But before the Soviet Union arrived, back in 1942 the Japanese arrived, and an unexploded shell crashed through the roof of a Linden Avenue home. For crying out loud, my office is at Linden Avenue and Ocean Boulevard! OK, so it was thirty years before I got there.

OK, Enough with the history lesson. Suddenly the cold war was warming a bit, and ships bearing the flag of the Soviet Union were calling on the ports of Long Beach and Los Angeles. Prior to 1977, ships bearing the flag of the Soviet Union were barred from entering many US ports. The restriction was lifted in 1977. I don't mean to make it sound like this was a really big deal because most people, in fact—other than people who worked in the harbor—had no clue Soviet flagged ships were calling.

Most of the Soviet ships carried general or bulk cargo and though seaworthy, generally in sorry condition. But all had a most interesting array of antennas and odd looking aerials. They attracted the attention of the Department of Defense, which of course meant yours truly. It was my task to get to know everything there was to know about these ships and their crew.

Through a local shipping company's patriotic generosity I was given a position as "shipping agent." I was given a quick schooling on bills of lading (which told you what was on the ship, where it came from, and where it was going), Coast Guard regulations, and all other paperwork regarding shipping and receiving. In other words, when the Soviet ship's captain needed something, I was his guy. Through my own agency, DFL, I was given a full set of identification, drivers license, business cards, insurance cards and a car registered to me Marc Bauer, Agent for Bergen Shipping.

Learning to drink vodka and mineral water like the Russians was one of those more difficult tasks. If you believe that, well I got some beach property in Arizona for sale. The most difficult task though, was dealing with the folks who physically dealt with the docking, loading, and unloading of each ship—the Longshoremen and Warehousemen's Union. The harbor was their territory, and new faces were not welcome—in this case the Soviet ships and me as their agent.

Other than that, life for me was quite pleasant. Let me say my work life was pleasant, my personal life was a fricking mess, and it was my own damn fault. Mid-life crisis, maybe. Wandering eye, maybe. Stupid, no doubt.

3

TO RUSSIA

January 1982

Part of my job with DFL involved direct communication and meetings with representatives of foreign governments, and in particular their defense departments. I had just returned from a month-long trip into the Soviet Union, and I was still recovering from the trip. I don't know why I thought it was going to be fun.

The United States and the Soviet Union were in serious discussions regarding an arms reduction treaty which would call for the destruction of all intermediate range missiles. The treaty would also forbid the future manufacture of those missiles. The treaty would involve inspectors from the Soviet Union to become a presence in the United States and inspectors from the United States a presence in the Soviet Union for the duration of the treaty. The duration time of the treaty had not yet been determined.

I was part of a team sent to the Soviet Union to survey the site where we would house our future inspectors. The site was 900 kilometers east of Moscow. To get to this site, it was a tedious journey. I would fly commercial to Frankfurt, Germany, where our team assembled and was briefed prior to going into the Soviet Union.

From Frankfurt, we flew military aircraft to Moscow, and then transferred all our baggage and equipment onto an Aeroflot four engine turbo-prop which took us to the city of Ishevsk. From there we were bused to Votkinsk. Votkinsk is the manufacturing site for the soviet intermediate range missiles.

Ishevsk is the home of A. Kalashnikov, two time hero of the Soviet Union and the Kalashnikov museum. You have probably heard of his invention the AK-47 automatic rifle. Votkinsk is the birth place of Tchaikovsky and a music and art school bearing his name.

Aeroflot is just not a fun ride. I noticed the tires bare, the interior shoddy, the seats threadbare, and the smell, omigod the smell —Russian cigarettes mixed with the smell of borscht—sorry, I'm getting sick just thinking about it.

I had been to the Soviet Union before, sitting in on talks with the Soviets regarding their upcoming presence in America and our future presence in their country. I made a request of my boss General Parker to make a stop in Moscow on my way out of the country. I wanted to touch base with the Commercial Attache at the US Embassy. I had some questions about the Soviet ships calling on the west coast ports. My request was granted so I made plans to travel as soon as I finished my part of the survey.

I finished my part of the survey a couple days early and was driven back to Izhevsk air field from Votkinsk. Instead of the turbo prop I got a seat on a Russian Yak 40 (think Russian Learjet) to Sheremetyevo Airport in Moscow. All the while the crew and I were in Votkinsk, we were escorted everywhere, so I was surprised that I was allowed to make the trip to Moscow without an escort. I figured surely there would be someone waiting for me when I arrived at Sheremetyevo. But, I saw no one. There must be someone watching me, so I did the best I could to check for any surveillance. But it was an impossible task, and why I really cared is beyond me. I mean, I was really in Moscow on an official visit to the Embassy. I had carried my bag on the Yak 40, so I got off the plane and walked straight through the terminal pretending to know what I was doing and hurried outside. Everybody hurries in Moscow. I have no idea why. There's nowhere to go, and when you get there, there is nothing to buy. I dashed out the door, and I hailed a cab.

A typical beat up rusty cab pulled up and I jumped into the back seat. The driver sat in the only front seat, the passenger seat was missing. He was a pleasant looking fellow who looked as though he might be from one of the southern soviet states.

I asked him "Do you speak English?"

He replied "*Da*." My limited Russian told me he said yes.

"Drive up to the next entrance and stop, and wait."

A few hundred feet later he stopped in front of the next entrance. I tossed him twenty rubles, told him to wait, got out of the cab and dashed back into the terminal. I waited a few moments to see if anyone came back in looking. No one. So, I walked out the door again and got back into the same cab. The cab driver introduced himself. He had reddish blond hair and wore a neatly trimmed beard.

"I am Dmitri, you are American? Did you forget something inside the terminal?"

"Yes, I am, and no, I did not, I thought I saw someone I knew. I'm staying at the Ukraina." Rubles, the official currency of the Soviet Union were worth nothing, and American cigarettes, Levis, dollars, in fact anything American was in demand. Use it just like currency.

Apparently sensing what I was thinking, Dmitri says "For you, the fare to the Ukraina is three packs Marlboro or one American dollar. Is better than rubles."

"Sorry, I don't smoke, Dmitri, so here's two dollars, and if you're available all day tomorrow, it's worth ten dollars."

"At your service Mr. American, but all day will cost you fifteen."

"OK Dmitri, how about you call me Ryder, and I'll see you at eight am for twelve dollars. And Dmitri, you're not working for the KGB or the GRU are you?"

"Oh, I see you are familiar with our most esteemed Soviet Intelligence pigs. I am Chechen. Any more questions Mr. Ryder? And so we agree to thirteen dollars, yes?"

"Oh alright. See you tomorrow."

After a hair-raising ride, we arrived at the Ukraina Hotel, an old Stalin-era hotel that was definitely not the Hilton, or the Marriot, or even Motel 6—where they, at least, keep the light on for you. I stepped up to the registration desk dreading the check-in procedure, because I don't really speak Russian.

Wait, I can speak Russian, I just can't understand it. So, I pled English only, and to my surprise the desk clerk spoke perfect English.

"Good afternoon Mr. Ryder, I shall need your passport and government voucher. Oh, I see you are traveling on a Diplomatic Passport. Perfect. I shall upgrade your room, and you shall be much more comfortable. Your room is nineteen forty. The floor monitor will have your key."

"Thank you, Sasha. The floor monitor has my key?"

"Yes, that is correct."

A floor monitor is not something all the hotels have.

Only in Moscow have I ever encountered floor monitors before. What's up with that? Nineteen forty. I figured upgrade means the room has more listening devices. The elevator had an operator, I got in and requested the nineteenth floor. I'm answered with a grunt and a scowl. I exited the elevator at the nineteenth, there were no other passengers, and there at a desk facing the elevator sat a stern-looking woman. I nodded and turned to head to my room.

"Excuse me sir. I will escort you to your room. I have your key. It is for security."

"Oh yes of course you have my key. Just give it to me, and there's no need for you to bother escorting me to my room."

"I will keep your key at my desk. It is for security. Simply come to this desk, and you will be escorted to your room. I, or somebody else will be here, and all you have to do is call for us. We will make your bed, clean your bath, and be out of your way. *Dobre Noche*."

"Yeah, good night to you, too, madam." She opened the door to my room, scowled at me, and marched back to her desk.

My room, or should I say my closet, was maybe eight-feet wide and 15-feet long. The actual closet was a free-standing armoire, and the bathroom was about the same size as the armoire. It consisted of a shower stall and a commode. The sink and a small mirror were on the wall outside the bathroom. The towels were about 18 inches by 36 inches and threadbare. Did I say towels, I meant towel.

The bed was a thing of beauty—about the size of a very small twin bed with a hand-carved headboard and footboard. I stand about 5'11" and could not lie down in the bed without bending my legs at the knees. Oh well, I should survive two nights.

Now, seeing as how I had been in the country for almost three weeks, the Cultural Attaché had requested a meeting at the US Embassy before I met with the Commercial Attaché. Basically, he wanted to pick my brain about who I might have met with and tell me not to cause trouble while in Moscow. But before that happened, I needed a good old-fashioned Bud Light. So, I made a little detour.

The bar at the Ukrainia served Russian beer—ugh—and vodka. The Plotnikov Pub, across the bridge on oto Novvy Arbot served Bud Light. I had about an hour to kill before my meeting with the CIA guy, I mean Cultural Attache. Pretend I didn't say that. OK, I found a seat at the bar and ordered a Bud Light, cheese, and bread.

Plotnikov Pub at 5pm was busy, and the clientele were mostly white-collar government hacks with a few military thrown in. It wasn't a tourist spot, even though I heard English being spoken. As a matter of fact, the bartender spoke pretty good English.

I casually looked around the room and saw three women sitting at a table. One of them, a real looker, looked familiar, but I couldn't come up with a name or where I would have known her. She happened to glance at me at the same moment, looked away, and then quickly looked back. I figured, she's thinking the same thing as me, "where do I know him from?" I was about to get up and walk over to her table when who should appear at my side but the Cultural Attaché himself.

"Hey Ryder, somehow I knew I'd find you here."

I greeted him and looked back at the table, but she was gone. Damn, why would I know her anyway?

"Look Ryder, something has come up and I won't be able to meet up with you later, but you should check in with the chief of station anyway. Anything or anybody that you need to talk about during your vacation in Udmurt Province?"

"Nope, nothing. I'll buy you a beer and then head over to the Embassy. Any fun things for me to do for the next couple of days?"

"Yes, but don't get caught doing them. I'll pass on the beer. Catch you next time."

He left, and I finished my beer and headed over to the Embassy—still trying to come up with an answer. Who was she?

4

MARINA

AUGUST 1981

OK, let's go back five months, and I can explain why that gal in the Plotnikov was so familiar. . .

Up to this point in time, there had not been any female crew members aboard Soviet freighters, if there were, I never saw one. This was going to change when I received notice that a Russian passenger liner, the MS Mikhail Lermontov was to be calling on the Port of Los Angeles, and Bergen Shipping was the agent. I also was notified that the Mikhail Lermontov carried a diplomatic pouch which was to be picked up by representatives of the Soviet Consulate in San Francisco. The pouch was in the form of two very large shipping crates.

I know what you are thinking. Two large shipping crates. The phrase diplomatic pouch brings to mind a large brief case or a large ladies purse. But in fact, almost anything can be declared part of a diplomatic pouch. It cannot be opened or inspected.

The Consul General of the Soviet Consulate in San Francisco was coming down to personally oversee the transfer of the pouch from the Mikhail Lermontov into two panel vans, driven down to Los Angeles Harbor from San Francisco. The transfer had to be done in Los Angeles because Soviet ships, cargo or passenger, were not allowed into the ports of San Francisco or Oakland.

The Consul General had to get special permission to drive to Los Angeles because the Soviets were restricted to a fifty mile radius of their consulate. Naturally this activity rang the alarms of all the three-letter agencies, who immediately appeared on the scene. Federal pandemonium!

The Mikhail Lermontov arrived on schedule, and I went aboard to meet the captain and first mate. The Mikhail Lermontov was a medium-sized passenger ship and a little worn around the edges, but a well-kept vessel. I was shown to the captain's quarters and was surprised when both the captain and the first mate greeted me in English. So, first things first, get the paperwork out of the way. The most important item was, of course, the diplomatic pouch. After assuring the captain, who could now assure the consul general, the pouch would be transferred off the soviet vessel into the custody of US Customs under the observation of Soviet officials and then be released to the authorized Soviets, we concluded our official business.

The captain said to me, "now we are finished with the paperwork, can I offer you a Russian refreshment? Maybe Russian vodka and mineral water?"

"Absolutely, please."

"You would prefer Absolut?"

"No, no, Stolichnaya is my favorite."

"We have Stolichnaya chilled and ready."

You know, sometimes the invisible teleprompter that I read from just makes me look stupid, so I clarified, "Stolichnaya, yes definitely Stolichnaya."

"Marina, we are ready for refreshments."

Marina swept into the room, and I was in awe, this woman was stunningly gorgeous! She did not appear to be Russian and spoke English with a slight British accent. She seemed more mid-eastern or from one of the southern Soviet States. She had long, black hair that shined, deep, dark brown eyes, and a light brown complexion. Couple this with a figure right out of *Playboy*, and well, I couldn't take my eyes off her. She left the room, and the first mate woke me out of my trance.

"She is quite beautiful, is she not?" he said.

"Uh, yes, quite beautiful."

The Captain said "Mr. Bauer, I would like to offer you a tour of our ship, if you have the time. I would also like to extend an invitation to lunch with the Consul General. He will be joining me, and I am sure he would like to meet our American business partner."

"It would be an honor. I'd like that very much."

He then asked "Marina, could you please take Mr. Bauer on a tour of our ship and have him at the dining room at twelve-hundred hours sharp."

She responded"Yes, Captain. Very well."

She then said to me "come with me Mr. Bauer." She pronounced Captain as *capeetan* and called me *Gaspedin* Bauer, which she pronounced *Gas-pah-deen.* Mister Bauer in Russian.

We walked all over the ship. I was shown the bridge, radio room, crew's quarters, ballroom, main dining room, and a typical passenger cabin.

I told her, "this ship is more luxurious than I expected. You must enjoy working for this company. What do you do when you are not at sea?"

"I live in Moscow and work part time at the GUM

department store. Are you familiar with Moscow? It is on Red Square across from the Kremlin."

"Yes, I know exactly where it is," I bragged.

"You have been to Moscow?"

"Yes, a number of times. Always in the winter. Very cold."

"Russians more prefer winter to summer. It is too warm and too many bugs in the summer. Also, it is not dry."

"Humid?"

"Yes, humid."

"Your English is very good."

"Thank you, I am multi-lingual. It is a good part of the reason I was offered this job. I speak German and Farsi and of course Russian."

"My Russian is basic, and my English a little better."

"You amuse me, Mr. Bauer. I have not met many Americans, but they all seem very happy people. The Russians are very self-depreciating and seem to have little hope for their future. But if you get to know them on a personal level, they are wonderful people."

"So, you are not Russian?"

She whispered, "No, I am from Afghanistan." Looking both ways and speaking quietly she confessed, "I would like to come to America. I am not happy in Moscow. I have information that could be of interest to your country's police. Maybe you could help me?"

Before I could answer, the first mate appeared out of nowhere and called me to lunch, and she said, "Goodbye, Mr. Bauer."

Holy Borscht! My mind was spinning... What kind of info could she have? How am I going to find her after I leave the ship? I don't even know her full name. Wait, crew list! I have a crew list, I can find her. I needed to think this out. Should I pass the info to the FBI, or pursue it myself? I decide on the latter, which meant maybe I'd see her again. The ship didn't leave until the day after next. With that I went off to lunch with the Captain and the Consul General. I know you're wondering what we had for lunch? Check this out!

First course was red caviar, roast beef with asparagus, and horseradish sauce. Then came Sturgeon and Potatoes Chateau. Chicken cutlets followed with a cheese board. Dessert was ice cream with *Cognac Aroma*. To wash it down, a choice of white wine "Gurguani," *Mukuzani* (a Georgian red wine), Armenian cognac, Stolichnaya vodka, and Borjomi mineral water, or all of the above. Delicious!

I was introduced to the Consul General. He was a tall, silver haired gent. He obviously bought his clothes in San Francisco as they were not the usual ill-fitting Russian variety. He looked the part of a Consul General. He spoke very good English and asked me if all arrangements had been made for the transfer of the diplomatic pouch from the ship to the waiting Soviet representatives on the dock. I assured him it was a done deal.

I'm thinking that lunch should last me for at least a couple of days. And when am I going to learn that I cannot drink vodka with these guys. We must have toasted everybody in the world from our family members on up to the president of each country. Oh man I'm not looking forward to coming down. I suppose I could just keep drinking.

As I staggered down the ship's gangway I try not fall into the harbor while all I can seem to think of is Marina. Marina, what a lovely name. Marina, what a lovely dilemma you have put me in. Do I go to the FBI with what she told me, or hold the info and see if I can find her and get more details?

I returned to the ship the next day to observe the transfer of the diplomatic pouch and to finalize paperwork with the captain. I was directed to the ship's purser, and Marina is not in sight. So now I have a dilemma, FBI or not?

5

MOSCOW

JANUARY 15, 1982

Alright, so let's return to the Plotnikov. . .

I finish my Bud Light, still trying to figure out who the looker was, and why I think I should know her. I make my way over to the Embassy and after making the rounds of folks I knew and have worked with, I subject myself to the chief of station. Surprisingly, he has very few questions and cuts me loose. Good, I'm ready for something a little stronger than Bud Light and head back to the hotel. That Russian vodka and mineral water chaser at the Ukraina bar sounds good.

January in Moscow produces a scene which can only bring depression. The overcast daylight hours are shortened by the smothering smog. The sun will not show its face. The sky is a steel gray, and by mid-afternoon the city is cast in darkness. It begins to snow. A small hope arises that the gray landscape will be covered with a white, clean blanket, but no, it quickly becomes a sickly looking slush that covers the walks and streets.

I exit the Embassy of the United States which is located on Bol'Shoy Devyatiinsky Pereulok #8. As I leave, the Marine security guard cautioned me of Moscow streets at night, so I stick to the shadows. To get back to my hotel, The Ukraina on Kutusovskiy Prospekt, I run down Kudrumskiy, take a right on Bol'Shoy through the commercial area oto Novyy Arbat and on to the bridge across the Moscow River. Just before I cross the bridge, I find a darkened doorway to stop and catch my breath and watch. My hotel lies just across the bridge.

She suddenly appears. Strikingly beautiful in a Russian fur hat and fur trimmed coat, it's the gal from the Plotnikov. As she passes, she whispers, "I'm Marina. Meet me at the Plotnikov Pub, at the Arbot in thirty minutes." The car comes out of nowhere. Two men, wearing masks jump out as it stops, knock her to the ground, pick her up, and throw her into the car. I hug the shadows as they look around and as quickly as they arrived, speed off. I'm wondering, what the hell, is there another duo waiting for me to show myself?

I wait. The January cold is numbing. A slight breeze has picked up, and coming off the river it cuts through my clothes. I wait just a little longer. A look to my left reveals nothing, however, I cannot see over the bridge. I decide to make a run for it.

The bridge is at least 200 yards long with a substantial rise. As I come over the center rise of the bridge, a car turns on its headlights, blinding me. I hear car doors slam, and before I can focus, two very large men wearing masks slam me to the ground. I'm handcuffed with my hands behind my back, and a bag is pulled over my head. I'm grabbed by my arms and thrown into the back of some type of a van. One person stays with me, hands on my back, and off we go. Before I can say anything, a foul-tasting rag is shoved up under the bag over my head and held firmly against my face. It smells like chlorine. I don't remember anything until someone punches me in the chest, and bingo, I am awake. This is not a good thing, as now I'm afraid the beating will really begin.

I'm dragged out of the van and into a room and the bag is pulled off my head. The room has no windows and a single hanging light bulb for light. I'm thrown on a cot, and one of my hands is cuffed to it. I try to get up, but I'm sucker-punched below the belt and as I bend over I'm given a knee to the chest, knocking the wind out of me. I fall backwards onto the cot and slam my head against the concrete wall. I try to get up again, and I'm met with a blow to the stomach and another blow to the head.

As I fall, I hit my head on the floor. Things are getting very blurry, and I've got double vision. Another big guy enters the room, and to me it looks like there are four of them. I'm pulled up off the floor and shoved back on to the cot, hitting my head again on the concrete wall. I plead, "What do you want? I'm Marc Ryder, US Department of Defense and traveling on a diplomatic passport. I demand to be set free." I'm set free alright, with a roundhouse right hook.

I don't know how long I'm out, but I awake with burning headache, and I'm back on the cot. The mattress is covered in blood. I grasp my forehead, and my hand is all bloody. I know I've been trained for this kind of situation, but I don't remember the drill with handcuffs on. Basically I've only got one hand free. I might get in the first punch but that most likely would be the last punch.

I'm frantically working on getting my hands free from this tangled wreck.

The door opens, and another body is thrown into the room. She lands heavily on her side, and the door slams shut. She rolls over, and it's Marina. She puts her finger to her lips, "say nothing" she whispers. Her face reveals she has been beaten. She gets up and sits on the cot beside me. She whispers, "I have told them nothing. I heard them talking and they have become worried about your claim to have diplomatic passport. They are going to release us shortly, as soon as they are sure there are no police."

"They are not police?"

"No!"

"Who are they?"

"We must not talk now. Wait until we are free and clear."

If they're not police, then who the hell are these guys? I've got a million questions. I wonder, are they going to release us dead or alive? I suddenly think to see if I have my wallet. That's a no, and that's not good. The door opens and the two large guys enter with masks on. Marina is cuffed and a bag put over her head. I get the same treatment. We are pulled up and shoved out the door and then through another door, where we're hit with the January midnight cold. A car door opens, and we're shoved into the back of a van again, and off we go. After about 20-30 minutes of what feels like driving in circles, we stop. The door opens, and we're dragged out and pushed down an embankment. The van drives off leaving us with bags over our heads and handcuffed. Damn it's cold.

As we roll down the embankment, Marina lands on top of me, and I am able to pull off the bag on her head with my teeth.

Marina says, "I think they threw my purse and some other things out of the van after us. If I can find my purse, I think I can get these handcuffs off."

"See if you can pull this bag off me so I can help you look."

"There," she says, "I see my purse."

She fishes through her purse and produces a bobby pin. We are free of the handcuffs a couple of minutes later.

"Do you have any idea where we are?" I ask.

"No."

"Do you have any idea who these guys were?"

"Mafia. Ukrainian Mafia."

"Ukrainian?"

"Yes. They are the ones who my brothers have been dealing with."

"Your brothers? Dealing in what?"

"Drugs."

"Drugs? Drugs! Smuggling? Where and with whom?"

It takes me a by surprise because I thought the information she had was technical or military. It never occurred to me that we were talking drugs.

"Why did they let us go?" I ask.

"I overheard them talking and they were looking for me and my brother, but because of my papers which are in a different name and your drivers license, they realized they had the wrong people, well almost the wrong people. Would you be able to recognize them if we saw them again?"

"Could you? I never saw a face."

"They both had blue eyes."

"Well that sure narrows it down."

We gather ourselves and our belongings—what we could find—and Marina points to some lights in the distance. Surprisingly my wallet was among the things thrown out of the van. My passport was of course in the safe keeping of the Ukraina Hotel.

"I recognize those lights, and I think I know where we are. Let's follow this road, and I think it will take us to the main highway where maybe we can find a taxi."

We hustle down the road and come to a main highway. Our luck holds as a taxi comes to our aid.

We hop in. Marina gives him an address in Russian, and off we go. We arrive at an apartment complex, and I pay the driver with three, crumpled dollar bills. We watch him drive off. I start for the entrance of the apartment building, but Marina stops me. "This is not my building," she says. "My building is two blocks away. I did not want to be dropped off in front of my building."

I'm thinking, she's a hell of a lot smarter than me. We finally get to her building and it's ten stories. Her apartment is on the 10th floor. The elevator doesn't respond, so we climb the stairs, ten stories. I ask her about the elevator, and she just shrugs her shoulders, "Sometimes it works, sometime not."

Finally, we get to the 10th floor and to her apartment. It's a two-room apartment with a bathroom, and it's very warm. It seems soviet apartment buildings have only one temperature, very warm and much warmer, which in one sense is good, but in another sense is bad because the smells of the building are overwhelming. Cooking smells, mixed with cigarette smells are mixed with toilet smells. Sewer systems and facilities are ancient. Awful, just plain awful especially when the temperature is in the mid to high eighties. Thermostats don't seem to exist.

We sit down, and she begins to tell me the story of her brothers and their drug smuggling business. She also tells me about the death of her brother Atta and begins to weep, but she quickly composes herself and continues the story. When she is finished, I have no doubt the FBI and the DEA will be interested, although I do not look forward to going to their office. She also described the Chechen who called himself Dmitri Shepelova. She said he owned a taxi company in Moscow.

"Wait, he owns a taxi company?"
"Yes, why do you ask?"
"Because I think I know him."
"You know Dmitri?"

6

DMITRI AND MARC

JANUARY 15, 1982

"OK, Marina, you have to tell me the whole story." After Marina tells me the whole story, I'm exhausted. No, exhausted is the wrong word, I am drained. I can't believe how I fell into such a situation—a family of international drug smugglers, a murder, an international scandal involving numerous countries, and of course, me. I should go back to the embassy and tell them the whole story. They would want names. They would want, aw crap, they would want everything that I can't give them. So, they would want me. I need to get out of the Soviet Union and get back home and figure out what to do. Damn, I hate this. Oh right, DFL, Defense Foreign Liaison, that's me. Liaising with drug smugglers, killers, and who knows what else?

Ok, first things first, I've got to get out of this country. I can't call anybody affiliated with the Embassy, but who else do I know? So, I'm thinking call a cab, and bingo—Dmitri, that's who I know. Marina has his phone number, so I make the call.

"Dmitri here. Where are you, and where do you want to go?"

I answer, "Dmitri, it's Marc, the American. Do you remember me?"

"Of course. Where are you, and where to you want to go?"

"Pick me up at the main entrance to University of Moscow."

"Didn't pick you for a student, Mr. Marc."

"Just pick me up and I'll explain."

I say goodbye to Marina and tell her if she comes to the US again, she should call me, and I will try to help her. We hug and I'm torn inside to leave her. She seems to trust Dmitri, so I am going to have to trust Dmitri to take care of her.

I head out for the entrance to the University of Moscow and hopefully on my way home. It's about a 15-minute walk to the University, and I had no more than arrived when Dmitri pulls up in his cab. I get in and tell him to take me to my hotel. I'm going to pick up my luggage, and then we'll head for the airport. On the way back to the hotel, I tell Dmitri what has happened and that Marina has told me everything. He doesn't say a word. We pull up to the hotel, and I ask him to wait He just nods his head.

"Dmitri, are you upset with Marina telling me her story?"

"It was her decision to tell you. She is in a very dangerous situation. Mohammed will think nothing of doing away with her, and the same goes for the Ukrainians. I have done the best I could to keep her out of harm's way. There is nothing between Marina and I, but I respect what she has had to put up with, and what she had to do."

"I feel the same way and will do my best to help her. I think we are on the same page of the book, yes?"

"Yes."

It takes me about twenty minutes to get my luggage and check out. I go out the front door, but there is no sign of Dmitri. As I'm about to go back inside, another cab pulls up. The driver gets out and says he will take me to the airport as Dmitri has been called to another pickup. I have no choice, so I get in, and he delivers me to Sheremetyevo.

I'm lucky, I get the last available seat on Delta to Atlanta. Bye-bye Moscow. I've got eight hours to think about what has happened and what to do. I think I need more time.

When I arrived back in the States I got in late in the afternoon. I decided I would go straight to my office and catch up on paperwork. I had barely sat down and the phone rang. It was Dmitri. He told me he returned to Marina's apartment after he dropped me off and demanded to know if she could recognize any of the men who grabbed her.

Dmitri related his conversation with Marina as best as he could recall. "She said that she would tell me if she recognized any of them. She only knew they were Ukrainians from their speech. She said she had told you her whole story because she wanted to leave this country. She wanted to go to America. She said she told you of her brothers working with the Ukrainians but that she did not tell you anything about me. She said that you called me because I was the only person who you knew in Moscow who could get you to the airport."

Dmitri continues I told her "I know Marina. I know. We are going to have to move you out of this apartment. I can't take the chance that they will find you. Pack everything of importance to you, and we will go to my place tonight, and I will find you a new place tomorrow."

Dmitri goes on "So I took her to my apartment and after getting her settled down, I told her I had to go out, make some calls, and check on my other cabs."

"So I left and went directly to a bar near the US Embassy and found the person I was looking for."

"OK Dmitri" I said "I would venture a guess at who that was but not on this line."

"So you know who I am speaking to at the bar?"

"Yes, I think so."

"OK, so the guy asks me, is he gone?"

"He's asking about me, right?"

"Of course, I tell him yes, my cousin delivered him to the airport, and he should be in the air shortly." I ask him "Do you know who these Ukrainians are?"

He responds "No, I don't. I'll talk to my source and see if he has any info on Ukrainians working in Moscow."

I asked him "You will keep me out of this, yes?"

"He said I might want to go back to Odessa and lay low for a while. I should take Marina with me and set her up there. He told me you know I can't do anything for her."

I answer "I know, I know, of course not. We will be gone tomorrow,"

"So I left and got back in my cab thinking, damn CIA, what are they good for anyway? I returned to my apartment and told Marina that we were leaving first thing in the morning."

"Marina has gone to bed, and I am on the couch when my phone rings. I answer it with my usual taxi lingo, Dmitri here, where do you want to go?"

It's the guy from the Embassy. He says "listen very carefully. I've got two names for you. They were here in Moscow today and have left already for Odessa. My source says they are dangerous men and handle the enforcement work for the Ukrainian mob in Odessa."

I tell him "This is not good. We are leaving early in the morning. Thank you."

He asked me, "Dmitri are we good?"

"I told him, we are good. The book is even."

"He said OK, be careful. These guys are dangerous. I am surprised Marina and your friend Marc came out of this alive."

"OK Dmitri" I say, "so the embassy guy knows I am on my way back to the states. What the hell is going to happen to the two guys in Odessa?

Dmitri is silent. "Alright my friend, *Dosvedanya*!"

I really don't want to know what happens in Odessa.

7

THE CONNECTION

JANUARY 1980

Down in Huntington Beach, California a local boy was heading for the big time, big time trouble that is. . . Robert Romano grew up in Huntington Beach. He was born there, and his parents owned a convenience store a half-block off Main Street and right around the corner from Jack's Surf Shop. He went to Huntington Beach High. His family lived only a few blocks from the high school. Although the drug scene in Huntington Beach was not inordinately excessive, drugs were available to those who knew the contacts. Robert and his brother and sister somehow did not become users. They all worked at the convenience store and became first-class beach bums. Robert loved to surf, so he always took the late shift at the store so he could spend his mornings on his board. It was on his board and in the surf that he met his future business partner, Loco Leo.

Leo Ortiz was a huge man and surfed on a long board. He was about 6'4", 300 pounds with coal black hair and beard. He introduced Robert to the rest of the group that hung with him, usually 12 guys who answered to an assortment of nicknames and met almost every day north of the Huntington Beach pier to surf for two or three hours. They came from as far north as Redondo and as far south as San Clemente. After surfing, they convened at a garage Leo owned on Adams Avenue. Leo's garage advertised car repairs, but the six-foot, chain-link fence surrounding it seldom had its gate open. A large parking area behind the building provided room for all the gang's cars. It was in this garage where the drugs were stored and then divided among the 12 distributors, who were also the sellers.

Leo was known behind his back as "Loco Leo" and for good reason. He had a temper to match his size and was known to carry a Colt 45 caliber pistol most of the time.

Robert had heard that Leo actually killed three men, but no one wanted to talk about it. One of the surfer guys, Frantic Freddy, told Robert when asked about it, "Don't campaign to be number four, man, and don't even think about asking anyone else. Zip it!"

Leo and his brother-in-law had brought the family business to California from Panama. They were not friends, and one was sent to watch the other. The two of them fought constantly, and one day the brother-in-law disappeared. Leo said he went back to Panama, and no one questioned him. As both of them were in the country under false papers, no one went looking for the brother-in-law.

Leo had connections with his family in Panama and was the "man" in the drug scene in Huntington Beach. As their friendship progressed, Robert became more and more interested in Leo's business and began to see ways it could be safely expanded and become much more lucrative. He and Leo began to spend a lot of time together, and Leo enlisted Robert as his financial man, nicknaming him the "CFO."

Robert took over the books and suggested to Leo a scheme to launder the money through the purchase and import of exotic cars. Using this laundry method Robert surmised they could double, maybe triple, their sales. However, this would require more of the product from Panama. After looking over the operation for six months, Robert thought they could increase their sales by seven percent.

Leo thought they should personally present this to their suppliers and suggested they both fly to Panama and meet with their suppliers. Leo failed to mention to Robert exactly who his "suppliers" in Panama were. It was at this point that Leo decided to take Robert into his full confidence.

Leo's supplier in Panama was located outside of Colon, close to the seaside town of Portobelo. Their travel took them from Orange County, California to Panama City, and on to Colon. Here Robert would meet Adolfo and Manuel Mendez, kingpins of the Mendez Cartel. Loco Leo's uncles.

The Mendez compound had more security than Robert had ever seen, and the houses of Adolfo and Manuel were palatial mansions. It seemed that almost everyone carried some sort of automatic weapon, and of course everyone wore dark glasses. Even Leo had brought his and put them on.

A meeting was set for late afternoon and Robert was invited to "please feel at home and explore the grounds." He found his way to a huge swimming pool and sat down to just enjoy his surroundings. A servant immediately appeared and asked if he would like something to drink, so he requested a Negra Modelo beer.

At about the same time the beer arrived, a young woman appeared at the other end of the pool and dropped her robe where she stood, revealing a black bikini on a gorgeous body. Without a word she dived into the pool and began swimming laps. The pool was Olympic-size, at least fifty meters. After about ten laps, the woman swam up to where Robert was sitting. She was beautiful.

"Hi, I am Rosanna, and you are?"

"I am Robert."

"Where are you from, and what are you doing here, Robert?"

Not sure who this woman was and what he should tell her, he paused for a moment.

"Robert, I am Adolfo's daughter, and I know what business my dad is in. Is that why you are here? You don't look like a cattle buyer."

"I'm afraid you have found me out, Rosanna. I am from Orange County, California, and I'm here to meet with Mr. Mendez and his brother Manuel Mendez."

"Trust me it will be boring. After your meeting you will be coming to dinner, so I shall see you there, and we can become better acquainted."

"I'll look forward to that very much."

Meanwhile in the office of Adolfo Mendez, he and his security chief Alfonzo discussed Robert and the wisdom of allowing Leo to bring this unknown into their world.

Alfonzo related, "My contact in Orange County has made inquiries with Huntington Beach Police and Orange County Sheriff have both said they have nothing in their records, and the address he gives, is in fact the home of his parents."

Adolfo replied, "OK, we'll go ahead with the meeting and see what it is they have to propose. If anything comes up before then, we will deal with it, and he will simply disappear. We will have dinner after the meeting. I have been told their plane does not leave until tomorrow late afternoon, so we need to get our assurances before they leave. What's your first take on him?"

"He's hungry and eager and seems to be cautious, but naïve. I'll be watching him closely and waiting for any other info from the States."

"Good. Why don't you go over his story with Leo one more time and see if you catch any mistakes. By the way, how do you feel about Leo? Is he OK?"

"Leo seems fine. He believes this Robert Romano has something to offer."

"Manuel and I are looking forward to the proposal he has brought us."

I assume the meeting will be in the library. I've got all the electronics and video set up, ready to go."

"Perfect."

8

TEQUILA

MARCH 1982

The Mendez Cartel had been transporting drugs to the US for almost twenty years. Their contacts in Mexico were long established. A significant stop between Panama and California was a little town just north of Guadalajara. The home of Tequila and aptly named the same.

The town of Tequila lies in the mountains between Guadalajara and Puerto Vallarta. It's about a one-hour drive from Guadalajara and a four-hour drive from Puerto Vallarta on a winding, two-lane road. Much of the terrain between Puerto Vallarta and Tequila is dense jungle and inhabited by simple people who grow agave for the tequila distilleries in Tequila. Most of these people are of the Toltec Indian Tribe and do not have much contact with the outside world. Consuela and Jose Tolctezx were such people. They often would walk to the local market just outside Tequila and pass by the small airstrip carved out of the jungle. Every once in a while they would stop and watch a small plane which occasionally landed there. It apparently stopped for fuel, filled quickly, and took off again. The plane appeared to be packed with burlap bags. The trail was hidden from the airstrip by the dense vegetation.

"What do you think is in those bags," asked Consuela?

"I don't know," answered Jose.

"Those men are not from the village. They look like big city people."

"They are probably from Guadalajara. They drive those big black cars."

"I asked Juanita if she knew who they were and what they were doing."

"Consuela, do not talk to anybody about those people. If they should find out we are asking questions, it might be bad for us."

"Jose, you think they are smugglers?"

"I don't even want to think about that, and I sure don't want anybody to think we might know something."

Much further south in Panama, Adolfo Mendez and Alfonzo Benitez were discussing the airstrip near Tequila. The airstrip was the second stop after leaving Panama. The distance from Colon to Tequila was not within the range of the plane, so an additional stop was required at a desolate air strip in Guatemala. The plane was a small twin-engine Cessna 414, and at each stop the tail numbers on the plane would be changed. The plane would leave the Tequila air-strip and fly to another seldom used air strip in the province of Nayarit and be unloaded in a concealed hanger. The goods would be repackaged with kilos of cocaine being wrapped in hemp with a signal device which could be activated by only one person. Only one person possessed a device to activate and receive that signal—Loco Leo.

From there the goods were loaded on a shrimp boat

and continued on their way to Guaymas on the Sea of Cortez. The goods were then trucked to the busy border town of Nogales, Mexico and unloaded in a warehouse not fifty feet from the US border. Inside the warehouse the cocaine was extracted from the hemp bundles and placed in backpacks.

The backpacks were strapped on human mules who would carry them from the warehouse through an underground tunnel to another warehouse in Nogales, Arizona. Then came the dangerous part of the trip, by truck to California. The kilos were packed into freezers of fresh fish and bound for the west coast.

"I'm telling you Adolfo, I think it's time to find a new airstrip. We've used it too long, and I am worried some of the local Indians will talk about it and bring the *Federales*."

"It's true, we have used it for quite a while, but we have had no problems. Maybe you should go up there and see if there is any gossip in Tequila about it. If there is, look for a new strip."

"I'll leave tomorrow, but it will take a day to get there. I'll call you in a couple of days which will be a couple of days before the next shipment is scheduled to arrive."

"You will stand out up there, Alfonzo, so use your contacts."

"I have someone in the Tequila police force who is going to handle any inquiry."

"*Bueno! Hasta la Vista,* Alfonzo."

Alfonzo exited and immediately had Adolfo's secretary book a flight from Panama to Guadalajara. He then went into his office and picked up the phone and made a call.

"Humberto, it's Alfonzo."

"Greetings my friend. It has been a long time. Are you in the area?"

"No, but I am arriving late today at Guadalajara International. Flight 224, AeroMexico."

"I shall see you there, Alfonzo."

"Humberto, can you arrange for a room at Hotel Casa La Gran Senora. Maybe two nights?"

"Done."

Alfonzo busied himself the rest of the day contacting his sources in California and searching through his maps of Mexico for any other airstrip they might use and preferably purchase. By mid-afternoon he had come up with nothing in California and nothing in Mexico.

He went to his casita and quickly packed a bag and called for the car to take him to the airport. He passed through Panamanian passport control and boarded for Guadalajara.

Alfonzo arrived at Guadalajara, grabbed his bag, exited the terminal, and looked for his ride. A Tequila police car pulled up, and he hopped in the front seat. The driver of the car, Chief Humberto Gonzalez, was about fifty years old with dark hair and full mustache. He wore dark glasses which covered his dark eyes. He wore his chief's uniform with four gold stars on his shoulder boards. He commanded a police force of fifty, and there was no higher authority in the city of Tequila.

"Hola, Humberto! How are you?"

"Very well, and you, Alfonzo?"

"Very well."

"What brings you to Tequila? I hope nothing is wrong with Tequila International Airport?"

Alfonzo busts out laughing and responds"we have used Tequila for some time now, and I want to make sure there is no gossip among the Toltec."

"I have four or five sources among the Toltec who work in the distilleries of Tequila. They do not mix with most

Mexicans but they seem to know everything that goes on within the community of Calle Primavera, which is very near the strip and just north of Guadalajara Tepic 15. Many of them walk to Tequila and it is possible to see the strip from their trail. One of my sources who we shall stop and see is on the way to Tequila."

About five kilometers outside of Tequila, Humberto turned off on a dirt road and continued another kilometer through dense jungle before they arrived at a clearing with four very primitive houses. Humberto pulled up in front of the most primitive one, and hopped out of the car. He motioned for Alfonzo to come with. About the same time, a woman opened the door of the house and stepped out on the porch.

"Hello, Juanita. How are you?"

"I am fine, Chief Humberto Gonzalez. What brings you here?"

"How is your family, Juanita? Your daughter must be young woman now. Is she working in the distilleries also?"

"She is fine, Chief Gonzalez. And yes, they are all working."

"Very good, yes, very good. We must look after our children. Working keeps them out of harm's way. It makes you feel safe, yes? I am wondering if you have heard any rumors or had any inquiries about the abandoned air strip near Calle Primavera?"

"I have heard nothing although I don't think the strip is abandoned because I have heard an occasional plane, and I think it landed and took off from that strip."

"Have you yourself seen this plane," asked Alfonzo?

Juanita looked at Alfonzo and then back at Humberto with a puzzled look on her face.

"Please excuse me, Juanita. This gentleman, Senor

Benitez, is with the Policia Federales and is also interested in any gossip about the air strip."

"No, I have not seen the plane and don't know of anyone who has. It does not affect our lives in Calle Primavera," answered Juanita. "I only hear it."

"Thank you, Juanita. Be sure to look after your daughter and take care of yourself. If you hear anything about the air strip, you know how to contact me, and of course, I know how to contact you."

Humberto and Alfonzo returned to the car and drove off, back towards the highway. Juanita turned and went back into her house. She waited a few minutes and ran out the back door to one of the other houses where she found Rosa out back washing clothes.

"Rosa, who was asking about the airstrip?"

"The airstrip? Why are you asking me about that?"

"Because that pig Humberto Gonzalez was just here asking if anyone had been asking me about it, or if there were any rumors or gossip about it. He had a Federale with him and he threatened my daughter! You must tell whoever asked you about the strip to say nothing more. Ask no more questions. I am scared he will return with more questions, and you have heard the rumors about what he does to young women."

"It was Consuela who asked."

"We must warn her to not ask any more questions. We do not want to have any problems with that pig Humberto."

"She will be home shortly, or maybe she is home now. Let's go over to her place and wait."

Consuela and Jose arrived at their home about the same time as Rosa and Juanita.

Consuela was completely surprised and asked, "What are you doing here?"

Juanita immediately told her of the visit of Humberto Gonzalez and the Federale, which prompted Rosa to say, "I saw him. He didn't look like no Federale to me. Just another well-dressed thug."

"It makes no difference Rosa, they are both dangerous men. Consuela, we are here to tell you to be very careful. Ask no questions about the airstrip and repeat nothing about what you may have seen out there."

Jose shook his head, "Don't you think you are maybe making a big thing out of nothing?"

"Jose," said Juanita, "you do not think Humberto Gonzalez is a dangerous man? Do you not wonder about some people who have disappeared from our village, especially young women? We must look the other way when passing the airstrip."

Meanwhile, Humberto and Alfonzo were driving on to Tequila. Humberto said, "Maybe I should pick up Juanita's daughter tomorrow, take her to the station, and question her. It will shake Juanita up and maybe loosen her tongue."

9

MANNY & THE UKRAINIANS

MAY 1980

Leo's disclosure to Robert about Manny and the Ukrainians is a major turning point in this story and operation. How did that ever occur? A Mexican forming a deal with a Ukrainian? Strange bedfellows indeed. . .

Loco Leo's cousin Manny Ortiz worked as a longshoreman in the Long Beach and Los Angeles harbors. His job was to be there when a ship came in and tie it up to the dock. He worked odd hours but on some days or nights, he might have only one ship to tend. If this one ship took only one hour, it didn't matter, he was credited for an eight hour shift. So he and his crew were free to do whatever. Whatever, usually meant stopping at the Anchor Inn. Manny had worked many years as a longshoreman and was well known among the union. On one of those wasted days Manny was hanging out at the bar at the Anchor and got into a conversation with Fedor Stanislovsky who he had met before at the Anchor Inn. Fedor worked with a couple of Manny's good friends on a different crew.

"Hey, Manny, how's it going?"

"Hey, Fedor. Life is good. How's life on the crane crew?"

"Work has been steady. How about you, Manny?"

"You know they come and go. It's been steady. I haven't seen you around in a while. Hey, Bo, how about another Bud for me and my friend here?"

"Thanks, Manny, I've heard some talk, and I was wondering if you might be connected to some people who would be interested in a product a friend of mine has for sale?"

"Product? I hope it's not something slipping around Customs or out of Customs custody?"

"No, this is a personal-use product."

Looking around to see who's listening, Manny said, "Personal use?"

"Yeah, like the product your cousin has for sale."

"I don't know what you're talking about, Fedor. I think you have the wrong Manny."

"Oh come on Manny. The stuff I have to move comes from Afghanistan. It is the best stuff ever to hit the west coast."

"You got the wrong guy."

"I don't think so. I met a guy down in Orange County a couple of months ago, and he said he could connect me with a guy named Leo. I did some further inquiries, and it appears he's your cousin. Now I don't know Leo and he never returned my call, but I know you. I'm telling you Manny, this is a money-making proposition, and I'm just looking for someone to sell the stuff I can provide. Let me leave you a number, you can call if you want more information. You tell Leo this is an offer he shouldn't pass up."

Manny nodded and turned to talk to the bartender, Bo, as Fedor walked away.

"Hey, Bo, what do you know about that guy? He's not a cop is he? He sure asked questions like a cop."

"No, he ain't no cop. He's in here a lot. I think he's part of a crane crew. I'm surprised you haven't run into him before."

"Oh, I have. He's friends with some friends of mine. We just never hung out together."

Manny finished his beer and headed for the pay phone on the wall by the men's restroom. He drops in a coin and dials Leo's number. Leo answers on the second ring.

"Leo, this is Manny."

"Hey, Manny, what's up?"

"I just got approached by a longshoreman, named Fedor who knew your name and wanted to know if you might be interested in a product a friend of his has for sale."

"I hope to hell he's not a cop. You didn't give him any info did you?"

"Hell no! I gave him the brushoff, but he did give me a number to call if you were interested. Bo says he's a legit longshoreman."

"Come on over to the garage tonight and we'll talk it over and maybe give him a call. Demand is exceeding supply right now, and I might be able to work this. Watch yourself when you leave the Anchor and especially when you get down into Huntington Beach. Fedor got a last name, by the way? Sounds Russian to me. Those bastards are difficult to deal with and deadly as well. "

"His name is Stanislovsky. He said he called and left a message on your answering machine and you never called him back. I'll check with these guys who know him and see what they say."

"I don't like the fact that he had my name. You know I think I remember a call from a guy named Fedor and I thought it was some kind of joke. We need to be careful."

"Right, talk to you later, Bro."

Damn, thought Leo, this could be a nice bump in the wallet.

Stanislovsky headed out the door of the Anchor and stopped at the first phone booth he saw. "Ivan, it's Fedor. I made the pitch to the Mexican, and I think it might have perked his interest."

"Perfect. We got a shipment coming this Friday, and I've still got last month's to get out. If we get a call, I'll be ready to deal at a real good price. We might be able to break the stuff down and make a real nice profit. "

Leo was interested and thus began a very lucrative but dangerous business with the Ukrainians.

Longshoremen are a close-knit group. The union kept an ear to the ground and not much happened in the harbor that didn't come to their attention. Drug dealers and smugglers were not tolerated. Rumors were checked out by their "Rumor Squad" and you didn't want to be the person they were checking on. They carried things that could hurt you and usually did.

The rumor squad mainly consisted of two people. Johnny Dudek and Mike Nichols, who were union stewards and knew everyone who worked on the docks, not just union workers. Because of that they heard every rumor, true or not. When needed they provided discipline and if needed muscle to handle a situation. They did not handle pilfered goods, nor were they involved in the drug trade. But they did demand their cut. If they heard rumors of a smuggling operation being operated without their approval, they would check it out. An operation like that could upset the whole order of things on the docks. They would not let this happen.

Dudek and Nichols had just run into the agent for Russian Shipping at the Anchor Inn and warned him about the general dislike amongst longshoremen for the Russian ships.

Dudek asks Nichols, "So what do you make out of the Bauer guy? Is he legit or is he some fed sneaking around under the sheets?"

Nichols replies "I did some checking and he's new at Bergen Shipping, which handles all Russian shipping, but he seems to know his job and he knows his way around the docks. I couldn't find anything on his past."

Dudek says "I don't know why, but I smell fed. Ya know that could work in our favor if these guys are moving stuff around us, know what I mean?"

"Yeah, I think we should lean on Manny Ortiz and see what we come up with. In fact where is he today? I think we should get on it right away."

Dudek reaches in his jacket pocket and pulls out the daily shift schedule. "I agree. Ortiz is scheduled for the day shift, but he's only got one ship and it comes in at one thirty this afternoon, pier ninety two, San Pedro. We can grab him as soon as the ship is tied up. Pier ninety two? Is it a passenger ship?"

"Pier ninety two has got to be. A Russian by the sound of its name. MS Mikhail Lermontov."

"Gotta be. Let's go do it." Some how they missed Manny.

So, they decided to call a union meeting for the next day. Mandatory attendance was required. To accommodate all shifts, the meeting was split with one session in the morning and one session in the evening.

Manny attended the morning session while Fedor attended the evening session. Dudek and Nichols walked up to Manny after the meeting and said they would like a word with him. Manny knew who these two guys were and didn't hesitate to accompany them to their car. Dudek and Manny got in the back seat and Nichols got in the front. Dudek did the talking.

Dudek said to Manny, "ya know Manny we been hearing some rumors about the Russian ships bringing some new drugs into the harbor. You know anything about that Manny? Rumor has it that you got a cousin down in Orange County who is a big time dealer. We don't like stuff like this happening in our harbor without us knowing about it. This is some serious problem. I think you better get with your cousin and discuss this Manny. When you and your cousin come up with a solution to this problem, like serious compensation for overlooking your operation, you call me. Do you understand what I'm talking about here, Manny?"

Manny nods his head as perspiration rolls off his forehead. Dudek opens the door and gets out and motions Manny to come out. Dudek slams the door closed and spins Manny around and slams him up against the car, twisting Manny's arm behind his back. Dudek leans up against Manny and quietly whispers in his ear, "you got forty eight hours to get back to me with the right answer or you will be floating with the fishes. You understand me Manny? Now get the fuck out of here."

Manny gets in his car and stops at the nearest pay phone and calls Leo. Loco Leo now becomes paranoid Leo.

Dudek and Nichols grab Fedor after the evening session and he is given the same lecture as Manny. After being let out of the car and sent on his way, Fedor goes looking for the nearest phone also.

10

THE BROTHERS NOOR

SEPTEMBER 19, 1980

The guys that Loco Leo had hooked up with were some colorful and dangerous people, and I'm not talking about the Mendez brothers.

A few thousand miles away, just south of Dubrovnik, Croatia, in the tiny seaside town of Herceg-Novi, the Brothers Noor—Ustad, Atta, and Mohammed—plotted. Herceg-Novi is a coastal town in Montenegro, located at the entrance of the Bay of Kotor. Between 1482 and 1797, it was part of the Ottoman Empire and the Albanian Veneta of the Republic of Venice. It has had a turbulent past, and a history of varied occupiers and occupations has created a blend of diverse people.

The brothers Noor were actually Afghanis who fled the Russians and brought with them their knowledge of the opium and heroin trade. Using an import/export business dealing in Afghan dry goods as a cover, they traveled throughout the Middle East and Southern Europe using Herceg-Novi, Montenego as their base and the Hotel Perla as their home.

They could be found most days, when not traveling, in the Café Bar.

On this day they were all irritated because of the news they had received from the United States, in particular, their cousin, Ahmed Sul Fazir, who worked as a longshoreman and fisherman in Long Beach, California. He had told them that the Ukrainians were breaking down their product, or stepping on it, and making it less potent. They were then selling the excess to another dealer. The cousin was told that the product was being diluted by the dealer in California, who was not happy.

So, it was in the Café Bar after too many ouzo's and talking a little too loud, that a bearded man with light complexion, reddish blond hair, and average build overheard bits and parts of the Brothers' Noor conversation. Dmitri, the Chechen, was a good listener.

Mohammed, Atta, and Ustad were trying to decide what to do about the information they have received. However, the ouzo was making them feel drunk with power and making unreasonable plans. They were definitely getting drunk.

Mohammed said, "The Ukrainians have skimmed off about five percent of the last shipment. After doing more calculations, I figure the Ukrainians had been doing this for more than two years and have cost us at least three million in US currency. This is going to stop."

Atta responded, "We should go to Odessa, confront them with our information, and kill them."

Ustad disagreed, "We should not involve ourselves. We should hire someone to kill them."

Mohammed interrupted. "You both are wrong. We must simply find a new route for our goods and cut the Ukrainians out of the loop. We must make a new deal with the Chechen for he is the one who packages and transports the goods to Leningrad. He does not fear the Ukrainians."

The Chechen was the transporter of the goods after it cleared Odessa. He made sure it got to Leningrad and was packaged and loaded aboard a Leningrad ship bound for the West Coast of America. But now, it appeared the best plan was for it to be loaded on another ship for transport to America out of Odessa. The Chechen would have to find another cooperating captain.

There was no love lost between the Chechens and Ukrainians. Dmitri, the bearded man was the Chechen, a Moscow taxi cab company owner on holiday in Herceg-Novi. Well that's what he told everyone. He actually wanted to observe the Brothers Noor close up. He and his associates were the Odessa to Leningrad transporter. He didn't much like the Ukrainians or the Russians and he began pondering how he could put together a new deal for the Brothers Noor.

"Atta," Mohammed said, "you and Marina will go to Odessa and find the Chechen and have him find a different shipping company to transport our goods directly from Odessa. We will cut the Ukrainians out of the loop. Seeing as how we do not deal directly with the Chechen, it may require some searching to find him."

"Why should I take Marina with me? She will only slow me down."

"Your documents will show you traveling as husband and wife. Your inquiries in Odessa will be much less suspicious."

"I don't like it. Can she be trusted to go along with this?"

"Marina, come over here and sit down. We have something to discuss with you."

This is the same Marina from the MS Mikhail Lermontov and the Plotnikov Bar and this is how she got to Moscow and eventually to Los Angeles Harbor. Marina was a thirty-year-old, classic, mid-eastern beauty with long black hair, dark eyes, a perfect complexion, glowing light-brown skin, pearly white teeth, and a knock-out figure. She was tall for an Afghan woman, about 5′8″ and carried herself like a princess. Of course, her brothers forced her to wear traditional Afghan wear which effectively covered her figure.

Unfortunately, or fortunately, there were no suitable Afghans in Herceg-Novi for her brothers to arrange a marriage. Marina knew there was no way she would ever escape the grip of her brothers. She considered them thugs and was subjected to physical abuse regularly. She loved Herceg-Novi, but she was literally her brothers' slave.

"Marina, I want you to go with Atta to Odessa. You will travel with documents showing you and Atta as husband and wife. We need to locate someone in Odessa, and this will arouse less suspicion."

"I do not like the idea of her going. It is a bad idea. We don't know if she can be trusted," argued Atta.

"Trusted," spat Marina. "What have I ever done to deserve that remark?"

"You are a woman. Mohammed, I don't like it."

"Atta, you don't have to like it. Just do it. Marina you will do as your brother says and not draw attention to yourself. Agreed?"

And so, the Brothers Noor went to work finding a Captain with a Black Sea Shipping Company in Odessa who might be interested in making some extra cash.

Because he had anticipated a possible future problem with the Ukrainians, the Chechen had already come up with a new ship and a captain who was always interested in making more money, especially money for his own pocket. The bulk freighter *Mikhail Novogrodov* and its captain,

Serge Danislovsky, would be a perfect pair for this deal. Danislovsky at first balked at the idea of carrying contraband of any sort, however, when he was told how much money he could make, he changed his mind.

It seems everybody had a cousin working as a longshoreman in the Ports Long Beach and Los Angeles. The Brothers Noor had Ahmed Sul Fazir. The Ukrainians had Fedor Stanislovsky, a crane operator. Leo once had his cousin Manny Ortiz. Dmitri Shepelova had his cousin Sasha Federakova, who was assigned as a crane operator's helper, and of course, assigned to Stanislovsky's team. Because of their Odessa roots Federakova and Stanislovsky became friends. Ahmed Sul Fazir was a fork lift operator and also became part of Stanislovsky's crew.

The men became friends and drinking buddies, and it was over a few beers at the Anchor that Stanislovsky told Fazir and Federakova about a scheme he had to rip off some drug smugglers. Federakova and Fazir readily agreed to help him.

They agreed to be available when the next shipment came in, which was in a couple of days. They talked some more about how they would handle it, and after a couple more beers, called it a night. After leaving the Anchor both Federakova and Fazir got in their respective trucks. Federakova drove west over the Vincent Thomas Bridge to San Pedro, stopping at the first pay phone he saw. Federakova called Shepelova, waking him up in the middle of the night, telling him what he had just heard.

Fazir headed east down Ocean Boulevard towards Long Beach, stopping at the first pay phone he saw and called Mohammed and told him what he had just heard. This caused a major eruption of anger on the part of Mohammed.

Mohammed abruptly ended the call, saying he would

call back with instructions. Fazir knew what those instructions would be. Mohammed was not a man to be crossed.

Dmitri Shepelova, the Chechen, received the information with thoughts of how he could finally rid himself of the Ukrainians.

11

THE CAFÉ BAR

SEPTEMBER 19, 1980

The Café Bar is crowded with tourists. The Brothers Noor are having a late lunch at a table near the railing overlooking the bay. They have made the decision that Ustad should go to Afghanistan and that Atta and Marina will go to Odessa. After some grumbling the brothers agree.

The Noor family grew up in the Kandahar Province of Afghanistan, near the city of the same name. They were traditional Afghans, but as the brothers grew up they wanted more, and those who had more were involved in the growing and harvesting of opium.

Mohammed, against the will of his father, took a job with an opium trader as a general laborer, but he was ambitious and hard working. He was soon given more responsibility. That responsibility was transporting the opium from Kandahar, across the border to the port of Karachi, Pakistan—a very dangerous job. The border guards on the Pakistan side had been bribed and look the other way, but there was always the chance of someone new or a disgruntled guard.

There seemed to be no end to the demand for opium, so Mohammed recruits his brothers, Ustad and Atta. The shipments of opium were carried from Kandahar to Karachi, hidden in Afghan dry goods, and portions of the route were by horseback or mule. Their route took them through the central Brahai and the Khude Hills of the Pab Range where they had to skirt around the small towns and villages. Any, and all, persons of authority were bribed.

Ustad, who was the most personable, handled all the bribes—hence the reason he was selected to go to Afghanistan, as there seemed to be some new people who needed to be brought into the fold.

Travel from Herceg-Novi is not easy. First, it's by car to Dubrovnik, then by regional airline to Athens where Ustad will fly to Istanbul and on to Karachi, while Atta and Marina will fly to Odessa. Over the years, Mohammed has accumulated a dozen passports for all, and for each trip a different one is used. Only Marina, who has not traveled before, needs new documentation. They decide to travel in one week and go about their ways to prepare. Mohammed and Marina head for Mohammed's friend who will prepare Marina's new documents.

Dmitri Shepelova, the Chechen, who had been sitting across the room in the café, lingers for a moment, then gets up and casually follows Mohammed and Marina. They walk towards the older, central part of Herceg-Novi and after a series of stairways, up and down, stop in front of a non-descript three-story building and knock on the door. They are greeted by an unseen person who lets them in and shuts the door.

Dmitri checks the time and waits for about thirty minutes.

He is about to leave when Mohammed and Marina suddenly come out of the building. He turns and walks down an alley and makes another turn, out of sight. He waits a few minutes and goes back to the building and knocks on the door. A bearded man, about 5'5", wearing an apron smeared with printer ink opens the door, "May I help you?"

Dmitri recognizes the language as Farsi, but he does not speak Farsi and asks if the man speaks French, to which he responds, yes. Dmitri tells him he is looking for a jeweler and thought this was the address. The man responds, no, he is a printer and the jeweler, Moshe Rothshak, is on the next street over. Dmitri thanks the man and goes on his way, planning how he is going to pay the printer a late-night visit after he watches the building for a couple of days.

Directly across the street, Dmitri finds a small hotel, The Kotor, and books a room overlooking the street, and of course the building.

After two days, he has determined that the printer lives on the top floor and that he goes to bed at 10 o'clock promptly each night. At two a.m. the second night, Dmitri pulls on black slacks, a black turtle-neck sweater, black watch cap, and black gloves. He carefully exits his hotel through the back, circles around through the alley, and comes up on the building from the rear. He unexpectedly finds a side door to the building, and to his amazement, it is unlocked. He finds himself in a back room with only a file cabinet and a desk. Lying on the desk is a folder. He opens the folder and there are the beginnings of at least five passports and ID cards. He spreads them all out on the desk, takes out his camera, and photographs all the pictures and paperwork. He carefully replaces everything and quietly goes out the door. He does not return to his room at the Kotor, but instead goes down to his room at the Perla. Tomorrow would be a travel day.

12

ODESSA & DMITRI

October 9 & 10, 1980

Dmitri arrives back in Odessa and immediately calls his cousin, a supervisor with the immigration service. He tells him that he is expecting a visitor he met on his trip to Herceg-Novi and asks if he could please notify him when this person arrives.

"It will not be a problem," says the cousin.

Dmitri then goes to work devising a plan to move the shipment from the Brothers Noor into his own warehouse, which was unknown to the Ukrainians. He then calls the Ukrainians and asks when he will be required to take a shipment to Leningrad. He is told they are not expecting a shipment but will call him when something arrives.

Three days later, his cousin calls and says Marina Sofia Noor had arrived in the company of her husband and was staying at the Hotel Marmara.

"They are traveling with Turkish travel documents which look good, but I spotted a flaw, and unless you have some purpose and appropriate compensation in mind, I will be obligated to report them to the Intelligence Service," warns Dmitri's cousin.

Dmitri silently curses, but says he indeed has compensation in mind and will deliver it the following day. He would dearly like to bury his knife into his cousin's neck, but business is business.

The Hotel Marmara is not far from the harbor and has a decent restaurant and pastry shop. Dmitri leaves word at the desk for Marina and her brother that he will be in the café at nine a.m. the next morning. The front desk passes the information on to Marina and her brother who are more than alarmed to receive the note.

"Atta, who is this man? Do you know him? How did he know we were here at this hotel, and how did he know you are my brother? Our documents show us as husband and wife," cries Marina.

"I don't know, Marina. I will call Mohammed and tell him of our situation."

"No, you must not. We have to handle this or Mohammed will order us home, and he will take this out on me, that I am to blame. That I must have made a mistake. I will not let that happen."

"Silence! You will do as I say. I need to go down to the café right now and look it over. I will then decide whether or not to call Mohammed."

"No, we will not call Mohammed. We will handle this meeting and see what this man wants."

Atta scowls at Marina. She has never talked to him like this before. Suddenly, he reaches out and slaps her face. He then grabs her by her hair and throws her on the floor. He curses her and then kicks her in the stomach. As she lay moaning on the floor, he grabs her by the hair again and warns her, "You will do as I say, or I shall make you disappear into the brothels of the Black Sea, you insubordinate bitch."

Marina is stunned. The brothers had always treated her as if she were a slave and would at times beat her for meaningless reasons, but they had never made such a threat. Marina makes up her mind that this will be the last time. If Atta ever lays a hand on her again he will pay for it. She will devise a plan and after their meeting with Dmitri Shepelova, she will decide what to do.

Then, Atta suddenly kicks her again and turns to go to the door.

"Where are you going Atta?"

"I'm going out. You will not leave the room. I shall meet with this Shepelova and make a decision of what to do."

He goes out and slams the door. Marina gets up and goes to the bathroom to see if she has any bruises. Her stomach aches and she suddenly feels sick and vomits into the toilet. She washes her face and changes clothes—donning slacks,denim jacket and a scarf on her head. She opens the door a crack, looks out, and doesn't see Atta anywhere, or anyone else for that matter.

The hotel is located across the street from a huge bazaar. It attracts many shoppers and is a place where one could buy almost anything. Marina slips across the street and disappears into the maze of vendors and shoppers. It doesn't take long for her to find what she is looking for. She asks the vendor for the price. After some haggling, they agree and she slips the item in her bag. After some more wandering, she returns to the hotel. After a couple of hours, Atta returns and says he has decided they should go down to the café and have something to eat.

"This will give me a chance to look the place over and decide if we should meet this Shepelova."

Marina had changed back into the clothes she had on when Atta left so he would not ask any questions. She says nothing to him and just sits on the bed waiting for his next comment. When he says nothing, she turns on the TV and pretends to watch. If Atta lays a hand on her again, it will be the last time. She is not sure of the consequences, but she does not care. She has her freedom from Atta in her bag.

After an hour or so, Atta tells Marina that he is going down to the restaurant and that she is to stay in the room. He returns almost three hours later and is obviously drunk. She starts to ask about the café when he suddenly slaps her across the face and shoves her onto the bed. He jumps on her and starts ripping at her blouse, all the while punching her in the stomach and around her head.

She attempts to resist him, but he is much stronger and his punching is taking its toll. "Atta stop!" she cries.

"Shut up, you worthless whore."

"Atta, it's me Marina. Stop. Stop, Atta." The beating worsens.

He continues his drunken rage as Marina reaches for her purse. The last thing Atta hears is the clicking of the switch-blade knife as it opens. The last thing he feels is the knife piercing his neck.

Silence. Blood everywhere. She pushes Atta off her and wails.

Marina crys outloud to herself "Oh my god! What have I done? Atta, why wouldn't you listen?" Marina collapses into uncontrollable sobbing. There is blood all over the bed and Atta is not breathing. She finally begins to realize what a hopeless situation she is in.

Talking to herself she says "I must gather myself. I must figure how to handle this. The police will throw me in jail and for sure they will discover my papers are forged. I must think clearly."

She gets off the bed and looks in the mirror. She is covered with blood. She strips off her clothes, gets in the shower, and scrubs herself clean. Looking at Atta, she tries to figure out what to do. She begins wrapping him up in the bedding, pulls him off the bed onto the floor, and drags him across the room behind the couch.

She continues to talk to herself "I need someone to help me. I can't do this myself. But, I know no one in this city. Wait, Shepelova. I will meet with him tomorrow and make an excuse for Atta and see who this man is and maybe he can help me. Yes, yes, that is what I will do." She looks at the bed and begins sobbing again. She cannot lie in this bed. This bed is where she killed her brother. She grabs a pillow and crawls to a corner, as far away from Atta as she can, and collapses.

She sobs to herself "Tomorrow I shall deal with this. Tomorrow."

The next morning, Dmitri arrives at the Hotel Marmara at 8:30 and finds a table in a secluded corner of the café with a view of the entrance. At 9:00 he watches as Marina enters the café by herself. He is puzzled, as he fully expected Atta Noor to come without his sister. She is asked by the Maitre d' if he can help her. Dmitri catches her eye and motions her to come back. She cautiously, but yet confidently, walks back to Dmitri's table. Dmitri stands and offers his hand which she firmly grasps and shakes.

"Please have a seat and join me Miss Noor. I am Dmitri Shepelova. Excuse me if I seem puzzled, but I fully expected to be meeting your brother. Waiter, please bring us coffee."

"Thank you, Mr. Shepelova, but I'm afraid I have a bit of a problem. First of all, I am not sure of who you are and what it is that you want with me and my brother. He has decided for reasons of our safety to remain in a position of observance while you and I discuss whatever business you think we have."

"That is a wise decision. However, you and your brother both know what we are here to discuss. The establishment of a new route for your Afghan merchandise. I am the man who transported your goods to Leningrad, and I will be the man who arranges for new transportation from here to America. So, please signal your brother to come in, and we shall begin as I have made almost all the arrangements, and we just need to negotiate compensation."

Marina is suddenly stunned and speechless. She did not expect to meet this man. This man, who was part of their organization.

"What is it Miss Noor? And what has happened to you? I see bruises on your face. Were you attacked on the street? Please call in your brother and tell me what happened."

"I am afraid I have a serious problem, Mr. Shepelova. It was my brother who attacked me."

"What? Why did he attack you? Where is he now? This is unacceptable. We are here to do business. You two must conduct your family problems in private. We cannot draw the attention of the authorities. Do you understand me? Go bring your brother, now."

"I cannot."

"Why not?"

"He is dead."

"Dead?"

"Yes, dead."

"What happened? An accident? Muggers? What?"

"He was drunk and began beating me and attempted to tear off my clothes. I tried to resist and fight him off, but he was in a drunken rage. I stabbed him in the neck, and he is dead."

Dmitri is stunned into silence. He whispers across the

table, "You stabbed him? And he is dead? And where is he now?"

"In my room."

"In your room. In this hotel?"

"I put the do not disturb notice on the door when I left."

"Let us hope they do not disturb your room until you are on the other side of the world!"

"I did not know what to do. I know no one. I cannot contact my other brother, he will kill me. Can you help me?"

Dmitri silently curses under his breath, and after taking a deep breath and gathering his thoughts he says, "I must help you. We have been seen together. My first inclination is to take you up to your room and do away with you, but I cannot condone what your brother did to you. Finish your coffee, and we will go to your room, and I will try to come up with a solution to this problem."

"Can I trust you not to kill me?

"Do you have a choice? Come, we must get up there before the maids."

Dmitri is stunned by this event but was always able to think on his feet and come up with a solution. This, he thinks, may be as difficult a problem as he has ever faced. He decides he will take care of Atta Noor and dispose of the body. He will need to hustle Marina out of Odessa to Moscow, his home base. He will make some calls to acquire an apartment for Marina. He will make another call to a friend who works for a Soviet passenger vessel company at their Odessa office about a possible job for Marina. When he tells her of his plan she is reluctant to accept the idea of going to Moscow. He tells her she will not be able to exist on her own in Odessa. She reluctantly agrees to go. He makes plans for them to travel the next day.

13

DMITRI AND MARINA

October 10, 1980

Dmitri and Marina go back to her hotel room separately. Marina goes up first and immediately breaks down sobbing when she enters the room and sees Atta rolled up in the bedding. A knock on the door startles her, and she goes to peek around the curtain. It's Dmitri. How did this happen, she wonders? How do I dare to put myself in the hands on this Chechen? He would as soon slit my throat as help me.

Another knock at the door.

"Marina, open the door."

She does, and he slips in.

"What were you waiting for?"

"I was scared it was the police."

"We must think clearly and intelligently now. I have a plan to remove the body, but it's going to cost money. Did you and your brother bring money with you?"

"I don't have very much. I cannot call my brother Mohammed and ask for more. It would be better if he thought we were both dead. But wait, Atta must have money on him."

They quickly go through Attas Pockets and to Marina's suprise they find fifteen hundred American dollars.

"Mohammed does not know where I am staying. You could call. Tell him who you are. Tell him Atta went out drinking and was found stabbed. There was no evidence of what happened to me. I apparently went looking for him and disappeared."

"I like that better. I will make the call and tell him you have disappeared after our meeting. We cannot make the call from here. There are many phones in the bazaar. After I get rid of your brother's body we will go and I will make the call."

"How are you going to get rid of my brother?"

"I think it best that you don't know. I want you to go out for a couple of hours. Go to the bazaar, and I will meet you at a Greek taverna called Gregori's. Two hours. Understood? Take only a small bag with your essentials and documents. You will not be coming back here. So, go now, quickly."

As soon as Marina left, Dmitri slips out and goes to a pay phone. He has a hushed conversation. Then, he returns to the room and begins preparing Atta's body for removal. A few minutes later, two men arrive with a shipping trunk and a hand cart. Within thirty minutes the room is like no one has ever been there. Dmitri goes out and crosses the street to a small café on the edge of the bazaar where he can watch the hotel. He watches for an hour and then heads for the Taverna Gregori.

Marina is waiting when he arrives. Dmitri is in personal turmoil over what he should do. This woman is a liability and a danger to his welfare, but he cannot be overcome with sympathy. Of course, the fact that she is so beautiful has nothing to do with it.

"Dmitri, I am beside myself. I am so sorry to bring this upon you. If we call Mohammed and tell him what I did, he will surely kill me. I cannot face him."

"I am going to call Mohammed as soon as I come up with a suitable explanation as to what happened to Atta. I know for sure you cannot stay here in Odessa. I will take you with me to Moscow, and we will make you disappear."

"Moscow! What am I going to do in Moscow? I know no one. I have no money and no place to live. I might as well let Mohammed kill me."

"We will not worry about that now. I must first call Mohammed and get him off our back. Give me the telephone number. I will call him now. It is best to get this off our mind so we can make a plan for your future."

Marina reluctantly gives Dmitri the number and asks what he will tell Mohammed.

"I will tell him who I am. I am the Chechen. I will tell him that we had a meeting planned and that Atta did not show. I have tried to get information from the police, but they have no record of Atta Noor. I will tell him that you were most likely kidnapped and sold to a prostitution ring. I will tell him that I am the one who has been packing and shipping his goods to Leningrad, and I will continue to be his shipping source in Odessa, but I cannot be involved in his family problems."

"But what am I going to do?"

"I have many contacts in the shipping world and I will find something for you. You must be patient. We will go to Moscow and work things out from there."

Dmitri exits the taverna and calls Mohammed. He explains what he knows. Mohammed is livid and says he will come to Odessa and find out what happened to Atta and find his sister Marina.

"Mohammed, listen to me. I have found nothing, and I have many contacts in Odessa. If you come here, you may arouse the interest of the wrong people and our working relationship shall end. This is a dangerous business we are in, and I cannot afford to take this additional risk. I shall continue to package and ship your goods, but if you come to Odessa, I shall disappear. Can we agree?"

"I agree. But, if some information should come to your attention, you will share with me, yes? I will want revenge at the point of my blade."

"Agreed. Tell me when to expect the next shipment. I have many new arrangements to make. I need to make sure everything is in order. I have to make sure our new ship's captain is capable of handling the delivery in America."

"You have handled our business safely and securely in the past, so I will trust you with this. The next shipment should arrive one week from today. Call me on this phone if it does not. I trust the delivery at the other end is still in place?"

"It is."

Dmitri returns to the Taverna and tells Marina he has convinced Mohammed not to come to Odessa.

"We will find a hotel for tonight, and tomorrow we will go to Moscow. I will try to find you a job. Have you ever worked, other than for your brothers?"

"No, but I am a good cook, and I have waited on them hand and foot since I can remember."

"So maybe you could be a waitress or a steward on a ship?"

"I could do that. I speak Russian, German, Farsi, and English."

"English! That is good. I have a very good friend who

is the captain of a Soviet passenger vessel, the *Mikhail Lermontov*. It sails out of Odessa but their main offices are in Moscow. They are always looking for people who are multi-lingual."

"What is multi-lingual?"

"One who speaks more than one language."

"I am such a person."

"That is good, Marina. That is good."

14

DMITRI'S REVENGE

LATE OCTOBER 1980

The trip from Odessa to Moscow is without incident, and Dmitri quickly sets Marina up in his brothers' apartment. His brother Serge will be gone for months. He makes a call to his cousin and gives him the names given to him by the CIA in Moscow.

Marina is hired on the spot by the shipping company and learns she is scheduled on the next sailing of the *Mikhail Lermontov*. She doesn't need to unpack but she does need some additional clothes so Dmitri takes her over to the GUM department store and she gets what she needs.

Dmitri's cousin calls back within the hour and has the information that Dmitri needed. He tells Marina he has some business to take care of and may be gone for a couple of days. The shipping company will transport her back to Odessa. He leaves, wishing her well on her cruise.

The two men Dmitri is looking for are back at their home in the harbor area of Odessa. They actually have a compound consisting of four separate houses and garages.

Dmitri estimates at least 15 people live in this compound. His sources say they are heavily armed. He decides he will watch for a day or so, and see where they spend their days. It didn't take long to find where the men went every day.

They had a warehouse near the harbor. All five of the Ukrainians went there every morning and then left in trucks or vans to pick up goods down on the docks and bring them back to the warehouse. The street entering the warehouse is downhill, and although there is a gate, it is made of wood and would not withstand a truck or van hitting it dead on.

He decides to load a van with explosives and park it up the street. When he is sure all five are in the warehouse, he will release the brake on the van and let it smash through the gate and into the warehouse where it will be exploded by remote control.

By the time this happens, Marina will be well on her way out of the Black Sea and into the Mediterranean. Dmitri wonders if she will ever be back.

Marina feels a sense of urgency and anticipated excitement as her ship heads for new ports of call and, eventually, Los Angeles.

Dmitri and his cousins load the truck and deliver it to the street leading into the warehouse. At seven a.m. all five of the Ukrainians are there preparing to make their rounds. Suddenly they hear a loud crash and a van smashes through the gate and into the warehouse. That is the last thing they hear.

Police are unable to find any witnesses, and the van had nearly been reduced to scraps. They find where the VIN number should be, but it had been filed off.

15

THE ANCHOR INN

APRIL 27, 1979

Let's go back a couple of years and let me describe the Anchor Inn. This place could be the perfect set for any movie Hollywood ever made that features a bar. It could be in any state or any country. When you walk in you feel like you've been there before. However, the eyes that look you over scream alien, you don't belong here.

The Anchor, as it is affectionately called, is just off West Ocean Boulevard and just before crossing the Vincent Thomas Bridge. The Anchor Inn, a crossroad and meeting place for all thirsty harbor workers—longshoreman, truckers, seaman, shipping agents, and anyone else who actually dares to enter—stop for a quick beer or some of the best food between San Pedro and Long Beach. Dark, smoky, and well worn, it's not a place to stop for lunch or a drink wearing a suit. It's always crowded with big, loud, husky men who best be left alone. As a shipping agent I found it a convenient place to meet other agents and to become acquainted with what was going on in the whole harbor. The place is generally full of longshoremen and truckers who were Teamsters. There seemed to be an unspoken order that the two did not mix—longshoremen to the left, Teamsters to the right. Seldom did I stop there when there wasn't some argument that was usually settled by one of the two very large bouncers. You start a fight, don't come back. You lose a fight, same rule.

Today, I am recognized by a couple longshoremen who operated the cranes, unloading ships and were also union stewards. As I step up to the bar, Bo Swenson, the bartender asks, "What'll ya have?" Before I can answer, the two crane operators edge their way to the bar, one on each side of me, and tell Bo they're buying my drink.

"Thanks guys. What's the occasion?"

"We saw you go aboard that Russian rust bucket. Are you Russian?"

"No, I'm an agent for Bergen Shipping. What's up?"

"So you're not a cop or a fed?"

"No. I just handle the paperwork. So who are you two?"

The guy on my left looks left and right and then at the guy on my right, who nods.

"We don't much care for seeing Russian ships in our harbor, that is, we longshoremen. What is even more annoying, we heard a rumor they were carrying drugs. Even a hint if that is true, and we'll shut them down and out of our harbor. I'm a steward of the longshoremen's union, and I can make that happen."

"I have no information that would confirm that. I mean both Customs and Coast Guard deal with that kind of info. I can put you in touch with the right people in either organization."

The guy on my right finally speaks, "We don't deal with cops, local, fed, military, or whatever. We might deal with you. Gimme your card, and if you check out we might have something for you. Whatever you do, don't contact the cops, any cop. We got some really rough guys down here who have no trouble busting a guy up. Understand Mr. Marc Bauer? Bo, give the man another. Be seeing you."

Holy Shipping! I can't believe what I just heard! I ask Bo, "Who were those guys?"

"Longshoremen, man, longshoremen, and union stewards, Johnny Dudek and Mike Nichols. You just met two of the most powerful and dangerous men in the harbor"

"Oh great, but how the hell did they know my name?"

"Marc, everyone knows your name. You're the guy who deals with the Russians." He sets up another beer and says, "On the Union. Be careful out there. Longshoreman pride themselves on having an accident-free harbor, but that ends on Ocean Boulevard."

I later came to learn that Johnny Dudek and Mike Nichols were indeed union stewards and knew everyone who worked on the docks. Because of that, they also heard every rumor, true or not. When needed, they provided discipline and muscle to handle a situation. They stayed clear of handling pilfered goods or being involved in the drug trade. The word was that neither man had ever been arrested or charged with any crime in the harbor. The smuggling operation that they suspected was being conducted without their approval could upset the whole order of things on the docks. They would not let that happen.

16

THE FBI

MAY 24-26, 1982

Back in California things are happening that will not please the Mendez brothers and most certainly not the Brothers Noor. Me, on the other hand, I'm getting ready to hang myself virtually and literally.

Drugs were not on the FBI's hot list. That was the DEA's territory. But when an informant came up with some info that a certain young hotshot was importing luxury foreign cars to launder drug money, Special Agent Frankie Koch's ears perked up. Koch, who worked in the FBI's Orange County office, was an up and comer in the FBI and seemed to have a nose for big cases. When his informant, a Huntington Beach local, told him of this young guy with too much money and a Panamanian wife, he was like a bloodhound.

Koch first opened a preliminary inquiry in early 1981, which allowed him to check any and all records. Then he did the federal search, which included all the three-letter agencies. When nothing came up, he knew he had something. He packaged it all together—the house in Huntington

Harbor, the cars, no job, and the Panamanian wife—and got a wiretap authorized. Bingo! The information started flowing in. These guys openly talked about everything on the telephone, and it didn't take long to identify all the players.

The main characters, Robert and Rosanna Romano were surrounded by a cast of characters right out of the movies—Loco Leo, Curly Corey Flynn, Wipeout Willy, Boardman Barnes, Smack Kowalski, Donut Duncan, and others with equally memorable nick names. The entire group consisted of the Romano's and 14 other drug peddlers.

Meanwhile, I've decided that the contact with Marina should be reported to the FBI, so I do. On Monday May 24 I knock on the door of the FBI office in Santa Ana, California. I receive rather a cool reception from the FBI. It's like I'm another kook in from the street, and unless they developed the information, it's not worth the paper it's written on. Give him the "paperclip necklace," and send him on his way. Oh, the paperclip necklace. Street people come knocking at the door of every federal office, and you have got to listen to them. We are public servants. A lot of them hear voices and receive radio signals from outer space. So, some genius devised the paperclip necklace. While the citizen is ranting about what his or her current threat to world is, you reach in the desk drawer and grab a handful of paperclips and start making them into a chain. You then explain to the concerned citizen that this necklace is high-tech government technology which repels all those voices and radio signals. You then escort them to the secret back door passageway to the street. Works wonders. OK, I digress.

So, I'm thinking about this while I'm telling the FBI everything I know about Marina, the *Mikhail Lermontov*, the diplomatic pouch, and the members of the crew I had met. They want to know what was on the menu for lunch. They want the crew list and copies of all paperwork regarding the ship. Now, I knew damn well they had already been to my office at Bergen and had all this stuff, but I agree to provide it again.

"So how are things over at DFL?" the agent asks with a smirk on his face.

I resist dressing him down. I mean, I am a Deputy Assistant Director, GS-15, and this guy is probably at most a GS-13, Special Agent. But if you are FBI, everyone else is your underling. I lean across the desk and slide my card across the desk with one finger. "Things are fine, just fine, Special Agent." I get up and leave, feeling quite proud of myself.

Well, that lasts about 24 hours until Frankie Koch calls me and says we need to talk. Turns out, Special Agent Smart—as in ass—and his boss Frankie had a talk after I left. It seems they needed me and when I received a phone call from Frankie Koch I sensed it. What I didn't sense was the fact they had just gotten some wonderful new photos.

My phone rings and I answer, "Defense Foreign Liaison."

"May I speak to Marc Ryder please. This is Special Agent Frankie Koch."

"This is Ryder."

"Marc, may I call you Marc? We have need of your services and I wonder if you might come over to our office tomorrow and discuss what we have in mind. I would like you to be part of a task force we are forming. I have talked to the Assistant Director of your organization and he supports it if you will agree. I am aware that you are a busy man, but we need your help."

Well this was more like it. "Sure, I'll be there at two o'clock sharp."

"Thank you." Click!

With all the information coming in from the wiretap, Frankie was given anything he wanted. He had surveillance of the house in Huntington Harbor 24/7 and who should pop up, but yours truly.

Frankie was given some photos from a big party on the night of May 21st in Huntington Harbor. The photos included some very clear and close up images of me in the surf. Naked, with a Panamanian beauty.

I am really screwed, figuratively and literally! Of course, I have no idea of the existence of the photos nor that I am the main topic of a conversation going on while I am standing at the door of the FBI at two o'clock in the afternoon, knocking. It's like asking the hangman for the rope. The same agent who I encountered the last time answers the door, "Hey DFL! How's it going? Come on in and join the party. We're just talking about you, and I'd like to show you some great pictures."

"Thanks, but I'm not into kiddie porn."

"Really? Not even when you're the star of the show?"

As the air left my lungs and my heart stopped beating, I tried to stand tall without holding onto the wall. There was no way I could not register complete horror on my face.

"Whoa there DFL, you look a little pale. Have a drink of water and try to calm down. Follow me into the conference room. We have some important things to discuss."

Spread out on the conference table are too many pictures of my late night's fun. As I collapse in a chair, Frankie Koch comes into the room and things really turn to crap.

"Marc, you don't need to say anything. We pretty much know it all, but there is something that concerns you that I don't think you know about. I know you're married to Janet, but how well do you really know your wife?"

"Wait a minute. What does this have to do with Janet?"

"Well, judging from these other pictures we have, I'd have to say it has a lot to do with her."

I tell them our situation. Married, but not. Single, but not. She does her thing and I work.

Special Agent Smart exclaims, "How come I couldn't be so lucky? My old lady watches me like a hawk. Damn DFL, I have come to a new height of admiration of you."

"Alright, let's keep this professional. It seems," says Koch, "that she has been doing her thing with the Romanos, and they have compromised her into giving them information about your job and contacts, especially with the FBI or DEA."

"Compromised her? What? How?"

"Marc, I don't want to shock you, but Janet has not been a good girl, and we have photos that Rosanna used to compromise her."

"I can't believe this. I want to see the photos."

"You're not going to like them." He hands me some photos.

"Ah, shit."

"Amen to that. Here's what we want. We want you on our task force. Your closeness with Rosanna could give us a real advantage. We are going to bring them down, and your relationship with her and Robert could be a big help."

"I'd have to clear this with the director."

"He's already given us the clearance to use you. Don't worry, we did not share the photos or any info other than it appeared you might have a social relationship with the Romanos through your wife."

"Well, thank you, for that. I guess I'm on your task force."

"Hey, welcome aboard DFL, and you can call me Biff," says Special Agent Smart.

17

THE PLUNGE

May 17-21, 1982

OK, let me explain all those perfectly ridiculous pictures the FBI had of me. Maybe I can loosen the tightness of the rope around my neck.

My first marriage got trashed by me between my midlife crisis and getting recruited by the Defense Foreign Liaison Office—DFL, damn I hate that acronym. After first thinking what a special job I had, my second wife, Janet, soon disinterested herself in me and my career. We lived in a house with two master suites and we lived two different lives. Single, but not. Married, but not. Both miserable. Our sex life was passing. Whenever we passed, "Screw you!" Janet was in therapy when I met her and she could only talk about how the world was against her and I should be more compassionate. I should join her in therapy. I should do this, I should do that.

"Marc, are you listening to me?"

"Yes, I am listening."

"You need to come with me to therapy this week. I told Doctor Theresa you would come."

"Alright, alright. I'll go with you."

"No, you don't just go with me. You participate. You act like you want to be there."

"Alright."

"By the way, Linda Wright was by today with a buyer for the house."

"Buyer? The house isn't even for sale!"

"I told her it was. For a hundred-ninety-five grand"

"A hundred-ninety-five grand! That's forty grand more than we paid, 12 months ago!"

"I know. She has a buyer who made a cash offer for that amount. So she figured we wouldn't turn it down and thought we would obviously be looking for another house so she showed me a place in Huntington Harbor. Fabulous. On the water, three thousand square feet and twin master suites, a three-car garage and thirty five-foot dock. Two hundred fifty five thousand! A steal!"

This was the beginning of the end. Going from Irvine, California to Huntington Harbor, California. Fast boats, fast cars—OK, I had one too—and fast people who had way too much money and the time to spend it. I worked and traveled. Janet found a new group of friends and a new job. I wasn't included in her new circle of friends. So, I worked at being single, but not and married, but not.

In the meantime, my life was becoming increasingly complicated. How the two of us came together is just another sordid tale of two people seeing the grass on the other side of the fence greener. After tearing your life apart while climbing over, or through, or under the fence, you realize it's the same old brown grass, just in a different pasture. Janet had it all, it seemed. Good looks, a seductive smile, blond hair, a terrific sense of style, and did I mention a taste for money. She wanted the gold mine and I got the shaft.

I had a full week at home with no travel, and it gave me a chance to catch up with all my sources and chums in the harbor. It also revealed how far apart Janet and I had drifted.

"Marc, Robert and Rosanna are throwing a party at their house Friday and invited us. I said we'd love to come."

"Robert and Rosanna? Have I met them?"

"You'll love them. He imports exotic cars from Europe and Rosanna has a clothing line made in Panama."

"What kind of cars?"

"I don't know. Fancy one's like that Porsche of yours that you're in love with."

Robert and Rosanna Romano live along the water in Huntington Harbor and have one of the more spectacular homes and locations. A driveway at the end of a cul-de-sac reveals what appears to be a 4-car garage but is actually an 8-car garage. As you walk around the garage through a gate to a courtyard bordered by Roman columns, you are presented with a glass house which allows you to see right through it to the harbor beyond. Decorated in every color imaginable, with colorful modern furniture and paintings, one can only wonder, how the hell much did this cost? And what does this guy do?"

Robert is a young, slick, fast talking sales type who never answers questions like what do you do, but always has something to say. He's 6-feet tall with dark wavy hair, a small moustache, a diamond-pierced ear. He reminds me of some movie star from the '40s. He wore a white silk shirt, black slacks, and some very expensive loafers. He speaks with a slight accent, which I can't place, more Italian than Spanish. Rosanna is just plain gorgeous. She's native Panamanian with almost waist length, coal black hair, and mesmerizing deep brown eyes which strangely made me feel uncomfortable. Like I have heard a woman say "he undressed me with his eyes." I had that feeling. Her one-piece pant suit showed off all of her, what can I say, outrageously sexy shape. I returned the favor and undressed her. With my eyes!

The party was catered and a very good jazz combo provided the background sounds. Janet, more or less, dumped me off on a couple who sold real estate, and to be honest, they were the only people I'd meet all night who actually told me what they did. I told Janet before we got there that I was going to tell anyone who asked that I worked as a shipping agent.

"Whatever. Just don't tell anyone you work for the government."

"You make it sound like a disease."

"Yes, well it might as well be. Being a government hack in this crowd will surely not get us invited back."

"That's pretty cruel. What have you told Robert and Rosanna?"

"I told them you're in public relations and that you deal primarily with foreign companies."

"They believed that?"

"Yes, but who cares what you do? Just have a couple of your favorite dirty martinis and enjoy."

So, I did. The party rolled on, and about midnight I found myself at the bar next to Rosanna. I tried not to undress her as we talked. We got to talking cars and boats, and Rosanna invited me to check out Robert's exotic cars. Drinks in hand, we wandered out to the eight-car garage—two Porsches, three Mercedes, two BMWs, and a Ferrari.

"I understand you yourself have a Porsche?"

"Yes, it is my pride and joy."

"What color is it?"

"Black, 911 Carrera."

"Oooh, black is my favorite. Did you drive it over here tonight?"

"Yes, I did."

She reached out and stroked my arm, "We should maybe go for a ride on PCH and get a cocktail at The Golden Bear. They might have some good music we could dance to, hmmmmm? Wanna go?"

"We'll be missed."

"We're going to get more ice. Janet is into the good stuff and won't miss either of us until tomorrow. Robert, he could care less. Let's go!"

Janet's on the good stuff? Robert could care less? What the hell was I doing? We went out and hopped in my Porsche and pulled out of Huntington Harbor onto Warner and headed for the beach. We hung a left on PCH and headed for Huntington Beach. About halfway there Rosanna said to pull into the parking lot of Bolsa Chica State Beach. Driving down PCH with the wind blowing her hair, she was, what can I say, wow! We pulled into the lot and she jumped out of the car and ran across the beach, and I know I must've been imagining this, but what few clothes she had on, were now on the beach and she was naked as a jay bird, diving into the surf.

"Come on in, Marc! It's wonderful."

I looked around and saw no one else of the beach so, I did. I just knew I was going to regret this. I waded out into the surf, it was cold as hell, I mean it is May. She jumped up on me, wrapping her legs around me. I've been seduced. I hated every minute of it, well maybe every other minute.

We wallowed around in the surf having a great time exploring each other. The moon was almost full, and we were the only people on the beach or in the water, I think. We decided to find our clothes and head for The Golden Bear. I think we had two dirty martinis each, or maybe three. It was late and no one paid attention to us at The Golden Bear, even though our clothes were sandy and wet. We obviously couldn't return to the party together, looking like we did. So, I dropped her off a block from the house and headed for home. Rosanna assured me they would get Janet home the next day, and we would plan another rendezvous.

I know, history is gonna repeat itself. Damn me!

I was overwhelmed by everything that had happened. I needed to get myself together. Would it have been obvious to everyone that Rosanna and I disappeared? I left the car in the driveway and I quietly opened the front door and silently slithered down the hall to the "other" master bedroom, just in case Janet had somehow made it home. No one there. I checked the rest of the house. No one home. I decided to spend the night on the boat. It was a 35-foot ChrisCraft I had bought for a song, and the only place I could get away from everything.

I thought about taking it out in the harbor and anchoring. It would give me more time. I needed more time. Much more time. Who were these people? What have I got myself into? What has Janet got both of us into? I did not have a clue, and I definitely had no idea what was going to happen next.

I decided not to take the boat out, but just lay down on the couch in the main cabin. I turned on the stereo system and put in a Willy Nelson cassette, "Stardust." With the night's activities swirling in my head I rested. The next thing I knew, it was daylight, 6:45 a.m., and the typical Huntington Beach coastal overcast was hanging overhead. I got up, turned off the stereo, and went in the house.

Still no sign of Janet, so I turned on the coffee maker and

went to shower and get dressed. I had to go down to the docks and finish up the paperwork on a Russian ship over in Wilmington Harbor and after lunch, go meet with the FBI at 2pm. As I backed out of the garage, I decided to swing by the Romano's. I slowly drove by their cul-de-sac and saw no cars in the driveway and the garage doors all closed. I'll call her later, I thought. I don't know why I was so worried or concerned. Hell, I hardly ever see her anyway.

I was off to take care of Bergen business. When I arrived at the offices of Bergen Shipping and found it deserted, that was fine with me. Small talk with other Bergen employees was difficult. I grabbed the needed paperwork off my desk and headed out. I drove right up to the ship, *Mikhail Novogrodov*, ran up the gangplank, and headed for the captain's cabin. Captain Serge Danislovsky greeted me like always, a long-lost friend. We shook hands, sorted out the paperwork and signed what needed signing..

He opened his cabin door and shouted something in Russian, and a sailor appeared with a bottle of Stolichnaya, four glasses, and a bottle of mineral water. Danislovsky said, "We must toast our friendship, yes?"

"Of course," I responded, "but I was thinking maybe I could treat you to lunch at the Anchor, yes?"

"Absolutely! We shall toast when we return."

He again opened his cabin and shouted something in Russian. The first mate appeared and was apparently put in charge as the captain and I left.

Danislovsky was wearing his captain's uniform and when we walked into the Anchor, a few heads turned, but only for a second. I glanced at the bar and recognized Bo Swenson and a couple of longshoremen I had previously met. They all nodded and the captain and I found a booth towards the back and sat down.

Bo came over and asked, "What'll it be, gents?"

The captain said immediately, "Two Buds."

Bo nodded and laughed and tossed a couple of menus on the table. The captain told Bo he wanted a good old American cheeseburger, and I said the same. We finished a couple of Buds before the burgers arrived. I excused myself to go to the restroom.

As I stood at the urinal, one of the longshoremen stood in next to me and said, "We need to talk. We've come up with something. I'll call you this afternoon at four-thirty, OK?"

I said, "OK."

This was the same guy who approached me before.

18

ROSANNA'S PLAN

MAY 21, 1982

A dark colored van sat not far from where Rosanna was dropped off by the driver of a black Porsche. The lone occupant of the van sat in the dark with a Nikon camera and a 300mm lens and captured Rosanna and the driver in a passionate embrace. Just like the ones he took at the beach, in the surf, on the sand, and in the Porsche. A portfolio of disaster for some poor fool.

Meanwhile another photographer, sitting in a light colored van, had also been taking pictures and those ended up on the desk of FBI Special Agent Frankie Koch.

In the dark van, a pager on the occupant's belt goes off. Recognizing the number, he pulls away from the curb and heads for the nearest pay phone. He punches in the number, and Rosanna picks up on the second ring.

"Did you get pictures of it all?"

"Oh yeah, beach, surf, and car. Just happened to catch the license plate too."

"As soon as you get them developed, call me and I'll have your fee. Don't drool all over the pictures."

"Hey, come on, I'm a professional."

"And, so am I. Remember that."

She hangs up and heads for the bedroom.

"Rosanna, did you get what I need" asks Robert?

"You know, I always get what I'm after."

Janet is lying on the bedroom sofa, in a drug induced dream world. One shoe on and one shoe off. Her dress up around her thigh and her hair falling down over her face. She is oblivious of anyone or anything.

"Janet, you should stay here tonight," says Rosanna. Janet does not respond.

Robert rolls over in bed, "Yeah Janet, stay here. Plenty of room between Rosanna and me." Janet moans something unintelligible and rolls off the sofa unto the floor with a thud.

Rosanna stoops down and helps Janet into a sitting position and gets behind her and grabs Janet under the arms and gets her on her feet. Step by step she steers her towards the door and down the hall.

"Robert you are such a comedian."

Rosanna struggles with getting Janet to a guest bedroom and returns to Robert.

"Robert, we've got to play this very carefully. Janet may see through our little scheme. We need her to probe Marc for any info he may have. If we blow this opportunity, the Ukrainians will never deal with us again. If my father and Manuel even suspect what we are doing and not cutting them in, we are in big trouble."

"Hey, what are they going to do, send a hit squad from Panama? They need us. Without our connections, their consumers disappear. Besides seeing Janet like she was tonight just made me laugh. She's out of her league, way out of her league!"

"Don't even think about joking about a hit squad. It's not funny at all. I would think by now you would have a healthy respect for Alfonzo and his goons. Janet may be out of her league but she may be our new best friend if she can keep us informed about what her husband is up to."

"Hey, come to bed and show me what happened at Huntington State Beach."

19

JANET & ROSANNA

May 22, 1982

The morning after the party, Janet awakes and finds Rosanna curled up next to her. She almost cries out but then realizes that she is quite comfortable. As she stirs, so does Rosanna who reaches back and begins to slowly massage Janet. The arousal is immediate, and within no time they are entwined in each other's embrace. Janet is overcome with passion and completely overwhelmed with Rosanna's lovemaking. Before Janet realizes, Robert slides into bed with them, and another level of pleasure envelopes Janet.

She doesn't know how long the exquisite pleasure lasts, but when she awakes again, she is alone. At first, she only remembers the pleasure she experienced, and then suddenly, the shock of what had just happened hit.

Getting out of bed and searching for her clothes, she discovers there are none. She grabs a bed spread and wraps it around herself. She peeks through the drapes, out onto the patio, and sees Rosanna and Robert having coffee by the pool. She thinks—how can I get out of here without talking to them? I've got to find my clothes—but before she can do anything, Rosanna walks in.

"Good morning Janet, I saw the drapes move, so I figured you were awake. There's a bathrobe in the bathroom. I put your clothes in the laundry. They'll be out in thirty minutes."

"Oh, OK, thank you."

Robert walks in and remarks, "What a way to wake up, huh?"

Rosanna agrees, "My perfect morning wake-up!"

Janet says "Uh, yeah, quite a surprise. I need to get going soon. Mark is going to wonder what happened to me."

Robert says, "He already called, and we told him you were still sleeping. He said he had some work to do and would call you later. So relax, let's have some coffee and plan our day."

Janet slips on a robe handed to her by Rosanna, and they find their way to the patio's breakfast table. Conversation is somewhat clipped, but finally Rosanna asks, "Did you have an enjoyable time last night, Janet?"

"Wonderful time. But I think I may have overdone it on the wine."

Rosanna explains, "Oh you only had one glass of wine. It was the cocaine that did you in. After a couple of lines, you were flying high and the life of the party. You told stories that had everybody in stitches. We had no idea that Marc had such an ultra-secret job!"

Janet cannot contain the look of horror on her face when hearing this. She stands up, almost knocking over the table, and says "I don't feel well. Excuse me. I need to go to the bathroom."

As she runs to the bathroom, her head pounds, and her

mind races... What have I done? I've got to get out of here. What am I going to tell Marc? Upon reaching the bathroom, Janet really does become sick, barely making it there before emptying her insides out. She strips off her robe, steps into the shower, and turns it on hot, then cold, then hot again. She feels a little better, but her head is still pounding, and her conscience is burning a hole in her soul. "What have I done?" she repeats over and over and over.

Rosanna finally knocks on the door asking if she is all right and saying her clothes are out of the laundry. Janet gets out of the shower, finds her clothes laid out on the bed and dresses. She puts on some makeup, and exits the bedroom, ready to go home and face the music.

Before she can escape, Robert suggests they drive on down the coast to San Clemente and have lunch at the Fisherman Restaurant on the wharf. Janet tries to beg off but soon finds herself in the back seat of their Mercedes, sailing down Pacific Coast Highway, through Newport Beach, on the way to San Clemente.

Oh, God, San Clemente... now there's another story. Janet had a little history there (without Marc's knowledge), and T Street did not exactly render pleasant memories for her. Lifeguards. Boy toys. Janet worries, why am I thinking of him?

Janet realizes she is going down, down, down. Getting close to Robert and Rosanna was not the best idea she had ever had. Their friends and associates were just a little too fast, and now she had maybe caused some serious trouble for Marc. Stupid secret crap! Why the hell couldn't he have been a doctor or a lawyer, or even a fucking plumber.

She would have to make a decision on whether or not to tell him. He would be furious. Ugh, I hate this, she thought, this whole thing is going to unravel and Marc's going to find about everything. The fling in San Clemente. The drugs. What am I going to do? And here I am going down that muddy road again., You would think I would know better.

She is shocked back to reality when Robert announces, "Here we are at the Fisherman."

"Come, Janet, I'm starving" says Rosanna.

Robert asks the waiter for a table out on the deck overlooking the ocean, for four people.

"Who's the fourth," asks Janet?

"Corey Flynn," says Rosanna.

Janet groans and thinks, Oh, God, the lifeguard boy toy. This is getting worse by the minute. They get seated at a table by the railing and Janet is hoping maybe Cory won't show. Then she hears his greeting. Crap!

"Hi guys. Perfect timing," says Corey as he swaggers up to the table. All six foot three of him with his blond wavy hair, tight fitting tee shirt and cutoffs. He wraps his arms around Janet and plants a kiss squarely on her lips, causing her to gasp.

"Oh, good. Haven't lost my touch, but you have obviously lost my number," remarks Corey.

"Uh, yes, uh, well, I've been really busy, uh, working, and uh, not much free time," stutters Janet.

Robert laughs and says, "Oh, come on, Janet. Busy doing what?"

A stern scowl from Janet ends that line of talk. Corey turns his attention to a pretty blond sitting a couple of tables over, walks over and exchanges pleasantries with her. He returns to the table and says "She's an old friend. She teaches Special Ed at San Clemente High. She once sailed half way around the world in a thirty two foot sailboat. Amazing."

Rosanna says " I guess my first question would be why?"

Janet says "doesn't sound like much fun to me. How many days does it take?"

Corey responds "days? We're talking weeks."

"With her as my crew it might not be a bad trip" adds Robert.

Groans from Janet and Rosanna. "I'm thinking the same thing" says Corey.

"Oh God. Let's order and change the subject. Please!" adds Rosanna.

As lunch progresses, the conversation gets lighter with the consumption of a couple bottles of wine, Janet finds herself slowly lowering her resistance to the charms of Corey Flynn.

Robert suddenly says, "Rosanna and I have some errands to run. Would you mind, Janet, if Corey gave you a lift back to Huntington Harbor? When you get there, just tell Rosa that you need to borrow one of the cars. Take a BMW. We'll see you soon."

Janet is speechless and can only nod, thinking, what am I going to do?

Corey grabs Janet by the hand and pulls her towards the exit. He turns and says something about sailing to his school teacher friend and out the door they go to Corey's '66 Mustang convertible. Corey doesn't say where they are going, and Janet doesn't ask. They pull out onto the coastal highway and head for Dana Point. Corey suggests they stop at the Dana Trader for a quick cocktail and then head for his beach house. Janet just nods and wonders how she ever got into this situation and what's going to happen if, no not if, when Marc finds out she has revealed his work life to the Romanos.

The quick cocktail at the Dana Trader turns into two or three. Laughing and giggling they leave and get back into the Mustang and head north for the beach house. Corey's beach house is on the sand in Laguna Beach and accessible only by parking on the PCH and then taking the stairs down to the cove where only five other small bungalows exist. Seldom is anyone down there and Corey is the only resident living there full time. The beach house which he inherited from his grandfather was probably worth a couple of million, and the taxes were more than most people's mortgages.

Corey sweeps Janet off her feet, carries her in, and proceeds to undress her after which she starts on him. As they fall into bed upon each other, the phone rings.

Corey groans and answers, "This better be important!"

The caller only replies, "We got a problem. Meet me at the garage in one hour."

Corey gets up, starts dressing, and urges Janet to do the same, quickly.

"What's wrong?" asks Janet.

"That was Leo. I have a work-related meeting in one hour. Gotta go quick."

"Should I wait here?"

"No, I'll drop you at Rosanna's."

"Why not just drop me near my house? I'm only a few blocks from Rosanna's."

They climb back up the stairs to the car and drive north on PCH to Huntington Harbor in silence. Corey follows Janet's directions and drops her off a block from her house and leaves, saying only, "Later."

As she walks down the street "What an unfulfilling experience that was," she thinks. Then she tries to compose the story she is going to have to tell Marc. She thinks I'm going to have to tell him that I told Rosanna about his job. He is going to be furious. I am going to have to plead that I had too much to drink, and so maybe Rosanna did, too, and she won't remember.

Janet tries the front door, and it's locked. She goes around the side of the house and tries the garage, and it's locked. She goes to the back patio's French doors, and of course, they're locked. Good news, bad news, she thinks... I'm locked out, but that means Marc is probably not home. More time to come up with a story to tell Marc.

Janet sits down on a chaise lounge and becomes overcome with the problems she has created for herself when she hears, "Hello. Anybody at home? Janet, it's me Rosanna."

"Rosanna? I'm on the back patio. It seems I'm locked out of my own house."

Rosanna makes her way to the back patio and asks "Marc isn't home? Do you suppose he went into work today? What a fascinating job he must have. Why don't we have a little talk about what you told me last night? You were just bubbling over with pride about how important his job was. I am so intrigued."

"Rosanna, you know it was the alcohol and cocaine talking. I probably exaggerated way beyond the importance of his job."

"Janet, what do you really know about what Robert and I do? Do you have any idea of how we make our living?"

"I thought you were in the import business, you know, luxury cars."

"Oh, we are in the import business. You sampled some of our best imported product last night."

"What are you saying? You import drugs? You are a drug smuggler? Are you fucking kidding me? You need to leave right now. I cannot believe this crap. Our friendship is over. I cannot and will not be associated with drug smugglers."

"Well Janet, you are doing just that, and we need your help."

"Never! I will not, ever!"

"Janet, let me show you some pictures I brought with me."

"Pictures of what?"

"You and Cory. What a delightful time you two had the last time you were together."

"Delightful my ass. He got drunk dumped me off on the street by my house. Just like he did today."

"Oh please, please stop with the denial. If you didn't fuck him, you were going to. You know it and I know it, so cut the crap."

"What are you going to do with those?"

"Nothing if you will help me, but I'm sure Marc would not be pleased to see these pictures."

Janet feels strapped. I've just got to play along with Rosanna and see where this is going, she thinks.

"What is it you want me to do Rosanna?"

"You don't need to really do anything Janet. You just need to keep your eyes and ears open. If Marc mentions anything about getting involved with smuggling or drugs, you just tell me so we can be more cautious."

"You promise nothing will happen to Marc. You won't harm him?"

"Of course, not. Is there something you want to tell me now?"

"Marc has been made part of some kind of taskforce, but I don't know what they are after, or who."

"Taskforce? Here in Huntington Beach?"

"I don't know. All I know is what I told you. I overheard him talking on the phone, and he said something about a taskforce."

"Well that doesn't sound too dangerous. I've got to run. Remember what I told you. Be very careful of what you say around Marc about Robert and me. Hey, how about I pick you up later, and we go down to Fashion Island? We'll do some shopping and catch happy hour over at Newport Country Club. I'll pick you up at about three."

Rosanna dashes home and pages Robert. He calls back almost immediately. "Robert, where are you? Janet just told me that Marc is part of a taskforce here in Huntington Beach, but she doesn't know what or who they are after."

"Taskforce? What kind of taskforce?"

"I don't know. He works for some federal agency so I would guess it's a federal taskforce."

"Dammit, that is not good news. I'll make some calls and see if I can come up with anything. I'm over at the garage getting things ready for the upcoming shipment. I should be home around seven or eight."

20

LOCO LEO

May 22, 1982

The Mendez brothers had always worried that at some point Leo would get out of control. As the operation in Huntington Beach got bigger and more prosperous it became evident Leo was starting to get harder to control.

Leo gets a phone call from one of his street corner hustlers. Someone is poaching on their territory. The hustler had set up just off Beach Boulevard and Talbert when he is threatened by this poacher. Leo gets all the information from his salesman and tells him that he will handle the problem.

Leo calls Corey Flynn and tells him to meet him at the garage and to bring his piece.

Leo is waiting for Corey when he arrives and fills him in on what he knows about the poacher. They decide to just confront the guy and return the threat. Corey suggests they grab the guy, take him for a ride in Leo's van, and find out who he is working for. They wait until 8:30 p.m. and slowly cruise down Talbert towards Beach. There he is, about a half-block off Beach, peddling his crap. Leo tells Corey, who's driving, to pull up to the curb like he's a buyer. Corey pulls up, leans over, and rolls the passenger-side window down. When the poacher comes up to the window, Leo slides open the side door of the van, grabs the poacher, and pulls him into the van. Another man steps out of the shadows and fires two shots of double-aught buckshot from a shotgun at the van. One shot hits the poacher who falls onto the street. The other shot leaves a dozen holes in Leo's van.

Leo returns fire with his Colt 45 and the man goes down.

"Drive, Corey, drive! Get us the hell out of here! Make a right on Beach and hang a *U* at the next intersection, and as soon as you can make a right off Beach into one of the neighborhoods."

"Goddamn it, Leo, are you hit?"

"No, just drive Corey, just drive. Where the hell did that son of a bitch come from? I never saw him when we were driving up. This is not good. We have got to ditch this van, I mean, like, forever."

"The brothers are going to be pissed. We've got to be ready for a real shit storm to hit us. Where are we going to ditch this van?"

"We'll stay on the back streets and take it to the garage and think this out."

"We better hope there were no witnesses and some fool didn't get our license plate."

The drive back to the garage goes without incident, and they lock the van inside the garage.

About the same time Huntington Beach Police arrive on the scene, and officers fan out through the neighborhood to try to find any witnesses. Detectives are summoned to the scene as it appears to be a double homicide. Detectives Dave Allen and Jim Thomas are veteran homicide investigators.

The scene is confusing as the crime scene investigators try to sort out who shot who.

Allen says, "It looks like the guy laying in the gutter was shot by the guy laying on the sidewalk. The guy in the gutter doesn't have a gun, so who shot the guy on the sidewalk?"

Thomas responds, "This looks like a drug deal gone bad. My guess is we'll find drugs on one or both of these guys. Hey, you crime scene monkeys mind if we check pockets before you take over?"

They're given the OK and start searching pockets. Allen takes the gutter victim and immediately finds a number of packets containing a white powder but no ID. Thomas finds a roll of twenty-dollar bills and a wallet on his victim.

"This guy has an Arizona driver's license. Bisbee, Arizona. Where the hell is that?"

"Jim, I'm going to call Frankie Koch and tell him about this. They're running a multi-agency drug taskforce in Orange County, and I wonder if either of these guys are on their radar."

Dave Allen goes off in search of a pay phone. He calls the Orange County FBI office, but it's after hours. So, he tries the main office in Los Angeles and tells the duty agent who he is, the situation, and the need to talk to Frankie Koch. He's told to hang on as the duty agent calls Koch and tells him who he has on the line.

"Get me the number he's at, and I'll call him right now," says Koch.

The duty agent tells Allen to hang up, and Koch will call right away. The phone rings and Allen picks up the receiver, "Dave Allen here. Is that you, Frankie? Taking the night off, are you? Oh wait the Feeb's don't work at night, I forgot."

"Yeah, yeah, at least we work during the day, Mr. Donut

Shop. So you got a couple of recently retired drug peddlers on your hands, huh?"

"Very recently retired. No ID on the one but the other guy has an Arizona driver's license. Simon Woodward, listing an address in Bisbee. Does that name ring a bell?"

"No, but where are you? I'd like to come over and have a look. Maybe the faces will be familiar."

"We're on Talbert, just west of Beach. Lots of colorful lights flashing. You can't miss us. Hey, there's a donut shop on the corner. We could grab a cup and a glazed piece of heaven."

"Right. I'm less than ten minutes from there. See ya shortly."

"OK, Jim, Koch is on his way. We come up with anything in the neighborhood canvas?"

"We might have got lucky. A gal coming out of the donut shop saw a black van moving very fast, made a right on Beach, and then quickly made a U-turn and headed north. It crossed three lanes of traffic, causing some horn honking and turned east into the neighborhood across Beach out of sight. She said the driver had long, blond, curly hair."

"Let's go talk to her. Is she still here?"

"Yeah, the uniform told her to wait for us."

Allen tells the crime scene investigators where they are going and that an FBI Agent will be showing up shortly and to let him take a look at the victims. Allen and Thomas walk down the street to the donut shop where a middle-aged woman is standing outside talking to a Huntington Beach officer, and she is quite animated. As Allen and Thomas walk up she suddenly spurts out, "1XYZ."

"Thomas asks, "What's 1XYZ?"

"The last four digits on the van's license," she says.

"Ma'am I'm Detective Thomas and this is Detective

Allen. Would you mind retelling what you saw? And I'm sorry, your name is what?"

"Baker, Maude Baker. I own this donut shop, and I was just closing down, and I came outside for a smoke when this black van comes racing up to the intersection, didn't bother to stop, crossed three lanes of traffic, and made a U-turn. Then he crossed the three lanes on the other side of Beach and made a right turn into that neighborhood across Beach. Almost caused a couple accidents over there. The driver had shoulder-length, curly, blond hair. Looked like a surfer and a surfer van."

"And you saw the license plate?" asks Allen.

"Yes, I did. It was the older-style California plate, yellow letters on black. I only remember the last four, because, well I had a car with a plate ending in those same digits, 1XYZ."

"Thank you Mrs. Baker. The officer will take a full statement from you."

"It's Miss Baker, detective."

"Sorry, but thank you again."

"Quite all right, detective. Come on in for coffee and a donut anytime. I like having cops around. Inexpensive security, you might say."

Allen and Thomas walk back to the crime scene where Koch has arrived.

"Hey guys. Down to get a quick cup and a donut?" suggests Koch.

Allen responds, "Hey, Special Agent Koch. I didn't recognize you. No wingtips and no tie? What would Mr. Hoover say to that?"

"Alright, good to see you guys, too. I don't recognize either of the victims."

Thomas says, "Well, Frankie, we might have gotten lucky.

The donut shop owner, Miss Maude Baker, saw a black van with a California plate and remembered the last four digits, 1XYZ. We're having it run as we speak."

"1XYZ? Black van?"

"Sound familiar?"

"Very. Loco Leo Ortiz. He's one of our main characters in the Huntington Beach ring we're looking at."

"You've got to be kidding me," says Allen.

"Did your witness get a look at the driver?"

"Shoulder-length, blond, curly hair."

"Sounds like Corey Flynn, a pistol-packing buddy of Loco Leo."

"You have got to be shitting me. This can't be this easy," says Thomas.

"We need to talk about this before you make a move to arrest these two. Let me get a couple of my guys who know these two well, and we'll meet you at your office, let's say in one hour," says Koch.

"OK," responds Thomas. "This is going to *make my day*. Hey, that has a nice ring to it. Who said that anyway?"

"I think it was Burt Reynolds" says Allen.

"No way, had to have been The Duke."

"Get out of here. When's the last time you saw a movie?"

"Hey, me and the missus go to a movie every Saturday night. You know like a date night."

"Date night? She can't do any better than you?"

"Hey don't knock it. You should've tried it and maybe you wouldn't be on your fourth bride. By the way has she turned twenty yet?"

"She was my third."

"Was?"

"Yeah was."

An hour later Koch and the two Huntington Beach

detectives sit down in the chief's conference room and Koch throws everything he has on the table.

"I believe we have everything that we need to bring down the whole ring," says Koch. "I've arranged for us to use a vacant hanger at El Toro for the briefing on the day before the raid and the morning of it. I have gotten commitments from all the police jurisdictions involved and all federal agencies, also. I'm going with ten-man teams for each location which means there are going to be close to 200 officers involved. I'm only worried about three of the locations, as far as possible confrontations, and SWAT teams from Orange County Sheriff, HBPD, and FBI will back those teams up. I'm asking you at HBPD to hold off on arresting Ortiz and Flynn so that we don't spook the entire group."

"I completely understand," says Allen.

Thomas nods in agreement, but adds, "However, this is not our call and the chief will have to sign off on this. You understand, we're talking homicide here, right? So, to use a famous FBI phrase, we'll get back to you on this."

Koch busts out laughing and Thomas with him. "We'll call him right now," says Allen.

21

THE PLAN

May 25-27, 1982

Frankie Koch was an organizer. He knew what to do and who should do it. After months of just plain, good old hard work and the voluminous amount of information his group had gathered via the wiretaps, he picked a date and decided that would be the day the Romano Ring would fall. Those included would be Loco Leo and Romano and the 13 other distributors that had been identified.

On the morning of May 25th, four days before the actual mass raid was to take place, Koch called a meeting for the team leaders and other key personnel. I was flattered to be invited.

The suspects lived in seven different cities, but all within Orange County, California. Koch invited the other feds, too, of course—the Drug Enforcement Agency (DEA), Alcohol Tobacco and Firearms (ATF), Internal Revenue Service (IRS), US Customs, and of course, yours truly, Defense Foreign Liaison (DFL). I heard at least a couple of cops asking who the hell was the guy from dead fucking last. I ever find out who named my agency, I'm gonna strangle him.

The plan was that the entire taskforce would assemble at five o'clock in the morning, Saturday May 29th. Each team would have a complement of at least ten. The makeup of the team would include police officers, sheriff deputies, feds, and of course, for the seriously dangerous suspects, SWAT.

It was decided that only three of the suspects were dangerous—Loco Leo, Corey Flynn, and just as a precaution, Romano. Seeing as how most of the suspects were living in the beach cities of Huntington, Newport, and Laguna, SWAT teams from those three cities would accompany the arrest teams, and the FBI SWAT team would be on standby for emergency assistance.

Koch then invites Detective Dave Allen to come up and relate the shooting incident at the intersection of Talbert and Beach. He tells us that it is assumed that the two people in the black van were Loco Leo Ortiz and Corey Flynn and that they were the shooters. HBPD has held off on arresting Ortiz and Flynn and plan to take them on Saturday morning and charge them with double homicide.

Of course, with my extensive knowledge of the Romano residence, I was assigned to that team. I'm over being embarrassed, so I just nod my head and keep my mouth shut.

Koch is explaining procedure and going over last minute details "OK, now we've got eyes in every neighborhood, and you guys know who you are. Do not miss a thing. This whole operation depends on surprise, not for us, but for them. Ryder, I know your wife was coerced into this thing but that doesn't let her off the hook. I know you don't like it, but you got to keep her close for the next few days."

"Consider it done."

"Ryder, do you have a problem with your assignment?"

"No, I do not."

"You are going to have to be our eyes in Huntington Harbor until Saturday. We are going to have to turn off the wire so we're going to be blind until we hit them. Has anything come from your source that we need to know?"

"My source? You mean, like, as in my frickin' traitorous, so called wife? No, nothing."

"I know this does not make you happy, but it is what it is."

"What if I just were to confront her with the whole thing? We might come up with something that would be a world of help."

"Don't even think about it. If you're having doubts or regrets already, I'm gonna pull you off the team and recommend protective custody for the both of you."

"Oh, for Christ sakes, gimme a break."

This frickin' taskforce is going to be my undoing; wait, I already undid myself. What a frickin' disaster. My wife's spying on me. I'm spying on my wife. I should have bit the damn bullet and got a divorce.

As I walk out of the meeting, I hear my favorite FBI agent Biff say "Yo, DFL, you've been assigned to my team."

I'm so excited I can hardly contain myself. Me and Biff on the same team.

Biff yells out, "listen up, I've got packets made up for all of us. We got HBPD, SWAT, DEA, ATF, IRS, US Customs and Immigration, and you DFL, our star. I want all of you to go over every document in that packet and know how it is to be used. Chances are, we're going to be confiscating large amounts of cash, drugs and definitely cars. DFL, take a look at the diagram of the house and see if you have any suggestions about breaching it. We don't anticipate Romano to be armed or violent, but we need to be prepared. Basically, DFL, we need you to plan this carefully. Questions?"

"Yeah, could you lose the DFL? I'm Marc, or Ryder, please."

I reach out my hand, and Biff busts out laughing and grabs it.

"You know what, Ryder, I liked you from that first photo I saw of you in the surf with that Panamanian broad. What a guy."

"Thanks."

Inside, I'm dying—dying for a Bud Light. I probably sound like an alcoholic. I'm not, alcoholics go to meetings. I don't know why that comes to mind except maybe it goes back to me and Danislovsky at the Anchor. The first time I went into the Anchor, I went with someone who knew the place and the bartender, Bo. They ordered me a Bud Light and Bo never forgets. Now when I walk up to the bar, Bo sets down a Bud Light. I never liked Bud Light that much, but it kinda grows on ya. Funny thing is, after three weeks in Russia I began to crave Bud Light; which of course led me to the Plotnikov; which of course led me to Marina and all these nice bruises all over my body.

Speaking of crap, my pager goes off. I look to see the number—Janet. Before I can even think about calling her back, my pager goes off again—Rosanna.

I call Janet first. "Hey Janet, what's up?"

"I have to talk to you. Where are you, and where can we meet? This is really important, Marc."

"OK, let's meet at El Torrito on Beach at eleven thirty, OK?"

"OK."

I hang up and call Rosanna, who has sent me another page.

"Hey, Rosanna, it's Marc. What's up?"

"I have to talk to you as soon as possible. Where are you, and where can we meet? This is important."

"I'm tied up until about two thirty. How about the Lounge at SeaCliff Country Club at three?"

"Perfect."

I grab my stuff and slip out of the office. When I get to El Torrito, Janet is already sitting at the bar, and I can see she has already had at least one shot of Hornitos.

"What the fuck took you so long? I said this was important. I should have called the goddamn FBI."

Did I mention that Janet was a major potty-mouth?

"Look Janet, I was at the FBI office, and I left right after you called. Now knock off the expletives and tell me what is so important."

"Expletives? Screw you."

"Well that would be something different for you, huh?"

"What the hell was that supposed to mean?"

"Hey, let's quit the verbal war here and tell me what is so important."

"OK, I'm sorry. I'm afraid I've gotten myself involved with some really bad people and unfortunately dragged you in with me. Robert and Rosanna are drug dealers. One of their sellers was involved in that shooting, I think last night, and he's being smuggled out of California down to Puerto Vallarta, Mexico. He and the guy who was driving the van are both being sent down there to lay low. Rosanna has some pictures of me and the guy driving the van and threatened to show them to you if I didn't snitch on what you were doing."

"Janet slow down. What are you talking about? What shooting? Who did the shooting?"

Janet says "A guy named Loco Leo."

I don't respond immediately and Janet pokes me in the chest. "Marc are you listening to me?"

"Aw for Christs sake. Yes, I'm listening.This gets worse by the minute. Who's the guy driving the van?"

"A guy I had a fling with."

"What the hell? Does he have a name?"

"Corey Flynn."

"Janet, these guys are both killers! Dangerous and crazy killers."

"Well shit Marc, I didn't know that when I met them."

"Ok, so I assume you have told her what she wanted to hear?"

"I told her about your dealings with the Russians and your travel over there, and I guess when I was drunk, told her about you being assigned to a drug taskforce. She had a lot of questions about that, but I didn't know anything, so I couldn't tell her anything. I'm so sorry. They are really nice people who are really bad."

"OK, I don't think there is any problem here for us, as long as we, that is, you don't have anything else to tell them. I'd be interested in knowing more about these two guys who they sent to Puerto Vallarta and anything else about their business here in California."

"Oh for Christ's sake Marc, I'm scared to death. You think I'm going to ask any questions about their drug dealing? These people carry guns and not for fun. The two guys they sent to Puerto Vallarta, Leo and Corey are crazy, in fact, they call the big guy, Loco Leo."

None of this is good news. "Listen, I have another meeting I have to go to, so go home and stay there. When I get home maybe I'll have some idea of what we should do. OK?"

I leave El Torrito and head for Huntington Beach. I pull into the parking lot at SeaCliff Country Club, and a bad feeling washes over me. I haven't seen Rosanna since our romp in the surf, and it doesn't bring back any good feelings. This woman is Panamanian and married to a drug dealer. This could be my last drink, ever. Damn, I've got to get control of myself.

I walk in, and she's sitting at the bar overlooking the golf course and looking dangerously gorgeous, with an empty shot glass and a half-consumed beer in front of her. As I walk in, she hops off her stool, throws her arms around me, and plants a very wet kiss on my lips.

"Marc, I am so glad you could come and meet with me. Let's go sit out on the patio where we can talk."

I follow her out on the patio which is almost empty and ask, "What's so important?"

The waitress comes over, and I order a Negra Modelo with a chilled glass and no lime.

"I am afraid we have a little problem, Marc. You see we were not the only ones on the beach that night, and the other person had a very good camera. This person is apparently part of a drug cartel and has already approached me with demands."

"Great, just great. What has he demanded? If it's money, he's shit out of luck. I don't have any."

"He wants information. He has somehow put you on a drug taskforce here in Orange County, and he wants to know who is being targeted and what the plans are. He has threatened my life if I don't come up with the information. Needless to say he also said he would send the pictures to the *Orange County Register*, with the names of the participants."

So, there it is, she just told me she is somehow involved in the drug trade. I've got to come up with something and like right now. She knows, thanks to my loving wife, probably more than I think she knows, so telling anything but the truth will not fly.

I feel like I'm still trapped in that damn snow bank in Minnesota.

I say, "Participants? That would be like you and me? OK, let me think about this. I have been assigned to work with a FBI taskforce, but it has nothing to do with drugs. That's the DEA's area. I can only tell you the taskforce is targeting an international money laundering ring. Rosanna, I have been included because of the contacts my agency has, the Defense Foreign Liaison Office. We liaise with defense departments in every country in the world. It has nothing to do with drug smuggling. This guy is blowing smoke."

"Blowing smoke? He threatened my life."

"OK, give him to me. I'll pass the info to the FBI, and they'll grab him. End of story."

"I don't know his name. All I have is the number he left."

"Give it to me, and I promise, they will find him and neutralize him."

"What about the pictures? If they find him, they will also find the photos."

"I will be able to handle that, don't worry."

Rosanna finally calms down, and we agree to let me handle it. She tells me she's got a hair appointment in thirty minutes down in Corona del Mar, blows me a kiss, and dashes out the door. Oh, OK, I'll pick up the tab. I call for the bill and I don't know, maybe I'm paranoid but something is raising the hairs on my neck. Somebody is watching me. I can feel it. I look around and because the SeaCliff patio is behind the main building, there is no parking, and there are no cars. So why do I feel nervous?

Whatever, I am frickin' exhausted, so I head for home and then I remember I told Janet to go home. I don't want to listen to her anymore this afternoon. Just then my pager goes off, it's the FBI. I don't want to talk to them either.

Dealing with those two women in the space of a couple of hours stressed me out. I pull into a service station and there's a pay phone. I call Koch's office.

Biff answers, "Hey, DFL, we were wondering when you would surface."

Ignoring his attempt at humor, I tell him what I have learned from Janet and Rosanna.

"Hang on, Marc, I'm going to get Koch in on this conversation."

What the hell, he actually called me by my name. I've come up in the world.

"Marc, this is Frankie Koch. Biff just told me what you told him. Are you sure that she said they sent Leo Ortiz and Corey Flynn to Puerto Vallarta?"

"Yes, I'm positive."

"OK, here's what I want you to do. I'd like to send you and Javiar Delgado, a DEA agent, down to Puerto Vallarta and hook up with the Policia Federale down there. You met Delgado a couple of days ago, right? We need the Mexicans to grab these two guys for that shooting in Huntington Beach, and you two guys can escort them back. We need you there to stress to the Federales that we would like them back here alive."

"I can do that. I've had numerous dealings with Estavan Rodrigues, the chief of the Policia Federal in Jalisco."

"Do you trust him?"

"Yes, he will cooperate with us as long as we follow his rules."

"What are his rules?"

"That's just it. They change frequently."

"God help us."

"Especially me and Delgado."

"I will make a call to the Special Agent in Charge over

at DEA and see if they will make arrangements for you and Delgado to fly to Puerto Vallarta. Call Delgado and get yourself over to Meadowlark Airfield. Can you make in one hour? I will tell the SAC to have them pick you up there. "

"No problem, I'm in Huntington Beach now."

"OK, now listen up. When you get to Puerto Vallarta and get a feeling on whether or not the Federales are going to work with us and have verified that Leo and Corey are there, call me. I'll bring you up to date on what's happened here. Good luck."

The DEA-arranged itinerary includes a helicopter ride from Meadowlark Airfield in Huntington Beach to Brown Field, a dusty airfield outside San Diego. There, we are met by a mustache-bearing guy with black hair and dark glasses who directs us to a large black Mercedes sedan. We speed out of the Brown Field area and head south on a road I did not know existed to a border checkpoint.

We are waved through and after a short drive arrive at Tijuana International Airport. We pull up in front of the departures entrance and are led by "Mr. Mustache" directly to the gate, bypassing about a hundred people standing in line, waiting to board. Mr. Mustache says something to the gate attendant who requests our passports. Without any questions, he stamps them and waves us on board. Just like that, I'm on Aeromexico, flight 2986, seat 1A, on my way to Puerto Vallarta.

The gal next to me asks if I am going on a holiday. Absolutely, I told her, absolutely. The last time I used that phrase I got Stolichnaya.

A couple hours later, we land in Puerto Vallarta. The plane stops a long way from the terminal, and I look out the window to see Estavan Rodrigues leaning against his pickup truck. Delgado and I are called to the front of the plane, and the door is opened. A staircase is already in place, and we walk down to be greeted by Rodrigues.

A wave to the pilot and we are on our way downtown to Policia Federal HQ. Rodrigues has already been briefed by his superior in Mexico City who was in turn briefed by the FBI legal attache at the US Embassy, Mexico City. He has learned that our friends Leo Ortiz and Corey Flynn have checked into a hotel down on Playa Los Muertos—Beach of the Dead, how appropriate.

I didn't know it then, but I was soon to find out.

22

ESTAVAN RODRIGUES

MAY 1982

Estavan Rodrigues grew up in Nayarit. Nayarit is the state immediately north of Puerto Vallarta, which is in the state of Jalisco. He is the son of a fisherman whose home port was Bucerias. His hero was his uncle who served as the sheriff, known as *El Jefe*. Estavan decided he would be an El Jefe when he grew up.

Thanks to his uncle, he was afforded the opportunity to attend the Provincial Police Academy and upon graduation was assigned to the local police department in Tepic. He did well in Tepic and gained a reputation as an honest lawman. Eventually, after achieving the rank of captain, he began to desire more authority and responsibility and looked towards the Federales.

His first application was turned down, but he was not one to give up and after waiting the mandatory two years before he submitted another application, he again applied and was accepted. He had to give up his captain's rank and was assigned as sergeant in the town of Chapala, which sits on the shores of Lake Chapala, not far from Guadalajara.

He again did well for himself and was credited with bringing down a prostitution and drug ring which plagued the small city. He did not do this without making some serious enemies.

It was here in Chapala where I first met Estavan Rodrigues. I had traveled to the US Embassy in Mexico City to talk with Military Attaché Dick Holder regarding the presence of Soviet merchant vessels calling on ports in the US and Mexico. Dick Holder was a US Army full-bird Colonel, and we hit it off well—probably because I was a former Army officer myself. After we finished our business, he asked me if I would do him a favor.

"I'm scheduled to go to a little town near Guadalajara to attend the promotion of a federale by the name of Rodrigues. He seems to be one of the few people we can trust, and the ambassador thought it would be a show of support if we sent an official representative. I can't go, do you think you could do this for me? It's a beautiful area and a nice trip."

"Sure, why not? I have nothing pressing back home, so I can stay a few days and handle this for you."

"Great, I'll call your director and then advise the ambassador."

I got to Chapala just in time for another situation involving yet another drug ring and, of course, Estavan Rodrigues. His promotion ceremony had been postponed, and he invited me to accompany him and his men on the arrests. When making the arrests of the main characters of the ring, a shootout ensued and Rodrigues was shot by one of his own men. I was not armed, but I picked up Estavan's gun and returned fire, killing the officer. No one except Rodrigues saw this happen, and he quickly grabbed the gun from my hand

and said, “I did the shooting. You observed me shoot Officer Munoz after he shot me. Agreed?”

“Yes I agree,”

After everything was sorted out, no one questioned the shooting. Rodrigues was promoted to captain, El Jefe, and given a new assignment as El Jefe in Puerto Vallarta. It became my favorite vacation place, and I found many reasons to visit El Jefe, and we became good friends.

So, I was not worried about having full cooperation from the Policia Federales when I was in Puerto Vallarta. Little did I know how much my future would depend on Estavan Rodrigues.

23

ROBERT & ROSANNA

JANUARY 1981- MAY 1982

It took about a week after Rosanna arrived in Orange County, California to knock Robert head over heels in love with her. She completely consumed him and called Adolfo her tenth day there. . .

"Papa, it's Rosanna."

"Rosanna, great to hear your voice. Is there something wrong? Do you need to come home?"

"No, Papa. It is the opposite."

"The opposite?"

"Yes, Papa. Robert and I got married here in California, and everything is going wonderfully well."

"But your mother always wanted for you to have a big wedding on the patio in the garden and have many people to come. A big party."

"But she is gone Papa, and I did not want a big wedding. We will come down to you and have a party. This way, I can apply for citizenship and get all the documents I need as an American citizen."

"You are sure about this? We have not known this Robert long and must be sure he is who he says he is."

"He is, Papa. He is."

"I trust you are right. I will tell Alfonzo when he returns from his trip. Everything else is fine, yes?"

A good part of a year has passed and Rosanna and Robert have established themselves as a couple who people want to be associated with. They are the "in crowd" of Huntington Harbor. Although they still enjoy each other, they also found they enjoy others. Robert has discovered that his new found wealth attracts more beautiful women than he can handle and Rosanna has her own lovers, both male and female. They both seem to welcome their "open" marriage. They have accumulated many new friends and it is not by accident that these new friends are attracted to the Romano's because of the lavish parties they throw.

It was a day after one of these parties that Rosanna picked up the phone and called her Papa.

"Papa it's Rosanna."

"Rosanna! It is so good to hear your voice. How are you?"

"I am fine and Robert is as well."

"So what is this surprise call all about?"

"We have a problem with Leo."

"What is it?"

"I think I should call you on the other phone, and Alfonzo should hear this also."

"OK, call back at eleven your time tonight."

"Love you, Papa."

Later, Rosanna calls her papa on a phone which is not known to the FBI. The phone is used exclusively for direct calls between Rosanna and her papa. Adolfo answers and says, "Alfonzo is also listening. Is there a problem with Robert?"

"No, Papa, it is Leo."

"Leo? What is it?"

"He found out we had someone poaching on our territory and he and Corey went to confront him. When they found the poacher they were going to snatch him off the street into Leo's van. As Leo was pulling the poacher into the van, another man stepped out of the shadows and fired a shotgun at the van, killing the poacher. Leo fired back killing the guy with the shotgun. Corey and Leo left the scene in a hurry but have no idea if there were any witnesses to what happened."

Alfonzo asks, "When did this happen? Have you heard anything on the news? Where are Corey and Leo now?"

"Yesterday and we haven't heard anything on the news except that there was a shooting, and no identifications have been made of either dead man. Corey and Leo are at the garage with the van locked inside and waiting for the right time to dispose of the van. It has numerous bullet holes in it from the shotgun."

Adolfo asks, "Where is Robert?"

"He is right here."

"Put him on the phone."

"Robert here, sir."

"Robert, I am going to have to trust you to handle this. I cannot send Alfonzo up there as we have another matter in Mexico we must attend to. Can you handle this?"

"Yes."

"Do you anticipate any problems you cannot handle?"

"Let's just say I feel uncomfortable. This is not something I am familiar with."

"The shootings?"

"Yes. But trust me I can handle it. I think we should send Corey and Leo out of the country. I'm thinking to Puerto Vallarta. If you agree I'll make the plans. I think they should lay low for a month or two until the heat dies down here in California."

"I am putting Alfonzo on now as he may have some advice and also some questions. Hold on for a moment while I speak to him. I like the idea of getting Corey and Leo out of the country."

Adolfo comes back on the line and says "I have spoken to Alfonzo and we agree on your plan. He would like to speak to you."

A moment later he hears Alfonzo, "*Buenos noches,* Robert.

"Buenos noches, Alfonzo."

"Robert this is an unfortunate situation. I like your solution, although it may only be temporary. We need to tighten up security in light of what has happened. Be sure to make all of your people aware of heightened police activity because of this mess. We have a shipment on its way as we speak, and it will be ready for pickup this Friday. Are you going to be able to handle it?"

"It's going to be business as usual. The packaging location has not been compromised, and it will be clear of the van tonight."

"*Bueno. Keep us informed. Adios.*" Click.

OK, goodbye to you, too, thinks Robert. He picks up a different phone and begins to make arrangements for his plan to fall in place. First, he calls Leo's cousin who does not answer. He then calls the garage and tells Leo to sit tight and that he is coming down to talk with him and Corey. When he gets to the garage he tells Leo and Corey about their upcoming travel. Leo tries to argue against it, but

Robert tells him it's a done deal, approved by Adolfo and Alfonzo. From the garage, on another phone not known to the FBI, Robert then calls each of his distributors and tells them a shipment is arriving on Friday and to plan a meet late Friday night. He then makes a couple of calls and makes the arrangements for Leo and Corey's trip out of the country, to Puerto Vallarta, Mexico. He also makes the reservation at the Hotel Cardenas, on Playa de Muertos. Robert sits back and mentally goes over the whole plan again. It's good, he thinks.

Meanwhile, Frankie Koch receives the latest transcriptions. There's a lot of activity and he picks up the info that a shipment is arriving soon. He immediately gets on the phone to the United States Attorney's office to update their information and get authorization to issue arrest warrants and search warrants for the Huntington Beach ring, one and all. The wiretaps are shut down and the plans for raid and mass arrest are set in motion.

Down in Panama, Adolfo, Manuel, and Alfonzo are meeting to discuss Leo and Corey Flynn.

"Damn that Leo. It has been a fortunate run we have had up until now. I am actually surprised we have gone this long without Leo doing something stupid," remarks Manuel.

Adolfo asks, "Alfonzo, what do you think we should do?"

"I think Leo has served us well, but he has now endangered, not only the business, but us, as well. I hate to be the one to say it, but he and Flynn have outlived their usefulness to us. By leaving them in Puerto Vallarta we leave an open door for the Policia Federale or the DEA to seek us. We need to close that door."

"I agree," says Manuel.

"Who do you have in mind to handle this?" asks Adolfo.

"The Bolivian," says Alfonzo. "I intend to also have her

go to Tequila and silence the gossip and that pervert, the chief of police."

The Bolivian, known by no other name, is a thirty-something, coldhearted killer—a very attractive woman with coal black hair worn in a pixie style, similar to Halle Berry. Her eyes are her most striking feature as they are a titanium grey and seem to glow in the dark, even during the day. She is about 5'5", 120 pounds, and almost always dresses in a dark-colored blouse worn outside her slacks of the same color. Her shoulder bag, carried with straps over her shoulder, contains her tools. Her tools vary with the job she has to do. She is known throughout Central and South America by people such as Alfonzo. There are no known photographs of the Bolivian, and as such she is almost invisible.

She grew up in the slums outside Caracas, Venezuela. Her father was a small-time criminal and was killed in a bar fight over a whore. Her mother was a whore herself and by the time her daughter reached the age of 14, her mother's customers were more interested in the daughter.

The first man who tried to have her, she killed with a knife to the throat. From then, she was on the run. Another run-in with a would-be rapist left him dead also. She left a note on him, "The Bolivian."

There were more killings, and each time she left a note. Soon, she was in the business of killing for hire, a bona fide assassin. It seems assassins were more in demand than she imagined, and her reputation became well known among people like Alfonzo Benitez. She left Venezuela and established herself on a Caribbean island where she purchased a very private residence and lived a very private and quiet life, that is, when she wasn't traveling.

"*Hola, Senorita*. It is Alfonzo. I have two situations for which I need your services."

"Fax the packets to this telephone number or send them to this address, Calle del Oro, numero cinco, Cuernavaca. Do you have a deadline? If the situations are in different locales, I will need more time."

"It will be sent by fax today."

The phone number was an international number with no address listed. Calle del Oro #5 is a post box serviced by a forwarding company in Cuernavaca who checked it daily. It is one of many she kept. All mail was forwarded from there to Oranjestad, Aruba by express mail.

"I would like this taken care of as soon as possible" Says Alfonzo.

"I will proceed as soon as I have the packets." Click.

Someday, I shall have her, thinks Alfonzo Benitez. Alfonzo, the dreamer.

24

THE BOLIVIAN & PUERTO VALLARTA

MAY 27, 1982

Once Delgado and I were briefed by Rodrigues we made plans to have the federales grab Leo and Corey. Rodrigues tells us he has kept them under a loose and distant surveillance since receiving a call from his superiors. He tells us that they have been wandering around central Puerto Vallarta most of the day and returned late afternoon and retired to their rooms in the hotel. Around 6pm they re-appeared and went to Dick's bar. After numerous margaritas, they walked to The Blue Shrimp near the Rio Cual for dinner. The Federales' plan to grab them after dinner the next evening. I question waiting until the next evening. Chief Rodrigues says he needs proper papers from Mexico City before he can arrest them. The paperwork is due the next morning. The chief assures us that he will have his men on them constantly and will be ready to make the arrest tomorrow evening.

Delgado and I check into the Las Palmas Hotel and agree to meet at the bar around 6 p.m. I find a pay phone in the lobby and call Frankie to give him the news. He says he has already faxed the paperwork to the US Embassy in Mexico City and a courier is flying over with it to Puerto Vallarta the next morning. I am to meet him at the airport at 10 a.m. Everything seems to be working well—especially at the bar. A gorgeous blond sits down just a couple of stools away. She smiles at me and asks if I have a light.

I grab a pack of matches off the bar and light her cigarette, "Can I buy you a drink?"

"Why, thank you, kind sir. Yes, you may. I'll have a vodka martini, straight up, two olives."

"Ah, my favorite drink. Bartender, may I have two vodka martinis, straight up with two olives? Oh, and make mine dirty."

"Dirty? What does that mean?" she asks.

"He mixes in a little olive juice and just a dash of vermouth. It gives it a nice bite."

"A nice bite? You are no doubt American, yes?"

"And you? I can't place that accent."

"Costa Rica."

"Ah, there's the reason. You probably speak English better than I. What brings you to Puerto Vallarta?"

"I am a consultant for a company that does accounts receivable auditing."

"Accounts receivable auditing? Sounds ambiguously vague and involving the possibility of loss."

"Yes, it is. Our audits often result in someone losing their job."

"Well, at least it is not their life."

She looks rather startled at my remark and downs her martini and says, "Thank you. I have another engagement."

"Well, you are welcome, and maybe I'll see you tomorrow."

"I am leaving early in the morning, but thank you again. Good bye." She turns and walks out passing Delgado as he comes in. He saunters over looking over his shoulder at the blond.

"Whoa, who was that? She was something!"

"Yes, she was. Said she was an auditor doing accounts receivable. But there was something about her I just couldn't put my finger on. Sure didn't look like an accountant to me."

"I noticed she was asking the doorman to hail her a cab when I turned around and watched her walk out. I agree, she didn't look like an accountant to me either. Let's go find some dinner. How about Mexican?"

"Are you serious?"

"Yes, I am. How about we take a cab, and we'll stop at Si Senors for a drink and dinner. Best Mexican food in town! Then we'll go over to the Marina Vallarta. There are a dozen night clubs over there to pick from. A couple of them have live music, and we can dance the night away."

"You've talked me into it. Let's *vamoose*."

"Hey, I didn't know you spoke Spanish."

We leave the bar and step out into the street just as the blond is getting in a taxi. I try to catch her attention, but she slams the door, and the taxi takes off. We wait a few minutes for the next taxi. Delgado tells him to take us to Si Senors.

After a couple of margaritas and dinner, we get another cab and ask to be taken to Marina Vallarta. Delgado asks him to let us off at the south entrance of the marina. It is only a short ride. We hop out at the south entrance and begin looking for a place to listen to music, have a drink, and maybe dance at bit.

I say, "You know the last time I was here, we found this place on the fourth floor that had awesome views, live music, and lotsa dancing ladies."

"I know exactly the place you're talking about. It's right up there in the next block of condos."

We walk down to the building and take the elevator up to the fourth floor. It is just as I remember. Janet and I had been here when times were better. Delgado and I find a table on the balcony overlooking the marina and sit down. The waiter takes our drink orders, Pacifico for Delgado and Negra Modelo for me.

Suddenly, Delgado says, "Omigod, there's the blond from Las Palmas!"

I turn and just catch a fleeting glimpse of the back of her head as she heads out the exit.

"Yes, that looks like her. Was she alone?"

"It looked like it. I didn't see anyone else."

Just then, I notice a really big fellow get up and head for the elevator. He looks familiar. I say, "I think I just saw Leo Ortiz get in the elevator."

25

PUERTO VALLARTA

MAY 27, 1982

The Bolivian has received the information she needs via fax from Alfonzo. She was conveniently in Mexico City and only a short distance from Cuernavaca. She responds to Alfonzo, leaving a message on his answering machine, that the job in Puerto Vallarta will be done within the next couple of days and then she would proceed to Tequila for the other matter. She immediately books her flight to Puerto Vallarta. She decides to fly regular tourist class and dresses down to make sure she doesn't draw attention to herself.

She arrives in Puerto Vallarta without incident and because it is not an international flight she does not have to pass through customs or immigration services. Before leaving the terminal she finds the personal storage lockers and puts one of the two bags she is carrying in it and pockets the key.

She exits the terminal and hails a cab to take her to the Marriott Casa Magna where she checks in and gets her room key. She has booked three rooms, one at the Las Palmas, one at the Marriott Casa Magna and one at the Sheraton, all under different names. She then goes to the Sheraton and checks in and gets a room key. Lastly she hails a cab to the Las Palmas and again checks in and gets a room key.

Up in Huntington Beach, Robert decides that he and Rosanna should go to Puerto Vallarta to celebrate their marriage. Rosanna calls her papa and tells him she and Robert are flying to Puerto Vallarta to celebrate their marriage on Saturday. Adolfo pleads with Rosanna to wait a week or two so that he and Manuel could fly up to join the party. Rosanna is adamant and will not change her mind, "We will celebrate when we come to Panama, Papa."

Robert catches the last few words of Rosanna's conversation and says, "Rosanna, I think after we have processed the shipment on Friday, we should grab our bags and book a suite at the Ritz-Carleton in Laguna Nigel for a night before we fly out Saturday. I couldn't get us a good flight out of John Wayne, so we're going out of San Diego. We are going to do very well this month, so let's live it up."

"I love it. I'll call right now. No, I won't. Take me out to dinner down in Laguna Nigel, and we'll stop at the Ritz for a cocktail and book the room. I think there's a jazz combo playing in the lounge."

"I'm in. All work and no play makes Robert horny! And this business with Leo and Corey makes me want to get out of town for a while."

"Horny? What doesn't make you horny?"

Meanwhile, the pager on the Bolivian's belt goes off, and she finds a pay phone just outside Dick's where she has decided to wait and see if her two targets show up. After arriving late afternoon, she has through a series of phone calls to the Puerto Vallarta visitors bureau found a L. Ortiz and a C. Flynn registered at the Las Cardenas Hotel. Dicks is adjacent to the Las Cardenas. She makes a call and listens to a voice message, "I am sorry to bother you, but I have another client I wish to pass unto you. I do not want his wife to be harmed. They will be contacting the other two clients, probably on Sunday. I've sent their information by courier today, and you can pick it up at the desk at the Marriott Casa Magna."

The Bolivian decides not to have dinner, but orders a drink and an appetizer. She decides to walk along the Rio Cual and stop somewhere for an after-dinner drink. She signals the waiter and asks for her bill. As she leaves the restaurant the waiter thinks to himself, don't get many blonds in here that speak fluent Spanish.

On her way out who should wander in but Leo and Corey. She recognizes them but they do not see her. They are seated and served by the same waiter, and Leo orders them both Dick's House Special Margaritas. The waiter brings the drinks and both Leo and Corey decide on the red snapper and, of course, two more margaritas. After finishing their dinners and yet another round of margaritas, Leo and Corey are well on their way to being really drunk. Corey signals the waiter for the bill which the waiter brings.

"Great dinner, *amigo*. Margaritas were awesome. Now me and my friend here want you to point us in the direction of all the beautiful women I've heard about here in Puerto Vallarta."

The waiter responds, "You should have been here a little earlier. There was a beautiful blond sitting right here. And looking very lonesome."

"Where did she go?"

"I think she maybe went to walk along the river."

"The river?"

"*Si*, maybe she is walking along the Rio Cual and will stop at the River Café. They have music."

"Point us in the right direction, *amigo*."

Leo and Corey, more or less, stagger out of Dick's and head for the path which follows the tree-lined Rio Cual. They continue until they hear music and find themselves standing in front of the River Café. Without saying a word, they nod their heads, walk in, and see what they came for.

Two very attractive ladies are sitting at the bar, and they readily accept Leo's offer to buy them both a drink. Leo sits down on a stool next to the one on the left, and Corey grabs a seat next to the one on the right. After initial introductions and small talk, it is apparent to Leo and Corey that these two are available and want to go dancing.

This makes Corey happy, but Leo, well let's just say, Leo isn't a great dancer. But, he feigns interest. So, the four of them make plans to grab a cab and head for Marina Vallarta where one of the ladies knows of a really good night club, called La Vista with a good bar, live music and awesome views of the harbor.

Sitting on the patio at the River Café in the shadows of a eucalyptus tree, the Bolivian watches and listens. The marina, she thinks, this could provide an opportunity. The two bimbos may be unfortunate casualties. As soon as the party leaves she pays her tab and returns to the river walk and finds a public restroom with a mirror. She tosses the blond wig, combs out her coal black hair, puts on a black beret, goes out, and hails a taxi.

Leo and Corey and their new best friends are already out on the dance floor at La Vista when the Bolivian arrives. The night club they have chosen is on the top floor of one of the bougainvillea-adorned, four-story condo residences surrounding the marina.

The restroom is inconveniently located on the bottom floor. Perfect, she thinks. I will wait there. She returns to the bar and watches. The ladies decide to take a break and head for the elevator. Leo and Corey sit tight, but Corey is fidgety.

The Bolivian heads down the stairs and opens the men's restroom door, "Anyone in here?" Nothing. She goes in and waits. Within a couple of minutes Corey enters and runs up to a urinal.

The Bolivian steps out of a stall and puts two rounds in the back of Corey's head. She drags him out of sight of the entry door and settles back to wait. She doesn't seem concerned about the blood spatters on the wall. Within a few minutes Leo comes in, "Corey, are you in here?" No answer.

The Bolivian eases out of her stall, when suddenly a hand reaches around the stall door and grabs her by the neck. Leo shakes her like a rag doll and throws her against the wall. Her head hits the frame of the crank-out window, and her gun goes flying. She feels the blood coursing down her neck. Leo reaches for her again and slams her on the concrete floor. She tries to get up, but Leo is a big man and he falls down on top of her. She can hardly breathe. His hands find her neck. Leo is much too powerful for her to overcome. She forces herself to go limp. She feels a slight relaxation in the big one's grip.

Another man enters the restroom and shouts something in Spanish. Leo is momentarily distracted. Before Leo can react, the Bolivian rolls to the left, and her hand falls on the grip of her pistol. Leo sees the gun in her hand but is kicked in the chest by the man who just entered, who apparently thinks Leo is attacking a poor defenseless woman. The Bolivian looks at the man and mutters, "*gracias*" before shooting him in the forehead and then pumping two bullets into Leo who again falls on top of her. She struggles to push him off and gets up as another man enters the restroom. He stops, looks at the three bodies on the floor, and is hit from behind with the butt of her gun.

What a mess, she thinks, and quickly slips out the door into the shadows. She hurries down the hall out onto the promenade which circles the marina. Many people are out for an evening stroll, but she is covered with blood and keeps to the shadows. She walks with the evening strollers until she gets to the walkway of Marina Parkway where she walks in the evening shadows to the entrance of Casa Magna.

She hurries through the empty hallway to the stairs and goes to her room. She takes a quick shower, changes clothes, puts on some dark-rimmed glasses and a black wig. She grabs her bag and a damp washcloth and wipes down the room.

She leaves the room, heads for the front desk, and asks if she has any messages. The clerk checks his book, turns, opens a safe, removes a packet, and hands it to her. She hurries outside and immediately opens the packet. She does not recognize the face of Robert Romano, but why would she? Robert and Rosanna Romano, Fiesta Americana Hotel, booked Saturday to Saturday. Out into the night again, she hails a cab for a short ride to the Hotel Las Palmas.

Having already booked herself into the Las Palmas and having checked in, she goes to her room. Once there she puts on a medium-brown wig and changes her blouse, adding a silk scarf. She leaves the room and walks two blocks to the Fiesta Americana to get a visual of the grounds. After grabbing a drink at the bar and slowly walking the grounds, she walks down to the beach and finds herself in front of the Las Palmas grounds and pool area. Perfect. She walks through the grounds, through the hotel, out the entrance, and asks the uniformed hotel employee to hail her a cab. The cab arrives, and she requests, "*Aeropuerto, por favor.*"

On the way to the airport she puts the gun in a plastic bag and, upon arrival at the airport, drops it into the first trash container she sees. In her small, MK bag she fishes out a locker key. She goes to the bank of lockers and opens one with her key. She removes a small athletic bag she had placed in there earlier and looks for a restroom. In the restroom, she locks herself in a stall and opens the bag which contains a 38-caliber, automatic pistol, a screw-on silencer, three full magazines, and a switchblade knife. Also in the bag are two wigs, two pair of sunglasses and a reversible light weight jacket

Back at the La Vista, Delgado and I are trying to figure out whether we should follow Ortiz out when all sorts of commotion breaks out down on the promenade.

We look over the edge of the balcony and see a couple of police cars pull up as more officers are running towards the building. Something has happened. We find the stairs to the promenade and hustle down. As we open the door to the promenade, we run right into Chief Estavan Rodrigues.

I ask, "Chief, what has happened?"

"I was going to ask you the same thing. My Lieutenant has told me there are three dead men in the restroom and another unconscious. What are you two doing here? I thought we agreed how we were going to handle this?"

"We just came here for drinks, and I saw Ortiz walk out. We agreed to do nothing, and then we heard all the commotion from our table up on the balcony, so we came down to see what had happened."

"It appears that one of the dead men is Leo Ortiz and another is Corey Flynn. The third fellow is Manuel Tenorio."

"Ortiz and Flynn are dead? Who is this Tenorio guy."

"Yes, Ortiz and Flynn are dead and we have no idea who Tenorio is. I want you to give a statement to my lieutenant and be sure to be thorough in what you saw. Also, anyone who you might suspect to be involved. We'll talk later as this is going to draw any, and all, media and newspaper types in town."

Delgado and I, after giving our statements to the lieutenant, hail a cab and head back to the Las Palmas. We decide to stop at the lobby bar and have a drink and discuss what we have seen this evening. We no sooner sit down and order our drinks when Delgado nods his head towards the entrance—a very attractive brunette dressed head to foot in Nike jogging attire is crossing the lobby, headed for the elevator. I glance over, oh my God, it's the blond in a brunette wig.

"Javiar, that's the blond that I talked with at the bar earlier."

"What the hell. What is she up to?"

"I think it's not a coincidence that we've seen her here and at the scene of three murders in two different wigs."

"I'll go get on the elevator with her and see what floor she's on, and we'll meet right back here and come up with a plan of action."

"Javiar, be careful. This one could be dangerous."

Javiar just barely makes it to the elevator before the doors close. The hotel has six floors, and she has already pushed number five, so he pushes number six. The elevator stops at floor number four, but no one gets on. The Bolivian reaches for the panel as if to push the close-door button, but she pushes stop.

Delgado is surprised, and before he can react she fires two rounds into his forehead. She goes through his pockets and finds his DEA credentials and badge. She takes out a key, drags Delgado out, and sends the elevator to the basement. She drags Delgado down the hall and manages to push him into a storeroom and then takes the stairs to the third floor. She checks the hallway and hurries to her room. She again gathers her belongings, wipes the room down with a damp cloth, and heads for the exit which will take her down to the beach.

I'm beginning to wonder what has happened to Delgado. He has been gone over thirty minutes. So, I decide to go to the front desk and ask for the security officer. He comes out of the back room with a scowl on his face and catsup on his mustache. He's about fifty-something years old, and I think Pancho Villa reincarnated. He carries a very large side-arm and a bad attitude. He and the desk clerk converse in Spanish, and he looks at me and motions me to follow him.

We go to the elevator Delgado got on and I immediately know something is wrong. I point the security officer to the floor. "That's blood," I say, "and it's still wet." He immediately gets on his two-way radio and shouts a whole lot of Spanish to someone.

We take the elevator back down to the lobby, and he tells me in English that he has called Chief Rodrigues and reported a possible murder. I just know one thing, this is all really not going to end well.

Crap, I haven't even called Frankie Koch. That ain't gonna be pleasant either. The rent-a-cop motions me to follow him into his office, points to a chair, and says, "Sit. Chief Rodrigues is on his way."

"Shouldn't we be looking for my associate."

"No. Chief said stay right here."

"Can I make a phone call? I'll pay for the call."

"Ask the chief when he gets here."

I guess that meant, no.

26

THE RAID

May 29, 1982

The Saturday morning has arrived. The entire taskforce will involve more than 200 law enforcement officers hitting 15 residences and Leo's garage. All members of the taskforce gather at the hanger on El Toro at five a.m. and are given packets of information. All pertinent information regarding those to be arrested, addresses, and vehicle information had been passed out to team leaders earlier. The purpose of this gathering is to furnish up-to-date arrest warrants and search warrants and any other new information that may be of interest. The meeting lasts 15 minutes and at 5:15 a.m. they are off and running. The raid commences at six a.m.

Janet is beside herself. She has not seen Marc, nor heard from him since they met at El Torrito. She tosses and turns in bed until she can no longer bear it. She gets up, throws on some clothes, and heads over to Rosanna's. It's 5:45 a.m. That's OK, she thinks, Rosanna is an early riser, and maybe she'll know something about Marc.

Janet pulls up in the driveway and walks around the side of the house, through the side-yard gate, and into the backyard. There are no lights on in the house. Trying to remember where the spare key is hidden, she notices the phone inside on the table blinking with what looks like eight or nine messages.

Outside, down the block in a black van, Biff radios Frankie at the raid command center, "Frankie, Janet Ryder just pulled up in the driveway and went around the back of the house."

"Crap, just what we didn't need. If she's still there when you go in, read her, her rights and hook her up. We'll just have to sort her out of this later. Alright, here we go. I'm switching to channel one. All team leaders, this is the CP, it is 5:59 a.m., good luck and be careful. CP out."

Based on the diagrams provided by Marc Ryder, Biff and his team surround the house and grab Janet in the backyard. Doors are broken open, and the team enters the house to find it vacant. No one is home. Biff calls the CP and says, "We have no one at home at target number one. I repeat, no one at home. We are executing the search warrant now, and I'll report if we come upon any info regarding the whereabouts of our main subjects."

Janet, in the meantime, is already screaming bloody murder and has to be physically restrained. Biff assigns two agents to question her.

The agent asks, "Do you know where Robert and Rosanna Romano are?"

"No, I don't. I came here trying to find my husband."

"Who is your husband?"

"Who is my husband? He's part of your fucking task-force, you idiot!"

"Again, what is his name?"

"Oh for Christ's sake, it is Deputy Assistant Director Marc Ryder."

"Thank you, and what are you doing here?"

"I told you, you jerk. Don't you listen? I came here trying to find my husband. The Romanos are friends of ours, and I thought maybe they might know where he is."

"Hey, John, could you go get Biff. I think we got a problem here."

Biff comes over and the agent tells him what he has learned, "and this woman claims to Marc Ryder's wife."

Biff says "I'll take it from there and turns to Janet, "Mrs. Ryder, I'm Special Agent Biff Kowalski. I am not at liberty to tell you where your husband is other than he is working with us on this taskforce."

"OK fine. Now get these damn handcuffs off of me so I can go home."

"I'm sorry about that, but the cuffs stay on, and I'm going to have you transported to our command post where you'll be asked some more questions about why you were here and your relationship with not only the Romanos but one Corey Flynn. Also, your purse was searched as we are executing a search warrant for these premises and a baggie with a white powdery substance was found."

"Wha, what? Corey Flynn? White powdery substance? Shit. I want a lawyer, and I'm not answering anymore questions."

"Suit yourself. That's probably good advice."

Janet suddenly realizes that she is in real trouble and wonders if Marc can get her out of this mess. . . by the way, where in the hell are you Marc Ryder?

Biff and his team find one hundred seventy thousand in cash stashed in boxes in the master bedroom closet. Other than the cocaine found in Janet's purse, they find no drugs.

In the garage, they find seven expensive sports cars, all of which are confiscated. The other fourteen teams hitting other residences make fourteen arrests without incident and confiscate more than two hundred thousand in cash. The team hitting the garage finds pallets of marijuana and cocaine. This might be the largest drug bust in US history. They also find a black van with bullet holes in it. It seems Robert got too busy planning his trip to Puerto Vallarta to dispose of the van. Well that and the fact that Manny, Leo's cousin, seemed to have disappeared and didn't return his calls.

27

THE COMMAND POST

MAY 29, 1982

By nine a.m. everybody involved in the raids had reported in, and there is a feeling of jubilation in the room despite the fact that word had gotten out to the teams that action had also taken place in Puerto Vallarta, and that news was not good. It was confirmed that Delgado was dead, and last contact with Ryder was last night. Without Ryder and Delgado, the primary source of information from Puerto Vallarta was Chief Rodrigues. An assistant counsel general from the US Embassy in Mexico City had arrived and told Koch, after talking to Rodrigues, that the Romanos had also disappeared. He also related to Koch that, in what he thought was an unrelated incident, the chief of police in the city of Tequila had been murdered. The new chief had reported an unusual phone call to the Mexican Attorney General's office, and they were sending investigators to Tequila.

So, the CP is relatively subdued when Janet Ryder is brought in, and all hell breaks loose!

No sooner does she enter the room than she begins ranting, "Who the hell is in charge here? My husband Marc Ryder has been missing for more than 24 hours, and you pathetic excuses for fucking agents are sitting around here counting the goddamn money. Somebody needs to tell me what the hell is going on, and I mean now. My husband is not some fucking street agent, he is Deputy Assistant Director of the Defense Foreign Liaison Office. I am not going to stop screaming until someone gives me some answers. Do you fucking hear me?"

Koch steps in, "Mrs. Ryder, we are as concerned about Marc as you. If you will calm down I will give you a synopsis of what we know."

"About goddamn time."

"Marc was sent to Puerto Vallarta, Mexico to assist the Mexican authorities apprehend Leo Ortiz and Corey Flynn. Javiar Delgado, a DEA Agent went with him. Delgado was murdered, and that was reported to us by your husband. He also reported seeing the Romanos at the Fiesta Americana Hotel. Unfortunately, we have not heard from him since."

"Oh, sweet Jesus, are you telling me he is dead too?"

"No, I am not. Now, I see your attorney is here, and unless you have any information you want to share with us, we're finished."

"Can I be released?"

"Mrs. Ryder, you were found at a known drug dealer's house with cocaine in your bag. Need I say more?"

A very subdued Janet answers, "No."

"Do you have any questions?"

"I want to talk my attorney."

"Take her away please and let her and her attorney talk."

After talking to her attorney Janet is taken away to be

booked into the Orange County jail to await transfer to the federal courthouse in Los Angeles for an appearance before a US magistrate. Let's just say, she is not a happy camper.

By the way, I warned you that she was a potty mouth.

28

CONFUSION IN PUERTO VALLARTA

May 29, 1982

I'm basically confined to the security office until Chief Rodrigues arrives. He informs me that he is getting rather annoyed at finding or looking at dead bodies and seeing me at the scene. But, he calms down, and I relate to him, again, the events of the entire evening.

He demands, "Why do you think this woman has anything to do with this mayhem? And where can she be found? I'm telling you, Ryder, you need to come up with more than just a suspicion."

"I'm sorry Chief, it's all I got. With the sudden disappearance of Delgado, my feelings are that she had something to do with not only Delgado's disappearance but everything else that happened tonight."

At that moment, the chief's two-way radio comes alive with some very rapid and loud Spanish.

The chief quietly answers and looks at me and says, "I am sorry, *amigo*, they just found Delgado in a storage room on the fourth floor. He has been shot and is dead. I am going to issue an all-points bulletin to all Mexican authorities. We will find this woman."

At this very moment Robert and Rosanna are grabbing a taxi at the Puerto Vallarta airport for the short ride to the Fiesta Americana.

The Bolivian has again changed her wig and facial make-up and has found a coffee shop adjacent to the entrance of the Fiesta Americana. She now has shoulder-length, dish-water-blond hair and rimless glasses. She decides she will wait for this Robert to check in, as she has already verified his arrival time. She will then attempt to take him in the elevator. If his wife interferes, she may become an innocent casualty of war. She waits and watches. A taxi arrives and a man and a woman get out. It's them, no doubt.

Robert and Rosanna enter the Fiesta Americana lobby and go to the front desk. The Bolivian immediately heads for the bank of elevators and finds a small alcove to wait. Security in the hotel has received a fax vaguely describing the Bolivian. The man in charge says to his corporal, "Let's take a walk around the lobby."

As they start across the lobby area, they see a man and woman, Robert and Rosanna, head for the elevators. "Let's take the elevator up and work our way down," says the security chief. As they approach the elevator, the man and woman start to enter and suddenly a woman appears from an alcove nearby and produces a gun with a silencer. The security chief shouts, in Spanish, "Stop! Police!"

Unfortunately, these were his last words, as the woman swivels and fires two shots at both security men—both head shots. Robert shoves Rosanna into the elevator as the doors close.

"What the hell was that?" screams Rosanna.

"I don't know," says Robert. "As soon as we get to the room I'll call security and tell them."

Chief Rodrigues and I are discussing what to do next when his two-way radio bursts to life again.

"Chief, this is Lieutenant Lopez. We have reports of shots fired at the Fiesta Americana, with two security men down."

The Bolivian is beside herself. She rips off her wig and glasses, stuffs them in her bag, and races out the exit towards the beach. She runs south along the beach to a large timeshare condo complex, Los Tules. No one is out in the pool area this late, so, she is unseen. She crosses the pool and patio area to the parking lot and goes through an unlocked gate out onto Revolution Boulevard. She calmly walks across the boulevard at the signal light and heads for the shopping center. At the shopping center, she looks for and finds a car rental office. Using one of her multiple identities and credit cards, she rents a car and tells the clerk she is headed for Nueve Vallarta and that she will probably be gone for a week.

She finishes all the paperwork and is given the keys to a Toyota Celica. She gets in, familiarizes herself with the car, starts it, swings out onto Revolution, and heads north on Mexico 200. It's late, but she is not the least bit tired. I'll be in Guadalajara in four hours, she thinks.

Back at the Las Palmas, the chief is gathering his troops to hit the Fiesta Americana and isolate the hotel.

I ask, "Mind if I tag along, Chief?"

"You might as well, you are the only one who might be able to spot this woman."

Everyone in the hotel is being questioned, and no one is allowed to leave until they are cleared by the chief. Who should appear to be questioned but Robert and Rosanna. As I watch from behind a one-way mirror in the security office, I'm wondering if they were also the target of this mystery woman. I decide it's a good time to call Frankie. He tells me the raid and arrests in California went smoothly except for the Romanos. They have disappeared and they have no idea where they have gone. Have you got Ortiz and Flynn wrapped up?"

"The Romanos just walked across the lobby of the hotel and are being questioned by Rodrigues' men. There was a shooting here just a few minutes ago. Now you might want to sit down while I tell you everything that has happened down here."

As I fill him in, I can tell he is almost hyperventilating.

"What the hell, we had no idea. Jesus Christ, Delgado is dead? Ortiz and Flynn are dead? Two cops and a civilian are dead? Holy shit, the consulate people, hell, the ambassador, crap, the president are all going to want be briefed on this. What a frickin' goat rope. You didn't fire a shot or get involved in anyway, did you? And the Romanos are at the hotel right now?"

"Yes, they are here right now. I've done nothing but provide the chief with what I saw, and what I believe, that there is this mystery woman involved, and that she is the shooter. Do you have any idea who can help us out on who this woman might be?"

"I'll give everything we got to DEA and Interpol. They are the only agencies who might have people on the ground down there to help out. But we're going to need more descriptive information than you just gave me. I'll get the chief of station in Mexico City on the phone, as soon as I can, and give him what we have and pass it all to Interpol, also. You need to alert Rodrigues about the Romanos and I'll get the paperwork rolling over in Mexico City to arrest them. Ryder, keep me posted."

I wander out of the office thinking Robert and Rosanna have left. They haven't. They are standing waiting for an elevator. As Rosanna gets on the elevator she glances back and sees me.

"Crap!" Murphy's law, if it can go bad, it will. One damn minute later and she would not have seen me. Got to find the chief quickly.

They get on the elevator and Rosanna grabs Roberts sleeve, "Robert, I saw Marc Ryder come out of the security office. What the hell is he doing here? He's part of that task-force, could he be here because of us?"

"Are you sure? If so, I need to call Alfonzo. We may need some assistance."

"Maybe we should leave this hotel?"

"No, I think it is better to stay put for now."

Robert calls Alfonzo and fills him in on what happened at their hotel and the other killings of Ortiz and Flynn. He adds, "Alfonzo, there is something else. Rosanna saw Marc Ryder at our hotel with the chief of police. Do you think he is here because of Rosanna and I?"

"Remind me who this Marc Ryder is."

"He is the American whose wife became my wife's good friend."

"Damn, that is news I didn't want to hear. I want you two to lay low and stay right where you are. I'll have a team there to clean up this mess. "

Alfonzo can't believe what a mess this has turned into. He calls Adolfo and Manuel to tell them what has happened. He has no idea what is going to happen in Tequila, and he is going to be even more frustrated, to put it nicely.

Adolfo tells Alfonzo "whatever you do, you make sure Rosanna is safe and gets out of the mess. Do you understand me Alfonzo?"

"Yes, I understand. I have someone in Puerto Vallarta who can help with this problem."

"Alfonzo, it is only going to be a problem if something happens to my Rosanna."

"Adolfo, I will not fail you."

"No you won't Alfonzo." Click

Alfonzo thinks "I will personally find this Bolivian and strangle her."

29

JORGE OF PUERTO VALLARTA

May 30, 1982

Jorge Padilla is a native-born citizen of Puerto Vallarta. He's about 35-years old and has lived in the northeast section of Puerto Vallarta his entire life. His father had worked as a waiter and bartender at Las Palomas restaurant his entire life until his recent death. His mother has worked as a hotel maid with various hotels in Puerto Vallarta her entire life. Jorge, the youngest of six children, was definitely the problem child. He was also the biggest child in the family. At age 12 he was almost six-feet tall and 190 pounds. He was not so much a bully as he was just plain mean to everyone.

It didn't take long before he was part of a gang and became the chief enforcer. By age twenty he was the leader of the gang, and it was rumored he had killed at least six times. Probably the only reason he was not in prison, not that he had never been in prison, was because of his cousin. His cousin was part of the attorney general's investigative group, and, at times, he needed the services of Jorge.

Therefore, as a return favor, he would make Jorge's problem go away.

Jorge has received the call from Alfonzo and as soon as Jorge ends his call with Alfonzo, he gets back on the phone and within minutes has located Robert Romano at the Fiesta Americana and Marc Ryder at the hotel Las Palmas. Jorge is still a large man and sports a drooping mustache and pockmarked skin. He calls out to his brother and number-one man, "Luis, bring everyone in." Luis looks almost identical as Jorge except for wearing his hair shoulder length. Both are covered in tattoos as are their three associates, Carlos, Diego and Joe. "We have work to do" Says Jorge.

Luis comes in, followed by the crew. The whole crew, including Jorge and Luis, are alumni of the prison in Hermosillo. They are all members of a notorious killer-for-hire group known as, Amigos de Muertos.

Jorge decides they will take care of Romano first. A plan is hatched to draw him out of the hotel to the beach area north of the hotel which is rarely used. He thinks they should move quickly because they also need to grab Ryder from the Las Palmas.

Jorge and crew arrive at the Fiesta Americana to find all kinds of police activity. Jorge goes to the bar, orders a beer and asks the bartender what is going on. The bartender tells him that there has been a shooting and two security guards were hit and may be dead. Jorge casually finishes his beer, goes back out the front door of the Americana, and finds his crew near a small outdoor café.

Jorge decides he will call Romano's room and tell him that he has further instructions from Alfonzo and would he please meet with him near the palm cabana on the beach north of the hotel. He instructs his crew where to secrete themselves and gives them thirty minutes to get in position. He then calls Romano, and Romano agrees to meet.

"Who was that?" asks Rosanna.

"Someone who Alfonzo has sent. He has some information and instructions for us and wants to meet out on the beach north of the hotel."

"I should go with you. I have met or seen most of Alfonzo's associates and may know this person. I do not trust Alfonzo."

"I don't see any problem with this. Why do you?"

"Because I do not trust Alfonzo."

"OK, but how about if you stay back in the shadows and just watch?"

"I won't be far away."

Robert and Rosanna take the stairs down to the lobby and walk out onto the beach. Rosanna hangs back and watches Robert walk to the palm cabana.

It's very dark out on this area. It's a grassy area adjacent to the beach and it is not lit by any type of light. Rosanna hangs back and watches from the shadows. Suddenly, she sees a masked man step out from behind the cabana and point a gun at Robert.

She screams, "Robert, look out!"

Her scream distracts Jorge, the masked man with a gun and Robert tackles him to the ground. Rosanna, however, is unaware of the man next to her in the shadows, and after she screams, Luis steps out and knocks her unconscious with the butt of his gun.

The other three members of the crew rush to the aid

of Jorge. Robert is strangled unconscious by Joe and is wrapped up in duct tape. He is dragged down to the water's edge by Carlos and Diego.

Jorge and Luis are unsure now what to do with Robert. Joe comes up and points out in the bay where a small boat is tied to a buoy. He says "we could use that boat and take him out in the bay and throw him over board."

Luis wades out into the water to a buoy. Tied to the buoy by rope is a small boat. Luis unties the rope and pulls the boat up to the shore. Robert is thrown into the boat, and Joe, Carlos, and Diego get in. Carlos grabs the oars and begins rowing the boat out into the darkness of the Bay of Banderas.

About ten minutes out, they take the duct tape off Robert, push him out of the boat and hold him underwater—drowning him. When, and if, he is found, they figure his cause of death will be deemed accidental drowning. They return to shore to find their other victim.

That would be me.

Meanwhile, Chief Rodrigues is overwhelmed by the events that have occurred in his city in the last 24 hours. Everything is out of whack. This is a resort city where people come to have a good time and relax. Now, pandemonium rings throughout.

"Chief, I just got off the phone with Frankie Koch, and Puerto Vallarta is not the only city with some odd events and murders happening," I announce.

The chief responds, "Do I really want to hear what you have to say, Ryder?"

"Probably not, but just the same, it may be of interest to

you. The chief of police in Tequila has been murdered. The new chief, Domingues Dosportes, reported to the Mexican attorney general that he had been called by a person who identified himself as Alfonzo Benitez. This person wanted to know if everything was OK and that he represented the Mendez brothers."

"Benitez I do not know, but one of the leading cartels in Central America, the Caribbean, Mexico, and the USA is the Mendez Cartel. They are some bad hombres. Do you think they are involved in what has turned my town upside down?"

"I am sure they are. I gave all the information I had regarding the blond woman to Koch, and he is going to try to come up with something for us to go on."

Out on the beach, Rosanna suddenly comes to and finds herself alone. She vaguely remembers seeing someone attacking Robert before everything went black. She feels the back of her head, and it is all sticky with blood—no doubt the reason for the splitting headache she has. She wonders if the man she saw was a policeman and if Robert has been arrested. No, that is not possible. He had a mask on.

Down the beach she sees some men. She can't tell what they are doing but three of them get in a small boat and one begins to row. Two other men are standing on the beach having an animated conversation which abruptly ends and they start walking back towards the Fiesta Americana. Staying in the shadows she makes her way to the poolside restroom. She goes into the men's side and walks to the last stall. She climbs up on the commode and squats down and waits.

Jorge and Luis who were having an animated discussion on the beach about what to do about Romano's wife and came to the decision that she must not be harmed, but captured and delivered to Benitez. They arrive back to the area near the Palm Cabana and the woman is gone.

"Damn" says Jorge, "she is gone. Will you be able to recognize her Luis?"

"Yes, she is very pretty."

"OK, let's go find her and tell her we were sent by her father."

She waits in the restroom until she feels it might be safe. She looks out into the pool area and does not see anyone. She washes the blood from her face and hair. She ties her hair up in a ponytail and heads down to the beach to the next hotel, the Las Palmas. She goes into the lobby area and finds a gift shop where she buys a baseball cap.

She goes out on the street and finds a small sidewalk café, orders a coffee and sits down where she can see the entrances to both The Americana and Las Palmas.

Two men approach her table. Jorge pulls out a chair and sits down while Luis stands in the shadows. She doesn't recall ever seeing either of them before.

"*Buenos noches, Senorita*. I am Jorge, and I have been sent by Alfonzo Benitez to see that you safely leave Mexico and return home to Panama. I have also been asked to rid us of an American federale, named Marc Ryder."

"I don't know who you are, but I am waiting for Marc Ryder, and I intend to kill him. I think he may have done something to my husband Robert."

"I have been hired by Alfonzo Benitez as I said. Robert is safe and we will pick him up on the way to the airfield in Tequila. As soon as we dispose of Ryder, we will drive you to Tequila and then you are on your way to Panama."

"Why didn't Robert wait for me?"

"We could not find you. He told us of being attacked on the beach. He fought off his attackers could not find you. So he thought you might have been kidnapped. He called Alfonzo Benitez and Benitez called me. I happened to be only a couple of minutes away. Alfonzo was deeply concerned about Roberts safety as well as yours. So we have him in a safe place.

"So you are going to, as you say, dispose of Ryder?"

"Yes we will."

"Yes, and as we speak, there he is getting in a cab."

Jorge produces a two-way radio and calls "Luis, bring the car."

A black, Chevy SUV suddenly pulls up, and they get in. Luis and Carlos are already in the SUV. Jorge does not bother to introduce them to Rosanna. They follow the cab to the malecon where they observe Marc Ryder get out and go into Con Orgullo Azteca Restaurante.

Jorge says to Rosanna "we will take him when he comes out of the restaurant. It would be a good plan if you could distract him enough so we might grab him. Could you do this for us? I don't think you would be in danger."

"Yes, I can do that."

I hail cab at the Las Palmas and tell the driver to take me to the Con Argullo Azteca. It's only a ten minute ride but I almost fall asleep. We pull up in front of the restaurant and I pay my fare and hop out. I'm starving and beat.

Even just sitting at restaurant table the heat is overwhelming.

It's almost one a.m., yet the air is so heavy, so humid. The bugs aren't flying but rather swimming through the air. The aroma of bougainvillea and jasmine fills the air with a freshness only a south of the border destination can fulfill. The malecon is still lively. I enjoy a delicious dinner and a couple of dirty martinis and after paying my tab, go out to hail a cab.

I exit the Con Orgullo Azteca Restaurant and stand in the shadows of Avenida Juarez. The Lady of Guadalupe Cathedral, illuminated with a silvery glow stands at my back and the Banderas Bay shimmers under a full moon to my front. Suddenly I'm grabbed by my arm and a woman pulls me close. I can feel the sharp point of a knife in my rib. A feeling of fear overcomes me as I try to make a quick decision to escape her hold and knife. But before I can react she pulls me in closer. It's Rosanna.

She says, "Hello, Marc. Fancy meeting you here. Come with me and meet my friend Jorge."

That's the last thing I heard.

Jorge says "well done, Rosanna. We are going to drive to Tequila and meet Alfonzo. I have given our friend something to keep him asleep. We will get you on the plane and out of Mexico, and I will dispose of our federale."

"Jorge, where will we pick up Robert ?"

"He will be waiting in Tequila."

"I thought you said we would pick him up on the way?"

"Sorry, I meant on the way to Tequila."

30

TEQUILA SHOTS

MAY 30, 1982

Humberto has been thinking about Juanita's daughter all day... had the mother, why not have the daughter? He waits along the trail, knowing when she gets off work, this is her route home. As she passes near the airfield, he suddenly steps out of the jungle brush and grabs her. She screams but Humberto hits her with a sharp blow to the head, knocking her unconscious. He drags her to a little clearing and rips her clothes off.

As he is about to have his way, she comes to and screams and begins to fight him off. He again hits her, and she falls to ground. He drops his pants and falls upon her. Faking unconsciousness, she feels a softball-size rock in the dirt beside her. As he falls on her, she grabs the rock and smashes it into his forehead. He falls off her, and she quickly jumps up, grabs her clothes, and runs off towards her home, stopping to put on what's left of her clothes.

Humberto lies still for only a few minutes before coming to and realizing what has happened. But, he is Humberto, and this will only put more fear into Juanita. He shakes off the dirt from his clothes and tries not to get blood all over himself, as he is bleeding profusely from the blow administered by Juanita's daughter. They both will pay, he thinks.

The daughter arrives home, thinking she will change clothes so her mother will not know. She is surprised to find her mother home and is forced to tell the entire story of what happened. Juanita calmly listens and tells her daughter to get cleaned up and not tell anyone what has happened. Juanita goes to her bedroom, opens a hidden drawer under her bed, and finds what she is looking for. She then goes to her closet, finds her finest dress, and puts it on. As she is leaving the house, she tells her daughter she will be back by dusk and heads down the road to Tequila.

Juanita walks straight through Tequila to the police building, walks up to the desk officer and asks to see the chief. The desk officer waves her right through, thinking she's another of Humberto's afternoon pleasures.

Juanita walks into Humberto's office and closes the door. She flirtingly lifts her skirt and says, "It's been a long time, Humberto. Maybe we should try it again?"

Humberto is surprised but thinks to himself, I didn't think this would work so quickly.

"Humberto, what have you done to your head? Come here, let me look at you. Don't tell me my little daughter did this to you?"

Humberto comes out from behind his desk and wraps his arms around Juanita.

She moans in his ear.

That is the last thing he hears before the click of the switchblade. The last thing he feels is a sharp sting as the blade penetrates his throat. He falls to the floor.

Juanita spits on him, "Pig!"

She walks to the door and sees the desk officer is gone. She goes out the door and runs home to her daughter.

"Pack everything you value up in a bag and pack your sisters things too. We are leaving for my sister's home in Manzanillo."

Juanita and her daughters have about a three-hour head start on the Tequila police because no one dares to walk into Humberto's office if they did not hear him say, after knocking to come in, especially when he is entertaining one of his afternoon delights. Finally, the lieutenant, second in command of the police force, makes the decision to just knock. No response. So he opens the door and finds Humberto lying on the floor in a pool of blood. The desk officer remembers he saw a woman going into the chief's office. He thought she might be a woman named Juanita who lived in the Calle Primavera neighborhood. His daughter and Jaunita's daughter were friends. Somehow, the lieutenant thinks, justice has finally been done in Tequila. Nevertheless, the whole police force swoops down on the Calle Primavera neighborhood of Tequila. They learn Juanita and her daughters are gone. No one knows where. Lieutenant Domingues Miguel Dosportes orders the entire community to gather and pronounces to them that he is the new chief of police. Things will be different, and he advises anyone who has information to come forth. No one does.

Dosportes returns to police headquarters and finds that Humberto has been transported to the mortuary and the office is relatively cleaned up. He starts checking the drawers in Humberto's desk and finds nothing of interest. He thinks that he will tackle the file drawer later.

Alfonzo has just landed at an airfield much similar to the one in Tequila but in Guatemala. While the pilot tends to the Cessna, Alfonzo finds a pay phone and calls the Chief of Police in Tequila.

The phone rings and he hears someone answer "Tequila Police."

Alfonzo replies, "This is Alfonzo. May I speak to the chief, please."

"This is the chief. How may I help you?"

"I'm sorry, I mean Chief Humberto Gonzalez."

"Chief Humberto Gonzalez has been murdered. I am now the chief, Domingues Dosportes, at your service. To whom am I speaking?"

"I am Alfonzo Benetiz, and I represent the Mendez brothers."

"I am sorry, but I know of neither you nor the Mendez brothers. What does this concern?"

"Uh, it is a personal matter. Sorry to bother you. Goodbye."

Alfonzo wonders if this is the work of the Bolivian. He only hopes that the shipment has cleared Tequila and the new chief. After calming down, he picks up the phone and calls a number in Puerto Vallarta. A woman answers, and Alfonzo asks for Jorge. The woman tells him that she does not know where Jorge is but she thinks he might be driving to Tequila.

31

TEQUILA SHOOTERS

MAY 30, 1982

The Bolivian arrives mid-morning in Tequila, exhausted from the drive from Puerto Vallarta. She intended to make quick work of this Humberto Gonzalez and make her way out of the mess in Puerto Vallarta, but the first thing she notices is the presence of too many cops. They seem to be everywhere. Why would such a small town have this many cops on the street at this hour? As she approaches the town square she realizes she is going to have to go through a checkpoint. Shouldn't be a problem, she thinks. She stops and three policemen approach her car. One goes to the passenger side and another stands directly in front of the car with his automatic rifle pointed directly at her. The third officer comes up to the driver's side window.

"Good morning, officer, what is happening here?"

"Your identification, and what is your business here in Tequila?"

"Here are my papers, and I am here to audit accounts at the Francisco Javiar Sauza Distillery."

"Where are you coming from?"

"Guadalajara."

After looking over the papers the officer tells her, "You may proceed."

"May I ask what has happened?"

"The chief of police, Humberto Gonzalez, has been murdered."

Humberto Gonzalez, her target in Tequila. Someone has cheated her out of a nice fee. The Bolivian proceeds through Tequila and spots a café which advertises *desayuno,* and she realizes she is starving and stops for breakfast. After a leisurely meal she finds her way back to the main highway to Guadalajara. As far as she is concerned, mission accomplished.

Arriving at the Tequila airfield just before the Bolivian arrived in Tequila are Jorge, his crew, Rosanna, and a unconscious Marc Ryder, trussed up in the back of the van. Driving up to a cleared area near the lone building adjacent to the airfield—a shed with sliding doors—the van stops. Alfonzo is due to arrive shortly in the plane from Panama.

Rosanna throws open the door and runs to the building. She pulls open the sliding doors, only to find it empty. She turns around and screams, "Where is Robert? You said he would be here. Did you lie to me, you bastard?"

Jorge motions Luis and Carlos to get her out of the shed. They manage to grab her and carry her back to the plane where she has her hands and legs duct-taped. After listening to her scream for a minute, Jorge decides to gag her. Let fucking Alfonzo deal with her when he gets there.

Now for the federale in the van. "Luis, take Diego and Joe and find a suitable place to bury him. Go down to the far end of the airstrip and just do it."

"Shall we kill him first?"

"Just dig a hole and bury him. He will die soon enough."

The conversation is interrupted by the sound of a small airplane passing overhead and circling for a landing. The plane also catches the interest of Consuela and Jose walking on the trail to Tequila from their home in Calle Primavera. What also catches their attention is a van coming down the strip towards them. "Consuela, come, we've got to hide ourselves. Maybe they saw us."

"Where will we hide, Jose?"

"Follow me. The jungle is thicker on the other side of the airstrip."

Consuelo and Jose run, hunched over, about a hundred yards from where they were and hunker down in the dense growth. They watch as the van stops and three men drag a man out of the back of the van. They carry him to the end of the strip and disappear grunting and groaning as they lug the body out of sight and into the jungle. Two of the men are also carrying shovels. Not more than thirty minutes later, they come out of the jungle, get in the van and drive back to the shed.

In the meantime, the plane lands, and one man exits the plane. He is greeted by the largest of the men in the shed and a heated conversation ensues. Finally, they seem to come to some sort agreement.

"Listen to me, Alfonzo, she was a screaming banshee. We had to tape her up. They could have heard her screaming in Tequila."

"Alright, Jorge, I believe you. What have you done with the federale?"

"He is buried in the jungle. He will never be found, trust me."

"All is well then, Jorge. *Hasta la Vista,* Jorge."

Alfonzo gets in the plane with the pilot and a tied-up

Rosanna in a back seat. "Rosanna, I will cut the tape from you as soon as we are airborne. You must promise not to struggle." He can see her eyes are welling up, and she begins sobbing and moaning. Alfonzo thinks, I knew this was going to happen the minute I laid eyes upon that American. Nothing but trouble.

At the end of the airstrip Consuela and Jose creep back to where they saw the men take the body. After a short search, they find a fresh grave and begin digging with their hands. Jose finds the body's feet and frantically begins scrapping dirt away. As Consuela continues to clear dirt from the upper torso, Jose grabs the ankles and pulls. The ankles and wrists are duct-taped, and Jose pulls out his knife and cuts them off. Consuela wipes the dirt from the body's face.

"Consuela, is he alive?"

"I think so, *Como esta, Senor*?"

She has got to be an angel. I must have died, and she is an angel. Everything hurts, especially my head. Wait, if I'm hurting, I must be alive. I don't think dead people feel pain.

"*Como se llama, Senor*?"

I am hurting all over. Throbbing in pain. I hear the woman say again "*Como esta Senor? Como se llama?*

What the hell did she say? My college Spanish kicks in and I respond in broken Spanish that I speak only a little Spanish and that my name is Marc Ryder.

She responds in English thank God!

"Where am I?"

"You are in the jungle near Tequila."

"I need to use a phone. Can you take me to a telephone?"

She says "we will tell you where you can find a phone, but we cannot go with you. It will be too dangerous for us."

Dangerous! Great, just great. I love danger. That's me, DFL.

At that moment, a small plane takes off and passes right over our heads and out of sight. Consuela and Jose continue to brush the dirt off me and discuss something in Spanish, which they don't seem to agree upon. Finally, Jose speaks, "Bad things have happened in Tequila. The chief of police has been murdered, and our good friend Juanita and her daughters have disappeared. I think it would be best for you to go to the police and tell them what has happened to you, and of course, who you are. We have had bad experiences with the police, mostly Humberto Gonzalez, who is dead. We do not know the new chief, Dosportes. We can lead you to the edge of town, and you can easily find the police station."

"I will be eternally grateful. Thank you. What are your names?"

"We think it better that you do not know."

Consuela and Jose lead me to the edge of the jungle. Before me lies a highway and Jose says to walk north about one kilometer where I shall find Tequila and the police. We say goodbye, and they disappear back into the jungle. I start walking, or I should say hobbling, towards Tequila, and I see a car approaching from Tequila. The car slows down, and I get a good look at the driver. It's the blond from the hotel bar but her hair color is different. She quickly looks away and speeds off to the south towards Guadalajara. What the hell has she been up to in Tequila?

I finally get to Tequila, and I'm stopped at a police checkpoint. The officers don't speak English, and I don't have any papers, so I am handcuffed, roughly shoved into the back of a police car, and driven to police headquarters. Once inside, I'm literally thrown into a cell, handcuffs still on. I say to the jailor, "I am an American citizen, a federal agent. I have been working with Chief Rodrigues in Puerto Vallarta."

The jailor disappears and shortly returns with another man who appears to be in charge. "Is your name Marc Ryder?"

I'm thinking, I'm in trouble, big trouble but I answer, "Yes, it is."

"I have spoken to Chief Rodrigues and told him that you are here. Juan, release this man. There is a restroom near the entrance, if you should like to clean up a bit before we hear your story."

"Yes, yes, thank you very much."

I look at myself in the mirror in the restroom and I don't recognize myself. My face is covered in bruises and dirt, and my clothes are torn, bloody, and filthy dirty. Nothing I can do about that, so I wash myself up as best as I can and head for the chief's office. I first get on the phone with Chief Rodrigues who expresses how happy he is to hear I am alive. I tell him how I was kidnapped off the street by Rosanna Romano and some guy named Jorge. Rodrigues seems to think he knows who I am talking about.

Rodrigues then tells me, "We found Robert Romano floating in the bay. It appears he drowned. We could not find wounds of any type. As far as that mysterious woman, she shall remain that way as we have found no trace of her anywhere."

"I think I saw her here in Tequila when I was walking into town. She was heading south on the main highway towards Guadalajara. She slowed down to take look at me, and I'm sure it was her. I thought maybe it was her who murdered the chief of police, but she was in Puerto Vallarta when that happened. She was driving a blue Toyota, maybe a Celica. Four doors and very plain. Looked like a rental. And, her hair was shoulder length and black this time, not blond."

"I will alert the highway police and other authorities in Guadalajara. I would like to talk to her about the mayhem here in Puerto Vallarta. You should call your office in California, as they are very concerned about what has happened to you, Marc Ryder. Goodbye, and *vaya con Dios, amigo*."

"*Gracious, el jefe. Hasta la vista*."

I call Frankie Koch and tell him the whole story. He puts Biff on the phone, and I tell it again.

Biff listens without interrupting, and when I finish he exclaims loud enough for everyone to hear, "DFL has definitely moved from DFL up to number one. Jesus, Marc, that is one hell of a story. You stay close to the police HQ there, and I'll have someone from Guadalajara up there within a couple of hours to pick you up and drive you to Guadalajara airport for a flight home. Don't worry about papers or ticket, you have made some powerful friends in the state of Jalisco. Give me your clothing sizes and shoe size and they'll bring them to you in Tequila. Have a good trip, my friend."

Biff called me, "my friend." I have definitely moved up.

Down the road near Guadalajara, the Bolivian pulls off the road and parks in a large lot. She finds a parking space in the far corner. This is the lot servicing the train station. The train runs frequently between Tequila and Guadalajara. She hurries into the station and into a restroom, takes off her jacket, and reverses it from black to plaid. She reaches into her bag, finds a strawberry-blond, shoulder-length wig, and puts it on along with a pair of white-rimmed glasses. She changes her lipstick to a light pink, calmly walks out over to the ticket counter, and buys a coach ticket to Guadalajara. The train arrives in 15 minutes, and according to the schedule, she'll arrive at the Guadalajara airport station in 25 minutes.

She arrives at the airport, and although there seems to be more police than normal, no one pays any attention to her. She goes to the AeroMexico counter and purchases a one-way ticket to San Jose, Costa Rica using a credit card and passport in the name of Dorthea Mann. Her luck is holding since the flight leaves in forty minutes. Boarding goes without a hitch, and in forty minutes, she is gone. The police arrive twenty minutes after her flight is gone and go from counter to counter telling them to be on the lookout for a woman, age 35, coal black hair, 5'5", slender, and no glasses. No one had any customers fitting that description.

Aero Mexico flight 2784 arrives at San Jose International Airport in Costa Rica. A beautiful woman with strawberry blond hair exits the plane and heads for the nearest ladies room. She finds a vacant stall and quickly removes her wig, replacing it with an auburn one, cut very short. She takes off her glasses and replaces them with green contact lenses. She again reverses her jacket, now black. She exits the restroom and goes to the American Airlines counter and requests a business class ticket to Oranjestad, Aruba. The male ticket agent smiles while looking at her credit card and Passport. "Nice passport photo and thank you for your business Ms. Jackson. Enjoy your flight."

32

HOME

May 31, 1982

My flight from Guadalajara back to California is a blur. I'm so tired, I fall asleep the minute I sit down in my seat which, by the way, is in first class. I don't even hear the flight attendant offer me a drink. I don't wake up until the flight attendant, Patrice, wakes me to tell me we are preparing to land at John Wayne International.

As I leave the plane Patrice is at the door and says, "Thank you for flying Delta." She reaches for my hand and slips a business card onto my palm. Smoothie that I am, I can only stutter, "Oh, uh, thank you. It was my pleasure. Uh, goodbye. Thank you." I'm sure she's standing by her phone waiting with bated breath for my call.

As I reach the gate and look for the exit, I hear some yell, "Hey, DFL, welcome home. You know you're a regular James Bond."

"Thanks Biff. It's good to see you too."

"Come with me, my friend, we're going to meet the rest of the gang over at the Crazy Horse Saloon and partake in a proper celebration for the return of the dead. Not dead fucking last anymore."

All those arrested that Saturday in Orange County would be making their initial court appearances, including my wife on the day after I got back. I spoke to her attorney, Al Storkey by phone and he said she would likely plead guilty to possession. She would probably receive one year of probation. Her lawyer also advised me the she was filing for divorce from me. I knew this story would have a happy ending.

The celebration at the Crazy Horse didn't last long for me. I could hardly keep my eyes open, so I called a cab to take me home to Huntington Harbor. It seemed like a year since I'd been home. I found the spare key and walked in to an almost bare house. There was one bed in one room, a couch in the living room, and a table and four chairs in the dining room. The walls were bare. The patio was bare.

Damn, my boat was still there, I didn't dare look in the garage to see if my Porsche was there, but it was. Thank God she couldn't drive a stick shift. As far as the rest of the house, it was "a pitiful pile of possessions," to quote a friend of mine.

I spent the next few days filling out reports and being interviewed by one FBI agent after another. DEA also had questions, as did the ATF, the IRS, and last but not least the CIA. Everyone wanted to know about the mysterious woman. Finally after what seemed like a weeks of paperwork and interviews, I had a free weekend to catch up on my own life.

I stumbled across the card that Patrice, the Delta beauty had given me and was looking at it when the phone rang. "Hello, this is Marc."

"Hi, Marc, it's Marina."

This may not be the end.

Part Two

33

FRANKFURT

JANUARY 10, 1983

Boris Bergraf was becoming a very wealthy man as the re-building of Germany gathered speed. From the end of World War II his family had held onto many pieces of property in East Berlin, all the while getting even more wealthy on their holdings in West Berlin. His family was gambling on the wall coming down and the re-unification of West and East Germany. Should the wall come down the family would become millionaires many times over. Boris who seemed to have the most business savvy was a relentless, cruel, and merciless man who would cut your throat on a spread sheet for a single Deutsche mark.

The massive accumulation of wealth caused more than a little mistrust and suspicion within the family. The Bergraf family consists of Boris, Franco, and Joanna. Boris, the eldest, was the most suited to take over the business from his father which he did. Franco was best suited to be a playboy, which he is. Generally, he can be found in Monte Carlo where he keeps his yacht. It is on this eighty-foot floating playground that he entertains the rich and famous of the world.

Joanna married a banker—Josef Feldman, a Jewish banker. Feldman became the Chief Financial Officer of the Bergraf family corporation. Boris does not like him, but he is Joanna's husband. Josef Feldman does not like Boris, but he is Joanna's brother. Neither of them likes Franco, who only sucks money from the corporation like a Kansas tornado. Nevertheless, Boris and Josef respect each other and their business skills. Rather than get Franco involved in the corporation, of which he had no interest except for his monthly check, they began to find ways to cut him back and reduce his draw on the company.

As things begin to get a little tight for Franco, the introduction to a businessman from Odessa opens a door to more money than he had imagined. Money that he does not have to share with his stingy brother and his Jewish CFO.

Franco's yacht parties are legendary in Monte Carlo's harbor. Invitations are coveted and flaunted. Sergey Shepelova had snagged an invitation through another yacht-party wannabe, Antonio Rotante. Rotante owed him a favor, that favor being a few thousand dollars or in this case rubles. Sergey's brother Dmitri had brought Sergey into his business, that being the import and distribution of heroin and marijuana. Rotante, a distributor in the south of France had been holding back payments, and Sergey was there to deal with him—but that would wait until after the yacht party.

I had been hanging around Monte Carlo for a few days waiting to make contact with a source. Source, a nice word for informant. The source was coming out of the Ukraine and supposedly had information about a pilfered nuclear warhead. This was a serious problem in the Soviet Union! Who's in charge of the nukes? DFL was involved because of the upcoming Intermediate Nuclear Forces Treaty. Actually, everybody working for a three-letter agency was involved because this was serious stuff.

I met my source, Sasha Paseeka, at the Casino of Monte Carlo, and she told me she had struck out on coming up on any information even remotely connected with a missing warhead. She had been traveling as part of her job with the Bergraf Corporation's joint venture with a Ukrainian company.

I was hanging around the craps table wondering if I even had enough money for one minimum bet when I feel someone slip in close and put their arm around me. We greet each other like old friends, of which we are and after catching up on our personal lives, neither one of us have one, we get down to business.

"I am so sorry, Marc. I was sure I was on the right track, and all the information I had checked out, but there was no warhead."

"Any problems with your cover being blown, Sasha?"

"No, the ID and papers you provided didn't cause anyone to look twice."

"If we come up with some new info, can you go back?"

"It should not be a problem."

"Well, if nothing else, Frankfurt is a pleasant city to spend time."

"Indeed. You should come to Frankfurt. I may even get you a tour of the Bergraf HQ."

"Bergraf might be a stretch, but I would have no problem spending time there drinking some Romer Pils."

"Speaking of Bergraf, I scored two invites to Franco's yacht party tonight."

"Get out of here!"

"Does that mean you'll go?"

"Let me think about it for a second. Yes."

Did I mention that my source is a gorgeous Ukrainian brunette who could double for Kate Jackson? And no, we were not lovers. Come on, really, I've put that philandering womanizer to rest. Being buried alive changed my whole outlook on life, and of course having a beautiful fiancé at home who dotingly spoils me rotten helps.

So, anyway, off to the party we go. Marina catches wind of this, I'm toast. I make a vow to myself to behave.

I know there is a word more appropriate than lavish, but that'll have to do. I have never seen anything in my life more extravagant and luxurious than Bergraf's yacht. The other guests are a people-watcher's delight. I would guess there are maybe eighty guests, evenly divided, men and women. There could not be forty more gorgeous women gathered in one place anywhere on earth.

Diamonds are a girl's best friend? What a gathering of friends was on display tonight! The dresses that these forty gals wore could *fully* clothe at least twenty women! Did I say skimpy?

Sergey Shepelova meets Josefina Archetta, aka, The Bolivian, at the Casino of Monte Carlo only hours before the party on Franco's yacht. Josefina had just sat down at the bar when Shepelova asks if he can buy her a drink. She accepts his offer to buy her a drink, and she orders a vodka martini, straight up, adding, "and make it dirty."

Sergey immediately inquires, "What's a dirty martini?"

"The bartender adds a little olive juice. Gives it a little bite."

"That sounds like an American drink."

"As a matter of fact an American turned me on to it."

"Here's to America. What are you doing here in Monte Carlo?"

"I am an accountant, and I do accounts receivable auditing. I have a contract with a company on the Greek Isle of Mykonos."

"You do not look like an accountant although I must admit, I don't know what an accountant is supposed to look like. My name is Sergey, and you are?"

Dressed in a stunning black cocktail dress she replies "thank you and I am Josefina."

"Josefina. I like it. How do you like your dirty martini Josefina?"

"Excellent. Thank you."

Small talk leads to another martini which leads Sergey to ask, "Josefina, I have an invitation to a party aboard the yacht of Franco Bergraf this evening. His parties are legendary in Monte Carlo. Would you like to accompany me?"

"I have heard of his parties. Will this attire do, or do I need to dress more formal?"

"Excuse me, but as they say in America, you look hot. So, that was a yes?"

"Yes."

"Splendid. Let's have another martini and catch the launch for the Berlin two."

"Berlin two?"

"Yes, that's the name of Franco's yacht. That's Berlin two, as in roman numeral two."

"Ahhhh, so what happened to Berlin one?"

"I heard it sank while at anchor off the coast of Portugal. It was only a fifty footer. Not big enough for Franco's ego."

When Sasha and I arrive at the yacht we are immediately greeted by none other than Franco himself. It was like we were long lost friends.

"Sasha, I am so glad you could come. And who is your friend?"

"This is my friend, Marc Bauer. He is with Bergen Shipping Agency."

I say, "Nice to meet you Mr. Bergraf."

"Please, call me Franco. Feel free to tour the boat and enjoy."

"Thank you, I'm sure we will."

The evening is beautiful. Everything is first class—music, food, and drinks.

Sasha and I spend most of the evening out on the open deck taking in the lights of Monte Carlo and just watching the rest of the people. We spend a lot of that time talking about her next trip though we couldn't plan much until the analysts back home went through all the information she had gathered and gave us some new leads to follow up on.

The evening goes by quickly. We see that a launch is just leaving, so we decide to catch the next one. As I watch the launch pull away, I can't believe my eyes. It's her. The mysterious woman from Puerto Vallarta. She's not blond anymore, but it is her. Even from a distance I could not mistake those eyes—platinum, almost glowing in the dark. She will be impossible to find in Monte Carlo, unless, unless she leaves another dead body behind.

I probably won't have long to wait.

As the launch pulls away, the Bolivian turns and looks back at the yacht and she notices a couple standing on the rail on the upper deck. The man turns and looks directly at her. It is him. It is the American. She sees that he recognizes her. How did this happen, she thinks... this cannot be. It must be just a coincidence. He could not have possibly tracked me here. I need to find out what he is doing here. It is not possible he knows about my contract, it's just not possible, unless, no, not possible....

34

ROMER PILS

JANUARY 13, 1983

I had finished with my business in Monte Carlo and I was still getting over the shock of seeing that mysterious woman from Puerto Vallarta. Her scary looking eyes gave me the creeps. Her look made me want to get drunk just to forget I saw her.

There's something about getting drunk that, uh, I can't remember what it was I was going to say. Oh yeah, it feels so good going down and we're not even going to talk about it coming up. I'd never been to Germany before 1980, and after now having been there a number of times, I must say I still get excited about going there. What the hell does this have to do with getting drunk, you're asking? Well it seems every time I went to Germany, particularly Frankfurt, I'd always get drunk.

The first few times I traveled there were job related and courtesy of the US Department of Defense. I would fly into Frankfurt for briefings before traveling on into the Soviet Union. I liked to get there a few days early so I could have time to explore. My first time there, I found Frankfurt a place of my liking. Not far off the Zeil on Romerberg, I found a little, locals type bar, simply called Romer Pils. The bartender was named Joe and he spoke pretty good English. I also found a nice little bed and breakfast next door, called what else, The Frankfurt.

As I walk in I hear "Inga, look who's here. It's your long lost son from America," hollers Joe.

"*God aften*, Joe," I say.

"Vee don't snucka norske! You're in Germany now. Hallo to you, you Norwegian vagabond."

"Ok, *hallo* to you, Joe. Where's Inga? She speaks my language."

"Inga!" He shouts, "your son wants wiener schnitzel and his Romer Pils."

"Hey, I haven't been in here for a while, maybe I'd like something else."

"Then I'll have to ask you to leave."

"Why would you do that?"

"Because you are pretending to be someone you are not."

"What? Just because I didn't order schnitzel and a Romer Pils?"

"You've never ordered anything else."

Inga comes over and gives me a hug, "Your schnitzel will be right out."

I would always get there, after a day of exploring nearby towns, around happy hour. Of course they didn't have a happy hour, but after my first evening there of drinking and eating, I always felt happy to be back there. Joe would dispense the Romer Pils, and Inga would cut me off after she decided I'd had enough and send me to the Frankfurt. I never seem to remember that part of the evening.

Over at the Bergraf Corporation, the executive committee and board members are discussing their attempted financial takeover of their largest competitor, Karllson-Brandt Incorporated. Lots of people are unhappy about this hostile takeover, and of course the most unhappy person is Werner Brandt, CEO, Chairman of the Board, and major stockholder.

About the same time at a meeting of the senior executives of Karllson-Brandt Inc., things are getting hot. In addition to the senior executives, the Chief legal advisor, and the CFO of the finance department are also present. Brandt is not happy.

"Damn it, what the hell do I pay all you over-paid lawyers for? If this deal goes through, the whole lot of you are fired. You financial twits will be selling pencils on the street." With that, Brandt slams his leather bound note book on the table and fires his cocktail glass at the fireplace. "Now get the hell out of my sight and start earning your money." He yells out to his secretary, "Get Schultz up here, now!"

Tomas Schultz, head of security, is a bull of a man. He is former military, German Special Operations and had trained with Russian Special Forces. He stands six-feet-two and is a trim 195 pounds. He wears his blond hair in a severe crew cut and sports a matching blond handlebar mustache. If this isn't enough to intimidate you, he wears a patch over his left eye and always seems to have a perpetual sneer on his face.

Tomas had worked for Brandt since he left the military. When Brandt wanted something handled, or to go away, Tomas was there.

A knock at Brandt's door, "Come on in, Tomas. Have a seat. I have a problem, and I need it to go away."

"At your service, Mr. Brandt."

"I have prepared a packet of information that only you and I have seen. As you will see the target is very high profile, and there will be a lot of interest. Take a look at it, and tell me if you have someone in mind to handle this."

Schultz scans through the two pages inside the folder and says, "I have someone who can handle this and disappear. It will be done discreetly."

"Good, time is of essence."

I get up the next morning and head off to my briefings at Rhein Main, and then I'll be off to the Soviet Union. I can't believe how much I looked forward to my first trip into the USSR, and now I can't wait to get in and get out! Little did I know what mayhem was going on until I arrived at Rhein Main and was told to call my office in Washington DC.

My orders had been changed, and I was to return to Los Angeles ASAP and call in on a secure line as soon as I got there. Man, I love all this secret stuff. I got the next available flight on Delta, and I would be chasing the sun for the next 12 hours. I almost hate to leave Frankfurt Airport. It's like a giant bratwurst and beer garden. I don't understand why all Germans don't weigh 250 pounds. I check in at the Delta gate and get my boarding pass for seat number 48F, groan, back of the bus. This is really gonna be a long flight. F is like friggin' middle.

I grab a seat in the waiting area and open my book—a novel, *Sunrise in Cozumel* by some guy I never heard of, supposedly an action/thriller author. I hear someone say, "Marc, is that you?" I look up and see the smiling face of Patrice, the Delta Doll.

"Patrice! What a surprise."

"Where are you going?"

"I'm headed back to Los Angeles, and you?"

"The same. What flight are you on, and where are you sitting?"

"Delta 78 and seat 48F. Are you working that flight?"

"All the way to Atlanta. Overnight there and then to Minneapolis and Los Angeles."

"Hey, great to see you, and I'll see you on board."

"Nice to see you, Marc."

She walks away, and I'm thinking really bad thoughts about what might have been. Oh well, back to my book. This guy ain't bad. I'm just getting into it when I hear my name being called, "Mister Marc Ryder, come to the Delta desk, please."

Oh crap, don't tell me my orders have been changed again. I present myself at the desk, and the Delta check-in person asks me for my ID and boarding pass. Before I can ask why she says, "Mister Ryder, we have changed your seat assignment to four A for the entire duration of the flight. Enjoy your flight and thank you for flying Delta."

Four A, first class! All the way home! Guess who my flight attendant is in first class?

35

DMITRI'S FIND

FEBRUARY 11, 1983

Dmitri Shepelova is angry. He is angry because his very lucrative smuggling business has gone away and Marina with it. He made out that he could care less about her but now that she was gone it made him angry. He decides that he is angry at Marc Ryder too. His cab business in Moscow is still doing well, but he feels as if he is constantly looking over his shoulder because of what he did in Odessa. The word in Odessa is that the Ukrainians have put out a hit on him, and he has no reason not to believe it. His business is licensed in a different name in Moscow, so he hopes they will not find him, and it appears they are concentrating their efforts to find him in Odessa and the Black Sea area.

Dmitri enjoyed considerable success in the smuggling business and was able to keep himself once or twice removed from the actual operations. A couple of weeks before Marc Ryder's scheduled arrival in Moscow, Dmitri recieves an anonymous call offering a very large sum of money to deliver a package to Los Angeles, California. The contents of the package, the size of the package, and any other details will be disclosed if, and when, an agreement is reached on the shipment. A call-back number is given, and an exact time is given to make the call.

Dmitri waits for the exact time and calls the number. A garbled voice answers and instructs him to go to a rundown bar near the main subway station just off Kutusovskiy Prospekt. "Take a seat at the bar and order a drink," the voice tells him.

Dmitri arrives at the bar and does as he is told. Shortly, two men sit down next to him, one on each side. Both bearded with the caps pulled down low. A voice from behind him says, "Don't look at them and do not turn around. I have an extremely valuable and sensitive package I would like delivered. I am willing to pay a large sum of money to have this package delivered."

"What's in the package? That will determine how much it will cost."

"You do not need to know. I have given you all the information you need until we have an agreement."

"I would be crazy to accept such a deal. You provide me with what I am shipping for you and I will provide how much it will cost you. It's very simple."

"Yes Dmitri, it is very simple. Either you agree to our terms or we will provide a certain Odessa businessman with everything he needs to know to find you and extract his vengeance for that nasty little bomb you sent him."

This sends a shiver down Dmitri's spine.

"OK" responds Dmitri "I have a source who can handle almost anything, but she will probably also have questions."

"She? Your source is a she?"

"What, you have a problem with skirts?"

"Set up a meeting with your source."

"She's going to be in Odessa shortly, we can make the meet there. Give me a number to call you, and I'll set it up."

"Sure, you would like my number, Dmitri. I will call you in 24 hours, and you will have made contact. We will then discuss when and where we will meet. You stay here at the bar for a few minutes after we leave, and we'll be in touch, Dmitri."

After his new friends leave, Dmitri calls the bartender over and orders another vodka and mineral water and asks the bartender if he knows the three guys he had been talking to.

"I have never seen them before, just like you."

"What do you mean, just like me?"

"Never seen you before either. At least you aren't wearing a fake beard like those clowns."

"They had fake beards? You could tell they were fake?"

"Oh yeah, along with that lousy accent."

"Accent, what accent?"

"Just like yours."

"Accent? I got an accent?"

"All you Ukrainians have an accent."

"I'm not Ukrainian, I'm Chechen."

"Even worse, and I wouldn't advertise that in this bar."

Dmitri downs his vodka, throws some rubles on the bar and leaves thinking, this is a bad deal and nothing good can come of it. I have got to call Olivia and set up the meeting. Do I really want to do this? I've probably already gone a step too far. Damn!

He doesn't notice the grey van across the street with the dark windows and, of course, can't see the man snapping pictures with a 300mm lens. Dmitri stops at a pay phone on the wall of the pharmacy next to the bar as the camera continues to take pictures. The cameraman has a clear view of the telephone keypad and sets the camera to automatic, and it takes ninety pictures per minute.

The van and its two occupants watch Dmitri disappear from view, and they drive back to their garage which is equipped with a dark room. Within an hour they have the pictures developed. After studying all the pictures in sequence, they come up with six different telephone numbers.

The first four are not operational numbers, the fifth is a laundromat, and the sixth is most interesting. A woman answers, "Senorita Duarte's Office, Export Division."

One of the men picks up another phone and dials an international number and waits for it to be answered, which it is. "General Vlasenko's Office. Major Yakov speaking."

36

A NEW PLAYER

February 15, 1983

Monte Carlo is an expensive playground, and one must have substantial means to spend time there, and if you are a player, you must have unlimited disposable means, or you eat in the buffet. Unlimited disposable means describes those who play in the casinos of Monte Carlo. And, there is no buffet.

Konrad Ilyavich Levorenchenko is not of either of the aforementioned financial categories. Konrad is a cold-blooded killer who goes by the name of KIL. He uses his skills as a former Soviet Special Forces operative to continue in his favorite pastime, killing people, and just happens to get paid for it.

He receives a call from a German Corporate Security Chief. He has a target but he has inadequate description or, for that matter, hardly any information other than the target called herself *The Bolivian.* Herself? A female killer for hire?

KIL knew of no female assassins in continental Europe or the Soviet Union. It didn't take long to get an answer from his contacts in the Americas. He had done business with the Mendez Cartel in Panama before, and so Alfonzo Benitez is the second person he calls.

"Alfonzo speaking."

"Alfonzo, this is KIL, we have done business before. Do you remember?"

"Yes, of course. How can I help you?"

"I am looking for a woman, she may go by the name of the Bolivian, and she is for hire."

"You and I are looking for the same person. She is probably responsible for murder and mayhem in Puerto Vallarta, Mexico. I employed her to terminate three problems, and it would seem she killed everyone who came in contact with her, and then she disappeared."

"How did you contact her to arrange the terminations?"

"I can give you a telephone number, a fax number, and two post office boxes here in Mexico."

"I'm sure the post office boxes have forwarding agents, but hopefully the telephone number is still good. Thank you, Alfonzo."

KIL calls the number and unbelievably a female answers.

"Buenos dias."

"Buenos dias, Senorita. I have a request."

"Were you referred by someone?"

"Yes, I was referred to your service, but of course I cannot reveal this person."

"Do you have a certain time or place for this job?"

"No, just want it done as soon as you can."

"Do you know where to send everything?"

"Yes, I have a fax number and a mailing address, Calle del Oro, numero cinco, Cuernavaca."

"Yes, that is correct. And do you know what information is to be included in the fax?"

"Yes, of course, it will not contain anything incriminating."

The entire conversation was recorded by the Bolivian.

The fax communications received in Cuernavaca are serviced by a private individual who forwards the faxes to a number in Orangjestad, Aruba. Another individual receives the material and faxes it on to an answering service on the island of light, Paros. Parikia, on the island of Paros is the ultimate destination of the information packet. The Bolivian who holds the password, calls on a dedicated line and requests the information packet to be sent by fax to a new number.

A day after the phone call from KIL, The Bolivian is looking at the fax from him and does not recognize the name of the target, but because of the Cuernavaca fax number she knows that snake Benitez is the one who furnished the address. Someone is trying to set me up she thinks. She first needs to find out who is this person who is trying to set her up. She replays the recording several times and decides the caller, who spoke to her in Spanish, spoke with an eastern European accent. Russian she thinks.

She makes three calls and the person she speaks to on the third call gives her a name and number. She calls the number and a male answers hello in what she decides is Russian. She says nothing and the person at the other end of the line says something else in the same language and hangs up. She is positive it is the same voice as the one on her recording. Konrad Ilyavich Lavorenchenko, also known as KIL.

Pondering a course of action, she decides she needs to go to Panama and close out this Panamanian drug puke. She decides to confront him face to face to tell him she knows who he gave her contact information to and then kill him and then send word to her associates in Panama that the Mendez Cartel can no longer be trusted.

This new person is someone she thinks is a loser, but she needs to find out more about him. Then he will soon to be a dead loser.

After receiving the packet from KIL in Parikia, she returns to Marmara and checks into the Hotel Marmara. She remembers that she hasn't checked her answering machine at her residence in Parikia. After remotely checking her answering machine in Parikia and hearing the recorded message from Gregory, she thinks, so I was right. The Chechen has possibly traced me here to Paros. She says to herself "I'll just play tourist here in Marmara for a week or so. But I think I will ride daily over to Parikia and observe. KIL may serve some useful purpose, but it will be bye-bye, Alfonzo."

37

HERCEG-NOVI

FEBRUARY 17, 1983

Mohammed Noor is livid. In the last eight months his whole world has turned upside down. First, his brother Atta is murdered in Odessa. Then he finds his sister Marina has disappeared and all the while his drug smuggling operation is unraveling. The Chechen in Odessa has also stopped communicating with him so he calls a cousin in Odessa and asks him to make some discreet inquiries about his brother and sister. He decides it is best not concern himself with the Chechen or the Ukrainian thugs he dealt with.

He calls Ustad and tells him to come to the Café and that he has a job for him. They do not exchange pleasantries when Ustad arrives.

"Sit down Ustad and listen, I have a job for you."

"I am more than happy to help you my brother."

"Good then, just listen. I want you to go to Odessa and meet up with our cousin Jerriz al Moudin. He is going to do some checking for me about the alleged murder of our brother Atta and the disappearance of Marina. Do not get involved with the search for information. Let Jerriz al Moudin do it all. When he has finished, do nothing without checking with me first. I want you to leave as soon as you can."

"I will leave tonight and I will call you as soon I have talked to al Moudin."

Ustad, thinking Mohammed had called him in to chew him out about something, makes a hasty retreat from his meeting with Mohammed. He quickly makes some calls and arrangements for travel to Odessa.

He catches the first available flight and arrives in Odessa late the next day and immediately calls Jerriz al Moudin.

"Jerriz, it is Ustad, what do you have for me?"

"Ustad, you are not going to like what I have found. Atta's body was found and he had been stabbed in the neck with some type of knife. The knife hit an artery and he died almost immediately. The police have no suspects but would like to talk to your sister Marina who was the last person to see him alive. However, your sister Marina took a job with a Soviet tourist ship and it seems she jumped ship in America and requested asylum."

"What? You think the police suspect my sister of killing Atta?"

"Police say they have a witness who heard them fighting in their room. Neither one has been seen since. They left the room without checking out."

"And Marina jumped ship in America? She was working on the ship?"

"You now know everything that I know. The name of the ship is the MS Mikhail Lermontov and she was last seen in San Pedro, California. The ship is part of the Black Sea Shipping company's fleet and currently here in the port."

"How do you know all this?"

"Your cousin and mine, Ahmed sul Fazir."

"Do you think I could get a job on this ship?"

"Yes, they are always looking for janitorial and maintenance help."

"Thank you Jerriz. I must call Mohammed and tell him what you have learned."

"Tell him he now owes me a favor."

"I do not think that would be wise. Mohammed does not like to be reminded of his debts, but I will pass on your regards."

Ustad finds a phone and calls Mohammed who picks up on the first ring. He listens in silence as Ustad tells what he has learned. When he finishes, Mohammed is silent.

"Mohammed, are you still there?"

"Yes my brother. Go find a Western Union Office where I can send you money. I want you to get a job on this Soviet tourist ship and go to America. I want you to find Marina and deal with her. She killed Atta I am sure, and she probably had help. When you get to America call and let me know. Then call our cousin Ahmed and he will help you. If you fail Ustad, do not come back to Herceg-Novi, understood?"

Ustad can't believe what he just heard. Marina possibly killed Atta? Don't come back to Herceg-Novi. But Ustad respects his brother, the family leader, and after the phone call, he immediately goes about finding a Western Union office. He finds one and calls Mohammed and tells him the address.

After collecting the money from Western Union he then presents himself at the offices of the Black Sea Shipping Company and applies for a job. He is lucky, the *MS Mikhail Lermontov* is in port and will not be leaving for 3 days. They are hiring janitorial helpers and kitchen helpers. No experience needed.

38

I'LL BE DAMNED

FEBRUARY 18, 1983

Mohammed Noor, the leader of the Brothers Noor is now being very careful in Herceg-Novi, Montenegro. He and his brother Ustad are still plying their trade of drug smuggling but are painfully aware that they have been careless.

Mohammed has tried to find the Chechen, Dmitri Shepalova, but he has disappeared. He's also decided it is not wise to go to Odessa and ask too many questions. Unable to go to Odessa and find a new shipper he has found his business at a stand still. He is determined to find Marina.

The drug business of the Brothers Noor to America has dried up. This makes Mohammed more than just angry and he puts all his energies into finding Marina.

It appears as if Marina has vanished in America, but that doesn't mean Mohammed is going to give up. As far as Mohammed is concerned, it is Marina's fault that his business failed. Mohammed reaches out to his cousin, Ahmed Sul Fazir of Long Beach, California to help him find Marina.

Mohammed's main man in Odessa, the Chechen Dmitri Shepelova, has broken all ties with the Brothers Noor and is himself keeping a low profile. He and his cousins blew up a warehouse in Odessa, killing 5 members of the Ukrainian mafia. The authorities have not yet come up with any clues or suspects. Dmitri has basically shut down his smuggling adventures in Odessa until things are clear in his mind about who he can trust.

While Dmitri may have escaped the authorities, he has not been overlooked by Leonid Petroflova, the boss of the Ukrainian mob in Odessa. Petroflova has put together the pieces of the Shepalova and Noor business and is making plans to avenge his cousins who died in the warehouse explosion. He has made a call to someone who can find Shepalova and bring him back to Odessa.

Dmitri does not know who to blame for most of his problems, and loss of business. It does not matter. He has discovered that Marina is most likely in the United States where she always wanted to go. He didn't realize that he cared for her until she was gone. Dmitri's cousin Sasha Federakova, a longshoreman who worked on the docks of Long Beach and Los Angeles harbors has gone missing, so he has no one to look for Marina. That damn Ryder is to blame for this.

Meanwhile down in Puerto Vallarta, Mexico another murder has *El Jefe* angry. Estavan Rodrigues, *El Jefe de Policia Federales* in Puerto Vallarta is not happy with the mess I left him and he calls me. I answer the phone "Marc Ryder."

"Ryder this is Estavan Rodrigues."

"Hey Chief, nice to hear from you."

"Ryder, this is not a social call. I have another murder on my hands. The word on the street is that the *Amigos de Muertos* have put out a contract on you."

"Me? Why on me?"

"The leader of the Amigos, Jorge Padilla has been murdered, and a card was found pinned to his chest with a knife, "The Bolivian." They seem to think you are connected with this mysterious woman who had caused such havoc in my city. Damn you Ryder."

OK, so I've been damned by just about everyone, Dmitri, Rodrigues, and a guy in Herceg-Novi, Montenegro that I've never met. Not to mention my ex-wife and the entire Longshoreman and warehouse union of the Long Beach and Los Angeles harbors. All this damning is bound to have a negative effect on my golf game.

39

MARINA AND ME

FEBRUARY 18, 1983

My adventures in Huntington Beach, Puerto Vallarta, Tequila, and Moscow are in the past, finally. I had been thoroughly debriefed by every three-letter agency in the country, as well as half a dozen police departments, and I finally had a weekend all to myself. I was trying to figure out what to do with my empty personal life when Marina called. It's been more than six months since that call.

Marina has become the most important thing in my life. She returned to Los Angeles on the Soviet passenger vessel, *MS Mikhail Lermontov*, went ashore in San Pedro, and never got back on. Thank goodness she did not. When she called she said she wanted to stay in the United States. She was in fear of her life if she returned to Odessa. I was able to find the right people to have her apply for temporary residence.

I suppose my title of Deputy Assistant Director of DFL might mislead you to believe I am an important person. Well I'm not. I'm a case supervisor and I have other agents working with and for me. These folks generally avoid me like the plague, they were all happy when I got assigned to the FBI task force. Even happier when the task force sent me to Mexico, and they love my extended stays in the Soviet Union.

The embassy passed a message on to me that I was not welcome in Moscow. This could be a problem as I have been tasked to go back and assist on the Intermediate Missile Treaty because I'm the Deputy Assistant Director for the Defense Foreign Liaison (DFL). You want to hear the rest of this story? Don't even think about making a wise crack about DFL.

I decide the best thing to do is just pick up the phone and call Dmitri. I'm sure he'll listen to reason. I'll meet him at the Plotnikov, and after two or three Stoli's I'm sure he'll listen to reason. First, I have to reason with Marina.

I guess I failed to mention that Marina and I are now living together. Things happen, you know? I finally get up the courage to tell her about my upcoming travel to the Soviet Union.

"I'm sorry, Marina. This trip just can't be avoided or put off. I'm going to try patch things up with Dmitri on my way through Moscow."

"I don't like this trip. You be careful, Marc. You remember what happened last time you went to the Plotnikov, yes?"

"This is different. I'll be on the books with the Defense Department and carrying a Diplomatic Passport."

"You were last time. Big help. Those bruises healed up yet?"

"OK, I understand your doubts, but I have to do this."

"I'll be here all alone."

"Oh come on, don't play that card."

"What if my brothers find me, and you're not here? They will kill me, and you will not even know."

"Marina, please stop. Roy and Jeff over at Long Beach PD will be checking on you all the time. They are just a phone call away."

"Do you promise to call every night?"

"Yes, every night."

"Will you miss me?"

"Of course I will, especially at night."

"Oh so you will miss me more at night. I am your bedtime toy."

"Oh migod, oh migod! I'm not going to win this am I?"

"No, my boy toy. Now come with me to my bed."

"I didn't think you would ever ask."

40

THE PHONE CALL

FEBRUARY 22, 1983

Marina and I had just spent a leisurely three day weekend and I had received Dmitri's warning about not being welcome back in the Soviet Union last week so I decide to call Dmitri on Tuesday morning.

"Hello, this is Yuriy."

"Yuriy? This Marc Ryder, I'm a friend of Dmitri."

"You are lying son of a bitch, you are no friend of mine."

"Dmitri Ivanovich, I thought that sounded like you."

"What the hell do you want?"

"At least I didn't call you a son of a *vich*, even though you are. Dmitri, I'm trying to be nice here. I am going to be in need of transportation when I arrive in Moscow, and of course I immediately thought of you."

"I am not in the mortuary business, and you will need a hearse."

"Come on, Dmitri. Neither I nor Marina had anything to do with the business problems you have experienced. But I may have had something to do with the fact you are not in the hands of our favorite three letter agencies that hang out at Lubyanka, the home for wayward Soviet citizens, if you get my drift?"

"I'm sure you will soon tell me something of importance. Something that will make us best friends forever."

"Do you have any idea or information about what happened to me in Puerto Vallarta, Mexico? There were too many coincidences involving an unidentified woman. She has perked the interest of a lot of people. I think you will also be interested when I tell you the story."

"Yes, as a matter of fact I know everything that happened down there."

"Let me tell you the story from my point of view."

"Forget it. You got yourself in way over your head, my friend, and I know your country's FBI and DEA made many powerful friends during this arrest and raid, but you also made many more powerful enemies. But, I know nothing of this woman."

"Serge Ivanovich Shepelova I think did."

"What? What are you insinuating? Are you telling me my brother was involved in your Puerto Vallarta fiasco. I have not heard from my brother in months."

"Dmitri, I am calling to ask for your help. There was a third party, and maybe even a fourth party involved down in Puerto Vallarta and Tequila for that matter. You probably don't know the chief of police in Tequila was murdered. Nobody has yet been identified as the killer. But there was a woman possibly involved, and this woman was recently on the island of Mykonos, in the company of your brother."

"You can't be serious. You have not identified her, but you have information my brother was with her?"

"Yes. The information came to us quite accidentally because of a murder which took place while your brother was there. The murder was a classic hit, two rounds in the forehead. Interpol tracks and monitors possible assassinations."

"Interpol?"

"Yes. Look, Dmitri, I've been assigned to the American taskforce to go back to Votkinsk, in the Udmurt Province, and do another survey. I will arrange to spend time in Moscow. We need to talk, and I would like to invite you to meet me at the Plotnikov to discuss something of mutual interest."

"Are you buying?"

"Some things never change."

"Give me the first topic of discussion."

"Assassins."

"Are you in need of one, or are you running from one?"

"I need to find one."

"To find one?"

"Yes, I think she, yes, I said she, is responsible for most of the dead in Puerto Vallarta."

"So this has now turned into a murder investigation, and you think my brother was somehow involved?"

"I'm sorry to have to say this Dmitri, but I think this mystery woman and your brother were possibly lovers, and she may have killed your brother."

"Damn you Ryder, how do you always find a way to ruin my day? Are you telling me that my brother Serge is dead?"

"I'm sorry Dmitri, I am very sorry to have to be the one to tell you."

"Damn you Ryder. Call me when you get to Moscow."

Damned again.

41

SASHA

FEBRUARY 28, 1983

Sasha Paseeka returns to Frankfurt after her trip to Monte Carlo. Her boss, Boris Bergraf, left a message for her to go ahead and make the planned trip to Odessa and that he is going to Greece to meet with some corporate people of the company they are attempting to take over.

She checks in with Josef Feldman to make sure the trip is still on and that travel funds are not a problem. Feldman is not in a good mood and suggests that Sasha cancel her trip, mostly because he is upset with Bergraf going to Mykonos without him.

"Mykonos! Why is he going to Mykonos?" she asks.

"That's where they want to meet."

"Who are they?"

"Corporate people from Werner Brandt's company."

"Don't you think that it's strange to meet there, when their corporate HQ is in Vienna?"

"Exactly what I told him. He said it was neutral territory, and he wanted to mix a little pleasure in with the business."

"Sometimes I just don't know what he is thinking. OK, I'm going to put together my proposals for our joint venture, and I'll be flying out tonight. I should be back by this weekend."

"I can't talk you out of this?"

"Everything is in place. I cancel this trip, and it'll take me three months to set it back up again."

"Alright. Keep me posted on our secure phone."

"Of course."

Sasha leaves with a bad feeling about Bergraf's trip to Mykonos, but nonetheless excited about her trip to Odessa. Her previous meeting with the Chechen exporter had left her somewhat uneasy, and she wonders when she returns what will be in store for her.

She had been told by Marc Ryder that dealing with Chechens was very unpredictable and dangerous.

When Sasha and I met in Monte Carlo, she related her contact with the Chechen.

I warned her, "Sasha, you must be very careful when dealing with a Chechen. What name did he give you?"

"Ivan."

"Ivan. That's it?"

"He said that was all I needed to know."

"What does he know about you?"

"I gave him my cover name, Olivia Duarte and showed him my Spanish passport. He wanted to take a photo of my passport and me, but I refused. It did not seem to bother him, especially when I described the capacity and speed of the new computers I was going to get for him."

"How did you get to the subject of nuclear warheads?"

"We went to a restaurant near the center of Odessa, which seemed to be frequented by the more affluent. After about an hour of casual conversation we were joined at our table by two men and a woman who spoke very good English and French. The men spoke only in Russian with a peculiar accent. I think they were Chechen."

"Did you get their names?"

"First names only. Yevgeny, Vladimir, and Katrina. I got the initial feeling that Yevgeny and Vladimir were ex-military, although none of them ever indicated what they did. Katrina had a very European look about her and smoked cigarettes using a long holder, like some old-time movie star."

"Zsa Zsa Gabor?"

"Exactly. We wile away the evening and the conversation eventually gets down to what Ivan and I can really handle in the export end of our relationship. Vladimir asks through Katrina if I am able, through my official capacity to get something through the German border security? I tell him that nothing going directly from the Ukraine could get through without serious and thorough inspection. Anything from anywhere behind the Iron Curtin would be subject to thorough inspection. However, by showing the original shipper as say, Italy or Spain, and the end user being a German manufacturer, I could work some magic. This was cause for some serious and animated conversation between Ivan, Yevgeny, and Vladimir."

"Did you understand what they were saying?"

"Hello, Ryder, did you forget who you are talking to? Sasha Paseeka from Kiev. Please do not make me believe that DFL does not only stand for Defense Foreign Liaison."

"Oh, for crying out loud! That is really cruel."

"OK, yes I understood what they were saying, but I sure

as hell couldn't let on that I understood. They decided that they wanted to do some checking and set up a meeting later in the week. They also discussed how the general was going to manufacture paperwork to get the nuclear device out of the warehouse."

"The general? One of them was a general?"

"Yes, when they started talking among themselves they addressed each other more formally, and I'm pretty sure it was Vladimir. I'm guessing that Yevgeny was either a major or a major colonel."

"How were they going to check you out?"

"They asked to see my passport, and Katrina took a long look at it. I suspect she memorized everything on it."

"You can be sure of it."

Dmitri is still upset with the demise of his collapsed smuggling enterprise but is encouraged with the new prospect of making even more money with his new friends, General Vladimir Vlasenko and Major Yevgeny Yakov, both officers in the Soviet Rocket Force . The biggest stroke of luck was finding a source with connections in Western Europe, Olivia Duarte. The taxi business was just too boring.

Sasha walks in the door of her apartment and hears the phone ringing. She drops her purse and coat on the couch and picks up the phone, "Hello, this is Sasha."

"Sasha, this is Joanna Feldman. We just received a telegram from Mykonos that Boris is dead and that he was murdered along with another man in his hotel. Josef needs you to come back to the office as soon as you can."

"Oh, my God, Joanna, what awful news. I'll come right back. Who was the other man?"

"He was not identified to us, but we inquired with Werner Brandt, and he knew nothing about a meeting in Mykonos. It appears to have been a setup to kill my brother."

"Good grief! I'm on my way."

42

PAROS

MARCH 4, 1983

The Mexican debacle convinced the Bolivian it was time to move on. She had replayed the events in Mexico over and over in her mind for the last six months. It is definitely time to move on. That American will probably not let this go. The questions cycle through her head... why did I turn to look at him on the road to Guadalajara? No, a better question, why was he walking on the road? He looked like he had been buried alive. He was filthy dirty. It was probably a given that he would remember me from that bar in Puerto Vallarta, the Las Palmas. That was stupid. A blond in a bar in Mexico. Well, that wig is history. Who the hell wouldn't remember that? Am I losing my touch? How could I be losing my touch? Did I not leave Puerto Vallarta with my marks dead, well two out of three anyway?

Then there was that fleeting moment that I turned and looked back at the yacht in Monte Carlo harbor. And there he was. On the yacht and standing at the railing looking right at me. Maybe I was just seeing things. It probably wasn't him.

She thinks about the German. She left him in a hotel room on the island of Mykonos. Too bad Serge Shepelova has to spend eternity there also, she thinks. It was an unfortunate circumstance that he had to walk into the room just as she put two rounds into the forehead of the German . The German, a very wealthy business man, had crossed the wrong people in Frankfurt and had become her mark. Serge became an unfortunate casualty. Now that could be a problem, yes that would be a problem should the Chechen's brother Dmitri show up.

But now she was back home on the island of Paros. The Island of Light. The house she had purchased in Parikia, a town steeped in history, was maintained as if someone lived there all the time. She was not able to spend as much time there as she would like, but she wanted to make sure it appeared that someone was always there.

Business was good, and she loved Parikia. The walkways and cobblestone streets were lined with shops which reminded one of the past residents, such as the Byzantine artists and the Venetian traders. Parikia's harbor was lined with restaurants and night clubs along the promenade. A lively place at night where ouzo flowed generously.

I must check my bank accounts and make sure those Panamanian crooks have deposited my fees and then I'll lay low for a while in Parikia, she thinks. Maybe I should think about retiring. Maybe soon, but this business is just too much of a thrill to give up.

She thinks about going somewhere for a week and concentrate on her marksmanship. I missed that mark in Puerto Vallarta as he got on the elevator in the Fiesta Americana. That was unforgivable, but it was partly because of the Mexican thug who got in the way.

It had made her so angry that she had returned to Puerto Vallarta, found the thug, and put two rounds into his forehead before she placed her card on his chest and plunged a knife through it into his chest. That was not a smart thing to do. I must not make my work personal.

She finds herself restless for some reason and decides to take a ride on her Vespa. The seaside town of Logaras is on the other side of the island but a scenic ride. There is a quiet beach and a beachside café. A nice Greek salad and a glass of the wine of the island is just what I need, she thinks.

After the relaxing ride to Logaras she finds a table in the corner of the seaside café. The waiter, Gregori, greets her and tells her he is so happy to see her again. They exchange pleasantries, and she orders a salad with feta cheese, olives and tomato, and Paros wine. Perfect. She finishes her lunch and wanders down to the beach, finds herself a spot to lay out her beach towel, strips down to her bikini bottoms, and stretches out on her towel.

The sun feels good. She doses off for a short nap and awakes with a start. A daytime nightmare? No, she can feel someone's eyes upon her. It's not unusual, she is a very beautiful woman, but she has never gotten used to someone staring at her. She sits up and casually pulls on her blouse, puts on her floppy straw hat and her sunglasses and takes a look around the beach. Not many people out on a weekday but she suddenly feels a tingling in her spine as she sees a man about fifty meters away turn and look at her. He has a light beard, a light complexion, reddish-blond hair, and an average build.

He could be Serge's twin brother; no, he could not be, she thinks, I am becoming paranoid! She gets up and casually walks back to the café and walks through the café and out the back door where she has parked her Vespa.

Dmitri waits a few minutes and walks to the café expecting to see her sitting at a table inside. There are two other couples seated, but the woman is nowhere to be seen. The waiter asks him if he would like to sit at a table and order something.

"No thank you. I was looking for a friend of mine. I thought she would be here."

"There was a woman here earlier, but she left to go lay on the beach."

"And she didn't come back here?"

"If she did, I did not serve her."

Dmitri turns and walks out of the café, looking up and down the beach. Nothing.

The waiter goes to the back of the café and picks up the phone and dials a number. He gets an answering machine, "This is Gregori. He came in asking about you and left."

43

LONG BEACH

March 27, 1983

It has been a few months since my Mexico adventure, if you call being buried alive an adventure. Marina and I have settled into a comfortable relationship and found ourselves a very nice cottage down in the Belmont Shore area. She found a job at my favorite pub, Joe Jack's, and I continue to do mine at DFL. Damn I hate that acronym. It's not even an acronym. It's like a millstone around my neck. I know, I know, shut up and continue with the story.

Spring brings the pageantry and excitement of the Long Beach Grand Prix. What fun to see the likes of Mario Andretti race through the streets of Long Beach. My office just happens to be at Atlantic and Ocean where they make the hairpin turn to head down Shoreline Drive towards the Queen Mary, but my friend John Flake has an even better office spot across the street. So, that's where we're heading on a gorgeous March day in Southern California.

Marina has never seen such an event and is excited to see and experience this new adventure. We leave my office building, which has underground parking and head out onto the street to John's office across Ocean Boulevard. As we stop at the corner, waiting for the rent-a-cop to wave us across, Marina suddenly freezes up, grabs my hand, and turns back towards my building.

"What's the matter Marina?"

"I just saw Ustad."

"Ustad? Your brother Ustad?"

"Yes, yes. He was in the crowd of people across the street with my cousin, Ahmed Sul Fazir."

"Are you sure it was him?"

"Do you not think I would know my own brother? Yes, it was him. They have found me!"

"I'm sorry. I didn't mean to question you, but this is unbelievable. This is not good. Take the keys to the car and go wait in it. I want to go back and see if I can pick them out. I'd like to follow them to see where they go."

"Ustad had a green baseball cap on. But Marc, listen to me. They most likely know what you look like also. This is a bad idea. They will kill us both."

"OK, take the car and go home. I'm going to call in a couple of favors from Long Beach Police and see if they will check them out and see what their story is and what they are doing here. Do you think either of them saw you?"

"I don't think so. I think they would have come after us if they had. And, I'm not going home without you. I will wait in the car until you return."

"OK, but sit in the back seat and hunker down. Keep the doors locked and I'll be down in a few minutes." Besides my Porsche we have a Jeep Cherokee with tinted windows in the back. A good place to hide.

"Marc, be careful. My brother Ustad is a dangerous man and he always carries a very sharp knife."

What the hell was going to happen next? Marina's brother and cousin in Long Beach. Not good, not good at all.

I pull my cap down low and walk back towards the corner, and I immediately spot a green baseball cap on a man with dark complexion walking with another similar looking man crossing the street. As I pass them, they are looking over the crowd of people but don't pay any attention to me. So, they are looking for a couple, or Marina herself, and not a single man. I let them pass me in the crowd of people and then turn and follow them myself. After a couple of blocks, I finally find a patrolman and show him my badge and ask him if Roy Henry or Jess Shaddack of Long Beach Police Intelligence are out on the street.

He gets on his two-way radio, and, lo and behold, Roy and Jess are less than a block away. Lieutenant Roy Henry and Sergeant Jess Shaddack and I were the bomb squad of Long Beach. We had all attended the FBI's bomb school at Quantico, Virginia and during the 70s had been called on many times for either bomb threats or bomb disposal. Professionally, we were very close friends. When faced with the decision to cut the red wire, or the blue wire, or the white wire, you better have confidence in your friends. We meet up at Pine and Ocean and I give them a quick synopsis of what I'm faced with.

Roy says, "Dammit, Ryder, you paint yourself into the most unbelievable corners. Are you carrying your gun?"

"No I'm not. Roy, I can't believe they traced Marina here. But she is positive it's her brother, and I recognized Fazir. He was a person of interest to the taskforce over in Orange County in that drug bust. He's worked as a longshoreman for quite a number of years and hangs out with the shadier section over in Wilmington."

"Alright, let's catch up with them and let Jess and I

handle the shake down. Jess, get on the radio and get us a couple of guys in blue to back us up in case these guys are armed. Ryder stay back and away."

Jess gets a couple of blues, and we head west down Ocean to catch up with Ustad and Fazir. We find them less than a block away, and Roy tells me to stay where I am while they *speak* with Ustad and Fazir. The two blues approach Ustad and Fazir from the west and Roy and Jess come up behind them. I can't hear what the blues say, but both Ustad and Fazir spin about and run directly into Roy and Jess. I see the flash of a large-blade knife and then hear at least two gunshots. Jess goes down and so does Fazir. The knife flashes again and one of the blues screams. It's pandemonium. People are screaming and running. In the midst of it all Ustad disappears in the crowd. I run to the scene and find Fazir already dead. Jess has a knife wound in his abdomen, but it appears to be superficial. The blue had been cut on his shoulder. Roy tells the other blue to stay with Jess and calls for more backup and an ambulance.

"Ryder, did you see where he went?"

"He disappeared into a group of people, and I think ran across Ocean. But there were just too many people running in all directions."

"Damn! I don't think I could even come up with a reasonable description of him, could you? I don't imagine Marina has a picture of this dirtbag?"

"I've never seen one. Unless he slipped into the country illegally, INS should have a photo of him, provided he didn't use a fake ID. I have no idea how he entered the country."

"Chances of INS having a picture are pretty slim, don't ya think? Hell we don't even know what name he used."

"It would be a waste of time."

"Holy fuckin crap. I can't believe this happened. The

chief is going to go batshit livid, and the city council, the business bureau, the chamber of commerce, and the race organizers are going to be looking for heads to roll! Shit, the race hasn't even started yet, and we got ourselves an incident. I can hear the Chief now, "'Lieutenant, tell me again why you stopped these two and started a gun fight on the streets of my city.'"

"Aw hell, Roy, I'm sorry. I don't know what to say?"

"I would lay low, very low for a few days, if I were you. Dammit, Ryder!"

OK, I've been damned again.

By the time I get back to the car and Marina, and we drive home, only about 45 minutes have passed. Yet, I have 12 messages on my answering machine. None of them are very pleasant. The last one was just plain disturbing.

"I will find you Marina. You and the infidel are already dead, but you will both still feel the tip of my blade, courtesy of your brother and I you murdering whore!"

I don't need to utter the profanity that I was thinking. I'm sure you have already heard it all, but damn it, we're in Long Beach, California. This ain't supposed to happen here. What I wouldn't give for a dirty martini right now!

44

SAN PEDRO

March 27, 1983

Ustad runs for his life. His mind racing—how the hell did this happen? What an unbelievable mess. Mohammed is going to be furious. Ahmed had to have lied to him. He must have gotten himself in trouble with the local police. How else would they have Identified and stopped them? I must get aboard the *Lermontov* and get back to Odessa.

Ustad runs west on Ocean until he gets to Pine Avenue and sees a cab sitting on the curb.

"Can you take me to San Pedro? I have dollars to pay."

"Whereabouts in San Pedro do ya wanna go? And I sure as hell don't take pesos."

"I need to get back to my ship the *MS Mikhail Lermontov*. It is at the pier."

"Well there's more than one pier in San Pedro. If I have to drive around looking for this ship, it's going to cost ya more money, bud."

"It's the pier under the bridge. When we go over the bridge, we will see the ship."

"Alright, get in. Where are you from anyway? You got quite an accent, but I can't place it, and we get a lot of foreigners here in Long Beach."

"I am from Montenegro."

"Montenegro! Now there's a place that I ain't never heard of."

"It is on the Adriatic Sea."

"Can't say I know where that is either."

"OK, no more questions please. Just get me to the ship."

Ustad is near panic mode. As he gets out of the cab, he pays the cabbie but does not tip him. He runs down the pier and up the ship's ladder, shows his ID to the boarding officer, and makes his way to his cabin. He begins to settle down and think a little more clearly. He wonders if Marina may have seen him, but what would she have told the police to make them stop Fazir and himself? Things happened much too quick. It must have been Fazir. He has to have done something for the police to be on the lookout for him.

Ustad is not aware that Fazir lay dead on the sidewalk in Long Beach. Hoping that Fazir also got away, he thinks, I will go out and call him later. I must also come up with a suitable story for Mohammed. I also will call Marina tell her she and her infidel lover are dead. Which he does.

Ustad thinks for a while and says to himself, that phone call was stupid. Maybe I should just take the money he gave me and stay here, or maybe go to Hawaii—the *Lermontov's* next port of call.

No, not Hawaii. Next port of call is Puerto Vallarta, Mexico. Much better idea. I will fit in much better there and the money will go further. Definitely something to think about. But first I will call Fazir and make him tell me why we were stopped by the police.

The cabbie is fully annoyed with this Montenegro jerk. No tip. Maybe Roy Henry might be interested in him. Louis Perkins, known to his friends and to certain members of the Long Beach Police Department as "LP" was a long time confidential informant of "LT," also known as Lieutenant (LT) Roy Henry, LBPD Intelligence.

The day after the ruckus on Ocean Boulevard, I'm sitting in LT Roy Henry's office when the phone rings.

He answers, "Lieutenant Henry." Short pause. "What's up, LP?" Long pause as LT Henry listens. "Where did you pick him up?" Another long pause. "OK, LP, I'll see if anyone is interested in this guy from Montenegro, and if so, I might owe you. Yes, I said might."

"Holy crap, Roy, are you going to tell me you know someone who knows a guy from Montenegro?"

"Don't get your shorts all twisted, Marc, but maybe it was our guy. A cab picked him up at Ocean and Pine and took him to San Pedro where the *MS Mikhail Lermontov* is docked. Don't you have the passenger list and a crew list for that boat?"

"I do, but not with me. I'll have to go down to my office at Bergen Shipping to get it. I usually go over the names, and I would think Ustad Noor would have jumped out at me, so I'm thinking he has to have used another name and ID."

"OK, let's go, and I'll call Captain Jim Neilson over at Los Angeles PD, San Pedro Division and let him know what we got going."

Meanwhile, Ustad has called Fazir at least a dozen times with no answer. The ship will be leaving San Pedro the next morning. He decides he will just stay out of sight until the ship is at sea. He decides not to call Mohammed until he reaches Puerto Vallarta to tell him what has happened. And, he decides he will definitely not tell Mohammed that he is staying in Puerto Vallarta, and he will use one of his other passports to stay in Mexico.

Roy and I hustle out of LBPD, definitely avoiding any contact with the chief, and take Roy's car to my office at Bergen. We find only the admin help in the office, and they hardly look up when Roy and I enter. We go to my desk, and I pull out the passenger list from the *Lermontov*. 467 passengers, listing their names, passport number, and country of origin. Roy takes half the pages, and I, the other half. Nothing.

We then go to the crew list. Roy says, "Bingo, Al Mohammed Lazzur, passport number 3762954, of Montenegro. Got to be him."

"Yes! Let's go visit the *MS Mikhail Lermontov*. We will have no trouble getting on board being an agent for

Bergen. I am good friends with the captain and I'm sure we can count on his cooperation. He was a little pissed when Marina jumped ship and requested asylum, but he got over it. "

45

THE LERMONTOV

MARCH 27, 1983

The captain of the *MS Mikhail Lermontov*, Anatoliy Tomilov, as you'll recall, is a former Soviet naval officer and had commanded a naval cruiser. He had reached the rank of captain, the equivalent of captain in the US Navy, when he retired and took command of the *Lermontov*. He had not lost his military bearing and is an imposing figure in his captain's uniform. He is almost six-feet tall and a trim 175 pounds. He wears his wavy hair, which is pure silver, in a neat, trimmed cut. He also sports facial hair which reminds me of Captain Nemo, from *20,000 Leagues Under the Sea*. I'm dating myself here.

Roy and I talk it over on the way to the *Lermontov,* and we decide it might be best to be up front with Captain Tomilov. We figure he won't mind if we take a man wanted for attempted murder off his ship.

We called it right. When told of the situation, Tomilov immediately calls his security chief, Victor Pavlov. Pavlov is former military, most likely some type of special forces, and it is evident in the way he reacts to Captain Tomilov—strict military protocol, including saluting, standing at attention, and locking heels.

Tomilov tells us Pavlov will take us to Lazzur's cabin and assist us in the apprehension. We start to protest that we will make the arrest, but the Captain reminds us we are basically on Soviet soil, and he is the one who makes decisions here.

We sheepishly back down and follow Pavlov to Lazzur's cabin, which we find empty. In fact, so empty, it appears this Lazzur has not used it. Pavlov immediately calls the housekeeping supervisor who reveals that someone had been using the cabin, but not last night.

Pavlov next calls his officer of the deck who records all activity at the boarding ramp. Pavlov declares that Lazzur left the ship early this morning and he returned less than an hour ago. So, allegedly, he is currently on board, but where? Pavlov shouts at his deck officer, "You are absolutely sure, Valeriy? Absolutely?"

"Yes sir, absolutely."

He said absolutely and that made me think of Vodka, Stolichnaya in particular. I could use one right now. This whole thing with Marina's brother is a nightmare. These cabins are much too small and remind me of that snow bank in Minnesota where I first got buried alive. I know that's a stretch but I think my claustrophobia would prevent me from being a sailor.

Five decks below, Ustad is putting on a janitorial uniform to make it look like he is getting ready to start cleaning. He stores his clothes in a suitcase and then stuffs the suitcase in a hidden crawl space next to the ship's kitchen. Several thousand miles away, it's late at night, and Mohammed Noor has no idea that his brother is now a fugitive.

It's also about the same time in Odessa, but Dmitri Shepelova is not sleeping. His mind is spinning thoughts of what he should do next... The American, I'd just as soon kill him as deal any further with him, but he may be my only lead to finding the killer of my brother. And then there's the Noor family, it was a mistake to become involved with them.

As Dmitri and his two cousins sit in a small, smoky bar in Odessa, they try to come up with a plan to deal with all of them.

Our search for Ustad comes up empty. It's like he has disappeared into thin air. The passport picture is poor quality, but we get it copied, and Pavlov and his assistants show it to every crew member. Again, they come up empty. Pavlov then plans a complete search of the ship, including passenger cabins.

Word has spread among the crew that there is going to be complete search of the ship. A crewmember, who works in the galley, slips out and goes to the crew's quarters. In the back of the crew's quarters is a small storeroom where crew members can put their suitcases and personal belongings.

"Ustad, it's me, Kahlil."

Ustad peeks out from the corner where he is hiding and says, "What do you want, Kahlil? You might have led them directly to me."

"You may have to abandon ship and make your own way back to Montenegro."

"What are you saying?"

"It is on the news. Fazir was killed in a shootout with police in Long Beach. Two cops were stabbed. They are looking for his accomplice and think there may be more involved. This search of the ship is definitely tied to that. I cannot do anything to protect you, and if they find that I was helping you, I'll go to jail. That is not going to happen. As of right now, you are on your own."

"Kahlil, I am in your debt. Could you please call Mohammed and tell him of my plight and of Fazir's death. I will stay hidden until I can escape the ship."

"I will make a call and see if someone can pass the news on to Mohammed. God be with you, Ustad."

Ustad hears the storeroom door slam as he is cast into darkness.

46

PUERTO VALLARTA

MARCH 31, 1983

The *MS Mikhail Lermontov* sails out of the port of Los Angeles with its first port of call to be Mazatlan and then Puerto Vallarta. By the time the ship passes Cabo San Lucas, Ustad is so hungry and thirsty he can hardly contain himself, and so at about three in the morning he sneaks out and goes to the crew's cafeteria. He finds a crewmember. He tells him that he has lost his ID and asks could he please just get him a bottle of water and a sandwich. He continues that he will go back and search for his ID as he is on duty in two hours.

The crewmember agrees but asks Ustad where he works because he doesn't recall seeing him in the cafeteria before even though he looks familiar for some reason.

"I was flown over to replace a sick custodian and just came on board in San Pedro," replies Ustad.

"Aah, that's why. Did you hear about all the ruckus and security searching the ship and questioning all of us?"

"Yes, I was questioned right after I came on board."

"OK, I'll get you your sandwich and water. Good luck in finding your ID."

Ustad hurries out the door and gobbles down his sandwich. I'm good to go, he thinks and makes a plan to get lost in Puerto Vallarta when the ship docks there.

The *Lermontov* arrives in Puerto Vallarta at six a.m. in the morning after leaving the Port of San Pedro three days prior and will actually spend the rest of the day there and not sail until six p.m. the following day.

Ustad decides to get off the ship as soon as possible. He realizes that he will need a boarding pass when leaving the ship. He has no trouble finding a careless passenger and takes his boarding pass. He goes back to the crew quarters and changes clothes. All of his belongings fit in a small gym bag he had brought with him. He checks to make sure he has all his belongings and heads for the exit on the wharf level. He mixes in with a large group and disembarks at eight a.m. and is holding his breath when showing his pass to the officer at the exit. The officer is only checking to make sure everyone has a pass to get back on board the ship. So, no problem, and he is amongst the throng heading for the taxi station and the tour busses.

He passes them all and heads down Avenida Mexico and, after walking what he considered to be a safe distance, hails a cab to Puerto Vallarta Centro. As they arrive at the north end of the malecon, he sees a McDonald's and suddenly realizes how hungry he is. He tells the cabbie to stop, gives him two American dollars, and heads out in seek of a double cheeseburger. As he is walking into the restaurant he suddenly feels exposed, as he knows no one and knows nothing about Puerto Vallarta. Fortunately, he had been forced to learn Spanish by his father who spent time in Spain. "A romantic language," his father had told him. Well, he certainly hoped so. As it turns out the McDonald's clerk speaks English.

"Welcome to McDonald's, sir. What would you like?"

"Cheeseburger."

"I'm sorry, cheeseburgers are not available until ten-thirty, only our breakfast menu now."

"Yes, uh, of course, then a sausage muffin, uh, *dos, por favor.*"

"Oh, *senor*, you speak Spanish. *Bienvenidos a McDonalds. Como esta?"*

"Bueno, I am *bueno*. And, yes, I mean *si*, I speak Spanish *poco a poco*. I mean I prefer *Ingles por favor*, uh *gracias*." Ustad is thoroughly flustered.

Florentina Alvarez-Rodrigues is equally amused and thinks, I must remember to tell papa that the cruise ship must be in.

"Did you arrive on the cruise ship?" she asks.

"The cruise ship? Uh, no, I am a dock worker. I did not come in on a cruise ship."

"So, you are not a tourist?"

"Tourist?"

"Yes. You are not on a holiday?"

"Holiday? No I am a dock worker. I work here."

"I see, but I have never seen you in here before, so I figured you were a tourist."

"No, I am not a tourist."

"Where do you usually eat?"

"Uh, I, uh, why are you asking me all these questions?"

"I'm sorry. Just making conversation while your order is getting ready."

After finally getting his order placed and received, Ustad with his fill of McDonald's heads down the malecon among all the other tourists. He has been told that across the Rio

Cual, in the older part of the city, there are inexpensive hotels. He has the money Mohammed sent him as well as what he was supposed give to Fazir, almost $5000. Having no idea what a room is going to cost, he stops at a kiosk advertising tourist information. He tells the woman behind the counter that he is employed by a shipping company and must find a place to stay for at least a month.

"Could you recommend a reasonable hotel?"

"Yes, of course, *senor.* I'm sorry I didn't catch your name, *senor.*"

"Estrella, Carlos Estrella."

"Where are you from, Carlos Estrella?"

"Baja del Norte, near Rosarita Beach."

"I would recommend Hotel Vallarta. It is just over the bridge that crosses the Rio Cual. If you are to be working at the harbor, it is a quick and cheap taxi ride and of course the buses run regularly. The hotel was owned by my cousin, Jorge Padilla, who was recently murdered right here in Puerto Vallarta."

"I am sorry for your loss, *senora*."

"You seem like a nice man, Carlos Estrella. Take my card and give it to the desk clerk, and she will give you a discount price. You tell her that Yvette Padilla-Gallegos sent you."

After profusely thanking Yvette he walks to the Hotel Vallarta and checks in without a hitch. After checking in he leaves the hotel and goes wandering down towards the beach and finds himself standing in front of a restaurant called the Blue Shrimp. It doesn't appear to be open yet, so he finds a table and chair on the deck and sits down to watch the ocean and suddenly becomes very mellow. He thinks to himself, I have escaped. I no longer need to worry about Mohammed or that whore sister of mine. I will do well here in Mexico. I will find someone to further help me learn the language tomorrow.

Later, Estavan Rodrigues walks in the door of his home in central Puerto Vallarta to find his daughter watching TV, "*Hola, papa*!"

"*Hola, Florentina*."

"The cruise ship must have come in today papa. The tourists were coming in."

"Yes, the Russian cruise ship came in today. Something happen?"

"Oh, I had this one guy who spoke lousy Spanish and lousy English. He said he was a dock worker and must have said ten times that he was not a tourist, that he was a dock worker. I just thought it was rather strange that he insisted upon repeating that he was not a tourist."

"And he said he was a dock worker? What time was that, do you remember?"

"Yes, it was about nine a.m., because we did not have our regular day menu up, and he wanted a cheeseburger."

"That's strange, because all the dock workers went to work when the ship docked at around eight, and then they will work shifts until it leaves at about six p.m. tomorrow. I'll have someone check to see if there were any absences today. What did this guy look like?"

"He did not look Mexican, and he wasn't a gringo. He looked like someone from Iran or India."

"So, he could have been from a Muslim country?"

"Yes, that's it. He had a two or three day growth of beard and looked like he hadn't had a bath in a week. His clothes were all rumpled and he carried a bag made of cloth with some unusual designs on it. Arabic writing! That's what it was, Arabic writing."

The phone rings and Florentina answers, "*Hola, casa Rodrigues*." She pauses and then asks "Marc Ryder, is this really you? Are you coming to visit? Do you have a new girlfriend? Papa, you want to speak to papa? And I thought you were calling to talk to me. I am so bummed."

I answer, "Florentina, your English is getting better and better and you are going to be a famous actress someday. Now let me speak to your papa."

"OK, Mister Ryder, here is papa."

Estavan answers, "I'm not sure I'm talking to you yet, Agent Ryder. With that mess you left me and then the murder of Jorge Padilla, you are lucky I haven't had time to put a hit squad on you. Of course, the resident assassin has been murdered, so you are lucky."

"Indeed, I am. I am sorry to hear about Padilla's murder, especially after you connected him with my kidnapping in Puerto Vallarta."

"Yes, I would have liked to personally put the handcuffs on him and gathered up the rest of his gang who have all gone to the wind. OK, enough of the BS, you must have called for a reason, yes?"

"I was calling to give you a heads-up on a situation we had here in Long Beach and Los Angeles involving the Russian cruise ship *MS Mikhail Lermontov*. Are you familiar with her?"

Silence and a long pause before he responds. "Yes. She docked here this morning and will sail out around six p.m. tomorrow."

"We suspect that the brother of my wife to be, Marina, was involved in the shooting of a police officer in Long Beach, and we think he secreted himself on board the *Lermontov* before it left Los Angeles."

Again, a long pause before he responds.

"Send me everything you can, a photo if you have it, and I'll do some checking around. If you think there is a murderer on that ship and he might be here in Puerto Vallarta, maybe you would be wise to come down here and pursue this matter personally."

"I took the liberty and everything I have is already on its way to you. Thank you in advance, Estavan. I will see if I can get permission from my agency to come down and hopefully help you. This is a little outside the purview of my agency but I may be able to spin it into a liaison mission. Plus the local police would be very happy. Tell Florentina I have two tee shirts from a U2 concert and a Long Beach Grand Prix tee. They should fit in my carry-on bag if I can make the trip down."

"She maybe will forgive you for whatever, but you'll have to do better than that for my forgiveness, Marc Ryder. *Adios, amigo.*"

I knew when he said, "Adios, amigo," he had already forgiven me. Something in his response told me that he already had some information about either the ship or the fugitive I was seeking. You know when you have a close friend, there is something between friends, that bond, that unspoken word, that inflection in their voice, or a pause in a response that makes them your close friend.

Now I just got to convince my boss of the importance of this trip.

"Papa, is Marc coming to visit?"

"He didn't say. He said he had been to a U2 concert, whoever they are, and the Long Beach Grand Prix."

"What is the Long Beach Grand Prix?"

"It's a car race."

"Racing? Who cares about racing. I want to go to a U2 concert. U2 concert, I would just die to go to a U2 concert."

"Die? I suppose I would have to use your ticket then, Florentina."

"Papa, you are *sooooo* dramatic."

"I suppose. Come let's have late lunch. I have to go out and check something down on the docks after lunch."

"Papa, can I go with? I promise I won't get in the way."

"We will have to check with mama to see about that."

47

COLON, PANAMA

MARCH 31, 1983

It is almost nine months since the Puerto Vallarta incident. The drug smuggling business of the Mendez Cartel has been interrupted by the series of mistakes made by their nephew, Leo Ortiz. Leo and his right-hand man, Corey Flynn, are now dead. Robert Romano, Rosanna's husband, who became the object of FBI attention in Huntington Beach is also dead. A decision was made by the Mendez brothers to hire another assassin to eliminate an American federal agent, Marc Ryder. The same assassin who eliminated Robert and thought he had taken care of the American agent.

Alfonzo Benitez was sent by Adolfo Mendez to fly up to Tequila, Mexico and bring Rosanna back to Panama. She was kept in the dark about what happened to Robert and threw a major tantrum when she was told Robert would not be traveling to Panama. Screaming and yelling, she was subdued by Jorge and his crew. She gave them no choice but to have them wrap her in duct tape. She kept screaming, so they also duct taped her mouth and awaited the arrival of Alfonzo.

When Alfonzo arrived, he questioned Jorge about duct taping Rosanna but he was assured it was needed . She was transported back to Panama a virtual prisoner. She was put into the small plane and buckled in to her seat and tied with duct tape. The duct tape was removed from her mouth and she immediately began screaming again. Alfonzo was forced to put the tape back on.

The flight from Tequila to Colon requires one stop for fuel in southern Guatemala, a nondescript air field not unlike the strip in Tequila. Alfonzo tells Rosanna he will remove the tape if she promises not to start screaming again.

"Rosanna, I swear I will leave you here at this jungle air strip if you start screaming again. Do you promise to behave?" asks Alfonzo.

Rosanna nods her head, and he removes the tape, "Alfonzo Benitez, if I find out that you have had anything to do with hurting my Robert, one day, I shall kill you. I promise you, Alfonzo Benitez."

The plane is refueled and continues to Colon and lands at the private air strip on the Mendez compound. Adolfo and Manuel are waiting when the plane lands and taxies up to the hanger. Adolfo opens the door, and Alfonzo gets out.

Adolfo sees his daughter taped up. "Alfonzo, what's the meaning of this?" he cries.

"She was hysterical and fighting with us, we had no choice but to tape her up."

"Please remove the tape and get her out of the plane."

"Yes, sir."

As Alfonzo removes the last of the tape, Rosanna leaps on him ripping her fingernails across his face and head. "You bastard. You murderer. You are a dead man, Alfonzo Benitez!"

Adolfo and Manuel grab Rosanna and pull her off

Alfonzo who is bleeding profusely from the facial scratches inflicted by Rosanna.

"Alfonzo, are you OK?" asks Manuel, who also calls for more help and someone appears with a first aid kit.

Adolfo leads Rosanna away towards an awaiting car. Rosanna cries to Adolfo, "I know he has had something done to Robert. I have to go back to Puerto Vallarta and find Robert."

"Rosanna, listen to me," says Adolfo, "we have received word that Robert drowned in the Bay. His family in California has requested his body be shipped home to be buried. There is nothing I can do."

"*Nooooooooooooo*. It cannot be! *Nooooo, noooooo, nooooooooooo*."

Rosanna collapses into the arms of her father and is carried into the house and put in bed. She appears to be completely out and is left to rest. As soon as everyone is out of the room, her eyes pop open, and she begins to plan. She realizes that Alfonzo works for her father and that she is going down a dangerous path. She does not think her father would order her husband's death but maybe, just maybe. The Mendez Cartel is more important than one person, and her father is the Mendez Cartel. I need someone to help me, she thinks. I need someone like Marc Ryder. Too bad they buried him in Tequila. He would help me avenge Robert's death. No way he drowned. He was murdered. I know it!

Between sobbing and falling asleep Rosanna begins planning her return to Puerto Vallarta to get the full details of Robert's alleged drowning. She begins a journal trying to remember every detail of what happened that night on the beach. The only name she has is Jorge. He has to be the killer. She does not remember having contact with anyone in the Puerto Vallarta police department but identifying herself as Robert's wife should give her access to information on what happened to Robert.

She is kept a virtual prisoner in the Mendez compound for almost nine months. Those months have passed slowly but an idea has been slowly developing in her mind on how she can extract her revenge. She decides she needs to contact Janet Ryder and see what happened in Huntington Beach after she and Robert left. Rosanna has no idea how surprised she is going to be at the news from Huntington Beach.

While Rosanna is plotting on how to get out from under control of Alfonzo, Alfonzo has been agonizing over the events in Puerto Vallarta and Tequila for months. He was surprised at the failure of The Bolivian and she can go to hell about expecting full payment for that botched job.

He then thinks that might be a mistake I might regret. Alfonzo decides he needs to go to Puerto Vallarta and maybe Tequila to develop new people to handle the Tequila airfield. He realizes that he needs someone within the Tequila Police Department.

This new character who calls himself KIL puzzles him. First of all, his name is a joke and second, who hired him?

Alfonzo tells Adolfo of his plan to go to Puerto Vallarta and Tequila to find new people to handle things.

"It has been almost nine months since those unfortunate events in Mexico Alfonzo. Do you think everything has quieted down? Do you think it is wise for you to go to Puerto Vallarta?"

"There is no one else I can trust. I need to find new people."

"OK, I agree."

Alfonzo makes his plans to travel to Puerto Vallarta.

Delta Airlines Flight 3201 arrives at Puerto Vallarta

International. It parks out on the tarmac several hundred meters from the arrival gate for international travelers. The passengers disembark and board a bus to be taken to the arrival gate. The passengers all hustle towards the baggage area and seek their bags, after which they head for the customs counter to have their baggage searched and their passport stamped.

The customs officer, Juan Comprisias, had little sleep and too much Tequila the night before. He passes on the bag search, but asks the tall man who stands at his window, "what is the purpose of your visit to Puerto Vallarta, and how long will you be staying?"

Tomas Schultz responds, "I am here for vacation. I needed rest and recuperation and I will be here for a week."

Comprisias, who could only think of his upcoming break, notices three things about the man which should have made him ask more questions, but he didn't. He has a patch over his left eye, he speaks Spanish with a German accent, and he has only one small carry-on piece of luggage. He simply stamps his passport which is in the name of Tomas Schultz.

Three gates down another bus carrying passengers on a Delta flight pulls up to the gate, and among the people who get off is a dark-haired man with a drooping Poncho Villa mustache and what seems to be a natural scowl on his face. He also must pass through Juan Comprisias' gate.

Comprisias asks "what is the purpose of your visit and how long will you be in Puerto Vallarta?"

The man replies "the Easter celebration. Just four days."

Comprisias opens the man's passport and stamps it. "Enjoy your stay in Puerto Vallarta Senor Benevides."

Alfonzo Benitez, aka Juan Benevides, passes through Comprisias' station without raising any suspicion. Unaware of each other, Tomas Schultz and Alfonzo Benitez walk together, almost elbow to elbow on their way to find transportation into downtown Puerto Vallarta. Had they known what awaited them, they both would have turned around and left.

But they didn't.

48

TUSTIN, CALIFORNIA

MARCH 31, 1983

Janet Ryder has moved on with her life. After making mine as miserable as she could, she suddenly is gone. Hey, I'm not complaining, I mean, it was almost like we were still married. Never saw her then either. Because we still had mutual friends I heard she had gone to work for a major department store, working in women's fashions. A perfect job for her. She, however, apparently also kept tabs on me.

After getting off work at six p.m. and stopping off to have a cocktail with a couple of friends, Janet arrives home at her townhouse in Tustin. She loves her townhome, a spacious two-level, two bedrooms, two baths, a fireplace and a two-car garage. As she walks into the kitchen from the garage, the phone rings. She gives thought to have the "machine" answer it, but she impulsively picks it up, "Hello, this is Janet."

"Janet, oh I am so glad to have found you. This is Rosanna."

"Rosanna?"

"Yes, yes, it's me, Rosanna. Please, please don't hang up on me. I need help, and I didn't know where else to turn."

"Rosanna, do you know the trouble you and Robert got me into? I almost got sent to prison. I don't know why you and Robert are not in prison, you should be."

"Janet, Robert is dead. Leo is dead. Cory is dead."

"Wha, what? What happened?"

"I think my father's security chief hired someone to kill them, and I think I may be next. I am confined to my father's house and have not been out of the Mendez family compound for almost nine months. I am actually afraid to leave my room for fear Alfonzo will find some convenient way to do away with me."

"OK, you have my attention, but still I am wondering what this has to do with me?"

"I am calling first to tell you I am sorry for the troubles I caused you. Sincerely, I am most sorry and beg your forgiveness."

"You sound sincere, Rosanna, but I sense there is something else you want. What is it?"

"I need someone to help me. I need someone to go with me to Puerto Vallarta and find out how my Robert was killed. I need someone to help me to then extract my revenge. I need someone like Marc."

"You have got to be shitting me. Why would Marc even think about helping you after what happened to him? Why would he do that?"

"Wait, Marc is alive?"

"Yes, he is alive. Some thugs, friends of yours he thinks, grabbed him in Puerto Vallarta and buried him alive near some podunk town north of Guadalajara. Some native jungle people witnessed it and dug him up before he died."

"I had no idea, really, I had no idea. They had me duct taped and gagged."

"You were there?"

"Yes, they were taking me to Robert, and when I realized he was not there, I went crazy. They duct taped me and gagged me. The last time I saw Marc he was also tied up with duct tape and unconscious. I thought he was dead. They strapped me into my seat in the plane and flew me back to Panama. I am now a prisoner here in my own father's house."

"Holy shit, Rosanna. You are living under a black cloud."

"Janet, I beg of you, I need Marc's help. If I could talk to him, maybe I could convince him that they tricked me into thinking he killed Robert, and he could help me find the real killer."

"You do not have a very good reputation for being honest, Rosanna, and I'm sure Marc will be very wary of entering into a questionable relationship with you. Especially since you were the last person he remembers seeing in Puerto Vallarta before he was buried alive."

"He told you that?"

"Yes, he did. He also shared some other things about you."

"Is there any reason we have to go there, Janet?"

"No, we don't. Enough of the chit-chat. What do you want? When this conversation is over, I don't ever want to hear from you again, agreed?"

"Agreed. Just give me a number to call Marc, please."

"Alright, here it is." Janet repeats the number twice. "Goodbye, Rosanna."

Janet hangs up and immediately dials Marc's number and gets the answering machine. She leaves a cryptic message, "Rosanna called and needs your help. She thinks her father's security chief is trying to kill her. She thought you were dead."

Life is about to become even more complicated for me, Marc Ryder, DFL.

49

BELMONT SHORE

April 1, 1983

Naturally, the call comes when I am not home. Marina listens to the message and immediately calls me at the office. She has no problem expressing her anxiety over the call and wants to know what I am going to do.

"I don't know what I'm going to do. I'm going to finish what I'm doing here at the office, and I'll be right home."

"This does not make me happy, Marc Ryder. These people are the cause of all the problems we have had. Hurry home. I have to be at work at four, and I want to talk about this."

"OK, I'm leaving in ten minutes, and I'll be home in twenty. Love you."

"Love you, too. Bye."

This is really unsettling and annoying. I had hoped never to see or hear of either Janet or Rosanna ever again. This may call for a double martini. Maybe two.

The minute I hit the front door Marina is right there in my face.

"Marc, what are you going to do? You cannot help this woman. She had you buried alive. Tell me you are not going to do anything crazy here. Tell me."

"Whoa, slow down a little bit and let me listen to the message. And could you mix me one of your wonderful dirty martinis? I think I could use one."

"OK, I will. You listen to the message and tell me you are not going to do something stupid."

I listen to the message and realize its Janet, not Rosanna like I thought and also realize I can most certainly expect a call from Rosanna. I thought I had gotten off this merry-go-round.

50

PUERTO VALLARTA AGAIN

April 2, 1983

Konrad Ilyavich had survived in the assassination business not because he was thorough and researched each assignment through and through. It was because he was just plain blessed with dumb luck. He was smart enough to familiarize himself with all aspects of his intended target. Being a fan of old American gangster movies he picked up some of the slang. When preparing for a job he thought he should "case" the location of the "mark." "Ya know what I'm sayin' here" he once told a client. The client happened to be an Interpol Agent working undercover.

His sense of fashion and wardrobe were, however, atrocious. As a former military officer who wore a uniform or a suit and tie for twenty years, he had no clue how to casually dress as a civilian without turning heads. His favorite outfit usually included a Hawaiian-print shirt and dark glasses—something everybody remembered.

His life saving attribute was that he trusted no one, and in the case of Alfonzo Benetiz, there is no doubt in his mind that he should be very careful. Unfortunately, vodka blurred his decision making at times.

Some in his line of work like to be colorful and leave subtle clues as to who perpetrated the hit. Some are quite bold and actually leave some sort of indentification. This woman, this so called *Bolivian* is one of those. It will catch up with her, he thinks, and Konrad Ilyavich may just be the catcher.

He decides he will travel to Puerto Vallarta, Mexico to see what he may find to pick up the trail of the *Bolivian* and to solicit whatever information he can from the local police about her style and methods. He has been to Puerto Vallarta before and befriended a local cop on the police force. He wonders if his old friend Estavan Rodrigues is still on the police force. So, he picks up the phone and calls the local police department of Puerto Vallarta. Konrad Ilyavich speaks passable Spanish, and the call is most informative and rewarding.

"*Policia*, Puerto Vallarta."

"*Buenos dias*, I would like to speak to Estavan Rodrigues please."

"I am sorry, *Senor,* you have the wrong number. Estavan Rodrigues, can be reached at his office, Policia Federale de Mexico, Puerto Vallarta District."

"Could you please give me that number?"

Konrad Ilyavich is given the number, and he immediately dials it.

"Policia Federale."

"*Buenos dias*, this is Yuriy Gorbachevsky. I am a friend of Estavan Rodrigues and I would like to speak with him please."

After a short pause, Estavan answers "Yuriy Gorbachevsky, what brings you to Puerto Vallarta?"

"Good to hear your voice Estavan. I am not in Puerto

Vallarta but will be tomorrow and thought I would call you before I got there. Possibly we could get together for dinner one evening and catch up on things."

"Of course. Please call me when you arrive, and I'll have someone pick you up and take you to your favorite hotel. Is this a business trip?"

"No my friend, just pleasure and *Muchas gracias,* Estavan. I will see you soon."

Konrad Ilyavich is more than happy. His friend is now the chief of the federales. This should be more than helpful. He did not bother to tell Rodrigues he was already in Guadalajara.

Estavan Rodrigues is more than surprised by the call from his former acquaintance and wonders what the real reason for his visit to Puerto Vallarta entails. Yuriy Gorbachevsky was a cultural attache out of the Soviet Embassy in Mexico City when they first met. Estavan always suspected that there was more to his job than that and felt he was being played. He suspected Gorbachevsky was most likely military intelligence, GRU, or maybe even KGB. But Gorbachevsky never asked him for any unusual information, nor did he ever ask him for any unusual favors.

When Gorbachevsky left the country, Estavan was invited to the Soviet Embassy for his farewell party. After the party he had been questioned by the Mexican intelligence office of the Federales as to his relationship with Gorbachevsky. Nothing ever came of it, as there was nothing to tell.

It was right after the farewell party that I was sent to Chapala and Estavan and I became friends. I am unaware of the phone call he received from Gorbachevsky until my phone rings.

"Hello, this is agent Ryder."

"Agent Ryder, this is Estavan."

"Hey, *amigo*. What's up?"

"I just received a phone call from Yuriy Gorbachevsky. Remember him?"

"Indeed I do. What did he want? I thought he had retired."

"So did I, but I wanted to alert you of the call, and maybe you could check your sources as to what he is doing now. In addition, I have discovered some information and evidence on our recent murders that I thought you should have a chance to take a look at."

"I was denied my request to make the trip down because it seemed more of a personal matter to my boss. I am going to go back to him with this information about Gorbachevsky and see if I can change his mind. I am going to guess he will change his mind. I'm going to go ahead and make arrangements to fly down. Could you arrange lodging at the Fiesta Americana?"

"Consider it done."

"Thank you. I'll call as soon as I have been cleared to come down and I have confirmed my flight."

I am intrigued by this out-of-the-blue call from Gorbachevsky to Estavan. I walk down the hall and knock on the boss's door and tell him about Gorbachevsky contacting Estavan Rodrigues. After a few questions he gives me the go ahead. I snag a seat on Mexicana Airlines for 8:45 the next morning, arriving in Puerto Vallarta around noon. I call Estavan's office and leave a message with the times and airline.

Marina was not happy with me going to Puerto Vallarta

and the usual parting conversation ensued. I won't bore you with it but just tell you that I have been told that if I don't come back alive she is going to kill me.

I arrive at Puerto Vallarta International with the tourists and pass through customs to find Estavan waiting on the other side. We greet each other warmly with bear hugs, and then I hear the squeal of a young girl, it's Florentina, who comes flying at me with bear hug.

After hellos, I reach into my bag and pull out the U2 concert tee shirts . After squealing her thanks, she tells me she can't wait to get home and phone her friends. Estavan tells her he is sending her home in a cab and that we will be there after dinner.

Estavan's driver pulls up, and we get in the back seat. Estavan asks me if I came up with anything useful on Gorbachevsky. I tell him we have nothing new on him since he allegedly retired.

Estavan tells me, "the call I received from Yuriy Gorbachevsky was just yesterday. I had not heard from him since he left the embassy and was transferred back to Moscow, at least that's where I thought he went. I later learned that he had retired from whatever government job he held and was working as a mercenary in the middle east. Rumor was that he had become a hired gun. There was also some confusion as to what his real name was, as it was suspected that Yuriy Gorbachevsky was a cover name."

"I remember that name from the brief time I spent at the embassy. I never had any contact with him, because I was sent up to Chapala to attend your promotion. I will see what our people in Mexico City can give me, and I will pass it on to you. When does he arrive?"

"He will call my office when he arrives."

"OK, let me get working on what we have in Mexico City.

Can you tell me why this has concerned you, and why you think I can help?"

"Marc, those killings, that mysterious woman, then the murder of Jorge Padilla, and now the sudden call from Gorbachevsky, something is going on, and you know this is something I cannot share with Federale Intelligence. I would be in handcuffs. And what the hell is this business with your wife to be? Her brother killed a Long Beach Police officer? Did you bring a warrant to arrest him?"

"Estavan, I have no idea how all this ties together, if it indeed does tie together. I actually found the mysterious woman, quite by accident and lost her in Monte Carlo. Her companion was found murdered on the Greek island of Mykonos. The brother of her companion is a friend of mine in Odessa, Republic of Ukraine. And no, I did not bring a warrant. I don't even know if he is here. The ship has already left, right?"

"Yes, it has, and I had the ship's passenger manifest checked but I found nothing resembling the name of your future brother-in-law. I had no authority to check the ship's crew manifest to see if he was on board or not. Unless a crewmember gets off the ship, we have no record."

"Where is their next port of call?"

"I think it is Acapulco."

"OK, I'll make some calls to Los Angeles and see if anything else has come up."

"Let me treat you to dinner tonight. How about we go to the Blue Shrimp and enjoy the beach as we dine?"

"Great idea."

"I'll have a car pick you up at eight o'clock."

"If you don't mind, I'll meet you there. After I make my calls to LA, I'd like to just wander about down on the malecon and soak up the flavor and sights of Puerto Vallarta."

"Always the romantic, just don't forget what happened the last time you went wandering on the malecon."

"Thanks for the reminder. See you at eight."

Estavan drops me off at the Fiesta Americana. I check in and stop at the bar to have a cold Negro Modelo to wash down the travel dust. I remember the last time in Puerto Vallarta I sat at the bar in the Las Palmas. I met the blond. The mysterious blond. I wonder where she is now.

My thoughts are interrupted by a tall, blond-haired man, wearing dark glasses and an outrageous Hawaiian print shirt, who orders a vodka straight up and a mineral water. His Spanish is good but with a definite accent which I pegged as Russian.

The man took his drink and left the bar to sit at a table out on the patio. I'm thinking, could this be Gorbachevsky?

Gorbachevsky sits down at his table and tries to come up with a reason the man at the bar is familiar to him. He appears to be American, but he did not hear him speak. I will ask the bartender after he leaves, he thinks.

I look at my watch and decide to go up to my room and change and then walk down to the malecon and enjoy the sunset. The downtown area, or El Centro area, of Puerto Vallarta has always been one of my favorite places since the first time I saw it—the shops, the street artists, the restaurants, and the people watching. I stop at Las Palomas and snag a table by the window, order a cold Negro Modelo, and settle back to watch the people.

After a few minutes a cab pulls up and the Hawaiian shirt gets out, looks around, and wanders south out of sight. I'm still trying to figure out whether or not he might be Gorbachevsky and decide to order another Negro Modelo.

I'm distracted by the waiter asking if I want to order food and almost miss the next cab which pulls up. A very shapely woman with dark hair, cut pixie style, gets out. I can't see her face as she has her back to me, but as she turns to pay the cab, I almost fall out of my chair. It's her. No doubt about it.

I slide my chair back from the window and wait a couple of seconds before peeking around the window post. She has crossed Avenida Mexico and is walking south on the malecon which goes towards the Rio Cual and Playa de Muertos.

I am stunned. I gulp down the rest of my beer and head down Avendia Mexico paralleling the mystery woman. She continues south on the pedestrian walkway which is at the end of the malecon. I cross the street to get behind her. There are many people on the walkway, so I'm hoping if she turns to look back she will not pick me out. We continue to walk south, and she suddenly stops and looks back. We are in a little shopping area made up of temporary booths, all offering Mexican tourist items. I duck into a tent selling Mexican silver, and before the woman behind the counter can say anything, I cautiously peek around the tent wall and sneak a look. She is gone. I don't dare go looking in each tent or booth, so I walk down to the beach and come up on the south end of the little shopping area just before the bridge across the Rio Cual.

I wait for about 15 to 20 minutes and decide that she has

already left the area and is probably up ahead of me headed for Playa de Muertos where there are numerous restaurants, including the Blue Shrimp and Dick's. I hurry down the walkway and realize it's a few minutes after eight, and Estavan is probably waiting. I walk into the Blue Shrimp, and I see Estavan waving from a booth by the window. I am hoping the mystery woman is not sitting in a booth watching.

I slide into the booth with my back to the door and quickly tell Estavan what I have just seen as well as the Hawaiian shirt guy. I describe both of them, and Estavan remembers that Gorbachevsky liked Hawaiian shirts, which he thought peculiar, and his hair was almost a white blond.

"But what about the woman?" asks Estavan.

"Her hair was dark and cut short in a pixie style. She was wearing a dark, loose-fitting blouse and dark slacks. She carried a purse with a shoulder strap that she wore like a bandolier—with the strap over her left shoulder and the purse hanging on her right. She must have gone down the Rio Cual walkway, maybe to one of the cafes along the river."

"If it was her, she will surely recognize both of us, most certainly together. You should go back to the beach entrance of the walkway, and I'll go up to the other end and start walking towards you. I'll grab one of my men to follow me, and if I spot her, I'll send for you."

"Be careful, Estavan. This woman is deadly."

"You can count on it. Marc, I almost forgot, my office got a call from the FBI, someone named Biff, and he asked that you call him when you have a chance."

Biff? What the hell could he want except to torment me? I can just hear him, "Hey, DFL, how are things back there, or should I say down there?" We did kinda patch things up after my burial in Tequila, but he still annoys me. I'll put this call way down on my list of things to do.

That annoying feeling of being watched... the tingling on the back of her neck. She thinks, I'm becoming paranoid. She stops suddenly and turns around and sees nothing but a throng of people. She continues across the bridge over the Rio Cual towards Playa de Muerto and again stops, turns around, crosses back over the bridge, and makes a right unto the Rio Cual River walkway. She walks into the first vendor's tent she comes to and pretends to look at the women's ware and jewelry while really watching who walks by. Nothing, no one, nobody. I'm definitely getting paranoid, she worries.

She waits and shops for the next 30 minutes, then continues up the walkway to where she can catch a cab, which she does, telling him to take her to Dick's. The cab drops her off near the beach walk to Dick's and she gets out and waits a few minutes and hails another cab. "Take me to the Marina."

51

BACK TO PUERTO VALLARTA

APRIL 2, 1983

The unexpected turn of events on the island of Mykonos didn't shake up The Bolivian, but it definitely annoyed her. Then, the appearance of Serge's apparent twin brother on her island of Paros really annoyed her. There must be a connection somewhere that she had not anticipated. Her first inclination is to eliminate the brother, but she quickly realizes that is not a good idea, thinking, this is my home now, and I do not want to leave here. If he does not leave the Island within a week, she will come up with a plan.

She quietly spends the next few days in Marmaras, checking with her sources and keeping tabs on the brother. She finds his name is Dmitri Shepelova. After the fourth day, she receives a call from her source at the ferry boat office that D. Shepelova has booked passage to Piraeus the next morning. She makes plans to observe him get on the ferry and leave, which he does.

She decides to leave Paros and makes plans to travel to

Aruba. She will spend a day or two on Aruba and then take a ferry to Curacao where she has a small apartment in the city of Willemstad. She thinks to herself, I'll just lay low for a week or two, and then I'm going to Panama and see what I can learn of the employers of Alfonzo Benitez.

So, using her Aruban passport she flies to Panama City and then to Colon, where she rents a car and drives to the town of Portobelo, home of the Mendez family. Portobelo is very small, but she stops at a small café for lunch. By sheer luck, she overhears some people talking in the cafe. Their topic of conversation is the Mendez brothers and their notorious strongman, Alfonzo Benitez. These people are planning something, and whatever it is depends on Alfonzo Benitez being away. One of the group says that he heard Benitez would be gone for most of a week and his destination was Puerto Vallarta, Mexico.

Changing her plans, she again uses her Aruban passport and flies to Mexico City and gets a hotel in Zona Rosa for two nights. She pays for the two nights and checks in. She takes the elevator to her room, messes the bed, throws the towels on the floor, and takes the elevator to the garage. She exits out on the street behind the hotel. She hails a cab and directs the cab to take her to the airport. At the airport, she finds a small local airline and gets a seat on the plane which leaves in one hour for Puerto Vallarta, no passport required. She feels confident that if she was being followed, the trail ended in Mexico City.

She lands in Puerto Vallarta, not at the international airport but at a small airstrip near Bucerias, north of Puerto Vallarta. The pilot tells her where to find a cab to the El Centro zone of Puerto Vallarta. Forty minutes later she is dropped off in front of the Marriot Casa Magna. The Marriot is on the bay and across the street from Marina Vallarta. She checks into the Marriot, collects her keys, drops off her luggage, and walks out into the courtyard and pool area. She finds a spot at the beach bar, sits with her back to the bay, and orders a dirty martini. She is watching. After an hour, she feels confident she is not being observed or followed.

She is not sure how she is going to find Benitez, if in fact he is actually in Puerto Vallarta. But if he is, she is sure she will find him.

She is feeling quite good about herself, yet she has lingering and annoying thoughts about what happened on Mykonos. She feels more disturbed about it than annoyed.

She thinks, "I must move on and make a plan to rid myself of these vultures. Who has hired this KIL character? Why is Benitez after me? And how does that truly annoying American constantly show up wherever I go? I'll go up and take a nice warm bath, put on some nice clothes, and go to my favorite restaurant on the Rio Cual—The River Café. I'll find a nice secluded table, listen to music, and have a nice dinner with a glass of wine. Yes, that's what I'll do and deal with the rest tomorrow."

After her bath, she dresses and takes the stairs to the main floor. As she has the doorman signal for a cab, the aroma from the Japanese restaurant tempts her to stay right there. But, she overcomes and tells the cabbie, "Las Palomas on the malecon por favor."

She gets out of the cab around the corner from the Las Palomas, pays the cabbie, and starts to cross the street when the hairs on her neck suddenly bristle... she turns around to see who is looking at her. No one, I'm getting paranoid, she thinks. She crosses the street and gets lost in the crowd of people heading towards Rio Cual and the restaurants in the beach area.

As she walks through the area filled with street vendors,

she again feels somebody is watching her and stops and quickly turns around. She sees a mass of people, but nobody looking at her. She thinks, this is crazy. She decides to walk up the Rio Cual walkway and catch a cab to Café Artistes, which she does. Where, instead of having dinner, she decides to have a margarita and leave. So, she grabs a cab back to the Marriot, goes up the stairs to her room where she grabs her bag and leaves via the stairway and side entrance to the street. She walks across the street to the marina and finds a sidewalk café to sit down and have a drink and watch.

52

MYKONOS MEMORIES

APRIL 2, 1983

The Bolivian finds a table at a café in the Marina and orders a dirty martini. She feels agitated or nervous for some reason and quickly downs the martini and orders another. She starts to relax and begins think about what happened just a couple of months ago.

Monte Carlo was fun. Seeing the American was unexpected, but she was not concerned. It did not take much to convince her new companion to leave Monte Carlo and fly to Athens. A pleasant night of food and wine culminated in a night of uninhibited sex. After the first round they don their robes and sit out on the balcony overlooking the Plaka, with the Parthenon majestically lit up off in the distance.

"Serge, would you like to come with me to Mykonos for a few days. I have to meet with some people and take care of some business. We could then be real tourists, do the nightlife and the Spanish side. Maybe take the boat over to Delos and wander about Cleopatra's old hang out."

"You are on. I need to take a few days off. I'll make some calls and tell my office I'm out for at least another few days."

"I like your spontaneity. I will make my appointment, which is two days from now, so we'll catch the ferry tomorrow morning, and then after my meeting, we'll become tourists."

The events forthcoming would certainly have discouraged Serge had he known, but he was in lust. This woman, Josefina, was the most mysterious and tantalizing person he had ever met. Being the handsome devil he was, he had had plenty of experience. He felt most comfortable with Russian or Ukrainian women, whom he thought were the most beautiful and alluring. They somehow knew how to put you at ease and make you feel like a Czar. But this olive skinned beauty went way beyond. He couldn't get enough of her. She was very vague about where she grew up. She did not care to discuss her family. She would only say her job involved accounts payable. Where did she come up with that?

In his mind, he knew it couldn't last. A chance meeting in Monte Carlo. A whirlwind weekend in Athens. Another fling on a Greek isle. He was right on, and then it happened. Josefina had been very vague about what business she had on the island of Mykonos, but Serge could really care less. He figured they would spend a few days enjoying each other and go their separate ways. Maybe someday meet again. Whatever.

The Bolivian had received a request from a former client, Werner Brandt. Brandt did not mix words and conveyed to her through her complicated contact system what it was he wanted—Boris Bergraf dead. He cautioned that he had given the task to his chief of security, Tomas Schultz, but that he was not sure he was capable of the task and knew Schultz would not do the deed but seek another party. Schultz said it would be at least two or three weeks to set up the hit.

Brandt wrote in his request, "Now is when it should be done." He furnished details of the document he had sent to Bergraf and the suggested clandestine meeting. The document from a non-existant source within Brandt's company promised ridiculous results and guaranteed the take over by Bergraf's company. Brandt furnished a copy of the document to the Bolivian. He also gave her the contact number for Bergraf to set up the meeting site and time. He suggested the Island of Mykonos.

The Bolivian thought having a male companion with her would be good cover as opposed to a single woman walking the streets of Mykonos. With the inside information she received from Brandt, she made contact with Bregraf and set up the exact time and place for the meeting. More documentation would be provided at this meeting she told him. The tidbits of information she gave to Bergraf had garnered his rapt attention. She stressed that the source of the document would not and could not be revealed and intimated the action as a result of this information should be initiated by Boris, and only Boris.

She requested a meeting on the island Mykonos in an obscure hotel and the deal would be consummated there. She warned Bergraf that after he had been furnished the complete scenario of the takeover, he must not keep any written evidence.

Bergraf could hardly contain himself. The inside information he got from this source made him salivate. He picked up the phone and called Josef Feldman. "Josef, this is Boris. I have received some most interesting information, and we need to talk. I think I have found an easy solution to our takeover action. Come up to my office and let me run it by you. I think you will be most impressed."

"I will be right up, Boris. Do you have some paperwork or documents for me to review?"

"No. This information comes to me through someone deep in the company, and it was given to me verbally."

"Boris, can you trust this person?"

"Josef, I don't know who the person is, but the information is more than solid and will be the dagger to the heart. I have been asked to meet this person on the island of Mykonos to be briefed on the rest of the available information and, of course, provide suitable compensation."

"Boris, this is crazy. What is suitable compensation?"

"One million dollars, US."

"Boris, you can't be serious? I am coming up and bringing Heinz Dorfmann with me."

"Josef, do not bring Dorfmann into this."

"For heaven's sake, Boris, he is our chief of security."

"Yes, he is, but do not bring him into this. Do you understand me, Josef? Do not!"

"I cannot condone this. This is madness."

"Josef, come to my office alone, and we shall talk."

"What about Joanna?"

"She does not need to know."

The meeting between Josef and Boris is, to say at the least, loud. In the end, Josef cannot dispute the facts and figures Boris has laid out. He is right, this is a dagger in the heart of Brandt's company. Boris is full of himself because of this and immediately makes plans to go to Mykonos.

He calls his secretary and asks her to find a particular hotel on Mykonos and book a room for a week, even though he does not intend to spend even one night there. Immediately after, he calls his transportation office to have the company plane readied for a trip to Athens and thereafter to the island of Mykonos. He then sends a message via telegram to the address requested by the confidential source. The message gives the date he will be at the hotel and confirms that requested compensation has been approved. The confidential source of course is the Bolivian. She now has the date confirmed and the hotel. She immediately goes to work booking the rooms she needs in the name of Serge Shepelova.

Serge and the Bolivian have checked into the hotel. Serge is looking around and asks, "Josefina, how did you find this hotel? I may never leave here. The views of the bay are without equal."

"Oh, Serge, I am glad you like it. When I booked it, I booked it in your name. Was that OK? I mean, I'll pay for it, but I thought it better to book it in a man's name. A Greek thing, you know?"

"I am glad you did, because you are not paying for a thing."

"It's not a problem. I can write it off as a business expense."

"Oh, so I'm a business expense now?"

"Well, I haven't seen your bill, but I fear it may be more than my expense account can handle."

"Well then, let me start reducing those expenses. You can start by taking off those boots while I pull back the bed covers."

"Two o'clock in the afternoon? Serge, you wicked and merciless man."

"Must I tell you again, off with the boots. And, while you're at it, the blouse. And the slacks." As the Bolivian strips off her slacks and exposes her undergarments, Sergey suddenly asks, "VS! Why do your bra and panties have the initials VS printed on them? Are you using an assumed name?"

Long sigh, "Serge, you need to get out more often."

"Excuse me, I'm out all the time."

"No, I mean out of Ukraine. Have you never heard of Victoria's Secret?"

"No, and this is taking much too long."

Serge throws her into bed, and the rest of the afternoon is spent with him wondering how long this can last and with her wondering how she is going to complete her task. But, she is not worried and, in fact, is quite pleased. Not only did she secure a very sizeable fee from Brandt, Bergraf will have one million for her efforts.

After receiving Bergraf's response, she booked another room immediately adjacent to Bergraf's, which was found by simply asking the desk clerk, if she could have a room adjacent to Boris Bergraf, her boss. The room was one floor below her and Serge. All she needs to do is slip out and go to the public lockers at the ferry boat terminal and collect the bag with her tools.

Serge did not see her slip a tiny pill into his glass of ouzo, and within minutes he is out cold. She slips into her clothes, silently leaves the room, and heads for the terminal. She takes the stairs to the first level and exits out the back door onto a cobblestone street. Walking away from her destination, she follows the cobblestone street to an alley which leads to the back entrance of the terminal. She waits in the shadows for a few minutes, and when she is sure she was not followed she goes into the terminal and collects her bag from the locker.

She then returns to the hotel by the same route taking the same precautions. She slips into the room and finds Serge still sound asleep. She gathers her belongings and grabs a damp cloth from the bathroom to wipe down all the surface areas she might have touched. Satisfied, she silently bids Serge goodbye and slips out the door.

Serge hears the door close and it takes him a few minutes to come out of his stupor. She is gone, but where? Maybe she left a note but he can't find any. He notices a crumpled piece of paper on the floor under the coffee table and picks it up. A four digit number is written on it. It's their room number. No, wait its twenty four twenty two, not thirty four twenty two. He goes out to check room twenty four twenty two. That's probably where she was meeting her client.

She again takes the stairs to the floor below and finds her other room. Engaging the dead bolt on the door before closing it, she causes the door to stay open just a crack. Then, she opens her side of the adjoining room door. She pulls up a chair, takes her silenced pistol out of the bag, checks the magazine, jacks one round in the chamber, and waits.

In a few minutes at precisely the correct time, Bergaf enters his room next door. She hears him checking out the room and then, per the instructions he had received at his office, she hears him opening the lock on his half of the adjoining room door. He is not prepared for what he sees as he opens the door. A woman with a gun pointing at his head. She says, "Mr. Bergraf, I presume."

He never hears anything else. Two shots to the forehead and one to the heart. She jumps up, steps over him, and grabs the bag he left in the middle of his room. As she steps back over him and drags him fully into her room, her door opens, and Serge walks into the room. Before he can say or do anything, he is felled by two shots to the forehead and one to the heart.

She exclaims outloud "Damn, damn, damn, damn! Why

couldn't you have stayed in the room? Why did you show up here? Damn! And how the hell did you find this room"

She quickly gathers herself and goes to the door. Finding no one else out in the hall, she unlocks the dead bolt allowing the door to close behind her as she again goes down the stairs, out the back, and onto the cobblestone street. This time, she heads directly for the ferry boat terminal. The next ferry leaving is headed for Piraeus in twenty minutes. Perfect! She buys a ticket and boards. The ferry has one stop at Island of Kea. She decides she will get off there and wait for the ferry to Paros. She will spend her time at the Taverna Kea with her friend Narvanos. He will say anything and nothing for her benefit. A true friend.

She is shocked out of her day dreaming by a mariachi band playing at the next table. Quickly she gets up and goes to the back of the restaurant and steps into the shadows to watch.

The day the German Boris Bergraf was to have his meeting on the Island of Mykonos, Josef Feldman was becoming more and more concerned. He waited until late that evening before he is sure that something has gone wrong. He calls Dorfmann and tells him to check up on Boris and tells him he does not have the name of the hotel on Mykonos.

"I don't care what you have to do Dorfmann. Find Boris."

It takes Dorfmann only one hour and he calls "Mr. Feldman, this is Dorfmann. I found the hotel, and Mr. Bergraf did check in. I asked them to please go to his room and check on him. They just called me back and his room is empty and doesn't look like anyone has been in there."

"Thank you, Dorfmann. He is probably on his way back to Athens and stopped to celebrate. Goodbye."

53

KIL'S MISTAKE

APRIL 2, 1983

KIL looks over his shoulder and cannot see the American at the bar. After a few minutes, he walks back inside and sits down at the bar. The bartender comes over, and he orders another vodka and mineral water.

"I saw a fellow sitting at the bar that I thought I may know. An American, I believe."

"*Si*, there was an American here a little bit ago. He went to have dinner, but I don't know where."

"Do you recall his name?"

"I don't believe I got his name. I only remember his generous tip."

"Is he here on vacation or business, do you know?"

"*Senor*, I may or may not know, but I know him from his previous visits, and I'm sorry I do not know you, nor do I like all your questions."

"Hey, I'm just being curious about a guy I might know."

"Are you a guest at the *Americana*, *Senor*?"

"No, I just stopped for a drink."

At that moment, a very large man appears and sits down at the bar next to KIL. He casually lets his jacket slip open, revealing a very large pistol stuck in his belt.

The bartender comes over and stands in front of KIL and leans over the bar. "Good night, Mr. Hawaiian Shirt."

"Hey, my friend, no reason to get hostile."

"I am not your friend, Mr. Hawaiian Shirt, and you have not seen me hostile. Reynaldo, find this man a cab."

"Thank you, I'll find my own cab, asshole."

He never saw it coming—a backhand blow from Reynaldo that knocked him off his barstool and sent him sprawling on the floor. Before he could react, KIL felt himself being picked up by the shirt collar and dragged out the door.

Reynaldo said, "*Buenos noches*," just before he delivered a solid kick to the ribs, and that's the last thing KIL heard until he woke up face down in the sand.

As KIL sits up, a sharp pain courses through his body. His rib cage is on fire. He recalls... what the hell just happened? Who was that American, and who the hell were those thugs in the bar? He gets up and limps around the outside of the hotel to the street where he catches a cab to his hotel—the Sheraton.

Staggering into the lobby's men's room, he looks in the mirror and does not like what looks back at him. He sneaks down the corridor to the elevator and goes up to his room. Damn I'm sore. How the hell did I let that happen? I'll take a hot shower and lay down for a bit and then go find some dinner, he decides.

A short time later, after a shower, KIL feels a little better. He puts on a clean Hawaiian shirt and shorts and heads down to the lobby bar. As he is getting off the elevator, a very attractive woman with dark hair cut in a pixie style gets on. She's dressed in a dark blouse, dark slacks, and dark glasses. He turns around for a second look but the doors have closed. "I'll have to keep an eye out for her. Gorgeous, just plain gorgeous," he says to himself.

The Bolivian finished her martinis at the marina café and walked out the south entrance to the marina and hailed a cab. She tells the driver "Sheraton Hotel please." On arrival at the Sheraton she exits the cab, walks across the lobby, and gets on the elevator, as she watches the man with an obnoxious Hawaiian print shirt exit. Somewhere in the back of her mind he looks familiar. She scans her memories, where have I seen that face before? I know I have seen that face before. Concentrate! Where and who was that? He looked like he had just been on the losing end of a fight.

KIL heads to the bar and decides maybe he'll just wait and drink, thinking, maybe the little lady with the pixie cut will show up. I need some diversion after that fiasco at the Americana.

An hour and a half later he is still at the bar nursing his third vodka. Sitting on the far side of the bar he can see the corridor that leads to the elevators and anyone who comes out.

Meanwhile, it was still driving her crazy... who was that guy? She changes her clothes and puts on a dishwater blond wig along with some rimless glasses and heads down the stairs.

She sees the Hawaiian shirt sitting at the bar, and she slips into a booth in a dark corner of the bar and watches. He seems to be having quite a conversation with the bartender, a very attractive Mexican gal of about thirty who wears a name tag. Maria it says. He orders another drink and, more or less, throws it down saying good night to the bartender and leaves. She waits thirty minutes and goes to sit at the bar.

"What can I get for you, ma'am?"

"I'll have a martini. Can you make it dirty?"

"I make the best dirty martinis in Puerto Vallarta. Would you like vodka or gin?"

"Vodka please and two olives."

"Coming right up." Moments later, "how does that look?"

"Perfect. This should relax me after a long day."

"Did you work today?"

"Yes, all day."

"What do you do?"

"I'm an accountant, and I'm doing an audit of a company here in Puerto Vallarta."

"I'm sorry. Sounds boring, but at least you are not boring. The guy that was sitting where you are now, he was boring."

"The guy in the Hawaiian shirt?"

"Yeah. He's here on vacation, and all he did was complain about the food, his room, the humidity, the cabs, everything. Typical Russian. Pig!"

"Russian, he said he was Russian?"

"Not in so many words, but he was definitely Russian."

"Did he introduce himself?"

"I believe he said his name was Colin, no Conner, no, let me think... Conrad, that's it."

"How interesting. Thank you, Maria. I'm going to go find a nice, late dinner and retire. Work again tomorrow."

"Maybe see you tomorrow night. Happy hour at five."

As The Bolivian walks away, she thinks, you have got to be kidding me. Could it be? Konrad Ilyavich Levorenchenko. Here in Puerto Vallarta. How convenient! The vodka has made him let his guard down. How many birds am I going to be able to kill with one stone? All I need now is to get that Panamanian pig, Benitez and that Ukrainian Shepelova here, and I can wipe the slate clean. I'll deal with the American later.

54

MOHAMMED

April 2, 1983

Mohammed Noor is livid. Not only was his cousin, Ahmed Sul Fazir, killed on the street in Long Beach, California, now his brother, Ustad, has also disappeared. After a tedious series of phone calls, it appears he is still on the ship *Mikhail Lermontov*, but no one can seem to locate him, and he has not responded to any of the messages left by Mohammed. Desperate, he tries his cousin, Jerriz Al Moudin, in Odessa. Al Moudin finally returns his call after two days. Mohammed wants to rip his heart out, but he needs Al Moudin's help so he tries to calm himself down.

"Thank you for returning my call, Jerriz. I am in need of your help."

Jerriz struggles to contain himself, for it is Mohammed who owes him a favor. He replies, "I am at your service, Mohammed."

"Ustad is apparently still on the Russian ship, but he does not return my calls. I have left messages with the shipping company that it is urgent to no avail. No one can seem to find him. Can you check with the ship's main office and see if they have any information for me? I also am wondering if you have any contacts in California who might do me a favor? Of course, they would be handsomely paid for their services."

"I can check with the ship's office without a problem. What is the favor you have in mind?"

"I want them to find my sister Marina and send her back to me."

"Send her back to you?"

"Preferably alive."

"Pardon me, Mohammed, this is more than a favor and could entail much planning. There would also be dangerous chances of involving the police."

Gritting his teeth and successfully stymying the urge to scream at Jerriz, Mohammed responds with a strained voice "I said they would be handsomely paid, Jerriz."

The tone in Mohammed's voice told Jerriz that he may have stepped over the line. He needed to end this call on a good note.

"I have a cousin in the Los Angeles area, and I shall contact him. I may travel there myself."

"I am already in your debt. I am going to wire you twenty-thousand dollars. And when the job is complete, I will send you an additional twenty thousand. I will also pay you any expenses you incur. Will this be enough incentive, Jerriz Al Moudin?"

"Yes, my Brother."

Mohammed slams down the phone and screams to no one, "Jerriz Al Moudin you are a dead man! Do you hear me? A dead man!"

During the next few hours Jerriz makes his calls and

books his flight from Odessa to Los Angeles via Athens. His Los Angeles cousin, Fahid Al Moudin, is given all the information that Jerriz has about Marina, and Fahid assures Jerriz that he will have located her by the time Jerriz arrives. Fahid, of course, has a cousin who works for the Immigration and Naturalization Service, so it should be no problem to find Marina. Jerriz cannot find any more information on the whereabouts of Ustad.

Jerriz arrives aboard a Delta flight at LAX, Los Angeles and is met by Fahid and two of his cousins. The three of them own a corner store in Wilmington. This is an unsavory part of Wilmington, controlled by the notorious, Mexicano gang Wilmas, whose graffiti is spray painted on the side of most buildings. It reminds Jerriz of the harbor area of Odessa.

"So, Fahid, have you located Marina Noor?" asks Jerriz, getting right to the point.

"I have found her residence, and by a stroke of luck I found where she is working thanks to a neighbor. I think it is better to take her at her place of work rather than her house."

"I agree. Where is her place of work?"

"A restaurant and bar on East Anaheim Street in Long Beach. It should be no problem to find out when she is at work. When do you want to grab her, and what are we going to do with her?"

"We should do it as soon as we can," Jerriz responds. "And you said you had an idea as to where we could keep her."

"Yes, I have a twenty-foot shipping container behind my store. The entrance is not visible from the street, and it is sound proof," replies Fahid.

"Perfect! I have made arrangements to meet a Croatian

ship off the coast of California in two days. It is going to Mazatlan and down the coast to the Panama Canal. It will stop at a couple of ports in Central America and then cross the Atlantic to its final destination, Odessa."

Fahid says that he needs to make one call to determine Marina's schedule, then asks, "How are we getting her out to the Croatian ship?"

"Mohammed provided me the name of a former business associate who owes him a favor. This person also owns a forty-foot fishing boat which regularly fishes in the Catalina Channel."

"Who is this man?"

"His name is Watermann, and his partner was a cousin of one of Mohammed's main distributors here in Southern California."

"So, you trust him?"

"Mohammed does. Do you want to question him?"

55

BIFF TO THE RESCUE

April 2, 1983

Before I leave the hotel to meander around Puerto Vallarta El Centro, I call home and realize Marina is still at work. So, I call Joe Jacks bar in Long Beach. Arnie, the bartender, answers, and I ask to speak to Marina.

"Who's calling?" asks Arnie.

"Arnie, it's me, Marc."

"Marc who?"

"Come on, Arnie."

"Hey, I gotta look out for my number-one waitress. You can't believe how many calls she gets, and that bum boyfriend of hers is always in Timbuktu or Wharethefugarwi! Works for some phoney outfit named Dead Fuckin' Last."

Long pause, and then hysterical laughter.

"Ya know, Arnie, you are going to regret that! Now let me talk to Marina."

"OK, what was your name again?"

"ARNIE!"

"Calm down. Here she is."

I hear giggling, and Marina answers "Hi, honey. Isn't Arnie a hoot?"

"Yes, he is a hoot. I thought I would call before I went to dinner with Estavan. I haven't found out any more about Ustad, and the ship has left. He didn't get off here, or I should say, at least, not legally. I'll call you tomorrow with an update. Is everything OK?"

"Everything except you are not here. Hurry home and be safe. I love you."

"Love you more. Bye-bye, Marina."

"OK, Arnie, I'm out of here, and I'll see you tomorrow at eleven in the morning" says Marina as she goes out the back door of Joe Jacks.

It's just past seven p.m. in Long Beach, and dusk has fallen as Marina goes out the back door of Joe Jacks to her car. Standing in the shadows, four men observe her as she walks across the parking lot. All four have ski masks pulled over their heads. As Marina reaches the center of the lot all four descend upon her. The first one to reach her is surprised as she spins out of his grasp and delivers a knee to the groin.

At the same moment two other men, customers at Joe Jacks, exit the back door and see the men assaulting Marina. They both shout for them to stop and charge the ski-masked assailants. Marina is now grappling with another masked man as the one she kneed in the groin is on the ground moaning. The other two masked men are fighting the two newcomers. At the same time, a car pulls into the lot, and its headlights light-up the parking lot.

The driver, Biff, sees four men in ski masks, one of them

on the ground in a fetal position, another with a strangle-hold on Marina, and other two going hand-to-hand with two men without masks. He jumps out of his car, pulls out his revolver, and shouts, “FBI! Everybody freeze now.”

All the combatants stop in mid punch except Marina, who delivers a haymaker punch to her attacker with a leather sap.

“Marina, it’s me, Biff. Go back inside and call Long Beach PD.”

Somebody has apparently already called Long Beach PD, as two patrol cars pull into the lot before Marina even reaches the door. Four patrolmen exit the cars and tell everyone to get on the ground, including Biff and Marina. Everybody is handcuffed, and they begin to sort out who is who, starting with Biff.

Three hours later, the good guys and the bad guys have been identified. The two guys from Joe Jacks are cut loose. Marina is able to identify her cousin, Jerriz Al Moudin, and with the help of Los Angeles PD, Harbor Division, Fahid and his cousins are also fully identified. LT Roy Henry, who was called in because Marina asked for him, assures Marina all four of her attackers will be in custody and that she is out of danger.

Biff and Marina are offered a ride back to Joe Jacks by the Long Beach PD patrol sergeant, which they accept.

They ride back to the parking lot in silence and thank the officer for the ride. As they get out of the car and start walking to Marina’s car, Biff asks, “Are you OK? If you want, you can come over and stay with me and my family tonight.”

“No, I’m fine. I just want to go home. I wish Marc were here, but I’ll be fine.”

“What really happened tonight, Marina?”

"I think they were sent by my brother Mohammed to either kill or kidnap me."

"Why would he do that?"

"He thinks I killed our brother Atta and ruined his drug smuggling business, and he is seeking revenge."

"He's the guy Marc told me about, right?"

"Yes."

"One more question. Where did you get that leather sap, and who showed you how to use it? They are illegal, you know."

"I have no idea what you are talking about Biff."

"Right. I think that I should call Marc and tell him what has happened and assure him all is well. Then, he can call you, or you can call him tomorrow. OK?"

"OK."

56

A NEW PLAN

APRIL 2, 1983

Just when you think everything is under control... enter the defense attorney. Within a few hours Fahid and company are on the street and back at the corner store. Fahid assures Jerriz that this is not over. They might as well commit suicide for their failure, because Mohammed will not let this lie.

"Jerriz," Fahid says, "we will meet back here tomorrow and make a new plan. You must call Mohammed and tell him what happened. Tell him we are not done and are making a new plan."

"He is not going to like this, Fahid."

"So he doesn't like it. What can we do different? That is what we must think about."

The phone rings, and Fahid answers.

"This is Ustad."

"Ustad? How did you get this number?"

"Ahmed gave it to me. He told me to call it if I could not reach him on his number."

"Where are you?"

"I am in Puerto Vallarta."

"Puerto Vallarta, Mexico?"

"Yes, Puerto Vallarta, Mexico. I got off the ship here and I was planning to work my way back home. I have been trying to reach Ahmed, but he does not answer his phone. This was the other number he gave me."

"Ahmed is dead, Ustad."

"Dead?"

"Yes, he was shot and died on the street in Long Beach."

"By the American?"

"No, Long Beach police."

"The Long Beach Police? Why?"

"He stabbed one of the policemen and they shot him."

"What else has happened?"

Fahid tells him of the failed kidnapping and of their arrest and that they are making a new plan.

"Fahid, I may have found a solution to the problem. The American is here in Puerto Vallarta and is being sought by a woman who I believe is an assassin. I saw her try to shoot him, and she shot a Mexican policeman instead. If I could somehow contact her, maybe she would agree to kill him and Marina for us, for nothing."

"Why would she do this?"

"Maybe because she does not know where he lives and I do and she seems to have some personal reason to kill him. I will give her Ahmed's phone number, and tell her to call it when she reaches Long Beach. I will tell her the person answering the phone will have the information on where to find the American and Marina."

"We have that so we can do this, but we will need to have someone at Ahmed's apartment to answer the phone. When do you think she will get here?"

"I don't know when she will get there. But she doesn't seem one to waste any time."

"I and my cousins will take care of this. Mohammed is getting anxious and that is not good. Jerriz is going to call Mohammed and bring him up to date."

"If he asks about me, tell him I am on my way back from Puerto Vallarta."

"I will, if he asks." Click.

57

COMPLICATIONS

April 2, 1983

Biff? What the hell could he want except to give me grief? I can come up with a million reasons not to call him, but the fact that he called and left his home phone number is curious.

We've obviously lost our girl, The Bolivian, so I decide to find a phone and find one near the restroom on the river walk and call Biff. The phone rings a half-dozen times, and I'm ready to hang up when a woman answers, "Hello?"

"Hello, this is Marc, and I'm returning Biff's call."

"Oh Hi Marc, hold on I'll go out to the patio and get him for you."

"Thank you." I wait a few minutes, and then I hear what I've been waiting not to hear.

"DFL! Hey man, I'm glad you surfaced long enough to call me."

"This better be important, and I'm charging you for this long-distance call."

"And I intend to pay, believe me."

"So what's so important that it couldn't wait until I get back in a couple of days?"

"It's about Marina."

"Wha, what about Marina?"

Biff proceeds to tell the whole story, and I am shocked speechless.

"Marc? Marc, are you still there?"

"Yes I'm still here."

"Good. She's OK, and I've got a couple of guys nearby, plus Roy Henry has requested patrol division to send a squad car on a drive-by every half hour. We are pretty sure all the bad guys are in custody and although Marina is definitely shook up about the whole thing, she is OK. I told her I would call you and fill you in on what happened. You think you can get out of there sooner than two days?"

"Well, I am certainly going to try. Let me tell you what has happened here."

I tell Biff everything that I have seen and that I have no idea what is going on but my quest to find Ustad is a bust.

Biff replies, "We got things under control here, partner. Find the quickest way out of there and come on home. Let Estavan and his federales handle Mexico. Call me at the office tomorrow morning with an update, and I'll fill you in on anything that happens here. But, I would say not to worry. I think we got it under control."

"Thanks Biff. I owe you."

"I already knew that, DFL."

"You know one of these days."

"Yeah, yeah, you're gonna get the best of us Female Body Inspectors, or are we Fan Belt Inspectors this week?"

"Friends, Biff. You and I are just friends."

"Oh, for crying out loud, don't get all weepy on me."

"Not a chance, Feebee, not a chance."

"Call me, and don't worry." Click.

I hang up and take a deep breath and thank God for Biff. I immediately call Marina and assure her that I will be home as soon as I can get a flight, warning her that it will be sometime in the morning. She tells me the whole story, and I still can't believe the incredibly lucky turn of events. Ustad and The Bolivian are the least of my concerns now. They probably do not feel the same.

After hanging up the phone, I am startled by two men emerging from the shadows along the river walk on the Rio Cual. I am relieved to see it's Estavan and one of his men.

"Estavan, you startled me. Did you have any luck in finding her?"

"No. She disappeared into thin air. I'm having one of my clerks run a list of new check-ins at all hotels for the last two days. We'll see what we come up with."

"Estavan, I've got to return home tomorrow. You will not believe what happened."

I tell him of the events surrounding the attempted kidnap of Marina, and he assures me that he will get me on the first flight home in the morning. I have a plastic bag in my hand with a couple of tee shirts, and it slips from my hand and falls on the ground. Estavan and I both bend over to pick it up when we hear a deadening thud, and Estavan's man keels over. We both dive to the ground and wait for whatever is going to happen next. Nothing, only Silence.

We slowly crawl behind a concrete block wall and peek over. Nothing. Estavan gets on his two-way radio and calls for help, "Officer down, repeat, officer down. All personnel in the area of River Cafe, converge on the river walk. We have an unknown person with a gun." At least that's what I think he said. My college Spanish just ain't cutting it.

"Damn it! Damn it! I can't believe they both bent over at the same time," The Bolivian curses under her breath as she disappears across the Rio Cual on the bridge.

Standing on the stairwell going down to the river walk is Ustad. He can't believe his eyes. He is sure it is him. It's Marina's American lover. His mind races... did he follow me to Puerto Vallarta? How did he know I was here? Who are those other two men? Are they police?

Ustad continues to watch from the shadows when suddenly, the American and one of the other men bend over to pick up a bag that the American has dropped and Ustad hears a strange noise. He sees the other man fall to the ground. It appears he has been shot. Ustad hears someone screaming in Spanish, something about a man or officer down. On the other side of the three men, Ustad notices a woman in the shadows. She has a gun, and she disappears into the trees. Ustad thinks, madness... this is madness! Maybe she was sent by Mohammed?

Ustad turns to hurry back to his hotel when he runs into two men with very big guns. One of them grabs him, throws him on the ground, and roughly handcuffs him. The other man puts the barrel of his gun in Ustad's ear and says something in Spanish like don't move. He is searched by one of them while the other runs over to where he saw the American and the man who apparently got shot.

Ustad is scared for his life, so when the man returns with one of the other men who was with the American, he starts crying and babbling about a woman he saw with a gun over near the river.

Estavan asks, "What is your name, and where to you live?"

Ustad replies, "Carlos Estrella, and I'm staying at the Hotel Vallarta."

"Are you visiting Puerto Vallarta?"

"No, I work here."

"Where are you from?"

"Baja del Norte, Rosarita Beach."

"Tell me Carlos Estrella what did you see?"

"I saw you and two other men over by the telephone, and you bent over to pick something up, and it looked like the one guy got shot. I saw a woman with a gun over there." He points to a spot about fifty yards away.

"What did she look like?"

"I could not tell. She was in the shadows, but I saw the gun, and she disappeared into the trees along the river."

"OK, Carlos Estrella, you can go back to your hotel. You better be there if I come looking for you, *comprende*? Where do you work?"

"I work down in the harbor."

Estavan has his man uncuff Ustad, and Ustad quickly disappears into the night.

Estavan redirects his men to search the area where Ustad claimed the woman had fled and comes back over to me and his downed man. An ambulance has arrived, and they seem to think Estavan's man will be OK. Estavan then tells me about the witness who saw a woman with a gun disappear into the trees along the Rio Cual.

"Who was the witness" I ask?

"His name is Carlos Estrella, and he works down on the docks in the harbor."

"If I have time tomorrow, I might go find him and show him a picture of Marina's brother, but I probably won't."

"Didn't you leave a copy of the picture at the office?"

"I did."

"I'll have someone find Estrella tomorrow and show him the picture. Maybe we can at least wrap that up."

The Bolivian finds a women's restroom and rips off her wig and glasses. Her hair under the wig is dark and short and wet from perspiration. She leans over to muss up her hair and ties a bandana around her head. She strips off her dark-colored blouse and turns it inside-out revealing a much lighter color with a flowery print. Satisfied, she heads towards the flea market on the other side of the Rio Cual and waits.

After a few minutes waiting and watching she heads on foot up a back street to the restaurant, Si Senor, where she goes to the second-story bar overlooking the street. She orders a cerveza and after waiting twenty minutes or so, she goes back down to the street and finds a small boutique where she buys a silky blouse and matching pants in a muted grey, matching sandals, a floppy straw hat, and some rose-colored glasses.

She tells the clerk she is going to wear her new outfit as she has a date for dinner and is going to give her old clothes to the clerk. She then has second thoughts and picks out a large straw beach bag and puts all her things in it. She is annoyed that she had to dispose of the gun in the Rio Cual.

Getting another gun would not be a problem, but she hated to lose the silencer.

As she exits the boutique, she runs right into two policemen. They profusely apologize and continue on their way, looking back at her backside, "*Muy bonita!*" The policemen had just finished a dinner break and had turned off their police radios. A violation of policy. As they turn their radios back on they hear Estavan's call for help and to be on the lookout for a woman on the run. He adds the description of The Bolivian. She, of course, looks nothing like that now as she slips into a cab, "Sheraton Hotel, please."

58

LET'S RE-GROUP

April 2, 1983

I am overwhelmed. What the hell is going on here? I ask Estavan if we shouldn't go back to his office, gather all our known facts, and see if we can find something we overlooked as to why this woman would be back in Puerto Vallarta. Why we haven't found any trace of Ustad, and if there is any co-incidence on the appearance of Gorbachevsky and the mysterious woman.

Estavan says, "I agree. We need to sit down and review everything. My men have come up with nothing on the woman. You also need to prepare to go home."

"I am going to, and with your permission, send all that we have to Biff and have them crunch the information to see if they come up with anything."

"I agree, and I will send what we have to my headquarters in Mexico City."

"OK, let's do it. Are we good to go here?"

"Yes, my people have it under control. Marc, I think it would be a good idea after everything that has happened for you to change hotels for tonight."

"Good idea, what do you suggest?"

"I know that you are not on a budget, but I can make a call and arrange for you to stay at the Sheraton, no charge."

"My kinda rate. As soon as we finish our conference back at the office I'll go back to the Americana and get my stuff."

"What do you have there? You probably didn't even unpack."

"No, actually I didn't."

"OK, I'll send Julio to grab your luggage and bring it to the Sheraton. Save some time, huh? Plus, it may be a good idea for you not to go back to the Americana. As you reminded me once, she is dangerous."

We go back to the government building in the shadows of the Cathedral and settle ourselves into the worn-out offices of Estavan Rodrigues, El Jefe. We cannot find any logical connection between the arrival of Gorbachevsky and our mysterious woman. We also cannot find or come up with any reason that she should return to Puerto Vallarta. Sorting through all arrivals at Puerto Vallarta Airport and matching them with all new check-ins at all Puerto Vallarta hotels reveals nothing. Being an international tourist destination brings people from all over the world. Unusual names and unusual points of departure are not unusual.

Estavan forgets to tell Julio to go grab my luggage at the Americana, but I don't remind him. I'll go get it myself. It'll give me some time to think. I need that.

Ustad is completely freaked out of his mind. He is sure that they, although he is not sure who they are, will find him at the Hotel Vallarta. He chides himself, why did I tell him that? What should I do now? His mind is racing... I will just leave the hotel. I left nothing there. I'll find another hotel in the tourist zone. Nobody will notice me there. I can hide in the open. He remembers the tourist office gal recommended the Sheraton. She had said the Sheraton was more expensive. He didn't care. He just needed a place to rest. He hails a cab for the Sheraton Hotel.

Tomas Schultz of Wiesbaden, Germany departs the Puerto Vallarta Air terminal and hails a cab to the Sheraton Hotel. He does not know how or why, but his instincts have told him she will be there.

After stopping at an information booth, Juan Benevides, aka Alfonzo Benitez of Portabelo, Panama exits the Puerto Vallarta Air terminal six minutes after Tomas Schultz. He hails a cab to the Sheraton Hotel, thinking, this is where I will pick up her trail and settle the Mendez account with this girl, this Bolivian.

The Bolivian feels confident she has escaped the federales in the El Centro area of Puerto Vallarta. I must have been crazy to come back here, she thinks, this has become a personal vendetta. Not good.

Konrad Ilyavich decided after he left the bar at the Sheraton, to just hit a couple of local bars along the beach and enjoy himself. After a couple hours he is thoroughly drunk, completely satiated with food and drink, and completely lost as to where he is. So, he hails a cab to the Sheraton Hotel.

Estavan and I are laboriously going through what seems

like endless piles of paper when a few things jump out at me. First, Wiesbaden is just on the outskirts of Frankfurt, Germany, home of Brandt Industries. A Tomas Schultz of Wiesbaden, Germany has just arrived in Puerto Vallarta.

Second, Portobelo, Panama is a small town just south of Colon, home of the Mendez Cartel. Juan Benevides, of Portobelo, Panama has just arrived in Puerto Vallarta.

Third, Carlos Estrella claims to be a dock worker. There's currently two cruise liners in port, why is he not working?

"Estavan," I ask, "why isn't Carlos Estrella, the dock worker, not working when there are two cruise liners in port? Could he have been Mideastern, maybe Afghan?"

Estavan gives me a blank stare and slaps his forehead, "It was him! It was Marina's brother. We had him and let him go. Come, let's go. With luck we can still grab him at the Hotel Vallarta."

Of course, we are too late. The desk clerk tells us that Estrella went out earlier and never came back. We search his room and find nothing.

"I cannot believe I let this happen. I was consumed by the shooting I never even thought about your brother-in-law. We will find him. Let me drop you at the Sheraton, and I will pick you up in the morning at seven for your flight back to California."

"First of all, he is not my brother-in-law and secondly, I was just a little consumed by the shooting too. Now, do you think there is anything that we might yet do tonight?"

"I have my people all alerted, and if anything develops, you will be the first call that I make, be assured."

I bid goodnight to Estavan after he drops me off, and I fight the desire to have a nightcap at the bar. I stop at the main desk to pick up my key, and ask if I have any messages. While I wait, I watch. A fellow carrying a Lufthansa bag walks across the lobby, and he catches my eye. He has an eye patch over one eye, very blond hair, cut in a crew cut, and a matching handle-bar mustache. Definitely former military. He disappears into the elevator corridor.

The desk clerk tells me I have no messages.

As I turn around another man catches my eye—a sturdy built, Hispanic man with slicked-back hair and a Poncho Villa mustache. He has a scowling expression on his face and gives the appearance of someone you would not want to mess with.

I'm about to head for either the bar or the elevator when none other than the Hawaiian shirt guy comes staggering through the lobby and in a very loud voice asks the concierge if he could direct him to the bar.

I hear the sound of music coming from the outside patio area and succumb to the calling of a glass of red wine. The cast of characters I have just seen come through the lobby would fit well into an old double oh seven movie. I decide before my nightcap, I'll make a couple of calls. So I find a house phone and have the operator dial the number for me and charge it to my room. The first one is to Sasha. I know it's the middle of the night, actually very early morning in Germany. The phone rings, and I can tell someone picks it up.

"Sasha, it's Marc. Are you there?"

"For chrissake, Marc, do you know what time it is?"

"Sasha, I'm sorry. But I have a question that only you can answer."

"What kind of trouble are you in now, Marc?"

"None, I just want to know if you know anyone with this description. White male, late forties, six feet, muscular, body builder build, military crew cut and a patch over one eye."

"You have just described to a tee, Tomas Schultz, Werner Brandt's security chief. A man you do not want to mess with. Where are you, and where did you see him?"

"I'm in Puerto Vallarta, Mexico. What the hell would he be doing here?"

"I don't know, but they call him the 'custodian' because he cleans up after Werner Brandt. I'd be very careful. I know we can't talk about our other job, but things seem to be at a stall."

"OK, I'm headed back home tomorrow. I'll call and set up a meet. Bye."

"Bye, Marc, be careful."

The next call I make is to DFL Headquarters in Washington. I ask for the duty agent and fill him in on what is going on. I ask him if he can give me a refresher on the description of the main characters of the Mendez Cartel, Adolfo and Manuel, and also if he has a description of any of their muscle men. He gives me five descriptions, and the fifth fits perfectly with the man I just saw in the lobby, Alfonzo Benitez.

"Do you have any idea why he would be in Puerto Vallarta?" I ask.

The duty agent says, "I will call over to DEA to see if they have anything going on with this guy and call you back."

"Thanks, but call and leave a message with my office in Long Beach. I'll be back there tomorrow."

"Got it."

I slip into the bar and find a table in the shadows behind a huge, ornate column where I can see and hear the band, see the moonlight on the bay, and of course see anyone who enters. Hawaiian shirt is sitting at the bar.

I wonder what more could possibly go down here Puerto Vallarta, but I don't have to wonder long.

59

TOMAS SCHULTZ

APRIL 2, 1983

Tomas Schultz is a dangerous man. He grew up behind the wall in East Berlin and was recruited at the age of 12 to attend military school in a secret camp near the Polish border. By the time he reached 18, he had been fully indoctrinated into the Soviet military, even though they wore the uniform of the East German Republic. He was trained to be a sniper, a hand-to-hand combatant, proficient in all forms of firearms, and completely without fear of dying. A robot. He served as an East German border guard for his early years progressing up the ranks and was eventually recruited by the secret police. Not since the Nazis had an organization been so feared and disliked as the secret police. They brought back nightmare images of Hitler's *gestapo*. Tomas Schultz thrived and rose through the ranks and was headed for a senior command position when an incident at the infamous Checkpoint Charlie derailed his career and sent him into retirement.

It was to be a simple exchange of spies. Bring your man,

and we will bring ours. They would meet in between the West Berlin gate and the East Berlin gate, better known as Checkpoint Charlie to make the exchange. Everyone would go home happy. That is until one spy, Wolfgang Gerber, held by the American and British agents overpowered his escorts, somehow producing a simple lead pencil and lunging himself at the East German escort, Tomas Schultz, yelling, "You traitorous bastard, may you die in hell!" Tomas Schultz had forced Gerber to spy for him by threatening him and his family. When Gerber had been caught by the American and British agents, Schultz had Gerber's wife and daughter sent to prison.

A melee ensued and seven people died. Two West Germans, two Brits, two Soviets, and one East German. Tomas Schultz lost an eye and was retired.

Like most deaths that occurred near or on the wall, they never made the newspaper, but there were those who made it their business to know about activity along the wall. Werner Brandt was one of those people. Through his contacts in East Berlin, Brandt hired Schultz at a considerable expense less than a month after he retired. What Brandt hired was a man who was not only grateful but dedicated to his master and would do anything he was asked.

The job Schultz had been asked to do by Brandt had been done. Bergraf was dead.

Brandt was very satisfied with the results but now requested that the assassin be eliminated as well. Schultz didn't know how he was going to find this person and had no leads as to where to look for her. A thorough search on the island of Mykonos came up empty. He kept on digging and found that someone fitting her description was wanted for murder and mayhem in Puerto Vallarta, Mexico. He decided he would see if he could pick up her trail in Puerto Vallarta.

And so, Tomas Schultz arrives in Puerto Vallarta to perform his custodial duties, as they are needed.

60

ALFONZO BENITEZ

APRIL 2, 1983

Alfonzo Benitez grew up in the slums near Panama City, Panama. Survival of the most fit prevailed. As with almost all the young boys in his barrio, they became members of a gang. Infighting was worse than fighting with rival gangs. Alfonzo became one of the youngest to lead his gang when, on a fateful night, four of the older leaders of his gang were killed by a rival gang. Alfonzo immediately stepped up to the front and called upon the gang members to appoint him as the new leader. He was almost a unanimous choice. Only one member voted no. Alfonzo called him out and congratulated him for his courage. He then shot him dead.

Realizing his small gang was a dead end, Alfonzo sought to expand, and he eventually united almost all the gangs in the outlying areas of Panama City.

To make money, one had to be in the drug business but Alfonzo had no such connections other than the local street peddler who would disappear whenever approached by his gang. He was not able to find the source. He did not know who the source was. Try as he might to wiggle his way into the trade, he reached a dead end. And then, a break. A local, street-corner drug peddler was robbed and beaten. His backup, and driver of the supply truck, came to his rescue, which he was not supposed to do. His orders were to just drive away, but he didn't.

Three of Alfonzo's boys came to the rescue of the rescuer and took possession of the supply truck. It contained more than two-million-dollars' worth of drugs and three bags of cash.

Alfonzo had the supply truck driven to a warehouse and then waited for news that the peddler had survived and had reported to his bosses what had happened. Alfonzo then came out from the shadows and revealed that his men had in fact, saved the lives of the dealer and the driver of the supply truck, and that he had the supply truck in his warehouse. The owner of the truck, through an intermediator, of course, asked what Alfonzo wanted for the return of the truck and its contents.

Alfonzo told him he thought it would be a good idea for the owner of the truck to meet with Alfonzo, and other than that, he wanted nothing. A meeting was set in the seaside village of Portobelo. Alfonzo said the location of the truck would be revealed right after his meeting with the truck's owner. The other side reluctantly agreed.

Alfonzo had never seen such a palatial estate. He thought, who are these people, and how do I become one of them? He was ushered into a lush courtyard featuring a cabana and a table and four chairs, beside an Olympic-size pool.

His thoughts were interrupted when he heard, in Spanish, of course, "Welcome, Senor Benitez. I am Adolfo, and this is my brother Manuel. I believe you have acquired a truck which belongs to our organization. I want to thank you on behalf of my brother and I, and all the members of our organization. Please sit down, and let me offer you some refreshment."

The conversation between the three never approached the subject of drugs, but instead, it mostly concerned the life of Alfonzo. Alfonzo does not realize this until, out of nowhere, Adolfo asks, "What would it take for you to come and work with us here in Portobelo? We are well aware of your reputation in Panama City, and we need someone of your repute to handle security for our organization. An incident, like what just happened, can open us up to only more such problems. We need someone to make sure this does not happen again and, if it should, to handle the reprisals. Could you do this, Alfonzo?"

And so, as Alfonzo now walks across the lobby of the Sheraton to the elevator, he is thinking about his past and how he got to this point in his life. He does not notice anybody else—a serious lapse for a security guy, for he is noticed by at least four other people.

I am enjoying a few moments by myself when I notice a man with a Poncho Villa mustache walk across the lobby. I also notice a bulge under his jacket. This guy is carrying a gun.

61

THE GATHERING

April 2, 1983

Ustad is totally confused and scared out of his mind. He is unable to decide if it is just a coincidence that the American is in Puerto Vallarta. He is not convinced that Mohammed has not tracked him here. He is completely lost in his own thoughts as the cab pulls up in front of the Sheraton. He is almost out of the cab when he notices a woman get out of the cab in front of him. She turns and appears to look right at him. She has unreal eyes. Even though they are covered by rose-colored glasses, they seem to penetrate through the glass like a laser. Those eyes are frightening and downright scary. He sits for a moment and watches her enter the Sheraton. He sits back in the cab and tells the driver to take him to the marina. He decides this is not a good place for him to stay.

As The Bolivian gets out of the cab she quickly dismisses the bell hop, "I've already checked in," and heads for the outside walkway down to the beach and the oceanside entrance to the Sheraton. Keeping to the shadows, she edges to the back side of the outdoor bar where the band is trying to play country music. She scans the patio bar area and sees not one but three people who interest her. The loud-mouth Konrad Ilyavich is sitting at the bar in his subtle Hawaiian shirt. Who he was hired by remains a question in her mind. Doesn't make any difference, he is history.

Tomas Schultz is sitting on the other side of the patio listening to the band. She did her homework on the Bergraf hit and knew it was Schultz who contracted her for Brandt. Schultz being here can be for only one reason, Brandt wants to close the loop.

The third person is the American.

She ponders the events leading up to her coming back to Puerto Vallarta and of course, these fools have come to Puerto Vallarta because of the fiasco surrounding my last trip here and the trip before it. They are here looking for me. I should have never come back. As she decides on how to deal with the Russian, the German and the American, another unexpected guest walks in and sits down at the bar. Alfonzo Benitez in the flesh.

I am sort of listening to the country band and watching the three guys I mentioned when I hear the unmistakable click of a switchblade knife. I feel a very sharp point in my rib cage, and I hear, "Do not move and listen to me very carefully, Mr. American. You are a dead man. I know you were following me tonight. You will stop. Why will you stop? Because if you don't, that bumbling cop you fumble around with will soon die and very painfully. Did I mention his family will die with him?"

A sharp blow to the back of my head causes me to collapse over my table and sends my drink, the lamp, and the glass candleholder crashing to the floor with me on top of it, and it probably caused quite a commotion in the bar. I don't really know because I'm knocked out. I come to and I'm being carefully rolled over by someone. It's Estavan, and through blurred vision I scan the crowd and I see the Hawaiian shirt, the one-eyed guy with a patch, and the Poncho Villa mustache guy all looking at me.

Estavan asks, "Marc, are you OK? Show me two fingers."

I do, and he asks "Do you remember anything? Who did this to you?"

"How long have I been out?"

"Only a couple of minutes. I was walking into the lobby when I heard the commotion."

"Estavan, it was her. She came up behind me and stuck a knife in my ribs and told me to stop following her, or I was a dead man. She also threatened you and your family. We have somehow got to find her and take this woman off the streets."

"Marc, you should not worry about such things now. You have a serious head wound, and you may have a concussion."

"Estavan, there are also three other people in bar who are nothing but serious trouble."

"Three others. Who?"

"First of all, Gorbachevsky. He's sitting at the bar and by the looks of it passed out drunk. Have you figured out what the hell is he doing here? Secondly, a German, Tomas Schultz, Chief of Security for Werner Industries. He is also at the bar on the other side."

"Werner Industries? Who are they, and why should it concern me?"

"I think this mysterious woman we can't catch was contracted by Werner to assassinate a man on the island of Mykonos. I called my office, and they told me Schultz is a dangerous man, known as the 'custodian' because he cleans up for Werner Brandt.

And thirdly, Alfonzo Benitez of the Mendez Cartel. He is also at the bar. I'm sure he contracted this mysterious woman we are chasing to kill Romano and his thugs. I don't have proof of this, but it fits. I also think that Jorge Padilla was hired by Benitez, and I would bet the bank that this woman we can't catch did the hit on Jorge."

"Marc, are you sure this blow on the head is not causing you to spin some dreams here. That's a lot of speculation."

"Maybe the blow on the head sorted everything out, Estavan."

"If that is the case, I'm calling in all my men, and we're going to take all these people into custody, and then sort it out. I'm going to have my family brought into the office, and I've got to try and close the loop on this woman. Got any idea what she was wearing or any description we don't already have?"

"I never got a chance to look before she hit me."

It is suddenly dark. The lights go out in the entire bar, patio, and lobby. Across the room amongst all the shouts and muffled questions, I hear a groan, and less than ten seconds later, two, quick gunshots and then two more. The emergency generator apparently kicks on, and the lights come back on.

Across the patio, the man with the Poncho Villa mustache lies on the floor with a knife sticking in his neck and a pool of blood gathering around him. At the bar, the Hawaiian shirt is slumped over the bar with two wounds visible in his back and a widening blotch of red spreading across his shirt.

On the other side of the bar, the man with a patch over his eye lies on his back with two bullet holes in his forehead.

During the pandemonium following the guns shots, The Bolivian loses herself in the throng of people rushing across the lobby and out the main entrance of the Sheraton, she finds a cab, but before she can close the door a man and a woman jump in with her. Before she can say anything, they tell the cab driver to take them to the marina. She says nothing, and they go to the marina. They request to get out at the south entrance, and she requests the north. After the couple gets out, she lets the cab driver go another two blocks, then asks him to stop, and she gets out.

She thinks, what to do now? In her wildest dreams she did not think she would be able to eliminate all three at once. I should also have finished off the American, she worries. But as she stands in the shadows of the marina condos, she knows she must now leave while the leaving is good. She turns to go find another cab at the north entrance but accidentally runs into Ustad and sends him sprawling on the sidewalk. She starts to apologize when he blurts out, "It's you. I saw you shoot him. I recognize you."

As he starts to get up, she delivers a kick to his head followed by a kick to the ribs. She flicks out her switchblade and grabs him by the hair. As she tries to jab the knife into his neck, he suddenly spins on his knees and, with his hands locked in a two-handed fist, delivers a blow to her abdomen, knocking the wind out of her and sending the knife flying into the shadows. She doubles over, and he delivers another blow to the back of her neck. She falls to the sidewalk, barely conscious and struggling to breath.

Muttering in a language she does not understand, he delivers two kicks to her groin and chest. He then reaches down and grabs her by the hair and spits in her face saying, "Infidel bitch!"

A group of people suddenly come around the corner of the building. Ustad lets her fall on the sidewalk and runs into the shadows. The people see the woman on the sidewalk and gather around her asking if they can help and should they call the police.

"No, I am fine. I just tripped and took a bad fall. I am fine."

One of the men asks, "Did I see someone running away from you?"

"Ah, yes, he is the reason I tripped. He frightened me. But, I am fine."

"You have a cut on your forehead. Are you sure we should not call for some help?"

"No, I am fine. Thank you, I am fine. My condo is right around the corner."

A rare occurrence... bested by an amateur... I'm getting careless. I need to get some rest, and then I should go home, she thinks... but, the American is not going to let this rest. He is going to have to be dealt with.

She mingles among the throng of tourists strolling along the marina until she gets to the north entrance where she picks up her pace and heads towards the Marriott Casa Magna. As she passes the Benihana Japanese Restaurant, she fails to notice a solitary figure in the shadows.

Ustad is still in a state of confusion, but some things are becoming clearer. He thinks to himself, none of this has anything to do with Mohammed, and it all has to do with Marina's infidel lover.

He ponders, who is this woman who shot the policeman, and what is her connection to the American? She is a stone-cold killer. She could possibly take care of the American and Marina for him. Then, I would be back in Mohammed's good graces. I need to find her and make a deal. I'll give her everything I know about Marina and her lover. She will kill them for me.

He can't believe his eyes. She is walking right past him into the Marriott. She walks up to the front desk and briefly talks to the desk clerk, then she turns and disappears towards the elevator corridor.

Ustad walks quickly up to the front desk and tells the clerk that he needs to leave a message for the woman who just left. He explains that he doesn't know her name but that she left her shopping bag at the restaurant where he works and that she had mentioned she was staying at the Marriott. He tells the desk clerk he will wait in the lobby bar while the message is delivered. He writes out a note, "I know the American's name. He lives in Long Beach, California with his lover who killed my brother. I am the man who saw you shoot the policeman."

As I sit and watch Estavan and his men go to work on the crime scene, my head throbs. Estavan insists I go to my room and stay there until he picks me up in the morning for the flight back to California. I offer no resistance and head for the elevators. I am dead tired and six a.m. is going to come too soon.

The phone rings. Had I even fallen asleep? I roll over and pick it up, "Hello."

"Marc, sorry to wake you, but I thought you would like to know I have come up with a name for our mysterious woman. Josefina Archetta."

"Do you have her, Estavan?"

"No. She has disappeared into thin air. I am sure, as I am sure you are, too, that the name is just an alias. She probably has a number of IDs and passports. I have already alerted the airport authorities to detain any lone female travelers who even remotely resemble our favorite killer."

"You think she would try to leave Puerto Vallarta by air? Kinda risky, don't you think? What about by car to Guadalajara? Or, even by boat out of the harbor?"

"I agree, amigo, air would be risky. Should she choose this, I will have her. Car, to Guadalajara? I have already put in place checkpoints on the only roads to Guadalajara. The only ferry boat out of Puerto Vallarta goes to Cabo San Lucas. I have already called my cousin, el jefe de federales in Cabo San Lucas, Aljandro Jesus Rodrigues, and he is anxiously awaiting the next ferry."

I think to myself, I have seriously underestimated Estavan Rodrigues and the expertise of the Mexican authorities. I'm going to feel a little better flying home. Not a whole lot, but a little better.

"Estavan, you continue to amaze and impress me. I'm wide awake now, so I'm going to come down to the lobby and find some more alcohol or coffee."

"Go for the coffee, gringo. I'll buy."

"What, are you really Mexican?"

"On second thought, gringo, you're on an expense account. I'll have the most expensive coffee drink the coffee shop makes. Happy now?"

"That's what I was going to offer you."

"I'm sure. I should have Florentina here to help me translate."

"Estavan, you know I am only having fun with you, right?"

"Gringo, you are so far behind, you think you are in front. Now, my coffee, please."

"OK, I'll be right down. Go ahead and order the same for me."

I walk into the coffee bar, and Estavan is waiting with two cups of something. Mine tastes wonderfully decadent, and Estavan is enjoying his. I think actually because I bought it.

I have thoroughly enjoyed this man's company, his family, and his professionalism. Again, I think to myself how I have really underestimated the ability and capability of his office. As we are enjoying our coffee and making idle talk about him bringing his family to visit and me bringing Marina down to visit, I suddenly remember a bag I left at the Fiesta Americana. It only contained some personal items, but I thought as long as I was up, I might as well go retrieve it.

Estavan thinks I should leave it, suggesting he could have one of his men pick it up, but he relents when I say it would be useless for me to go back to the room and try to sleep.

I would like to just walk over to the Fiesta Americana, but it is late, and so I take a cab. I have the cab drop me off a block from the hotel. It's late but the cafes and bars are all open and busy. It is a relaxing and peaceful walk. Listening to the chatter of the sidewalk cafes and the relaxing music coming from those cafes is worth the trip to Vallarta.

What happens next is not.

62

A NEW PARTNERSHIP

April 2, 1983

The Bolivian had hardly entered her room when a knock at the door startles her. Having taken a gun from Alfonzo Benitez, she holds it behind her back and hugs the wall as she inches towards the door to look out the peep hole. It's a young woman in a Marriott blouse with a name tag, Alicia.

"What is it?" she asks.

"I have a message for you, *Senorita*."

The Bolivian opens the door and is handed an envelope. She tips the girl and rips open the envelope. She is shocked. It's from the man who saw her shoot the policeman. He knows who the American is and where he lives. This is too good, too easy, there has to be a catch. The note says that the man will be waiting by a house phone in the lobby, number 15,and that she should call within the hour or he will be gone. She makes sure no one is watching and closes the door.

Ustad is as nervous as a man awaiting the gas chamber.

He thinks, she could be watching me right now and waiting for the right moment to shoot me. He picked house-phone number 15 because it is in a secluded end of the lobby where he can stand hidden in the shadows while awaiting it to ring, which it suddenly does.

He steps out of the shadows and picks up the phone, *"Buenos noches."*

He hears, "I don't know who you are, but I know you are not Mexican because you speak lousy Spanish, so let us dispense with this nonsense and get to the reason you sent me the note. Why should I want to know where the American lives? What is your interest? Why should I not hunt you down and kill you?"

"I think you were intending to shoot the American and accidentally shot the policeman. I don't know why you want to shoot the American, but I want you to shoot him because his lover, my whore of a sister killed my brother. If you kill me, you will probably find it difficult to find the American."

"All very interesting. What is it you want from all of this?"

"I want to see the American and his whore dead."

"You don't want money?"

"No, I want revenge for my brother."

"Do you have a name for this American and his whore?"

"Marc Ryder and Marina Noor."

"So give me the information I need to find them."

"I will give it to you one week from today in Long Beach, California."

"Long Beach, California? You want me to travel to the United States? You want me to risk that travel before you give me the information? Why should I do this?"

"Because Mexico is going to soon become a very dangerous place for you."

"Really? And why is that going to happen?"

"Because if you turn me down, I will hang up and call the federales and tell them where you are and that I am the one who saw you shoot the policeman."

"You are close to being a dead man walking. I know what you look like, and I would have no trouble finding you. It is only because you are not a threat that I allow you to talk to me this way. Give me the details on how you will pass the information that I need once I get to Long Beach."

"You will call this number, 213-931-5869, and you will be furnished with the address of the American."

She repeats the number and the line goes dead.

She thinks, You too will soon be dead you amateur. She then picks up the phone again and calls the front desk telling them she must check-out tonight, a family emergency.

The desk clerk replies, "No problem, Senorita Archetta. May we call you transport to the airport?"

"No, thank you, I have already arranged transport."

"Goodbye then, and thank you for staying at the Marriott Casa Magna."

She grabs her small bag and wipes down all the surfaces that she may have touched with a damp cloth. Slipping out the door and down to the stairs, she heads to lobby bar and finds a table in the shadows. It's a typical tropical evening, and the smell of the tropical plants is relaxing. I'll just have a martini for the road, she thinks.

The phone at the Marriott front desk rings, and the clerk answers, "Good evening, Marriott. How may I help you?"

"This is Estavan Rodrigues, El Jefe, Puerto Vallarta Policia Federales. I am looking at your check-in list for the last three days, and I see a reservation for a Josefina Archetta. Was she with someone, or was she alone?"

"It appears she was traveling alone."

"Please give me her room number. I need to speak with her tonight."

"She was in room eight-seventy-eight, but she checked out about an hour ago."

"Checked out? Where did she go?"

"I have no idea. I offered to arrange transport, but she said she already had it arranged."

"Do not let anyone go into room eight-seventy-eight. I am sending over two of my officers."

"As you wish, El Jefe."

Ustad is proud of himself. He will call his cousin in the morning and let him know what he has done. He thinks, I will tell him to give her the address for Marc Ryder, and she will take care of them. He decides to wait near the entry courtyard and watch for her to come out. After a few minutes and she doesn't come out, Ustad decides to go find a room for the night. He hails a cab and asks what hotel he would recommend. The cab driver first says the Sheraton. Ustad responds no, somewhere else.

"How about the Fiesta Americana. It's very nice and not too expensive."

"Take me there so I can look at it."

The driver takes Ustad up the street to the Fiesta Americana and Ustad likes what he sees and asks to get out.

OK, I need go over to the Fiesta Americana and get my bag.

You know the feeling. You are not tired. You feel fine. Then, all of a sudden, it hits you. You are so tired you can hardly stand up. All you want to do is get into bed and sleep.

My senses are all messed up. As I pass a steak house, I'm thinking, when and what was the last thing I had to eat? I check, they're closed. OK, focus here, let's go to the concierge and get my bag.

I am surprised there are no cabs in front of the Americana.

The entrance to the Americana is a horseshoe driveway, about 100 yards up to the entrance and 100 yards back down to the street. The bellhop explains that for security reasons they do not allow cabs in their horseshoe entry after midnight.

That sure sounded reasonable, and I walk down to the entrance of the horseshoe loop, past the steak house, and to the street. Out of the darkness, I'm slammed to the ground.

I should have stayed at the Sheraton.

63

ESTAVAN

April 2, 1983

The phone rings, and Florentina Alvarez-Rodrigues answers in Spanish.

"Florentina, please, go find you mother and get her on the phone."

"Papa, you sound upset. What is it?"

"Florentina, just go find your mother and get her on the phone, now."

A moment later, Claudia, Estavan's wife of twenty years, answers, "What is wrong, Estavan? Florentina said you were upset and you sound very upset."

"Claudia, listen to me very carefully, and please, do as I say. We have a killer loose on the streets of Puerto Vallarta, a female killer, and she has threatened me and my family. I am sending a car to pick up you and Florentina and bring you here to the office. I want you to stay here in the visiting officers' quarters until we have this person in custody or she is dead. She is very dangerous."

"Why can't we just go to my fathers?"

"Because, I can't protect you there. Do you understand?"

"No, but we will do as you say."

"Thank you, Claudia."

Estavan returns to the bar area of the hotel which is now a beehive of activity. He calls to his chief crime scene investigator "Raul, have you come up with anything?"

"No, El Jefe. It seems no one but your American friend had any contact with the woman and everyone was throwing themselves on the floor when the shooting started. The victim at the table by the door died from a knife to the neck, and he appeared to have been carrying a gun of some sort, but we have not found it. I would guess the victim at the bar and the victim on the other side of the bar were both shot with the same gun, most likely taken from the first victim. Shell casings we found are 38 caliber. No way to know what type of gun other than it had to have been an automatic pistol."

"Anything from the outside investigators?"

"No leads at all. Everyone was too busy just trying to keep from getting shot."

"OK, keep at it. I'm still checking on all hotel check-in's for the last four days. Not a lot of single female travelers, and I've got a couple of names that look good, so maybe we'll get lucky."

"We're due for some luck."

64

BILLIARDS ANYONE?

APRIL 2, 1983

Second Street which cuts through the heart of Belmont Shore, the hip section of Long Beach, is only a block from the little house that Marina and I call home. A spacious, palatial mansion of about 1,200 square feet. It is Marina's domain, and decorated in a fashion that I'm sure would have pleased Czar Nicholas or more likely Pancho Villa. I would bring home trinkets from my much too frequent trips to the Soviet Union, and she would give them all away to her best customers at Joe Jacks. Whatever.

Marina and I had settled into a very comfortable life in Belmont Shore. We enjoyed walking up to Second Street several times a week, and after dining at one of the numerous eating establishments on Second, we would adjourn to Belmont Billiards and shoot some pool. My friend Bobby is the manager, and we would get into some serious money games—loser buys the next 25-cent game and Jagermeister shots.

Everybody wanted Marina as their partner. Not only

because she is unbelievably good at billiards, but she is also a very affectionate and beautiful partner. She delighted in teaming with Bobby and thrashing me and my partner, whoever it was, at eight-ball. I always felt comfortable leaving town and knowing Marina could wander up to Belmont Billiards. God forbid anyone make a move on her. Bobby and his friends, Tommy, Ketch, and Burr Head were like her personal Iron Curtain.

Nevertheless, her attempted kidnapping shook up my sense of security, and I was glad to be heading home tomorrow. This trip to Puerto Vallarta was not what I expected it to be as I had not found Ustad, only someone who might have been Ustad. The mysterious woman had again created havoc for Estavan, and I think he was going to be very happy to put me on a plane bound for California, or anywhere for that matter.

65

AMERICANA MISTAKE

APRIL 2, 1983

The Fiesta Americana is just north of the Sheraton along the ocean. It is much more than a casual walk, so I hail a cab and have him drop me off on the street leading to the Americana. I thought I might as well enjoy myself and soak up the ambiance of Puerto Vallarta. I wished Marina was with me to enjoy this romantic spot.

I am lost in my own thoughts and not looking for or paying attention to anyone. I'm just another late night stroller.

The street which leads to the Americana is more or less like a tunnel because of the large trees lining the street. There are no street lights and the only illumination comes from landscape lighting to accentuate the scenery.

I head across the street towards the entrance and driveway to the Americana. I enter the hotel and check in with the concierge, telling her that I left a bag in my room. After giving her my name and room number, she calls for the bell hop. She tells me to wait at the lobby bar and the bell hop will retrieve my bag for me.

Sitting on the far side of the lobby, in an overstuffed chair in the shadows, sipping a dirty martini, The Bolivian almost drops her drink.

I can't believe it's him. What is he doing here? This just might save me a trip to California, she thinks. She watches as the bell hop brings him a bag and he turns and walks out towards the lobby exit. He doesn't appear to be in a hurry, nor does he appear to be looking for anyone. She waits for him to go out the door and gets up to follow.

The bell hop brings me my bag and asks me to check it and make sure it is mine and that all my belongings are there. I do and thank him. He asks if he can call me a cab, and I tell him I'm going to walk down the street and maybe have a late-night cocktail before I retire. He tells me Carlos and Charlie's has a nice band and generous cocktails.

Standing outside in the shadows, just over the wooden bridge by the pond in front of the steakhouse, Ustad is trying to make up his mind what to do. He is about to leave when he sees the American come out of the Americana and head right in his direction. He decides he will take care of this right now. I will send this infidel to his death, and Mohammed will be proud of me, he thinks.

I have just crossed over the wooden bridge in front of steakhouse, and I'm now out of sight of the front of the Americana when I am tackled and thrown to the ground. I am being pummeled by my attacker's fists. It's dark, and I can't see who I am fighting, but I get in a couple of good punches to the groin. I'm on my back, so I fake a twist to the left and roll to the right. He throws a haymaker punch at my head, and as I duck I grab his left hand. I get a good hold on his hand and fingers. I swing around under his arm, holding onto his fingers, and I feel and hear a couple of pops and a scream of pain. He screams at me in a foreign language, and I suddenly realize I am fighting with Marina's brother Ustad.

I grab for his hair, but I get his cap only, giving him a chance to regroup and hit me with a swivel kick, which catches me square in the chest. I tumble over backwards into some shrubbery, and he comes at me with a kick to my groin. I manage to block the kick and grab hold of his foot. The shrubbery has given me just enough leverage to spin to my left and throw him to the ground.

As I get up, I stomp on his ankle and hear a pop and scream of pain. I fall on him with my knee and knock the wind out of him. I roll him over as he is screaming and get him in a hammer lock. I tell him I'm going to yell for help and that I will break his arm if he doesn't stop struggling.

He stops, and I catch my breath and am about to yell for help when I feel something cold pressing against my right temple. There are no words to describe the feeling of a gun barrel pressed against your head. My mind is spinning trying to process the feeling of helplessness. There is no time to plan my next move. The time for the bullet to travel down the gun barrel into my brain cannot be computed. I'm a dead man. Stall, I have got to stall. I say "OK, you have me. What is it you want?"

"Your life, Americano. You are not going to be so lucky this time. I do not know who that animal you have pinned underneath you is, and I don't care. You are both going to hell tonight."

"Wait, at least tell me who you are."

"I am your worst nightmare."

"You must have a name?"

"You first, American."

"Marc Ryder."

"Pleased to meet you, Marc Ryder, soon-to-be-dead government agent. I am the Bolivian."

"That's not your name."

"Where you are going it will not matter."

My life is passing before my eyes. I'm trying to come up with something to stall her when I feel the pressure of the gun against my temple disappear and hear two shots fire in quick succession. The gun has a silencer, but it's still loud next to my ear. Ustad is obviously the recipient of those two shots as he goes limp under me. I then again feel the barrel against my temple, "Bye-bye, Marc Ryder."

Click. Click.

Nothing. The gun is empty. Before I can react, she hits me in the head with something.

Sudden, quick pain explodes in my head, and I fade into darkness.

Estavan is yelling, "Damn it, Ryder, wake up."

"Come on Ryder don't you dare die on me. Come on Ryder, I am not going to put you on that plane unless you talk to me."

"Come on Ryder, damn it! Wake up!"

The Bolivian can't believe what just happened. She silently screams at herself... I can't believe I didn't check my gun beforehand! Maybe I hit the American hard enough to kill him? I should have used the first two shots on him! At least, the meddling scum who smelled like he slept in a barn is dead. He will tell no one what he knew.

What to do now, she wonders. The fight has caused a commotion, and people are yelling for the police. If the American is still alive, he now has to be eliminated. I will go to California, deal with the American, and then go home to Paros and just stay there.

Oh my God! Oh my God! I open my eyes and God looks just like Estavan. God yells at me, "What the hell happened here, Ryder? I got another dead body, and again you're right next to it. Where did you get the gun, and where is it? Is this my witness to the other shooting?"

Oh my God I'm not dead it's Estavan.

"Estavan, it was her again. This has to be Ustad underneath me. He jumped me as I was leaving the Americana.

We fought, and I had him under control when she came up behind me and put a gun to my head. She then turned the gun on Ustad and fired two shots to his head. She put the gun back up against my head and said bye-bye and pulled the trigger. The gun was empty, so I think she hit me with it and knocked me out."

"I'm going to start calling you, El Gato, although you have more lives than a cat."

"Great, just great. Just what I need, another nickname."

"Would you rather use your other nickname? DFL?"

"Oh, for chrissake's, Estavan. Gimme a break."

"What you need, my friend, is to stay at my office until I put you on the plane tomorrow. Don't even think about protesting. You can give a statement to us when we get back to my office, and you can keep Florentina company."

"Can't you just put me in solitary confinement?"

"Not a chance. You need to be punished."

66

ON THE RUN

APRIL 3, 1983

The Bolivian is beside herself. She is lamenting to herself. I am losing it. I cannot believe what just happened. I've got to take a chance and go to the airport and get my bag out of the locker. Then I'll head for Bucerias and out of this place. Why did I ever come back here?

She is lucky and quickly finds a cab and tells the driver to take her to the airport. She pulls her cap low and hopes he does not get a good look at her. He drops her at the departure entrance, and she quickly finds her way to the huge bank of storage lockers on the lower level.

She locates her locker and takes her bag to the ladies' room where she finds an empty stall on the far end. She pulls out some Nike running shoes, black tights, a gray short-sleeve sweater, a reversible jacket, a brunette wig, lightly shaded glasses, and a small clutch style purse. The purse contains three passports, French, Dutch and Canadian, all in different names. She quickly changes, peeks out to see there is no one there, and slips out the door, stuffing her discarded clothes in the trash.

She hails a cab and is about to request to be taken to Bucerias, but she changes her mind and tells him Galleria Vallarta. It is only a short ride, and although she knows the shops are closed or about to be closed, she tells the cabbie to hurry. She hops out at the west entrance and watches the cab leave. Immediately, she hails another cab and requests to be taken to Bucerias El Centro, the center of town.

Thirty minutes later, she hops out of the cab in Bucerias El Centro and hails yet another cab to the airport. She is somewhat disappointed when she arrives and sees the flight schedule on the wall. She will have to wait at least four hours for the next flight to Guadalajara. The building is more or less deserted. She goes to the restroom and removes her wig and puts on a California Angels baseball cap.

She decides to stay in the restroom for at least 45 minutes. When time is up she goes out to the ticket counter and finds it closed. Now the building is completely deserted. She finds a dark corner where she curls up to await the morning ticket clerk.

She is awakened by voices. The ticket counter is open. Still wearing her California Angels baseball cap, she purchases two roundtrip tickets to Guadalajara, in the name of Jose and Juanita Lopez.

Three hours later, she is standing at the Mexicana Airlines ticket counter in Guadalajara, purchasing a ticket to Tijuana in the name of Lupita Manueloza.

I am exhausted but too tired to sleep. I feel like I have

been beaten with a baseball bat. It's after midnight, so I tell Estavan that I'm just going to go to the airport. I'll find something to eat and then go to my gate and wait. Estavan looks at me and says, "You are going to go with me back to my office. You will stay there until I take you to the airport in the morning. I will have something brought into my office for you to eat. I'm sure Florentina is starving. Do not even think about protesting and do not argue with me, or I shall put you under the protective custody of my daughter until I dump your sorry butt on that plane. *Comprende*?"

"Oh, for chrissake's, must you always be so dramatic?"

"Special Agent Ryder, I have already forgotten how many dead bodies you left me on your last trip here, but right now, I'm counting four on this trip. So, I'll be as god-damned dramatic as I please."

Whoa! I don't believe I've ever heard Estavan use such strong language, at least not in English.

"Sorry, Estavan. I apologize, and you are right."

"Thank you. And, no offense, but I will personally escort you onto that plane, not because I fear you would try to get off, but to make sure another dead body doesn't pop up before you take off."

"Oh, for chrissake."

Back to his office fortress we go, where I am wined, dined, and entertained by Florentina until I fall asleep sitting up in a swivel chair behind someone's desk. I wake up some time later and find myself covered with a comfy blanket and Florentina curled up on the couch in front of me. The lights are out in the office we're in, but there is a lot of activity in the office adjacent to us.

I get up and walk out to the other office where I am greeted by Estavan's number one technical service man, "*Hola, Senor* Ryder."

"*Hola*, Julio. Have you come up with any good leads?"

"Nothing, absolutely nothing. We have no idea what name she is using, so we are basically looking for single women travelers. We have nothing for the morning flights, and there was nothing out of Bucerias either."

"What time am I being taken to the airport? Wait, Bucerias? There's an airport in Bucerias? Do they have flights to the US?"

"No, it caters to only local or regional destinations."

"OK, so we'll be leaving soon?"

"Estavan should be here momentarily. Help yourself to come coffee."

Four hours later I am on the ground at Long Beach Airport.

I breeze through customs, immigration, and passport control. Nothing like having a diplomatic passport.

I exit the terminal and fall into the arms of Marina, "I want to hear the whole story, start to finish. Don't leave out the gory details, and I know there are some."

"OK, but can we go somewhere and have a cheeseburger and a cold drink while I tell you? Why is it I always crave cheeseburgers when I'm in Mexico?"

"We will stop and pick up a cheeseburger and then we are going to go straight home, and you can tell me the story after I mix you a dirt martini, boy toy."

"Dirty, not dirt, but I love it when you talk dirty."

"You ain't heard nuttin' yet, boy toy."

How my beautiful Afghan has changed. Got to be time spent at Belmont Billiards. I'm gonna have a talk with Bobby, Ketch, and Burr Head.

Mexicana flight 3637 from Guadalajara arrives at Tijuana International Airport. The Bolivian does not have to deal with customs or immigration or passport control. She is still in Mexico. Now, getting out of Mexico into the United States is another matter. She exits the terminal and sees a line of cabs and spots the one she wants—San Diego Cab Company. Hopefully, they can get her to California. She gets in the cab and says, "San Diego, *por favor.*"

As they get in line with hundreds of other cars headed for the US Border checkpoint, Tijuana, Mexico, the cab driver tries to assure her they are in an express lane for commercial vehicles. She reminds him they haven't moved in twenty minutes.

"*Senorita,* these things always happen when there is an alert, we should be moving soon."

"Alert. What are you talking about? What kind of alert?"

"Do you see the lights above the roadway? Each one means a varying level of alertness. The amber light is now lit, which is level two."

"What are they looking for?"

"I am not sure. We will find out when we get to the border officer."

She decides she needs a new plan to cross the border.

"I understand. What is your name?"

"Manuel Ortega, *Senorita.*"

"Manuel, I must use the restroom, can we pull over?"

"I cannot, but there are restrooms two lanes over. I will turn on my cab light so you know where to come back and find me."

She hands him a twenty-dollar bill and grabbing her bag, slips out of the cab, and pretends to trip and fall but is only pulling her baseball cap on while smoothly removing the brunette wig.

Jesus Alvarez Trujillo has worked for the Mexican Border Authority for almost 15 years and is one of the senior officers. Unlike most senior officers who spend their days sitting behind a table and attending to "official" business at Manuel's Cantina around the corner, Jesus likes to get his hands dirty and get involved. The amber-level alert has caught his attention, and he goes into the main office to have a look at the details of the alert.

"Pedro, let me have a look at the alert you just received."

"It's pretty vague, chief. We were furnished with two names, but we turned up nothing on our computer. It's a woman with only a vague description, but she is wanted for at least four and possibly as many as eight murders in Puerto Vallarta. The San Diego Field Office of the FBI, the DEA, and the US Consulate office in Tijuana are checking their computers as well."

"Keep your eyes and ears open, and stay at your post. Immediately notify me of anything remotely connected. This woman is a one-woman crime wave."

Another officer rushes into the room, "Chief, we just had a cab driver report that he had a woman passenger get out of his cab after he explained the alert, claiming she had to use the restroom. The description he gave could fit the woman we are looking for."

"Where did he let her out?"

"He was in lane eight about 200 meters from the border."

"Get Captain Mendoza of the Policia Federales on the line and tell him what you just told me. Pedro, call Sergeant Arenivas and have him bring his SWAT squad and meet me over on the other side of lane ten near that restroom. Tell him I want them now."

Getting across lanes nine and ten are no problem for The Bolivian as traffic is at a standstill. The front of the restrooms are hidden by oleander bushes so it is impossible to see anyone come or go. She slips around behind the building to find an eight-foot, chain-link fence topped with barbed wire. Going back around to the front of the building, she encounters a Mexican woman who has been out on the street selling souvenirs car to car. She asks the woman about her wares, and the woman sets them down on the ground, saying she must use the restroom and asking if she would be so kind as to watch her wares.

The Bolivian graciously agrees, and as the woman turns she knocks her down with a vicious chop to the side of the neck. She quickly drags the woman behind the building, then picks up her tray of souvenirs and walks out into the stalled northbound traffic. She quickly makes her way across all ten lanes and heads back towards Tijuana.

The northbound traffic and the southbound traffic are separated only by a median, and she is soon a kilometer away from the border. On the other side of the southbound lanes is a huge flea market. Dodging traffic, she manages to get across with her tray of souvenirs. The first booth she comes to sells the same type of souvenirs, and the vendor, who is pitching a customer, does not see her place the tray under his table.

At about the same time, twenty Mexican policemen show up at the restroom. They find a woman unconscious behind the building. When they finally revive her, she can only say a very attractive woman offered to watch her wares while she used the restroom. The Mexican officers agree they have missed their chance but decide to send two officers down each lane, checking all vehicles before they even get to the border.

After wandering about in the flea market for the better part of an hour, The Bolivian happens to overhear two older ladies and one man discussing some concerns about a drive down to Ensenada since they are unable to speak or read Spanish.

"Excuse me, I couldn't help but overhear your conversation about driving to Ensenada. I need to return to Ensenada myself, and, well, the cab fare is quite high. I was on a cruise ship, and they had a bus tour up here, but I missed the return bus. I speak and read Spanish, and I would be more than happy to accompany you all down there, and I will pay you for the privilege. My name is Miranda Brown, and I'm from Canada, here on vacation."

The man holds out his hand and says, "Well, I'm pleased to meet you, Miranda. I'm Arne Larson, and this is my wife Sonja and her sister Kirsten. We're from Minnesota. You look like a trustworthy young lady. You're not going to rob us, are you?" he asks, then breaks into hysterical laughter.

Sonja says, "Arne, are you sure this is a good idea?"

"Well, Sonja, we were just discussing our doubts about driving that road, you know."

Kirsten says, "I think if Miranda can show us her ID, you know, I think that would be just fine then."

Arne says, "You betcha, that would seal the deal. I suppose you have a passport, don't you then, Miranda?"

The Bolivian responds in her best Northern Minnesota Norwegian brogue, "You betcha, I do, but it's in my luggage on the cruise ship, you know. All I have in my bag is a change of clothes and my makeup kit you know."

Sonja says, "Oh, you poor thing. You're here and your luggage is in Ensenada? It's settled then. You're going with us to Ensenada."

"Gosh darn tootin," says Arne.

"Watch your language, Mr. Larson," says Sonja.

"Aw, Sonja."

67

SAILING NORTH

April 4, 1983

The Bolivian could not believe her luck. Traveling with Arne, Sonja and Kirsten was a real treat. Arne was constantly cracking jokes about some Scandinavian couple, Ole and Lena, with Sonja and Kirsten giggling. Then, Sonja would say, "Oh, Arne," to which he would reply, "Oh, Sonja," and Kirsten chiming in with, "Oh, for crying out loud, you two. You're embarrassing poor Miranda." And so, it goes, down Highway One, through Rosarita Beach, past Puerto Nuevo, and on to Ensenada.

She had not yet come up with a plan on how she was going to get across the border, but felt she was much safer in Ensenada than in Tijuana. She also had to ditch her new-found friends, although they indicated they were only going to be down for the day and then back to San Diego.

She found a parking spot in central Ensenada and bid her new friends goodbye, telling them she had to hurry and get back to the ship.

As The Bolivian walks away, Arne says, "Boy oh boy, wasn't she a looker?"

"Arne Jack Larson, you are just a shameless dreaming philanderer, aren't you?" says Sonja.

Kirsten says, "She was really beautiful, but you know there was something almost scary about her. I think it was her eyes. They were almost silver in color and sometimes seemed to change with the light."

"Her eyes?" says Arne.

"Yes, she had eyes, Arne. I know you never saw anything above her chest," says Sonja.

"Aw, Sonja."

"Don't you, aw Sonja me, Arne Jack Larson."

Kirsten says, "Come on, you two, let's do some shopping and find a place to eat."

"Hey, how about that place across the street, Hussongs, it looks like a jumpin' place," says Arne.

As The Bolivian walks away she sees a sign indicating two kilometers to the harbor. The harbor, she thinks, that's where I'll find a way to California.

Marshall Reginald Buckman, the third, was a trust funder. His trust fund was huge. The key word being, *was*. Getting on towards the high end of his forties, he was losing his playboy look and was far less choosey when it came to his women. The fact of the matter was, there were just less women. He had sailed down from Newport Beach, California on his 50–foot schooner, with a female companion, Emiley Clark. He had filed a departure clearance with the New Port Beach Harbor Master and listed himself and Emiley as crew. Emiley didn't have a passport, only a birth certificate which was all she needed.

Once they arrived in Ensenada and Buckman had filed the proper paperwork with the Mexican Harbor Master,

Buckman requested and was given a slip for three days. He maneuvered his schooner into the slip and after tying up, went back to the Harbor Office to finish the paperwork.

While he was gone, Emiley Clark grabbed her bag and headed for the parking lot where she found a pay phone and dialed.

The phone was immediately answered by her boyfriend who asked "How was the trip?"

"Oh my God he is such a bore. All he thinks about is sex. He can't get it up. It's like a strip of paper flapping in the breeze. Of course the good thing is that it causes him to drink like a fish and he soon passes out. Thank God I know how to sail."

"Ok, I'll be there in five minutes."

Five minutes later the boyfriend arrives "OK, hop in the car. We are out of here."

Hugs and kisses follow and then "Oh crap I left my purse. It's got my birth certificate in it. Dammit!"

"We'll come back later and sneak aboard and get it. Shouldn't be a problem. OK?"

"Yeah, you're right. He'll be passed out stone drunk by eight or nine o'clock. OK, let's go."

The Bolivian stands for a moment upon entering the yacht club to let her eyes adjust to the dark, smoke-filled room. There are only a half a dozen people in the room, and three of them sit at the bar. She goes to the far end of the bar and sits down. The bartender comes over to her, and she orders a dirty martini.

"Excuse me," says the bartender. "My name is John, are you a member here?"

"Oh, I wasn't aware this was a private club."

"Do you have a boat out in the harbor?"

"No, I'm sorry. I'll just leave."

"Do you know anybody here who could be your sponsor?"

"No, again, I'm sorry to bother you."

"Excuse me. I couldn't help overhear. I would be happy to sponsor you. My name is Marshall Buckman, and you are?"

"Why, thank you, kind sir. My name is Miranda Brown."

"John, please take Miss Brown's drink order and put it on my tab."

"Thank you again, Mr. Buckman."

"It is my pleasure. Call me Buck. All my friends do."

"Buck, if you don't mind I just want to enjoy a good martini and forget today."

"Then that is what we shall do. I get you did not have a good day, although I would say having a martini at the end of the day to me would indicate a good day."

"Buck, I really don't want to burden you with my problem and would just rather enjoy this martini."

"Well, Miranda, I can't imagine that your problem is worse than mine. I sailed down here on my boat with a friend, only to find she was just using me to get down here and meet someone else. As soon as we arrived here at the marina, I went to the yacht club office to rent a slip for a few days. When I got back to the boat, she was gone. She left a note which said, "Bye-bye, MRB3."

"She just left you, just like that? What's MRB3?"

"Marshall Reginald Buckman, the third. If you laugh I will spill your martini and not buy you another."

"Buck, how could I possibly laugh when your story is almost identical to mine?"

"Excuse me? Are you saying you have been ditched here, too?"

"Yes, me too, by my Huntington Beach surfer buddy."

"Miranda, this could be the start of a very revengeful relationship."

"Right after you buy me another dirty martini, maybe you could explain that comment?"

"I am leaving tomorrow to sail back to Newport Beach, and I could use a deck hand to get me there. If you know anything about sailing, with you helping I'll get us both to California where we can pursue the ditchers."

"I am not believing what I hear. You would take me on as a crewmember back to California?"

"We leave at six a.m. and with good sailing conditions, we should arrive in Newport Beach by late afternoon."

"Buck, there is one problem. Surfer boy also has my purse, and it contains my passport, credit cards, and all my cash except what I have on me."

"Miranda, you are as good as standing on the 17th street pier right now. That scamp left her purse on my boat and it has her birth certificate in it. You have now just become Emiley Clark."

Buck and Miranda continue getting better acquainted and feast on Ensenada's fresh-caught seafood until the midnight hour. Miranda tries to excuse herself to find a cab to take her back to her hotel, but Buck will hear nothing of it. He tells her his yacht has two comfortable sleeping cabins, a fully stocked bar, and is only a hundred feet away.

Staggering down the dock to his boat, Buck does not realize that Miranda poured most of her martinis into the sink over the bar of the yacht club. Miranda contemplates ending her relationship with Buck... just push him in the water. He's too drunk to swim. No, not a good idea. He's been here too many days, and we spent way too much time at the bar tonight and he is my ticket to California. I'll just drag him back to his boat and tell him I'm going to screw his brains out tonight. Tomorrow, I'll let him take me to California.

She helps a blubbering Buck onto his boat and puts up with his vain attempts at kissing her. She gives in to his groping once they're in his cabin. As she helps him undo her blouse, and he is slobbering all over her chest, she slaps his head with the palms of her hands, like she is playing the cymbals. It knocks him out cold. She proceeds to undress him and throw his clothes about the cabin. She finds a terrycloth robe inside a closet and proceeds to take off her clothes and throw them about the cabin. She spends the next hour searching every nook and cranny of the boat. A secret panel under the companion way leading to the engine room reveals a stash of twenty-thousand dollars and a Beretta PPK with two extra clips. "California, here I come," she thinks.

"Good morning, lover boy. It's almost six and we are burning daylight, captain. Here's a cup of coffee and a fresh donut. You ready to hoist the sails, Bucko?"

"Are you always this cheerful in the morning?"

"What's not to be cheerful about? We're heading home. After all those romantic things you said to me last night, why shouldn't I be cheerful?"

"What romantic things? What the hell are you talking about?"

"You don't remember? You want to marry me. You think I'm pretty. You want to have children with me. You want to spend the rest of your life with me. You were so sweet, and wow, what stamina. I can't remember how many times we did it."

"I said what? Stamina? Wait, did I take more than one pill?"

"Pill?"

"Yes, the little yellow ones. They're for erectile dysfunction. I can't take more than one because of my heart. If I have an erection for more than four hours I might die."

"Do you have one now?"

"What?"

"An erection."

He looks down, "No."

"And you're obviously not dead, right?"

"Who the hell are you? How did you do it? How did we do it?"

"Bucko, listen to me very carefully. We drank. We had sex. We are now going to have coffee and donuts, and then we are going to sail to Newport Beach. Is there anything in that statement that should alarm you?"

"Well no, it's just that I've had this problem for so long, and I know that's why that bitch left me."

"Bucko, it seems I have solved that problem. Shall we get under way, captain?"

"Yeah, OK, I just wish I could remember getting under way last night."

"Captain, let's just say your sails were full, and your spinnaker, oh my, your spinnaker!"

"Spinnaker?"

"You know that wiggly little thing between your legs."

Marshall Reginald Buckman, the third, has no clue what his new crewmember has in mind for him. MRB3 really can't believe his luck. Although if he had any clue what his luck was, he might have jumped over board before they even left the dock.

68

CALIFORNIA

April 4, 1983

Watching MRB3 handle his boat on the sail back up the coast to Newport Beach was a treat. This man knew his boat and knew how to sail it. The Bolivian had only to keep a fresh pot of coffee brewing and to hang on. Only when he changed course or adjusted the sail did he ask her to take the helm. What a thrill! The wind blowing her hair, the sun at her back, and the surge of power as the wind filled the sails.

"OK, mate, I'm going to hoist the spinnaker."

At first, she thought he meant the little spinnaker dangling between his legs but then realized he was actually hoisting a spinnaker. "Aye aye, captain."

"Bring her to a heading of 315, and hold on."

"315."

"Here we go. We are flying now."

"What a rush. I suppose raising another spinnaker is out of the question?"

"We'll engage the auto pilot and see what you got, mate."

"Will this be kinda like the mile-high club of flying?"

"Not even close, mate, not even close."

"Where are we going to do it?"

"Right here in the cockpit, mate."

"Oh, how appropriate!"

No matter what, nothing happened. The spinnaker went limp in the wind and the captain with it.

"Come on, Bucko, it's not the end of the world. I still cherish all the sweet things you said last night. Maybe it was the dirty martini?"

"You think that might be it? I'll mix up a pitcher as soon as we enter Newport Harbor. Now there's something to look forward to."

"If you only knew, Bucko, if you only knew."

"Miranda, you are the only person who has ever called me Bucko."

"Fitting don't you think, Bucko, seeing as how I'm the only one to get your spinnaker up and full?"

"If only I remembered."

"You will this time, Bucko."

I'm home. I'm in bed. It's not even two o'clock in the afternoon. There's a gorgeous woman next to me doing things to me that I shall not describe.

"Nice to have you home, boy toy."

"I need to leave town more often."

"The more time I get to spend at Belmont Billiards."

"On second thought, I need to stay home more."

"My thoughts exactly."

"Could we pretend I just got home one more time?"

"Are you sure you're up for it?"

"Oh, ha ha. Very funny. Time for an equipment check."

"Well, sailor, it appears you've been saving up for shore leave."

"Oh, for crying out loud. You are getting too good with the American lingo. Do you have a sister back there in Pakistan?"

"Very funny, Americansky. That's the wrong stan. It's Afghanistan and don't make that mistake again or I will demonstrate to you the new defensive tactic moves your friendly FBI guy taught me."

"Augh! I give up. I submit to your sadistic sexual desire."

"Aren't you even going to ask about the FBI guy?"

"Who else but Biff?"

"Oh, they got a new defensive tactics instructor. Young, blond, buff, tall, muscular, tanned, strong, gentle, and handsome."

"Oh, for chrissake's, knock it off."

"OK, boy toy, you are back in the center ring. Up, up, up and away. Whee down into the depths of sin. I love you, Marc Ryder, Special Agent DFL."

"Groan..........."

The phone rings. Louder groan.

"Hello, this is Marc."

"Oops, sorry, wrong number."

"Oh, for chrissake's, I know it's you, Biff."

"Oh crap, I gotta learn another accent. Glad you're home, DFL. You sure left a mess for our foreign liaison guys to clean up down there in Puerto Vallarta. Rumor has it that you are not being considered for a travel poster."

"You know, I wish I could say I was sorry, but none of it was because of me. That woman, she is a one woman crime wave. Slippery as a cat."

"That she is. I just wanted to let you know we think she slipped through the net at the border."

"The border?"

"Yes. Estavan thinks she took a flight from Bucerias to Guadalajara and from there to Tijuana. She bought two tickets and of course they were looking for a single female traveler. She used the same name on the tickets to Tijuana. The airline cabin people said a woman was traveling alone but had two seats reserved in the name of Jose and Lupita Manueloza.

They put out an alert at the border in Tijuana, and a cabbie reported a female passenger, bound for San Diego, left his cab about a hundred yards from the border to use a restroom. She never returned.

Tijuana police found a female vendor, who sold tourist junk car to car, unconscious near the restroom with her tray of wares gone. Another vendor at a nearby flea market found the woman's tray of wares under his table and reported it to police. So, we think it was her and she disappeared in Tijuana. She left no trace, but at least she didn't leave any dead bodies, that we know of."

"This gets really strange. You don't think she is coming after me do you?"

"Yes, we do."

"Why?"

"Because you are probably one of a very few people she has left alive who can identify her. By the way we have come up with nothing on that name she gave you, The Bolivian, but we sent all we had to Interpol and we'll see what they come up with."

"What's next, Biff?"

"We're thinking we need to put you and Marina up in a safehouse and wait to see if she shows up in Long Beach. I'm sure Marina is going to be relieved on one hand and grieving on the other over her brother. Does she know about Ustad yet?"

"No. It's up next."

"Aw, shit. I'm sorry. Call me back as soon as you can, and we'll work out a plan. I'm sorry, Marc."

"Thanks for that, Biff. God knows I'm in your debt for what happened at Joe Jacks."

"I am damn glad I was there. Talk to you later." Click.

Marina who has been listening to my half of the conversation asks, "Who was that?"

"Biff."

"I know you don't much care for the FBI, but let me tell you Marc, I love that man Biff."

"Me too, Marina. I have bad news about Ustad."

"That pig. The bad news would be that he is still alive. The good news would be that he is dead."

"He is dead."

"Dead?"

"The woman who everybody seems to be chasing, shot him in Puerto Vallarta."

"The woman? But why?"

"Ustad was in Puerto Vallarta, and last night he jumped me outside a hotel and was trying to kill me. Somehow the woman happened to be at the same hotel and saw us fighting. She came over and put a gun to my head, then turned the gun on Ustad and shot him. Then, she turned the gun me again and pulled the trigger twice, but it was empty. So, she used it to knock me unconscious. Someone called the police, and Estavan found me and more or less stayed with me until he put me on the plane for Long Beach."

"I know this is the short version, so start from the beginning. Do not worry, Marc, I am not going to shed any tears over my cowardly brother. Ever!"

I tell her the whole story. She does not shed a tear. I call Biff and set up a time for us all to meet. Marina and I walk down to Second Street and have lunch at Panama Joe's. It's good to be home. It's good to be sitting across from the love of my life. Everything feels good.

But if I know anything about my life, it never stays good for long..

69

JUMPING SHIP

April 4, 1983

The spectacular California coastline greets them as they approach the entrance to Newport Harbor. Buckman's first priority is to check in with the Harbor Master and advise them of his return from Ensenada. He and the Bolivian encounter no problems as she uses the birth certificate of Emiley Clark. The Bolivian is forming a plan to lose her sailing companion. She had already decided not to kill him. No reason to alert the authorities and have people asking questions about Bucko. No, she will just slip away. She has the money and the gun she found. She is ready to find Marc Ryder and maybe go into semi-retirement.

She tries to show enthusiasm for all the sights that Buck points out and expresses her desire to go ashore and shop for some new clothes before they go out to dinner later. Buck points out the Balboa Pavilion and says there are a number of little shops near it, or they could go on Balboa Island where there are numerous shops. She surely could find something there, and they could have dinner at the Village Inn.

"Balboa Island sounds like fun, Bucko. Let's go there and then come back to the boat for nightcaps."

"I like your style, Miranda. Let me get the boat tied up and ship shape, and we'll take the Zodiac over to the island."

"The Zodiac. What's that?"

"That little inflatable boat that we have been towing. That's the Zodiac. That's how I get to shore."

"So you tie up on that floating ball and just leave the boat out here?"

"Correct. It's somewhat of an inconvenience but a hell of a lot cheaper than renting a slip. We'll lock it up and it will be perfectly safe. I have never had a problem."

"Also, more private too, in case we attempt to raise the spinnaker in the cockpit after dinner, captain."

"We must remember to get the makings for dirty martinis. It must be the ingredient required for raising the spinnaker."

"Aye aye, captain."

This is going to be easier than she thought... She mentally makes a plan. I'll get the clothes I need, I'll learn how to operate the Zodiac, I'll get him drunk, and I'll be gone. I need to rent a car so I need to find a car rental office, but not close. I'll find a cab to take me to a rental car office away from the harbor. This is going well. I'll call that telephone number in Long Beach tomorrow, and maybe by the next day I'll be on my way home. Home is where I should have stayed.

The evening goes as planned. She coaxes Bucko to let her operate the Zodiac. She finds all the clothes she needs on Balboa Island. They have cocktails and dinner at the Village Inn where everybody seems to know everyone else. She wears her hair without a wig but buys a cute little painters cap to wear and a new pair of rose-colored glasses to disguise the color of her eyes. Although she is a beautiful woman, there seem to be beautiful women everywhere on the island, and her eyes—her most distinguishing feature—are now covered.

Bucko seems to know quite a few people and says hello to many. No one seems to take note of his companion, and she does not try to involve herself in any conversations other than with Bucko. After his fourth martini he begins to slur his words a bit, so she suggests they return to the boat and mix up a pitcher of dirty martinis. He has not noticed her switching his empty glass for her full one, and he picks it up and downs it, saying, "Less go, 'randa."

They stop at a liquor store on the way back to the Zodiac, and while Bucko visits the restroom she picks out a bottle of vodka, a bottle vermouth, and a jar of olives. Bucko comes staggering out of the restroom and almost falls down, catching himself at the last second on the counter. He immediately claims tripping on the floor tile as the reason.

As they walk the short, couple of blocks back to the Zodiac, Bucko is rambling on about everything and not making any sense.

As they climb down the ladder into the Zodiac, Bucko almost falls into the bay twice before finally tumbling into the front of the Zodiac. She hopes he will not pass out before they get back to the boat because she has no idea how she would get him into the boat.

Suddenly, it dawns on her... the boat, where is it? It's dark now and everything looks different. It is somewhere past the ferry boat crossing, so she will just have to cross the channel and work her way north until she finds the MRB3—at least she remembers the name. As soon as she crosses the channel and has gone no more than a hundred yards, bingo, there it is. She pulls up to the ladder, ties up the Zodiac, and climbs aboard taking the martini ingredients and her new clothes.

Bucko is sound asleep. She puts all of her things including the money and gun into the oversized bag that she purchased and puts the bag in the forward cabin's closet.

Back on deck in the cockpit she mixes up a pitcher of dirty martinis. Climbing back down into the Zodiac she notices Bucko has rolled over and is now snoring soundly. She grabs him by the shoulders and starts shaking him until he wakes up somewhat.

"Bucko, you need to wake up and climb up the ladder into the boat. I can't get you up there. Bucko, do you hear me? Wake up! WAKE UP!"

"OogK, oogK 'randa. I'm 'wake."

As he gets up, he almost falls overboard again, but Miranda catches him, almost falling over herself. She decides she should climb aboard and help pull him up the ladder which is only five rungs. First, she gets a glass of water and throws it in Bucko's face. That seems to bring him around.

"Come on, Bucko, grab the ladder, and I'll grab you and help pull you up."

"OogK, oogK, 'randa. Here I come." As he gets to the top of the ladder he falls into the cockpit. Miranda helps him up on the bench seat and hands him a martini, which he downs in one gulp. She refills the glass, sits down beside him, and hands him the drink which he also downs in one gulp.

"Randa, I hafta go to the head really bad."

"OK, Bucko, I'll help you down to the head."

Bucko barely makes it to the head, dropping his pants on the floor of the cabin. He staggers out of the head, falls face down on the bed, and is out cold. Within two minutes he is snoring loudly. She pulls the bedspread out from underneath him and covers him up. "Bye-bye, Bucko."

The question now is, where do I go? The Bolivian makes up her mind quickly. She will take the Zodiac back to Balboa Island and tie it up. Then, she will take the ferry boat back across the channel and find a cab. She loads her bag into the Zodiac, unties it from the MRB3 and starts the motor. She decides to tie it up at the same dock they used previously. She feels proud of herself as she motors across the channel. Finding the same tie up is no problem and she climbs up on the dock and heads north on the walkway to the ferry. She only has to wait a few minutes for the ferry to arrive and she gets on as they head back across the channel.

She walks off the ferry and immediately finds a cab. She tells the cabbie that she needs to rent a car, and he suggests Seventeenth and Newport, saying he knows of at least three or four rental car agencies in that area. She asks if they will be open this late and the cabbie says they are open twenty four hours. It takes about ten minutes to get there, and the cabbie is right, she can see three rental car offices from where she gets out of the cab.

She starts to walk towards the Hertz office when she notices a lot advertising cheap rentals and notes that their cars are older and maybe not in perfect condition. She starts checking out the cars and finds a Honda Accord just as a man wearing a Cheap Rentals logo shirt walks up and offers his assistance.

"I need a car for the next few days. How much for this one?"

"Twenty-five dollars a day or one-hundred-twenty-five dollars a week. You leave with a full tank and bring it back with a full tank."

"Sounds like a deal, and I'll pay cash."

"Great, come in the office, and I'll fill out the paperwork. All I'll need is your driver's license."

"I'm sorry I don't have a driver's license, but I do have a passport and another hundred dollars."

"OK, I'll just waive that, as I see your passport indicates you are a licensed driver," as he winks at her. "I only have one set of keys for this baby, so don't lose them."

"Do you have a map of the area? I'm going to Long Beach."

"Long Beach? Sorry, I don't have a map, but as you leave the lot, make a right on Newport Boulevard, and head towards the ocean. You'll see a sign, Highway One, Pacific Coast Highway, also known as PCH. Make a right on it, and it will take you all the way to Long Beach."

She gets in the car and waves to the rental guy and heads for Long Beach.

I awake with a start. I look at the clock, it's two in the morning. Marina is sound asleep. I roll over, but I can't go back to sleep. Did something wake me, or am I still on Puerto Vallarta time? Now, that is ridiculous. I slip out of bed and head for the kitchen. Maybe a nice glass of something bubbly or deep red will help me go back to sleep. It's probably just the pace of life that has caught up with me. The couple of days I spent in Puerto Vallarta seem to have lasted at least a week, and I don't remember sleeping.

70

HARBOR CITY

April 5, 1983

Fahid and his cousins come up with a plan to occupy Ahmed's apartment in Harbor City and monitor his phone. Harbor City is a mostly commercial neighborhood situated in the Los Angeles Harbor Region between Wilmington and San Pedro. Ahmed's apartment is only a few blocks from the Anchor Inn.

It's just after lunch as Biff comes by my humble abode with his "moving" entourage to relocate us to the safehouse.

I say, "Look, Biff, do you really think this is necessary?"

"Yes."

"That's it, yes?"

"It answers your question. Was there something else?"

"Dammit, Biff, you're being evasive."

"Marc, there is nothing that I'm not telling you. We are

simply taking precautions based on the fact that someone in Mexico tried to bury you alive. Someone took a shot at you and wounded a Mexican policeman. A woman tried to shoot you in the head and has vowed to kill you. So, before you go flying off the handle with me, let me tell you, these orders come from much higher up the ladder than our respective resident agencies. And let me tell you, that two-star general who commands Defense Foreign Liaison has even more powerful generals above him, and they have made it very clear. Get you and Marina out of the line of fire."

"So, I guess that's a no."

"Yes, no."

"Another no."

"You are impossible. Marina, could you come here please and be a part of this one-sided conversation I'm having with your significant other?"

Marina comes into the room not looking very happy and says, "Marc, we need to do this."

Biff responds, "Thank you, Marina."

I am annoyed but can see the look on Marina's face which tells me, Biff is right.

"OK, Biff. OK, Marina, let's do this."

Fahid has drawn the morning shift at Ahmed's apartment, and he is just about ready to hand over the duty to his cousin when the phone rings.

"Hello?"

A woman responds, "I was told to call this number when I reached Long Beach and that the person at this number would have some pertinent information for me. Do you have it?"

"Yes. It is one-seven-one-eight Argonne Avenue, Long Beach. You can find this?"

"Yes, I can find it."

"Do you have any message from Ustad?"

The Bolivian has no idea who Ustad is but quickly realizes he must be the man she encountered and killed in Puerto Vallarta.

"Ustad said he was going home, and I believe he has already left."

"Is there any assistance you need from us, Madame?"

"No."

She hangs up the phone and looks at a map she got at a 7-Eleven. "It appears that I'm in Seal Beach," she says to herself. Next stop, Long Beach.

Continuing north on Pacific Coast Highway she sees she is approaching Second Street which will take her directly into Long Beach. According to her map the address she is looking for is just off Second Street at the northern end of an area called Belmont Shore.

Could I be so lucky as to find him standing out in the street in front of his house, she wonders. As she continues down Second Street she sees that the residential side streets are one-way and at the same moment sees Argonne and makes a left turn onto it.

Gotta be getting close, she thinks. She notices two men leaning against a white van. Another man finishes putting a suitcase in the back of the van and turns to walk away. The man walking away is the American, and walking across the front yard towards the American is a beautiful dark-haired woman carrying more clothes and another suitcase.

The Bolivian pulls into a vacant parking space next to the curb, pulls out her pistol, and checks the magazine. She slips the magazine into the pistol and checks the other magazine.

71

THE SHOOTOUT

APRIL 5, 1983

"Come on you two, let's get this move done today," orders Biff. He is obviously getting anxious and jittery about evading this mysterious woman who is bent on killing me. I plead with Marina to just take enough stuff for a couple of days, and then we'll be back in our home.

"Marc, I am taking everything that I need. Do not say you will buy me new clothes or jackets or top coats. I want my own clothes. I am almost ready. Take these two suitcases, and I'll bring the rest."

"OK, I'll be out front with Biff and Paul."

Biff has checked out a big, white Ford van from the FBI car pool to move us to the safehouse. It's parked right in front of our house. We have a driveway which leads to a one-car garage behind the house, and my Porsche is locked in there. Marina and I will ride with Biff and Paul, and we'll leave our Jeep parked in front of the house.

As I walk out of the house with the two suitcases, Biff is

standing beside the van and Paul is leaning against it. Who knows why, but for some reason the hair on the back of my neck stands up and gives me a tingling feeling. I notice an older model Honda Accord slowly driving towards our house and the van. The Honda pulls over next to the curb between two cars on the other side of the street about three car lengths in front of the van. A woman steps out of the car.

I yell at Biff, "Lookout."

Biff turns around just in time to see the woman get out of the car. It all seems to happen in slow motion.

The woman stands behind the open car door and takes aim with her shooting arm resting on the door. Her first shot catches Paul in the chest. Even though he wears a bullet-proof vest, he goes down. The second shot catches Biff in his left shoulder, missing his vest, and knocking him to the ground also. I dive for the ground behind the van and grab Paul's revolver from his holster. I crouch behind the van and start to work my way around the van hoping I can get a clear shot.

She fires again, and I hear her curse as she fires yet again, then I hear a scream.

I turn and look at the doorway to my house and see Marina slumping backwards into the house and out of sight. My fury overtakes me, and I yell "NO, NO, NO," and jump up and start firing in the direction of the Honda. I fire all six rounds and hear glass breaking and bullets hitting metal.

Silence. I must have hit her. I turn and run towards the doorway to our house, and when I have taken only four or five steps, I hear a hysterical laugh and the woman saying, "Bye-bye, Marc Ryder." Then, I hear two gunshots, followed by a burning pain in my shoulder and head. Darkness follows.

The Bolivian touches her left side, and it feels warm. As she takes her hand away, she sees it is covered with blood. In the distance, she hears the wail of police sirens and quickly gets back into her car and drives away. She takes a left at the first intersection, East First Street, goes two blocks, and takes a left on Granada. After two more blocks, she comes to East Second Street where she makes a right and heads eastward towards Orange County.

She stays on East Second until she crosses PCH where she turns into the parking lot of the Long Beach Marketplace. She parks, locks her car, and throws the keys into a cluster of oleander bushes. She waits for only about five minutes when she sees what she is looking for—an elderly man pushing a shopping cart towards his Ford Bronco. As he is loading his grocery bags into the back of his Bronco, she approaches and offers to help him load his groceries and take his cart.

He is very appreciative. As he turns to grab the last bag, she hits him very hard at the base of the neck, and he falls forward into the back of his Bronco. She looks around to see if anyone is watching. She sees no one, so she lifts his lower torso into the Bronco and closes the door after fishing the keys from his pocket. Calmly she walks around to the driver's side, slips into the driver's seat, and opens the first aid kit she found in the back. The bleeding does not seem too bad and the wound is only superficial. She puts some pain relieving salve on it and covers it with a large band aid.

She reaches toward the rear compartment to grab her purse and notices the old man is stirring, so she hits him again, then starts the car and looks for a way to get on PCH southbound.

Marina tells me later that no less than four Long Beach patrol cars, two firetrucks, two ambulances, one EMT truck, and three FBI cars showed up at our house. The EMTs transported Biff and me to St. Mary's Medical Center to treat our gunshot wounds. Biff was conscious, but I was not. The bullet grazed my skull. At the scene, they administered first aid to Paul and Marina. Marina said she became hysterical and seemed to have forgotten English. Biff later told me that she was screaming in French, Russian, German, Spanish, and Farsi, depending on who she was screaming at. The bullet meant for Marina hit the door frame to her right and ricocheted into her suitcase, scaring the hell out of her as she half dived and half fell back into the house.

In the hospital, I am bouncing around in my dreams between being buried alive in the snow of Minnesota to being buried alive in dirt of Mexico. I vividly see a gun being fired at me, and I'm watching the bullet come at me in slow motion.

Every law enforcement department, local and federal, is on alert. Both radio and TV stations are broadcasting a description of the female shooter and her car.

A citizen calls in to Long Beach police that she saw a

woman, matching the broadcasted description, leave an older model Honda at the Long Beach Marketplace and throw something into the bushes.

Another caller reports that her elderly father went shopping at the Long Beach Marketplace and hasn't returned. She provides a license plate number of her father's Ford Bronco.

Heading southbound on PCH, The Bolivian's mind is swirling in muddled thoughts... this whole idea was stupid. I need to come to my senses. I vowed not to ever let this become personal and look what I have done. She decides she must get rid of this car and get off PCH. She makes a left turn onto Warner Avenue in Huntington Beach and begins looking for a place to ditch the Bronco and find another car. She sees a sign that reads, Meadowlark Golf Club, and turns in to find a large parking lot almost full of cars. Perfect.

As she pulls into a parking spot she sees two women get out of a Ford sedan and without apparently locking the car, they go into the clubhouse. She grabs her bag and jumps out of the Bronco and is almost hit by another car. The driver yells something at her, but she ignores him and gets into the Ford sedan. As she slams the door shut, the car keys fall onto her lap from the sun visor. How convenient, she thinks, and is on her way.

She pulls back out on to Warner and heads towards the ocean. She takes a left on PCH and heads south towards Newport Beach and Orange County Airport. The Ford Bronco is found when the injured, elderly man staggers into the Meadowlark clubhouse. The EMTs and Huntington Beach PD are called and the injured man tells how he was assaulted by a woman at the Long Beach Marketplace. At the same time, two women who had just enjoyed lunch at the Meadowlark Grill discover that their car is gone and report a possible theft to the Huntington Beach police officers. The make, model, and license plate number of The Bolivians new ride is immediately broadcast over all police radios.

The Bolivian pulls off PCH and parks behind a restaurant which is closed. Reaching in her bag, she pulls out her map and unfolds it. She studies her options, thinking, maybe I can just drive to San Ysidro and walk over the border into Mexico. I don't think the Mexican authorities check identification coming into Mexico. I could then fly to Mexico City and disappear into the world of International travel and eventually home.

After a knock on the door, it opens slightly, "Hey, Marina. How are you doing?"

"Biff, what you doing up and out of your room?"

"Actually they said I could go home, but I thought I'd stop by and see how you and Marc are doing."

"They say he's doing fine, but he's still out and seems to be having some very violent dreams. They gave him something to settle him down. Has that killer been caught yet, Biff?"

"Not yet. She's on the run, but I'm sure she will sooner or later make a mistake, hopefully before someone else gets hurt."

The hours stretch into days, and I am still out. As soon as whatever drugs I had been given begin to wear thin, I begin to have dreams again...

It's January in Minnesota. The winter is in high gear. The snow is coming down hard, and the northerly wind is driving the temperature down. The wind chill factor is most likely minus 35, but children like me seem to be immune to the cold. It is recess at Riverside school, and the game is on—after the fox. Blindly running along the ridge above the coulee, I fall head first over the top of the snowbank into the soft, new fallen snow. Buried. I struggle, but I can't move. I'm gagging with snow in my mouth, nose, and eyes. Someone grabs me by my shoulders and holds me still.

"Marc, Marc! It's me. It's Marina."

I open my eyes. The light is blinding. I squint and blink. No snow. No dirt.

"Marc, do you hear me? It's Marina."

"Marina. You're OK? You're alive? You weren't shot?"

"No, but you were, and I am so happy to have you back from wherever you have been. I love you my, boy toy!"

"And I love you, Marina. How long have I been out? Is she alive? Did they catch her? Is Biff OK?"

"You have been out for almost seven days. Biff is OK, but she is still alive, and no, they did not catch her."

"So this is not over."

After ditching the Ford sedan in a long-term parking lot near the Orange County airport, The Bolivian found another car with the keys in a magnetic box in the wheel well. She drove out of the lot after paying and got on the 405 freeway headed for San Ysidro. Traffic was light and she saw three or four California Highway Patrol cars parked along the freeway on the way to San Ysidro. They're looking for either the Bronco or the Ford sedan no doubt. She found a parking lot near the border and parked. She grabbed her only possession, the bag she bought in Balboa, and calmly walked across the border into Mexico.

She decided not to chance going to the airport and flying to Mexico City. Security could be a problem. After finding a second-hand store, she bought herself a complete outfit of washed out denim, including a well-worn pair of leather sandals. She put her other clothes in a worn out woven bag she bought and discards the bag from Balboa. She then found her way to the bus station and bought a ticket to Hermosillo. After four days of travel by bus and train, The Bolivian arrived in Mexico City. She immediately stopped at a pay phone in the train station. She dialed a number which was answered by a Spanish speaking male. They conversed in Spanish for about two minutes. They haggled on a price and after agreeing to a number, she was given instructions on where to pick up the documents she just ordered.

Two days later, a very attractive woman with auburn hair, wearing dark glasses, hiking clothes, a California Angels baseball cap, and carrying a backpack boarded a Brazilian airliner headed for Rio. After staying just one day, the same woman, now with very dark hair, wearing Nike workout clothes, rose-colored glasses, and a New York Yankee baseball cap boarded Air France flight to Paris. Arriving in Paris, she discarded everything except her new passports and the remains of her money. With new clothes on her back, and Puerto Vallarta and California in her rear view mirror, she boarded a Greek airliner bound for the island of Mykonos.

From Mykonos, it is only a ferry boat ride to the Island

of Light. Rest and relax and maybe, just maybe, retire. As she arrived at the Island of Paros, the sun is setting over the Mediterranean. She walked off the ferry boat and headed for her condo. Many people are out strolling along the boardwalk and many more are sitting out on the patios of the sidewalk cafes and tavernas. This is home and she felt herself beginning to relax. She did not notice a bearded man of light complexion with reddish blond hair and a medium build sitting in the shadows on the terrace of a taverna. But he noticed her, and he knew who she was.

Dmitri followed her for a short distance and watched her enter a condominium on the first floor of an old refurbished building only a few hundred meters from the harbor.

He watched until the lights went out, and then retreated to the taverna. He ordered a glass of the red wine of Paros and made up his mind on what to do.

I'm sound asleep, and why not? It's 4:30 in the morning. "What is that damn ringing?"

"Marc, the phone is ringing. Don't answer it."

"I have to, Marina, you know that."

"This does not make me happy Marc Ryder!"

"I promise Marina I am not going anywhere. I promise."

"OK. But if you leave this bed and don't come back alive I will kill you."

" Ohmigod, Hello, this is Marc."

"Marc, it is Dmitri. I have found her."

CPSIA information can be obtained
at www.ICGtesting.com
Printed in the USA
FFOW02n1327140318
45697039-46547FF

9 781478 793472